THE
DAWNING
OF DESTINY

THE DAWNING
OF DESTINY
CHANNING HALL

Finding God in the
Vicissitudes of Life

TATE PUBLISHING *& Enterprises*

Published by Tate Publishing & Enterprises, LLC
127 E. Trade Center Terrace | Mustang, Oklahoma 73064 USA
1.888.361.9473 | www.tatepublishing.com

Tate Publishing is committed to excellence in the publishing industry. The company reflects the philosophy established by the founders, based on Psalm 68:11,
"The Lord gave the word and great was the company of those who published it."

Book design copyright © 2009 by Tate Publishing, LLC. All rights reserved.
Cover design by Travis Kimble
Interior design by Nathan Harmony

Published in the United States of America

ISBN: 978-1-60799-267-7
1. Fiction: Action & Adventure
2. Fiction: Historical
09.04.01

Chapter 1

The sign ahead read, "Meadowview City Limits, Population 525." Just before reaching the sign, the farmer who had given Ken a ride turned his truck off the highway onto a dirt road that wound through the rolling farmlands.

"Good luck, son. Wish you would change your mind and come to work for me for the summer," said the burley farmer in the faded overalls.

"Thanks. I really appreciate the offer and the ride, but I guess I'd better go on to the job the orphanage arranged for me. That farmer is expecting me. Good luck to you too. I hope you don't have too much trouble finding the help you need," Ken said. He jumped down from the truck and watched as it slowly picked up speed and gradually disappeared over a low hill.

He sort of wished he had accepted the job. The slight acquaintance he had acquired with the farmer over the two-hour ride was appealing since the person he was on his way to work for was a complete stranger. *Oh well. Too late now,* he thought.

He started into the little town with a bag containing all his earthly possessions slung over his shoulder. The discomforting feeling of facing the world alone that had begun when he left the orphanage rose up within him again. That was the only home he could remember in his seventeen-year lifetime, and it was hard to get used to the fact he was leaving everyone and everything that was familiar to him and could no longer consider the orphanage his home.

His life there had been pleasant overall, but, especially in his younger years, he had felt a longing to be in a real family. During his most adoptable years, adoptions had been few. The country was going through a serious depression, and people were not inclined to take on another mouth to feed. His longing for a father and mother had been somewhat moderated by a warm relationship with some of the staff members, although it was unusual for any of them to stay at the orphanage more than a few years.

Over the years, the staff had found Ken to be congenial and always ready to help with anything that needed to be done. They marveled at his concern for the welfare of the other children. Even at the age of six or seven, when the adult personnel on duty got up during the night in response to some child crying, they would find Ken already by the bedside trying to soothe the one in distress. As he grew older, some of the younger children would often go to him for comfort when they were lonely and for help when they were having trouble with their schoolwork. He never seemed to be bothered by their requests for his time and attention.

Big for his age, for several years he had helped with work on the small farm the orphanage maintained to provide produce and dairy products for the orphans. He had known no other life, and over time his desire to be adopted had faded. He was content with his role in helping the orphanage provide a sanctuary for other motherless and fatherless children.

But as much as he cherished the feeling of "belonging" the orphanage provided, he knew he could not avoid the year 1942, which loomed ominously on the horizon. He would be eighteen in August of that year and, in compliance with state regulations, would have to leave to make room for younger children.

Then, on December 7, 1941, the bombing of Pearl Harbor set in motion events that affected the lives of almost all Americans. Although life in the orphanage was not directly affected, it created additional uncertainty as the time Ken would have to leave drew closer. Then the day he was dreading came even sooner than he had expected, in late May 1942.

"I'm sorry, Kenneth," Mr. Tanner, the new administrator, had said sympathetically. "I know you don't want to leave, and technically you should be able to stay here until your eighteenth birthday. But last week we had to take some new children that we don't really have the required facilities for. We really shouldn't have taken them yet, but it was a desperate situation. We've made some temporary arrangements for them, but we can't go long without getting back in compliance with the state regulations we operate under.

"But the good news is that because you have shown you are such a good worker, I was able to arrange for you to work for a farmer I know near my hometown for the summer. I've been told that is something we have not been able to do for many of those who have had to leave in the past. This could be a blessing in disguise. It will give you a little experience with what life is like outside the orphanage, but with the security of a temporary job. You will be eighteen in August and will have to register for the draft, and it's pretty likely that you will have to spend some time in one of the military services. If you do, it will give you time to decide what you want to do with your life. Hopefully the war will not last too long.

"You have been a good student. I have heard Congress is considering legislation that would pay the college expenses for those who serve in the military during the war. That may be a good way to get to go to college if you decide you want to do that, and with your scholastic record I would certainly recommend it. I think you would make a good teacher."

Ken left Mr. Tanner's office with mixed emotions. Knowing he had a job to go to and the other positive aspects Mr. Tanner had mentioned made the unwelcome news easier to take but did not eliminate his feelings of regret.

A staff member had taken him to the Greyhound bus station that morning and had dropped him off.

"You shouldn't have any trouble getting your ticket," he had said. "I would stay with you until you leave, but some social workers that I have to meet with are supposed to be at the orphanage in about twenty minutes. They give us enough trouble already. We can't afford to alienate them. So long. We are really going to miss you. Hope you enjoy that farm job!"

With that, he had driven away.

It had been hard saying good-bye to his friends and the staff members he especially liked. He was also going to miss some of the children who seemed to depend on him so much. But even though he dreaded leaving the comfortable familiarity of the orphanage as he entered the bus station, he was filled with sort of an apprehensive excitement over what the future held for him. He hadn't realized it, but he had an adventurous spirit within the recesses of his mind that had never been acknowledged or satisfied in any way. This had probably been suppressed by his strong sense of duty, which kept him involved in the day-by-day tasks that needed to be done.

The bus station was crowded, and he felt uncomfortable with the jostling while making his way toward the ticket line. His hand was in his pocket clutching the eighteen dollars the administrator had given him for a ticket and food. The station wagon driver had cautioned him to be careful with the money, telling him pickpockets often hung out in places like bus stations where there were crowds. He glanced around wondering if any of the people near him were pickpockets.

Being in a crowd of adults made him ill at ease. He felt much more at home around children. Everyone seemed to have store-bought luggage. The rough bag he was carrying made him a little self-conscious, not only because it made him different but also because he kept bumping people with it. One man angrily voiced his annoyance and didn't seem to be appeased by Ken's apology.

He reached the end of the ticket line behind about two dozen people. There was argument going on near him, as well as shrill complaining from a woman at the ticket window. The strong smell of body odor permeated the stuffy air, and the heavy concentration of tobacco smoke made his eyes burn. He wondered if this was a sample of what he would experience on the bus. There were a few people he saw that he especially hoped would not be on the same bus he would be on. One was a man who was seized with a fit of coughing from time to time and seemed to make no effort to cover his coughs. Another old man with a heavy, dirty-looking beard was puffing on a pipe. The slow-moving line was prolonging his discomfort.

Ken's thoughts turned to the money in his pocket. It gave him a good feeling to have it, even if it was only for a short time. There had not been many times when he had even a few coins in his possession, and eighteen dollars seemed like a huge sum. His mind idly wandered over possible ways the money could be used if it were not already committed.

As he shuffled along in the slow-moving line, a man somewhere behind him said, "Good night! What's the holdup? At this rate I could get there faster walking!"

This thought made Ken wish his destination was close enough that he could walk and get away from this crowd that was making him so uncomfortable. Then he suddenly thought of Larry. Larry was a charismatic young man in his mid-twenties who had worked at the orphanage for a short time a few years before. He had frequently told some of the older children about his adventures hitchhiking.

"Great way to travel anywhere you want to go, and here is the only ticket you need!" he said with a smile, holding up his thumb.

He was a good storyteller, and his vivid accounts of some of his travels held the children's attention. Those who enjoyed hearing about his adventures were disappointed when he left the orphanage suddenly, perhaps to further satisfy his wanderlust. No one seemed to know his plans for sure.

Ken felt a sudden thrill of excitement as he thought about Larry and his hitchhiking. The opportunity to see what it was like was open to him at this moment! But just as suddenly his enthusiasm melted away. There were just too many uncertainties. Larry had laughingly told of times when he had a hard time getting a ride, times when he had spent the night sleeping by the side of the road, once while it was raining.

Ken quickly discarded consideration of the idea, but it immediately popped back into his mind. Larry had seemed to think even the difficulties were a great adventure, and some of the experiences he described sounded attractive enough to outweigh the difficulties.

Ken's mind struggled with the pros and cons. One consideration was that if he didn't take the bus he would still have the eighteen dollars that seemed to offer a measure of security to his uprooted life. He wondered if he would be violating the trust of the orphanage administrator if he didn't use the money in the way it was intended. Then he reasoned the purpose of the money was to get him to his destination, so as long as he accomplished the purpose, it shouldn't matter if he didn't use the money to get there.

Finally, as the man in front of him reached the ticket window, he made up his mind. Tingling with apprehension over the possible consequences of his decision, he abruptly stepped out of the line and made his way out of the station. It was a relief to get away from the crowd, and, once he was on his way, he felt sort of good about his decision but still had a little gnawing feeling of anxiety.

Ken was not sure how to get to the highway that led to his destination. He had only been in the small city on a few occasions and was not familiar with its layout. He thought he knew the general direction he should go, but failing to find the highway after about twenty minutes, he was beginning to wonder if he had made a mistake deciding to hitchhike; then a friendly looking man who was buying a paper at a newsstand gave him the directions he needed.

When he got to the city limits, he stood by the side of the road ready to hold out his thumb when a car was coming, feeling a little selfconscious. There were not many cars leaving town, and for what seemed like a long time those that did come by seemed to ignore the thumb he was extending. He really couldn't blame the women and the older people. They saw a person nearly six feet tall dressed in rather shabby clothes, who appeared to have the ability to harm them if he were so inclined. A Greyhound bus went by that was probably the one he would have been on if he hadn't decided to try hitchhiking.

He was starting to get a little anxious when a farmer in a truck loaded with sacks of grain stopped, brakes squealing, and beckoned for him to get in. The farmer was very friendly and seemed glad to have company. He asked Ken where he was going, and Ken explained his situation. After they had talked for a while, the farmer said, "I really need to hire some help. How would you like to change your plans and come give me a hand for the summer?"

Ken was surprised and sort of pleased with the offer but felt he should follow through on the arrangements Mr. Tanner had made for him.

The business section of Meadowview, where Ken's ride had ended, extended about three blocks along the highway. The town, with its rather unpretentious stores that served the needs of the community, probably seemed pretty commonplace to those familiar with it. To Ken, whose world had been comprised of the orphanage buildings and grounds, it was quite interesting. As he entered the town, he passed a Texaco gas station, and then a rather plain brick building on his right announced it was the city hall. Next to the city hall was a fire station with an ancient fire truck parked in the driveway.

He passed a small grocery store and came to a drugstore. There was a young man sitting on a stool at the soda fountain drinking something out of a glass with a straw. Ken wondered what he was drinking and was intrigued with the thought that, like that young man, he could now go into a store and ask for something he wanted rather than having no choice in his food and drink. He felt an impulse to go in and order the same kind of drink the young man had but quickly dismissed it. If the hitchhiking didn't pan out, the money might still be needed to buy a bus ticket, so it was probably wise not to spend much on nonessentials.

The town had a homey feel that was appealing. The few people he met greeted him warmly, but he was sure they recognized him as a stranger and were probably curious about his reasons for being in their town. He felt a little envious toward the people who called this their hometown and wondered if he would ever be a part of a community like this.

Next to the drugstore there was a used furniture store that also advertised mortuary services. A hardware store, a cream collection station, and a feed store were on the other side of the street. In a vacant lot ahead there was a billboard, and five or six young boys were watching a man as he was putting up a new advertisement. Apparently this was the most exciting thing going on in the little town. The billboard was advertising Camel cigarettes. When he read the slogan, "I'd walk a mile for a Camel," he knew that viewpoint sure didn't apply to him. The walking he was doing was to get away from the tobacco smoke among the other conditions in the bus station that had bothered him.

He passed a small café and a telephone office. The clicking of billiard balls punctuated the loud music that was coming from the open pool-hall doorway. On the other side of the street, after a few vacant lots, there was a newspaper office, a post office, and a bank. Just beyond a vacant lot beside the bank, he saw a small building with a sign that read "Hot Dogs—Pop—Ice Cream." It had been five or six hours since breakfast, and he felt a slight pang of hunger.

Might as well get something to eat here, he thought. *"There's no way of knowing how long it will be before I have another chance.*

He crossed the street, went in, and asked for two hot dogs. There was a frosty box behind the counter that had the colorful image of a soft drink on the side. It looked good, and he was a little thirsty, so he asked for a bottle of the displayed drink. The hot dogs cost ten cents each, and the ice-cold bottle of orange Nehi soda cost a nickel. He carefully put one of the paper-wrapped hot dogs in his bag and proceeded toward the edge of town munching on the other one between swigs of soda. Neither the hot dog nor the soda lasted long.

When he reached the city limits, he stopped and resumed his hitchhiker's stance. It was not long before a battered pickup stopped, and the smiling driver opened the passenger door and beckoned to Ken. As he got into the pickup, he saw the driver was a pleasant-looking Hispanic man not much older than he was. Ken wondered if he may have had his own experiences hitchhiking and felt sympathy for someone who needed a ride.

Both Ken and the driver soon gave up attempts to communicate, and after five or six miles, the driver turned off on a side road and stopped. Ken jumped out of the pickup and waved his thanks, although he was wishing he had not accepted the ride since it was so short. It seemed probable people would be more likely to stop as they left town before they reached highway speed.

He turned toward the highway and had gone a few steps when he heard a soft whine. Looking toward the sound, he saw a little brown-and-white puppy lying by the body of a mature dog that was apparently the puppy's mother. Ken thought she had probably been hit by a car and had managed to crawl off the road a ways before dying. As Ken approached, the puppy looked at him and crouched fearfully. Ken was smitten with sympathy and reached down to pat him. The puppy drew back, but when he found the touch was gentle, he jumped up and licked Ken's hand, vigorously wagging his little tail. Ken looked at the mother and thought she had probably been dead for at least a couple days.

"Tough luck, little fellow," he said, "but what am I going to do with you?"

Knowing the puppy must be hungry, he set his bag down and took out the hot dog he had saved. The puppy ate it ravenously, part of the bun as well as the hot dog, and again enthusiastically licked Ken's hand.

He is probably really thirsty too, Ken thought.

Looking down the highway, not far away there was a line of trees roughly perpendicular to the highway, which could be an indication of a stream of water. He picked up his bag and the puppy and made his way toward the trees where, as he had hoped, there was a nice stream running under the highway.

He made his way down the steep bank, and after setting his bag down, he filled his cupped hand with water. The puppy drank it eagerly. It took several handfuls before the puppy's thirst was satisfied. Obviously refreshed, the puppy again licked Ken's hand and, wagging vigorously, tried to climb up his leg.

Poor little guy. Now that he has lost his mother, he needs someone to take care of him, but I don't see how I could keep him. I have enough worries already! Ken thought.

But he sat down on the bank of the stream and took the puppy in his arms, trying to decide what to do with him. The puppy showed his desire for affection by snuggling up against Ken. He was surprised at the feeling of pleasure he felt from holding the warm puppy. The puppy yawned and completely relaxed.

You look really sleepy. I'll bet you haven't slept for a while, Ken thought, and almost immediately the puppy appeared to be asleep.

As he was trying to decide what to do with the puppy, he heard voices, and soon two boys appeared from under the highway bridge. Both were carrying fishing poles, and they each had a forked willow branch holding several fish. When they saw Ken, they stopped and eyed him curiously.

"Hi, fellows. It looks like fishing is pretty good today!" Ken said.

"Yeah," one of the boys said as he proudly held up the fish he had caught. "Look at this big one! I'll bet he is a foot long!"

"Sure looks like it," agreed Ken. "That will probably make a good meal for a couple people!"

"Well, if my dad gets hold of it, he will eat the whole thing. He really likes fish. You like fish? I can give you a couple little ones if you want them."

Ken laughed. "Thanks, but I don't know what I would do with them! I'm hitchhiking, and I might get thrown out of someone's car if they got to smelling too much! Right now I'm trying to decide what to do with this puppy I found up the road a ways. Which one of you would like a nice puppy?"

The boys came closer and looked at the sleeping puppy.

"He sure looks like a cute little guy," one of the boys said, "but we have three dogs already, and my mom complains about having so many. She would kill me if I brought home another one."

"I'll take him," the other boy said. "My folks really like dogs, especially puppies."

Ken felt a slight pang of regret as he realized he had sort of been hoping the boys wouldn't take him, but no doubt this would be the best for both him and the puppy. He arose and handed the puppy to his new owner.

"Take good care of him," he said.

"Sure, I will," the boy said. "Guess I'll take him home now. I've had enough fishing for today. Come on, Billy. Let's go. Thanks, mister."

The boys started down the stream away from the highway. The new puppy owner was carrying his fish and fishing pole in one hand and the puppy in his other arm. He had gone a short distance when the puppy began squirming vigorously, and the boy set him down. The puppy immediately started back toward Ken.

"Come back here, you little rascal!" the boy yelled, but the puppy continued toward Ken and tried to climb up his leg.

Ken picked him up, and the puppy wagged joyously. Ken felt a surge of affection.

"Ah, he wants to stay with you," the boy said. "You better keep him."

"Yeah, I guess I will," Ken said, wondering how much this would complicate his life. "Thanks anyhow for trying to help."

The boys waved and went on their way.

"Okay, buddy," he said. "We need to get going. I guess us orphans need to stick together, but I hope you won't keep me from getting rides."

He slung his bag over his shoulder and, holding the puppy against his chest, climbed up the bank to the highway. "Buddy" had been a term that had popped into his head on the spur of the moment, but as he thought about it, he decided he would name the puppy Buddy.

When he got back to the highway, he looked down the road for ride possibilities. He didn't see any cars approaching, but a couple hundred yards away, he saw a rather old, faded, blue car by the side of the road with its hood up. It had not been there when he had walked past that spot ten or fifteen minutes before. A man was looking under the hood, and three other people were standing beside the car. There was a luggage rack on top of the car, implying the passengers were on a trip.

After a few minutes he decided to see if there was a problem he could help with and started walking toward them. As he drew near, the man who had been peering into the engine compartment straightened and watched him warily. Ken realized they might be a little apprehensive about his intentions, so he slowed his pace and smiled. He was impressed with the man's dignified bearing and appearance. A woman whom Ken assumed was the man's wife had long, jet-black hair, a fair complexion, and was quite attractive. A teenage girl was a younger version of the woman. The last of the four was a preteen boy, who looked at the puppy with great interest.

"Hello," Ken said. "It looks like you are having trouble."

"Yes, much trouble," the man said with an intriguing accent. "The motor, it will not go!"

"Are you sure you have not run out of gasoline?" Ken asked.

"I do not believe that to be the case," the man said, "but perhaps it should be verified."

Ken put the puppy down and removed his bag from his shoulder. The boy came over smiling and gestured toward the puppy in an obvious plea to hold him.

Ken said, "Sure. Go ahead. You can hold him."

The man said something to the boy that Ken didn't understand, and the boy smiled his thanks as he picked the puppy up. Ken went to the rear of the car and removed the gas cap. Peering into the tank, he thought he could see gasoline but wasn't sure. Bouncing the car yielded the sound of sloshing liquid.

"You do seem to have fuel," he said. "Do you mind if I look at the engine?"

"Please," the man said. "I do not know what to do."

Ken had occasionally helped the handyman work on the balky tractor at the orphanage, so he felt he had a chance of being able to fix the old Chevrolet. The main recurring problem with the tractor engine had been with the ignition points, so that's where he looked for the problem with the old car. He removed the distributor cap and looked at the points. Sure enough, they had a residue buildup that prevented them from opening and closing properly.

The handyman had explained this condition kept the spark plugs from receiving the electrical charge needed to make the engine run. With the knife he had received for Christmas the previous year, he removed the residue from the points and scraped the rotor contacts. He made sure the ignition wires were seated firmly in the distributor cap and reattached the cap to its base. Then he asked the man to try starting the engine. After an initial hesitation, the engine sputtered to life. He closed the hood and looked up to see relief and admiration on the faces of the three older persons. The boy was engrossed in playing with the puppy.

The man got out of the car, grasped Ken's hand, and said, "We are much in your debt! What can I pay you for this service?"

"Well, sir, I don't want any pay, but if you could give me a ride, I would appreciate it. I do have my dog with me, if you wouldn't mind having him in your car," Ken said.

"We would be much honored for both you and your dog to ride with us," the man said. "I am Jacob Meyer. This is my wife, Rachel; my daughter, Rebecca; and my son, Benjamin."

Although he didn't know what to call it, Ken was impressed with the evidence of culture he could see in this family. They all smiled warmly as Ken told them his name and how he had acquired the puppy.

Then Mr. Meyer somewhat hesitantly said, "I do not like to ask to impose on you further, but could you drive this car? I am ill, and my wife does not drive." His pale face and obvious signs of distress provided visible indication of his illness.

"Yes, sir," Ken said. "I will be glad to drive for you." He turned to look for Buddy and saw that the boy was still happily holding him.

"I believe there will be space for your possessions in the rear storage compartment," Mr. Meyer said as he handed Ken the car keys and wearily got into the passenger side of the front seat.

His wife and children immediately got into the backseat. Ken put his bag in the trunk and got into the driver's seat, glad to be able to help and for the opportunity to experience driving a car on the highway.

As they traveled down the highway, Mr. Meyer told him they were originally from Frankfurt, Germany, where he had been a professor at the Johann Wolfgang Goethe University of Frankfurt.

When the Nazi persecution of Jews had become increasingly oppressive, they had tried to obtain visas to the United States. After waiting for almost a year, they realized there was no way of knowing when they would receive visas, if ever, and they finally decided to abandon their home and go to Switzerland. They learned not long after leaving Germany the persecution had escalated into outright violence. There were also rumors of the systematic killing of Jews, and they were grateful they had left when they did. Professor Meyer had readily obtained a teaching position in Switzerland because he could teach several languages and almost any course in mathematics. However, they still had a desire to go to America, and they eventually succeeded in obtaining visas to the United States.

After their arrival in New York, with the help of an organization established to help Jewish immigrants, Professor Meyer had submitted applications for teaching positions to several colleges and universities. While they were waiting for a response to his applications, they went on a tour of New York City, and in their absence someone broke into their apartment and stole all the money and valuables they had left there.

Shortly after this he was offered a position with a small college in Ohio. Someone on the staff had known Professor Meyer in Germany and had recommended him highly, so he was offered the position of teaching summer classes without a personal interview. The family was now on their way there in the old car, which had been donated to the relief agency and in turn had been given to the Meyers along with some traveling funds.

"And what is your destination?" the professor asked.

"I'm sort of in the same situation you are," Ken said. "I'm on my way to a job with someone I've never met, although I guess I will be using my hands instead of my brain!"

He told Professor Meyer about the summer job that had been arranged by the orphanage. The professor seemed genuinely interested and asked about life in the orphanage and the circumstances that had resulted in his being there. Ken said he couldn't remember not being in the orphanage, but when he was about ten years old, he asked one of his favorite staff members if he could tell him why he was there. The staff member said he didn't know but took him into the office, and, after getting the permission of the administrator, they opened his file.

According to the records, he had been there since he was a year old. His parents had both been killed in an automobile accident. Miraculously he had escaped almost unscathed. The authorities had been unable to locate any relatives, so they had placed him in the orphanage. He had been registered under his father's name, Kenneth Ryan, which they obtained from his driver's license.

"So I guess I don't even know my own name for sure," Ken said with a laugh.

Suddenly there was the sound of a loud explosion accompanied by screams from the backseat, and the car bumped to a stop. Everyone jumped out of the car, and they saw the right rear tire had blown out. It had a large hole with fragments of the inner tube showing. The tire tread was almost all worn away, so it was not surprising that it had failed.

"Do you have a spare?" Ken asked the professor.

"If you mean an extra tire," the professor said, "there is one in the storage compartment."

Ken found the spare tire had very little air in it.

"Do you have an air pump?" Ken asked, compressing the tire to show it needed air.

"No," said the professor slowly. "No, I do not believe we have such an implement."

Ken could tell he was very concerned and seemed to be feeling worse.

"Well, no problem," said Ken cheerfully. "I'll take it back to the town we went through a few minutes ago and get it pumped up."

The professor seemed somewhat relieved there was a solution to the problem.

"I will be most appreciative if you are willing to do that," he said. "I would go with you if I was feeling better."

"I'll leave my bag and dog with you so you will know I won't forget to come back," said Ken with a smile as he started rolling the tire down the road. "I should be back in about an hour or so, I think."

Chapter 2

As he rolled the tire along the highway, Ken's thoughts dwelt on all the troubles the Meyer family had been through, and he was glad he could be helping them through this relatively minor problem. He rolled the tire into the service station at the edge of town, inflated it, and started to roll it back down the highway.

Just then the old station owner came out of his office. "Hey, kid," he said. "That tire don't look none too good. You better put it in that tank of water over there and see if it's going to hold air."

"Thanks, I should have thought of that," Ken said as it dawned on him there must be a reason the tire had so little air in it.

He rolled the tire over to the tank of water and put it in. As he rotated the tire to submerge each section, he was dismayed to see a stream of air bubbles rising to the surface.

"Oh no!" he exclaimed.

The station owner came over and looked at the bubbles.

"Afraid of that," he said. "When a tire gets that thin, it punctures pretty easy." He rotated the tire until the source of the bubbles was on top then took a pair of pliers from the pocket of his coveralls and pulled out a rather obscure part of a thorn. "We could patch the leak, but this tire don't look worth usin' even if the tube is in good shape, which ain't likely. Let me show you a pretty good used tire that's the same size."

Ken rather reluctantly followed the station owner to a rack of tires where he pulled out a tire that did look in much better condition than the one that Ken had brought in.

"A feller bought a couple tires yesterday, and I gave him a dollar off for his old ones since they are in pretty good shape. I'll sell you one for fifty cents. The tube is not real good, but I'll make sure it doesn't leak, and I'll even mount it on your rim."

"Well, it's not my car. I'm just a hitchhiker, but I guess I owe the owners for giving me a ride," Ken said slowly. "I'm pretty sure they don't have much money. They have had a pretty rough time of it. They are refugees from Germany and were robbed a while back. The old car they have was given to them by a relief agency."

"Yeah, from the looks of that tire, I would say they must be pretty hard up," said the station owner. "I hope their other tires are in better shape than this one. I'll bet they don't have no spare neither, or you wouldn't have come rollin' this one in here."

"This is the spare," said Ken. "I started to put it on to replace one that blew out."

The station owner rubbed the stubble on his chin thoughtfully. "Well, I've come through some pretty rough places a few times myself when someone helped me out. Tell you what. If you will give me fifty cents for this tire, I'll give the other one to them as a spare. Just have them come back in, and I'll mount it on their rim."

"That is sure kind of you," Ken said. "I'll be glad to give you the fifty cents, and I think they would really appreciate knowing they have a good spare!"

Without another word, the station owner took the tire into the garage section of the station, let the air out, and removed it from the rim. Surprisingly, the tube was in pretty good condition. He quickly patched the hole in the tube and tested it for leakage. He started to put it into the tire, but just then a car with what looked like tourists drove up to the gas pump.

"Fill er' up," the man said as he opened the car door, got out, and stretched. The station owner went to the car, took the gas cap off, and began filling the tank. The woman on the passenger side rolled her window down and emptied an overflowing ashtray onto the station's pavement. The mound of debris looked out of place in the otherwise tidy appearance of the station. The station owner frowned but said nothing.

A woman came bustling out the office door with a broom and dustpan and started sweeping up the cigarette butts and ashes. Ken was impressed with the woman's display of industriousness. When all the debris was swept up, she opened the back door of the car, emptied the dustpan on the car floor, and went back into the office. The station owner chuckled, but the woman in the car had an ugly expression on her face.

"We'll never stop in here again," she said.

The station owner smiled. "Well, we've been in business here almost twenty years," he said pleasantly. "I reckon maybe we might be able to get by a while longer." Then he raised the hood to check the oil, but after looking at the dipstick, he seemed satisfied that it was all right.

The man seemed embarrassed by his wife's actions and words but seemed willing to share the blame. "You know, that was pretty inconsiderate of us. We deserved what we got. I just wish we could give up this habit, and we wouldn't have to worry about getting rid of all our cigarette butts," he said. He meekly paid for the gasoline, and the car drove away.

The station owner was still smiling as he went back to finish mounting the tire for Ken. In a few minutes the job was complete. Anxious to be on his way, Ken handed the station owner fifty cents and reached out to take the tire just as a pickup pulled into the station and stopped by a gas pump.

"Now don't run off," said the station owner. "This feller will give you a ride." He rolled the tire over to the pickup and threw it into the bed. "Henry, this kid needs a lift back down the road toward your place."

"Sure," said Henry cheerfully. "Hop in. We'll leave as soon as I fill up."

Thanks to the unexpected ride, Ken was back sooner than he thought he would be. He got out of the pickup, removed the tire, and thanked Henry for the ride. Henry lifted his hand in a farewell salute and drove away.

The professor noticed it was a much better tire than the one Ken had left with and commented on it. While Ken was putting it on the car, he told the professor the station owner had been very generous and would give them another tire for the spare if they went back to town. The professor looked at the big hole in the tire that had blown out.

"It would no doubt be wise to have an extra tire for emergency," he said. "I think we should do as you say, although I do not wish to impose further on that person's generosity. Perhaps he will accept some payment."

From Ken's words, the professor got the impression the first tire had been a gift too, which was what Ken intended to convey.

The station owner met them as they arrived at the station and quickly removed the ruined tire from the rim and replaced it with the good, used tire. Then he checked the rest of the tires and made sure they were inflated to the proper pressure. The professor offered to pay for the tires, but the station owner waved him off.

The professor expressed his thanks and said, "Well, at least we can purchase some of your fuel," and asked for the tank to be filled.

When the tank was filled, the professor paid the station owner and said, "May the good Lord bless you for your kindness."

As they resumed their journey, the professor spoke again of his gratefulness to Ken and the station owner for resolving what he thought might be a serious problem, but then didn't seem to feel like talking, so Ken didn't try to involve him in conversation. Actually, he was glad to have a chance to just enjoy looking at all the new things he was seeing without any distraction.

The nice spring day along with the pleasure he felt with the new experience of traveling made him feel a little euphoric. The lush farm-lands on both sides of the road added scenic beauty. Ken was curious what the crops were that he was seeing. There were fields of several different green plants just on the other side of the fences, but Ken was not able to tell what most of them were. He did see several fields of corn.

Then he saw a field where there was a horse-drawn hayrack piled high with hay. A pleasant smell was wafting into the partially opened car window. A man was using a pitchfork to throw hay to another man, who was spreading it around on top of the load. The horses were being driven by a small boy. There was something appealing about the scene, and Ken hoped that might be part of his duties on his new job. This thought started him wondering just what kind of work he would be doing for his employer. No doubt he would be outside, and he liked that thought.

There were many interesting-looking farmhouses of various sizes along the way that usually had inviting porches. There were almost always barns some distance behind the houses and most of the time a number of smaller structures. Some of the farms had tall, cylindrical-shaped structures he learned later were called silos. He saw many green pastures with cows, horses, and sometimes sheep grazing. Looking at these peaceful scenes added to his feeling of contentment.

For almost a half hour, the highway went alongside a wide river. Ken saw several boats on the river, including a large one with two decks where there were several passengers standing at the rails. There seemed to be some sort of party going on. He heard the faint sound of music. Then he saw a sign on the side of the boat that said, "River Excursions."

A speedboat towing a man on water skis zoomed past on its way up the river. That looked fun. Other smaller boats seemed to be just drifting with the current with the people on board holding fishing poles. He also saw a few people fishing from the banks. It all looked very inviting, and he hoped someday he could experience the activities he was seeing.

Finally the highway crossed a bridge over the river and was once again traveling through farmlands. Seeing all these new sights was of real interest to Ken. The regret for having to leave the orphanage was beginning to fade.

Occasionally there was a low conversation taking place in the backseat in a language Ken assumed was German. He marveled over the fact that the jumble of confusing sounds obviously meant something to those who knew the language but were completely meaningless to him. Glancing in the rearview mirror, Ken saw that the boy seemed to be asleep still holding the puppy, which was also asleep. He was pleased that the car engine was humming along much better than he might have expected from its age. With the progress he was making toward his destination, he was feeling good about his decision to hitchhike. The only cause for concern was that the professor seemed restless and uncomfortable.

Some time later, out of the corner of his eye, Ken saw the professor clench his teeth and stiffen with pain. It happened again a short time later, and a low groan escaped his lips. Ken asked, "Is there anything I can do to help you, sir?"

Professor Meyer looked into the backseat and tried to smile away the obvious concern of his wife.

"Well, it seems I will need medical attention," he said heavily. "I do not want to do this because we have little money for doctors, but perhaps it is necessary to find one."

Ken pressed the accelerator down a little farther and hoped they could find a doctor in the town he could see in the distance. He could tell the professor was in constant pain. A few minutes later, they reached the town, and two blocks inside the city limits, he saw a sign labeled "Hospital" with an arrow pointing off to the right. Ken turned the car in the direction of the arrow and soon stopped in front of a freshly painted building with a sign identifying it as a hospital.

Ken turned to ask Professor Meyer if he could help him into the building, but he was doubled over with pain. Ken jumped out, ran into the building, and told the receptionist there was immediate need for emergency care. Minutes later a nurse was wheeling Professor Meyer into the examination room. The faces of Mrs. Meyer and the children reflected their anxiety.

Fifteen tension-filled minutes went by before the nurse returned and told them the professor had to have his appendix removed immediately, and then she went back to assist with the operation. Mrs. Meyer was looking even more panic-stricken, and Ken realized she had probably understood little of what the nurse had said. He repeated the nurse's words slowly, not knowing if she understood anything he was saying, but he supplemented his words with gestures, pointing to the appendix area. He smiled and nodded his head as he did this, trying to convey that this was a problem the doctor would be able to correct. He was glad to see some relaxation of the strain in her face, but it was obvious the wait was very stressful for her and her children.

Some time later the doctor appeared, still dressed in surgical garb. He said the operation was over, but there was a real possibility of complications since the appendix was badly infected and had ruptured.

"He will need to stay in the hospital several days and then be available for observation for at least two weeks. He has a remaining infection that could be serious if we don't treat it properly and make sure it has cleared up," the doctor said.

"Now I know this will impose a real hardship on you folks. Mr. Meyer has told me you are traveling and that he doesn't have the funds to pay for the operation nor the hospital stay, so I have a suggestion. The cherry harvest is just beginning in this area, and I've heard with so many men going into military service the growers are having a hard time finding the help they need and are paying higher wages than usual. If all of you could work in the harvest for two or three weeks while Mr. Meyer is recuperating, you should be able to pay a good portion of the hospital bill."

Ken realized the doctor assumed he was a part of the family, and he started to tell him he had to go on to his destination. Then a cascade of thoughts tumbled through his mind. He thought of his obligation to the farmer he was supposed to work for and the assurance of a job that would replace the security the orphanage had provided. Then he glanced at Mrs. Meyer and saw the anxiety on her face. He thought how frightening it must be for her with her husband unable to help her when she was in a foreign culture where she didn't even understand the language. To make matters worse, she apparently had little money, and yet she had the responsibility for providing for her children. Someone needed to help this poor woman, and if he didn't have a commitment, he would like to help. But who would help her if he didn't?

Suddenly, with a feeling of reckless exhilaration, he decided he was going to stay and try to help them and not worry about the consequences. He would just telephone the farmer and explain the situation. With this decision made, he told the doctor the suggestion to work in the harvest sounded like something they should consider. But Ken wondered what the Meyers would think about it when they understood the suggestion. He couldn't picture them doing manual labor.

"You can see Mr. Meyer now, but he probably won't make much sense for a while," the doctor was saying. The nurse was passing by, and the doctor asked her to take the family in to see Mr. Meyer. Then he turned and left to see another patient.

"Come with me," the nurse said, and started down the corridor.

Ken gestured to Mrs. Meyer that she and the children were to follow the nurse. Ken sat down in the waiting room thinking about the developments. When he had first thought of hitchhiking, he wondered if he would have any of the kind of experiences Larry had talked about, but none of the adventures Larry had related were anything like this! He smiled as he thought someday he might be telling children of his hitchhiking adventures like Larry had.

He suddenly thought about Buddy. Benjamin had probably left him in the car, but he knew he'd better check on him. When he got to the car, Buddy seemed glad to find out he hadn't been abandoned. Ken put him out of the car and let him run around a while. Then he thought the Meyers might think he had run off and left them if they didn't see him the waiting room, so he put Buddy in the car and went back inside. Finally Benjamin came into the waiting room and motioned for Ken to follow him.

The professor was still groggy, but he gave Ken a weak smile and said, "My young friend, I am most grateful for your help. I wish I could repay you for your kindness, but we have little money, and now we have this extra expense for which we cannot pay. Also my family will need someplace to stay until we are able to travel again. God must show us what we are to do."

Ken told him of the doctor's suggestion that they work in the cherry harvest to help pay the hospital bill and added, "I will try to help your family find a job in the harvest if they want to do that."

The professor did not seem to be at all enthusiastic about this suggestion. The idea of having his family work when he had always been the breadwinner was obviously foreign to him, but there seemed to be no alternative. "Would there be danger?" he asked finally.

"No, I don't think so," Ken said. "I don't know much about picking cherries, but it doesn't seem to me there would be any danger other than from something like possibly falling off a ladder. I will try to watch out for them. I might as well work here with them instead of going where I was scheduled to go."

The professor seemed somewhat relieved. "That would be so good of you!" he said. "I will be even more in your debt if you are willing to do that. I feel very helpless not being able to care for my family. It seems God has sent you to us as a guardian angel!"

He turned and talked to his wife and children, evidently asking them if working in the cherry harvest was something they would be willing to do. Mrs. Meyer, somewhat apprehensively, slowly nodded her head, not knowing what would be involved. Then the professor apparently told her Ken had said he would work with them because she flashed a smile in his direction.

While the professor was still talking with his wife, Ken went to the reception desk and asked the middle-aged lady there if she knew of an inexpensive place the Meyer family could stay.

"Well," she said, "there are three motels in town, but I have no idea what they charge. You could check with them, I guess. You would probably be better off trying Mrs. Schmidt's boardinghouse. She is a widow and keeps the boardinghouse as a means of support. I don't know if she has any vacancies, but it's a nice place, and she does serve meals."

The boardinghouse sounded like a good option to Ken, so he asked for directions to it. Armed with this information, he went back to the professor's room and told him what he had learned from the receptionist.

"That is good," said the professor. "We will pray there will be space available and the cost will not be too great. Would you be so good as to take my family to investigate?"

"Yes, sir," Ken said. "I will be glad to do that."

Mrs. Schmidt was a warm, motherly type. When she came to the door in response to Ken's knock, he greeted her and asked if she had room for a lady and her two children to stay until her husband got out of the hospital and was able to travel again. Mrs. Schmidt read the fearful, strained look on Mrs. Meyer's face and reached out and took both of her hands in hers.

"Yes, I do have a vacant room with a double bed and a nice shed where your boy can stay. Come right on in, and I'll show you the room!"

Mrs. Meyer understood the welcome more from the attitude than the words and blinked back tears of gratefulness.

"They don't understand much English," Ken said. "They are from Germany."

"Land sakes!" said Mrs. Schmidt. "My parents emigrated from Germany, and we spoke German at home until I was about in the sixth grade. Then my parents decided we should speak only English! I haven't spoken German for years, but let's see if I can remember any of it." She haltingly began to address Mrs. Meyer in German, interspersed with a few English words.

Mrs. Meyer burst into tears and spontaneously hugged Mrs. Schmidt. The two talked for several minutes with the children listening intently. Then she apparently told the Meyers to go with her to look at the room because they started into the house.

Mrs. Schmidt turned to Ken and asked, "What about you? Do you need someplace to stay?"

"Well, I guess I'll ask them if they would mind if my puppy and I sleep in their car," Ken said. "I've decided to try to stick around and see if I can help them."

"Nonsense!" said Mrs. Schmidt. "We can make up two pallets in the shed. Your puppy will like having the backyard to run around in. You may as well put him back there now and let him get some exercise. Oh my!" she said suddenly. "I must get supper on the table. My boarders will be coming to eat soon. I don't suppose you folks have eaten, have you?"

Ken shook his head.

"Well, I'll set some places for you. I'll show them the room, and then I need to get busy." She turned and spoke to Mrs. Meyer, and together they went up the stairs. In a few minutes, they reappeared. To Ken, Mrs. Schmidt said, "She wants to go back to the hospital and tell her husband they have a place to stay. She says he will be worrying about them and wants to know if you will take them."

"Of course," Ken said. "Anytime they want to go."

Mrs. Schmidt translated Ken's reply, and Mrs. Meyer looked at him with a smile. The friendly reception she had received from Mrs. Schmidt and the knowledge they had someplace to stay seemed to have lifted her spirits considerably. She beckoned to her children and started for the car, and Ken followed.

"I'll have something for you to eat when you get back," Mrs. Schmidt called after them.

Those words were music to Ken's ears.

In a few minutes they were back at the hospital. Ken sat down in the waiting room and tried to subdue his growing hunger pains, which had been stimulated by Mrs. Schmidt's mention of food. The hot dog was the only thing he had had to eat since breakfast, and his stomach was reminding him of that fact.

He shuffled through the stack of magazines on the table beside him. He hadn't realized there were so many different magazines published. The first magazine he picked up was a farm journal. Since he expected he would eventually be working for the farmer when the Meyers' crisis was over, he thought he would see if there might be something that would help him understand his job better.

There was an article about different brands of farm implements and testimonials by farmers who had used them and another article about the equipment needed for new methods of irrigating. There was a section where a question was asked about what to do about an infestation of a corn crop by corn stalk borers along with the answer by an entomologist as to the best way to deal with the problem. There was a lengthy article about ways to increase the quantity and quality of various kinds of produce. This article included color pictures of beautiful-looking vegetables, fruits, and berries, which made him even hungrier. He decided to lay that magazine aside and look at something that would distract him from his hunger.

He picked up a *Saturday Evening Post*, thumbed through it, and looked at the cartoons. Then he found an issue of *Popular Science* that had an interesting article that told of some of the revolutionary new products that were foreseen as a result of recent scientific discoveries. He had just about finished the article when he became aware that Benjamin was beckoning him to come with him to Professor Meyer's room.

Professor Meyer was much more alert than when Ken had last seen him. He greeted Ken warmly and said, "I just wanted to thank you again, my young friend. I'm very grateful that you have found such a good place for my family to lodge. You have truly been a blessing sent from God. May your heavenly reward be great! But I must let you all go. My wife tells me food is being prepared for you at your place of residence. We must not let the dear lady who is providing it become distressed that you and my family are not there to partake of it."

With that, he bid his family good-bye and told them to go to their meal.

Back at the boardinghouse, Mrs. Schmidt greeted them with her pleasant smile. Her regular boarders had already eaten, so she ushered them into her cozy kitchen and seated them at a large, round table. She gave them each a big bowl of stew with some hot biscuits and honey. Ken's hunger made the stew taste exceptionally good, and the biscuits and honey were a real treat. He was thankful when Mrs. Schmidt refilled his empty bowl. Then she served them a piece of delicious apple pie.

While she was busy washing her boarders' supper dishes, she carried on a conversation with Mrs. Meyer.

Finally, as she was finishing the dishes, Mrs. Schmidt looked at Ken and said, "I fed your puppy a while ago. He is really a cute one! But these ladies look tired. We had better let them get some rest. I will fix beds for you and Benjamin now. You can help if you want to, but first why don't you bring in their luggage?"

"I will be glad to do that," Ken said. "Would you ask Mrs. Meyer if she wants all their things brought in?"

When Mrs. Schmidt relayed this question, Mrs. Meyer indicated she would go to the car with him, and Rebecca jumped up to join them. Ken opened the trunk and took out his bag. Mrs. Meyer took out a small suitcase, and Rebecca lifted out an overnight case. Mrs. Meyer then pointed to a larger suitcase she wanted. Ken set the suitcase out, closed the trunk, and handed Mrs. Meyer the car keys. She smiled as she took the keys but then handed them back.

Carrying the suitcase, Ken followed the ladies to the upstairs bedroom. When he got back downstairs, Mrs. Schmidt handed him some blankets and two pillows. He followed her into the backyard and helped make two pallets on the floor of the shed.

"This is not going to be like sleeping on an innerspring mattress, but you young fellows look tough enough to be able to sleep without all the frills," Mrs. Schmidt said.

"I'm sure we will be fine," Ken said. "It looks mighty inviting to me."

Ken had noticed a drugstore on the main street a few blocks away from the boardinghouse and thought they might have a public telephone he could use to call the farmer, who was expecting him. Mr. Tanner had given him a slip of paper with the farmer's address and telephone number. He told Mrs. Schmidt he was going to run an errand but should be back in twenty or thirty minutes.

The walk was a pleasant change after riding so long. The drugstore did have a public telephone as he had hoped, and he asked a clerk for change for a dollar. He put a nickel in the pay phone as instructed by the posted notice and dialed the operator, who promptly asked for the desired telephone number. In response to her instruction, he deposited twenty cents. As he listened to the ringing phone, he hoped it was not too late to be calling. He had heard that farmers got up early, so they went to bed early. The farmer might really be angry with him if he was in bed already. It was bad enough to have to tell him he was not going to show up when expected.

When the farmer answered the phone, Ken identified himself and told him a family was in desperate need of his help for a while, so he wouldn't be able to show up when planned. Mr. Williams was not pleased with the news, but after hearing Ken describe the situation, he grudgingly agreed that Ken should stay and help them through their crisis.

Then he said, "But I do need help. Get here as soon as you can."

Ken agreed to do that and hung up, glad the farmer hadn't objected too strongly. He hoped if Mr. Tanner found out about the delay he would not be angry that he had not followed through with his plans. If he had taken the bus as intended, he would never have become involved in this situation, but he didn't regret his decision to hitchhike.

As he started out of the store, he saw a display of peppermint sticks. On an impulse he bought one, thinking it might be a way to help him become better acquainted with Benjamin since they were not going to be able to communicate much verbally.

He stepped out of the drugstore and looked up and down the street. What a nice town! It was much larger than Meadowview, which had impressed him on his way through. The streets were wider and cleaner, and the store buildings had an inviting look. With the exception of the drugstore and a restaurant, all the other businesses he could see had closed for the day. There were a few people coming out of a restaurant and some others a couple blocks away, but other than that the streets seemed deserted. Daylight was beginning to fade, and a few lights were coming on.

The peaceful scene reminded him of a picture he had seen somewhere. He had been so focused on finding medical help for Professor Meyer he had not noticed the name of the town when they came into the city limits. He knew he would find that out later, but whatever the name, he liked its looks.

Benjamin was sitting on the threshold of the shed playing with Buddy when Ken returned. Mrs. Schmidt had given Buddy a bone left over from the stew, and when Benjamin pretended he was trying to take it away, Buddy seemed to enjoy the tussling. When Ken handed Benjamin the peppermint stick, he smiled his thanks then laid it on his pallet and went to the hydrant just outside the shed, where he rinsed his hands. Ken was glad to see him do that after handling Buddy's bone and knew he was seeing evidence of good training.

Benjamin removed the cellophane wrapping from the peppermint stick, broke it in half, and handed one of the halves to Ken. Ken had not been expecting him to share the candy, but he took it, and they enjoyed the treat together.

Ken had not been back long before Mrs. Schmidt came to the darkening shed with a lighted lantern.

"It wouldn't do for you fellows to get lost and not be able to find your way to bed. This light should help," she said with a smile.

Ken thanked her for her thoughtfulness, and she bade them good night and went back into the house. The lantern cast a cheerful glow over the shed's interior. The rustic shed with the fragrant smell of pine wood made a pleasant, cozy atmosphere. It was such a contrast to the orphanage dormitory with its rows of beds. Ken was glad to be staying in the shed instead of the house.

Benjamin seemed intrigued with his shadow cast on the wall by the lantern and watched while he went through a variety of motions and used his hands to create shapes that looked like birds and other creatures. Ken was amused with the performance and watched until Benjamin tired of making shadow images. Ken thought they needed to start somewhere in being able to communicate, so he pointed to various objects and told Benjamin the English words for each item, and he seemed to appreciate the opportunity to learn. Finally Ken blew out the lantern, and they crawled into the comfortable pallets.

"Good night, Benjamin," he said.

Benjamin seemed to understand the greeting and repeated it back to Ken. With his hands clasped behind his head, Ken looked through the open door of the shed at the friendly, twinkling stars and smiled as he thought about what a different day this had been. He fell asleep with a mixture of emotions swirling through his head, but predominate was the satisfied feeling he was doing the right thing.

Chapter 3

Ken awoke from a sound sleep with Buddy licking his face. It was daylight, and he could see the morning dew sparkling in the sun on the bushes in the yard. It took only a few minutes to dress and wash up at the outside hydrant. The fresh morning air was invigorating, and he felt a twinge of excitement wondering what new adventures the day held. It surprised him to see how refreshing it was to break out of the routine at the orphanage. He went to the screened back porch, opened the screen door, and went in. The sound of rattling dishes was coming from the kitchen; Mrs. Schmidt was up and preparing breakfast.

When Ken rapped on the kitchen door, Mrs. Schmidt opened it and said, "Land sakes! Just come on in. I never lock the doors!"

"Good morning," Ken said as he entered the kitchen. "Is there anything I can do to help you?"

"Why yes, there is," Mrs. Schmidt said with a smile. "I need some more eggs. You could go out to the henhouse and gather the eggs for me. That would be a big help. Just a minute and I will give you something to put them in." She turned and picked up a pan, which she handed to

Ken. "Don't take the eggs from the farthest nest from the door. That big red hen is hatching some chicks for me."

Ken found nearly a dozen eggs in the various nests. This was a task he had done many times at the orphanage. When he had finished gathering the eggs, he saw the chickens' water container was almost empty. There was a bucket hanging on a nail on the side of chicken house, which he used to refill the container.

When he took the eggs into the kitchen, Mrs. Schmidt said she was going to scramble them and asked him to break them into a bowl she handed him. While she continued preparing breakfast, Ken told her about the doctor's suggestion that the Meyers work in the cherry harvest to pay for Professor Meyer's hospital bill and asked her if she had any suggestions as to where they should apply for jobs.

Mrs. Schmidt listened sympathetically. "Well, there are several places you could try," she said, "but I think a good place to start would be at Bill Dalton's place. He has a packing shed where the fruit is processed for shipment. The girls might like to try to get on working in the shed rather than picking. I doubt that they are used to manual labor. Those ladders can get pretty heavy by the end of the day. By the way, I have some overalls and work shirts I used in my fruit-picking days. They are too small for me now, but they should fit Rachel fine. They would be pretty big for Rebecca, but maybe she could get by with them. They certainly would be better than a dress."

Ken asked if she could give him directions to the Dalton farm, and Mrs. Schmidt quickly sketched a rough map and handed it to him.

It was nearly seven o'clock and almost time for breakfast. Ken went to the shed to make sure Benjamin was going to be ready for breakfast and found he had almost finished dressing. Soon after he had reentered the house, two female teachers who were staying together at the boardinghouse came into the dining room and sat down at the big table. They were followed shortly by a smiling, elderly man, then by a younger man who worked for the telephone company. They all in turn wished Ken a friendly good morning, and he returned their greeting.

Mrs. Schmidt asked Ken to get Benjamin then went to the foot of the stairs and called to the Meyer ladies to come to breakfast, and soon they joined the others in the dining room. Mrs. Schmidt introduced the Meyer family and Ken and explained the reason for their being there and mentioned the Meyers didn't understand much English. The regular boarders welcomed them sympathetically. The Meyer ladies shyly sat down at the table. Mrs. Schmidt went into the kitchen and returned with large platters of scrambled eggs, ham, and pancakes.

Miss Susan Crawford, a middle-aged schoolteacher, looked at the ham, turned to Mrs. Schmidt, and softly said, "Clara, Meyer sounds like a Jewish name! They may want something else to eat."

"Goodness," said Mrs. Schmidt, "I didn't think about that!" She turned to Mrs. Meyer and spoke to her in German. Mrs. Meyer answered with a smile, and Mrs. Schmidt seemed relieved. She asked more questions that Mrs. Meyer answered to her apparent satisfaction. She turned back to Miss Crawford and said, "Deborah says they are Messianic Jews and don't feel they necessarily have to follow the Jewish dietary laws, but they do think they are good laws to follow, partly because she believes they are healthful. She says that some Messianic Jews do feel like they should eat only kosher foods, but others believe it doesn't matter as long as they are grateful to God for the food. She says not to worry about what I fix to eat. I'm sure glad of that. I wouldn't know how to cook if I had to go by all those Jewish food laws!"

Ken was curious about the term *Messianic* but didn't want to ask what it meant. He noticed that Mrs. Meyer didn't eat any ham, but Rebecca and Benjamin did.

Ken enjoyed the breakfast and the pleasant conversation between the other residents. Occasionally they would ask him a question, and he knew they were trying to make him feel welcome. Mrs. Schmidt asked him if he wanted some coffee. He had never had any before, but it smelled so good he didn't object when she poured some into the cup before him. When he tasted it, he was a little disappointed that it didn't taste as good as it smelled, but after adding a teaspoon of sugar and some cream, he enjoyed it.

The rest of the boarders got up from the table to go about their activities for the day. Ken had sort of an inner compulsion to help out when he saw anything that needed to be done, and when Mrs. Schmidt started stacking the breakfast dishes, he began helping and carried the stack of plates into the kitchen. Mrs. Schmidt smiled her thanks.

"I think you are going to turn out to be a real blessing around here!" she said.

Then she disappeared up the stairs and returned a short time later with two pairs of faded overalls and two long-sleeved shirts. She handed them to Mrs. Meyer and explained they would need clothes like these, that it was just not practical to wear a dress while working in the cherry harvest, especially if they were climbing ladders. Mrs. Meyer seemed a little uncomfortable as she looked at the overalls, and Ken suspected she had never worn anything besides dresses. Mrs. Schmidt asked if Benjamin had some appropriate clothes to wear, and Mrs. Meyer said he did but asked if he wouldn't be too young to work.

"No, I don't think so," Mrs. Schmidt said. "It's not too unusual for children his age to work in the harvest if they are with an adult. They can't handle the ladders very well, but they can pick a lot of fruit from the ground and from inside the tree. I've never seen a boy yet who didn't like to climb around in trees!"

Ken asked Mrs. Schmidt to tell the Meyers he was ready to take them to look for jobs any time they wanted to leave. When Ken's words were interpreted, the ladies immediately went to change into the clothes Mrs. Schmidt had given them. Ken and Benjamin went to the shed and changed. Although the clothes Ken put on were not much different from the ones he had been wearing, they did show more evidence of wear.

They went back into the house, and soon Mrs. Meyer and Rebecca came downstairs looking quite different than they had a few minutes before. Ken had trouble keeping from smiling at Rebecca's appearance. She had been so neat in a nice dress, but Mrs. Schmidt's clothes hung on her loosely, and she had turned up her pants legs and shirt sleeves. She or her mother had also tied a sash or cloth belt around her waist to pull the gaping overalls next to her body. He could tell she felt very uncomfortable, and it was probably only the urgent need to help the family in their crisis that made her willing to endure the humiliation. Mrs. Meyer, who had the air of a gracious lady of refinement, also seemed out of place in the faded overalls, although they did fit fairly well. She did look as if she was a little embarrassed to be dressed in what she probably considered to be men's clothing.

Mrs. Schmidt looked at Mrs. Meyer's and Rebecca's long hair and immediately left and returned with two cloths that she used to pull their hair up into not unattractive head coverings. Benjamin appeared to be eager to go. He seemed to think it was going to be great fun to work with the adults.

Ken asked Mrs. Schmidt to tell Mrs. Meyer they could stop by the hospital to check on the professor if she wished, and she promptly did as requested. Mrs. Meyer looked at him with a smile and nodded.

Ken hoped the hospital visit would be short; he knew it was important to the Meyers to find a job as soon as possible so they would be able to pay their bills and go on to their destination. When the others got out he remained in the car, which he hoped they would take as an indication he didn't expect them to stay long. He wondered what the professor would think when he saw them in their working clothes.

A scant ten minutes later Mrs. Meyer and her children reappeared, ready to begin their job search. From their attitude Ken gathered they must have felt the professor was feeling all right. After looking again at the map Mrs. Schmidt had made for him, they started out and ten minutes later arrived at the Dalton farm.

"You bet!" said the Dalton foreman. "We sure can use some more help. Have you ever picked before?"

Ken said that he hadn't and didn't think the others had either. He mentioned they didn't speak much English, so he couldn't ask them.

"That's okay," the foreman said, referring to the lack of experience. "It's not like it is complicated. I will just have to do a little more explaining."

Ken asked if there was any chance the ladies could work in the packing house.

"Well," said the foreman, "our greatest need is for pickers, but if the rest of you pick, I could use another person in the shed. I guess I would like to have the older one for that. Of course, packing shed workers get paid by the hour instead of how much fruit they handle."

In spite of this possible disadvantage, Ken told the foreman he still thought it would be a better job for her. He just couldn't picture Mrs. Meyer carrying a ladder around. When he asked how much she would be paid, the foreman said it would be thirty cents an hour—about what an average picker would make. Ken vowed to himself he would try hard to do better than average and was excited to learn he could be earning so much.

The foreman took them all into the packing shed and gave Ken and the children pails with a hook on the bail and loops of rope. He told them the rope could be placed around the neck and the bucket hung from the loop or on a belt to allow the hands to be free for picking. He then gave each of them a set of tags with numbers on them. Each picker would have a different set of numbers that they would put on the boxes of fruit they picked. This provided a means of knowing who to credit with the work. Their assigned numbers were entered in a ledger, which was used to record the amount of fruit each worker had picked and provided the basis for their pay.

The foreman told Ken he would take them to the area where they were to start picking as soon as he showed Mrs. Meyer what she was to do. She would be working beside two other ladies who at that time were busy packing fruit picked the previous day into boxes for shipment to grocers in the nearby city.

Although some pickers were already at work, most of the packing shed operation had not yet started. The foreman motioned for Mrs. Meyer to follow him and led her to a conveyor belt and showed her where to stand. For training purposes, he didn't start the belt right away but spread some cherries on the belt to show her that she was to pick out bird-pecked, damaged, and not quite ripe cherries and toss them into the waste container beside her. Then he spread some cherries over a section of the belt and started it moving slowly. He watched while Mrs. Meyer deftly picked out the defective fruit, and he nodded his head in satisfaction. He then pointed to a box she could sit on until regular operations began then turned to his new pickers.

Before they left the shed, the foreman showed them there were restrooms in one end of the shed. As they were leaving, Ken signaled to Mrs. Meyer he would watch out for Rebecca and Benjamin. The foreman led Ken and the children to a flat bed, open cab truck used in the orchard to gather the boxes of picked fruit and instructed them to sit on the edge of the truck bed. He got into the driver's seat, drove to the side of the packing shed where there were several ladders leaning against the building, and threw two of the shorter ones on the truck bed.

"There are three varieties of cherry trees on this farm," he said. "The ones we are picking now are the earliest, and the trees are smaller than the others. For now, these ladders will be tall enough. When we get to the other orchards, you will need some that are longer. I guess one long one would be enough for you folks, just so someone in your group is able to reach the high limbs."

The truck wound its way through the extensive orchards until they came to a section where there were some pickers already at work. They looked curiously at the new arrivals but smiled a welcome. The foreman took them to the tree next to one that was being picked and took the ladders off the truck.

"Be gentle with the fruit, leave the stems on, pick the tree clean, and when you finish picking this tree, go to the next tree in this row that isn't being picked," he said. "When this row is done, start back up the next row. Remember to put your tags on the boxes you put your cherries in," he said, pointing to the empty boxes that had already been placed under the trees. "You are probably going to get thirsty. There will always be a container of water with some folding paper cups in the row being picked or close to it. That's about it. You show the kids what to do," he said to Ken. With that he got into the truck and headed back toward the packing shed.

Ken demonstrated to Rebecca and Benjamin that they were to pick the cherries by grasping the stem. He then picked a cherry without the stem, shook his head, and showed them the fruit was bruised by his grasp. They nodded their heads in understanding. With that Ken climbed up his ladder and started picking. Rebecca and Benjamin immediately followed suit.

Ken was impressed with the enthusiastic way they went to work. They did not show the slightest reluctance to energetically involve themselves in manual labor, which was most likely foreign to them. Their family's financial problems were no doubt a motivating factor. He was especially impressed with Rebecca. She had quick hands, which somewhat made up for her limited reach. However, she was hampered with having to occasionally re-roll her pants legs and sleeves, but did this quickly and without complaint.

They let Benjamin pick all the cherries he could from the ground. Ken concentrated mainly on the fruit that was the highest, and Rebecca picked the fruit that was out of Benjamin's reach but lower than Ken was picking. Sometimes Ken helped Rebecca move her ladder. She was able to do it herself, but he wanted her to save her energy so she would be able to continue working throughout the day. When they finished picking a tree and started past the trees being picked by others, Ken carried both ladders.

They had picked several trees and were walking to their next tree when they saw the large, five-gallon water jug that the foreman had mentioned. Ken didn't know if they were thirsty, but he wanted Rebecca and Benjamin to know the water was there for them to use, so he stopped at the jug, filled a paper cup with water, and held it out to Rebecca, another one to Benjamin, then had one himself.

With the three of them working with zeal, it didn't take long to finish picking a tree. Ken felt like it was a challenge to try to pick more trees than the other pickers, who were mostly women and usually working in groups of two, although there was one elderly man who was by himself. Ken took pride in making sure the tree was stripped clean and at first occasionally checked Benjamin's cherries to make sure he was leaving the stems on.

As they worked, Rebecca would sometimes point at something and ask, "What is English?"

Ken would tell her the word for that item and would occasionally ask her for the equivalent German word. Because she obviously wanted to learn, Ken sometimes voluntarily pointed out objects to her and told her what to call them. Once she heard the word, she seemed to have no trouble remembering it. Ken was impressed with the maturity she displayed as a young teenager, particularly with her consistent concentration on the job she was doing. Benjamin worked pretty steadily too but would pause occasionally and eat a few cherries.

Ken was so absorbed in his work that he was surprised when the foreman came around with the truck and announced it was lunchtime. He instructed all the pickers to leave their picking gear and get on the truck bed. Everyone sat on the edge of the bed while the truck made its way to the packing shed where they had left their lunches. Mrs. Schmidt had thoughtfully prepared lunches for Ken and the Meyers.

Mrs. Meyer was obviously glad to see her children again. Ken thought she had probably been a little worried seeing her children go off to work without her and was relived to see no harm had come to them. She also probably felt rather isolated not being able to communicate much with the other workers. As they sat on some packing boxes and ate their lunches, they talked excitedly. Ken heard the children mention his name occasionally, and sometimes Rebecca would mention an English word she had learned.

Soon the lunch period was over, and it was time to go back to work. The foreman again gave them a ride back to where they had been working. As Rebecca slid off the truck bed, she tripped over her dangling leg of her overalls and twisted her ankle. She uttered a little cry of pain, hobbled for a few steps, and stopped to rub her ankle and re-roll the unruly overall leg. She limped for several steps but didn't seem to be hurt badly, but Ken knew something needed to be done about the oversized clothes.

The afternoon went rather quickly for Ken. He could tell Rebecca and Benjamin were getting tired, but they kept working doggedly. Around five thirty, the foreman came around with his truck picking up the boxes of cherries and told them it was time to quit for the day.

"Just leave your picking gear and ladders here, and you can finish the tree you are working on in the morning. Leave one of your tags on an empty box so you will know for sure which tree you were working on," he said.

Ken was proud of the amount of cherries they had picked and wondered how much money they had made. They walked back to the packing shed where Mrs. Meyer was waiting for them.

As they came into town, Mrs. Meyer indicated she wanted to stop at the hospital again. Ken waited a few minutes to give the family some time together. Then he went in, greeted the professor, and asked if he would mind if he used their car to run a quick errand.

"Please do," said the professor. "You have been so kind. We will be happy for you to use it."

"Thank you," Ken said. "I should not be gone long."

He had seen a dry goods store on the main street across from the drugstore, and he went directly to it. The clerk was about to close the store but allowed Ken to go in.

"I need some overalls for a slender girl about this tall," Ken said, holding his hand at the height he estimated for Rebecca.

The clerk led him to some stacks of overalls and picked out some she felt met his description. Ken held them up and agreed they should be about right. He then asked for a work shirt for the same person. The cost of the new clothes was a little less than three dollars. As he paid for his purchase, once again Ken was glad he had not spent the money the orphanage administrator had given him. With the money he was making, it would not take long to replace the three dollars. He quickly made his way back to the hospital.

Professor Meyer again thanked Ken for helping his family find a job so promptly and for watching out for them.

Then he said, "I think you should now return to your place of residence for your supper so the dear lady there doesn't become impatient."

Ken nodded, and the professor told his family they should go. Ken knew he was partly concerned with the obvious weariness on the faces of his wife and children.

As they got out of the car at the boardinghouse, Ken handed Rebecca the sack with the new clothes in it. She looked at him questioningly then looked into the sack and took out the overalls. She uttered a little cry of pleasure as she held them up to her body. The clerk's guess about the size had been a good one. The shirt also looked like it would fit pretty well. Rebecca had a happy smile and sparkling eyes as she looked at Ken and spoke two of the English words her father had taught her— "Thank you!"—clutching the new clothes to her bosom. Mrs. Meyer also smiled her appreciation and laid her hand on his arm.

Mrs. Schmidt knew the harvesters would probably be late for her regular supper time and had set the kitchen table for them. The fried chicken and mashed potatoes and gravy tasted heavenly after a hard day's work. Mrs. Schmidt asked Ken how things had worked out, and Ken told her they had followed her suggestion and had gone to the Dalton farm and been promptly hired.

Mrs. Schmidt started talking to Mrs. Meyer in her broken German. Mrs. Meyer seemed so grateful to have someone to talk to in her language. They talked for some time, apparently sharing their experiences of working in the harvest. At one point there was a pause in the conversation, and both ladies sat looking at Ken with big smiles on their faces. Ken felt a flush creep over his face as he realized he had been the topic being discussed.

After the Meyer ladies had gone up to their room, Mrs. Schmidt came over and gave Ken a hug.

"That was sure thoughtful of you to get those clothes for Rebecca," she said. "Rachel was telling me how good you have been to them ever since they met you. It's so nice to know you are not just handsome; you have a good heart."

Ken was embarrassed and pleased at the same time.

A sequence of days had begun that were some of the happiest Ken could remember. It gave him a feeling of satisfaction to be earning money for the first time in his life. He enjoyed the challenge of seeing how much fruit he could pick, the fresh smell of the orchard, the cama-raderie with the rest of the harvest crew, and the good feeling he had about being the protector of the Meyer family. He marveled over how rapidly they were learning English, particularly Rebecca.

Rebecca's new work clothes had provided an obvious boost to her self-esteem, and she was able to devote her full time to picking instead of having to stop and re-roll her overall legs and shirt sleeves. As the days went by, Ken could see her changing from a rather shy, quiet girl into a laughing, fun-filled person.

Ken began to feel she was sort of a little sister and started calling her "Becky." She seemed pleased with the nickname.

Benjamin had an obvious admiration for Ken, and they enjoyed each other's company both while they were working and when they had left the others and had gone to their cozy, private quarters in the backyard. Benjamin had found an old baseball in the hospital parking lot, and sometimes while it was still light, they played catch for a little while. They also had fun throwing a stick for Buddy to retrieve. Buddy always seemed overjoyed when they were playing with him.

Mrs. Meyer was always so pleasant and seemed to be trying hard to show her appreciation for Ken's help. The more Ken and Mrs. Meyer, Rebecca, and Benjamin were able to communicate, the stronger the bond between them became. Ken's respect for Professor Meyer also continued to grow as he became better acquainted with him. He seemed to have a wide range of knowledge about so many things. Ken was sure he must have an exceptionally high degree of intelligence.

After over a week in the hospital, the doctor had released Professor Meyer to go stay with his family in the boardinghouse, but he still had to go back to the doctor every few days to make sure he was recovering from his infection. Mrs. Schmidt had fixed a pallet on the floor of their bedroom for Rebecca. The family was obviously happy to be together again.

The one dark cloud was in regard to Professor Meyer's employment. While he was still in the hospital, he had telephoned the college that had offered him a teaching position and informed them he was not going to be able to be there on the date summer school started as planned. A college representative had called back a few days later and said they had employed someone else, so they no longer needed his services. In spite of this, Professor Meyer remained optimistic.

"God will provide," he said.

Each week the Meyer family paid Mrs. Schmidt for their board and room then applied the rest of their cherry-picking income to the hospital bill, supplementing the rather small amount of money Professor Meyer was able to give them.

With the growing esteem and concern he had for the Meyers, after he had paid Mrs. Schmidt, Ken also went by each week and applied some of his earnings to the bill. When this was discovered, the Meyers were astonished. They protested, but Ken told them that was what he wanted to do. He felt amply rewarded by their friendship and the sincere appreciation they showed, and since he was used to not having any money, the amount of his pay that he kept for himself seemed like more than enough.

By the end of the third week, the hospital presented them with the bill marked, "paid." Ken felt sure they had reduced the charges to make paying the bill achievable. Having that obligation out of the way was a big boost to their morale.

The cherry harvest was coming to a close. The crew reduced in size as some quit to take other jobs that would last longer. The foreman asked Rebecca to work with her mother in the packing shed to take the place of a woman who had quit, which delighted them both. The next morning the foreman announced that there were not many unpicked trees left and estimated they would finish the harvest by noon.

As Ken and Benjamin were picking the last few trees, Ken was surprised to see Bill Dalton, the owner, approaching him. He was a distinguished-looking man about the same height as Ken. He walked with a slight limp. He held out his hand and introduced himself.

"Ken, I hear you are an exceptionally good worker, and I would like to have you work for me the rest of the summer if you are interested."

"Thank you, Mr. Dalton," Ken said. "I think I would like that. But I was supposed to go to work for a farmer near Riverdale over three weeks ago, and when the Meyer family needed help, I called him and said I wouldn't be able to show up for a while. He asked me to get there as soon as I could, and I agreed to do that. He may still be counting on me, so I guess I owe it to him to call and ask if he still needs me."

"Well, do what you have to do," Mr. Dalton said, "but if there's a chance you don't have to work for him, I would like to know as soon as possible. My hired man has just left to go into the army, so I need to hire someone right away. The fellow who was acting as the harvest foreman was working for me on a temporary basis. He has his own farm but doesn't have any cherry orchards, so he was available to help me out. When I asked if he knew anyone who I could hire, he recommended you." Then he asked, "What are the Meyers' plans? I suppose they will be moving on soon."

Professor Meyer's medical problem and Ken's help to the family had become well-known in the community.

"They are not sure what they are going to do now," Ken said, and he told Mr. Dalton the teaching job Professor Meyer had been counting on had fallen through because he was not able to start when they wanted him.

"That's rotten luck," Mr. Dalton said. He paused in thought. "Do you know what he was going to teach?"

"He said he was going to teach French and two mathematics classes," Ken said.

"Well now, Mrs. Kline is teaching math at the high school, but she is expecting a baby in a few months. She didn't want to teach summer school, but we weren't able to find anyone else to do it. I'm on the school board, so I get involved some in hiring teachers," Mr. Dalton said. "Tell Mr. Meyer if he is interested to go talk to the principal. If he has been teaching math on the college level, he would certainly be qualified to teach it in high school. That might turn out to be a good solution for him and Mrs. Kline both."

"Boy, that sounds great!" said Ken. "I sure will tell him."

Mr. Dalton looked at the ground in thought then said, "Say, I'll make you a really good deal. There's a three-bedroom house on my property where we lived before we built our new house. My mother has been living in it for the last few years, but she died a few weeks ago. If you will take the job, I'll not only pay you good wages but let you and the Meyers stay in the house the rest of the summer rent-free."

The thought of living in a real house, not under someone else's control, struck a chord with Ken. It sounded so attractive Ken was tempted to just forget about his other job. He wished he hadn't made a verbal commitment to Mr. Williams, but he felt he had to follow up on it regardless of his preferences. Hopefully things could have changed in the weeks since he talked to Mr. Williams.

"Mr. Dalton, that is really a great offer," he said. "I will agree to work for you unless the other farmer insists I go to his place!"

"Fine," Mr. Dalton said. "Come over to my house and make your call. We may as well get this settled right now if you have the telephone number with you."

"I remember it," Ken said. "It's pretty simple." Mr. Williams' number consisted of two letters, which happened to be the first two letters of Ken's name and a simple sequence of numbers—KE 2424.

It took about ten minutes to walk through the orchards to Mr. Dalton's home. As they entered the back door of the house, his wife looked up from the bread she was slicing and greeted Ken pleasantly. The fragrant aroma was evidence she had just removed it from the oven, and Ken saw six or seven delicious-looking loaves cooling on the counter. Mr. Dalton led Ken to the wall telephone.

"Don't worry about the charges," he said. "They will just go on my bill."

Soon the long-distance operator had the line connected to the farmer's number. The phone rang several times, and Ken was about to hang up when a woman's voice answered. Ken asked to speak to Mr. Williams.

"He is out at the barn right now. I'm his wife. Can I help you?" the woman asked.

Ken explained who he was and asked if her husband still wanted him to come to work after the unexpected delay.

"No," the woman said. "He has hired someone else. I'm sure he doesn't need you now."

Ken thanked her and hung up the phone with a feeling of relief.

"Well, I'm off the hook," Ken said. "I'm free to work for you."

Mr. Dalton held out his hand and Ken shook it, sealing their agreement.

"Just call me Bill," he said. "Everyone does." He took a key ring out of his pocket, took off a key, and handed it to Ken. "That will get you into the house," he said. "It is in one of the orchards, almost due north of here, maybe an eighth of a mile. You have probably gone past it on your way to some of the orchards you were picking. I would like for you to come over here tomorrow morning. I have an old orchard that doesn't produce very well anymore. I would like to get you started pulling out the old trees so we can plant some new ones."

"All right," Ken said. "I'll be over first thing in the morning. Thanks, Mr. Dalton!" He held out his hand again.

"Bill," said Mr. Dalton with a smile as he took the offered hand.

As Ken made his way out through the kitchen, Mrs. Dalton asked him if he would like to stay for lunch. Ken thanked her but said his lunch was waiting for him in the packing shed.

What a nice, friendly person, he thought. He marveled that she would invite him stay for lunch the very first time she saw him, and it gave him a warm feeling.

Ken felt exuberant over the developments. He had been dreading leaving his new friends that he had grown to care so much about, and he was quite impressed with Mr. Dalton. He seemed like a great person to work for. The large farm he had seemed to be evidence that he had been an intelligent, hard-working man, and Ken admired him for the concern he showed over the Meyers' needs.

Ken was glad the work day ended early. He was eager to share the developments with the Meyers. He joined Mrs. Meyer and the children, and together they picked up their last pay and headed back to the boardinghouse. When they arrived, Professor Meyer was at the dining room table writing a letter of application to another college, hoping to find a teaching position for the fall term.

After greeting him, Ken asked, "Professor Meyer, have you ever considered teaching in a high school?"

Professor Meyer laid down his pen. "No, I guess not," he said. "Since I am qualified to teach on the university level, I have never really considered high school. Why do you ask?"

Ken told him Mr. Dalton had suggested he talk to the high school principal about teaching mathematics for the summer. The professor was immediately interested.

"My, it certainly would be nice to find immediate employment," he said. "I think I would enjoy finding out what teaching high school children is like. I will go talk to the principal right away. Would you like to go with me to find the high school?"

"Yes, sir. I will be happy to go with you," Ken said. He had sort of become the family's chauffeur, and any time they went somewhere in the car, they expected him to drive. Ten minutes later they were entering the high school office, where Professor Meyer asked to speak to the principal.

Bill Dalton was held in such high regard in the community that when the principal was told he had suggested Professor Meyer talk to him about teaching, the door was wide open. The principal was also impressed with Professor Meyer's credentials and genteel bearing, and after a short interview he told him they would be glad to give him the job of teaching the summer school math classes unless Mrs. Kline had changed her mind about not wanting to teach. He called her in and told her she could turn over her teaching responsibilities to Professor Meyer if she wanted to. She was very glad to give up the job she hadn't wanted. She showed Professor Meyer the algebra, geometry, and trigonometry texts she was using and described how far along each class had progressed in the short time since summer school began.

Mrs. Meyer was excited to hear the news. She knew they had very little money left and had been a little anxious about their future, so she was very pleased with the new development. It was also evident Professor Meyer was pleased. He remarked about how once again Ken had helped them, and he was very grateful to him. He told Ken the debt they owed him continued to grow, and he saw no way they were ever going to be able to repay him for all the help he had given them. After the excitement had died down, Ken asked Professor Meyer if he would be interested in seeing where his family had been working.

"I would indeed," said the professor. "Perhaps it would be good to go now since I will begin my teaching responsibilities tomorrow."

Without further delay, the Meyer family and Ken got into the car and drove to the Dalton farm through the orchards to the now silent packing shed. The family kept up a running conversation with the professor along the way, telling him about their activities. They got out of the car and went into the packing shed, and Mrs. Meyer showed the professor where she worked and described what she had been doing, working on the sorting belt and sometimes packing cherries for shipment. She also apparently told the professor of some humorous incident because at one point he gave a hearty laugh.

When the conversation had died down, Ken said, "Why don't we go now? There is something I want to show you."

They got back into the car, and Ken drove through the orchards toward the back of the house Bill Dalton had said they could use. The front of the house faced a county road, which was a short distance away. When they went around the house to the front, the ladies exclaimed over the attractiveness of the place. The house was shaded by several large walnut trees, and a swing hung from one of the large limbs. A wide, inviting porch ran across the entire front of the house and down one side. In front of the porch was a flowerbed with several different colors of blooming flowers. A pretty stream, which was really an irrigation ditch, ran across the front of the large lawn.

Ken got out of the car and beckoned for them to follow. As they did they were greeted by the fragrant smell of lilacs. Benjamin had brought Buddy along, and he ran around happily smelling everything. Ken led them up on the porch, and they watched wonderingly as he took the key from his pocket, unlocked the door, and told them to go in. As they entered, the ladies exclaimed over the warm, homey appearance of the house interior. They looked at Ken mystified. Ken was enjoying the moment and was anxious to see what their reaction would be to his news.

"I will be working for Mr. Dalton this summer, and he said we could stay here for the rest of the summer rent-free!"

The ladies looked at him without comprehension. They had learned a lot of English, but they were unable to digest his statement. Professor Meyer also looked as if he could hardly believe what was said, but he translated Ken's words for them. As the words sunk in, the ladies clasped their hands and went from room to room chattering excitedly. After lodging in a room in the boardinghouse and sharing a bathroom with the other residents, getting to stay in a fairly spacious house seemed too good to be true. And as much as Ken had enjoyed staying in Mrs. Schmidt's shed, he was excited with the prospect of staying in this nice house with the Meyers and being able to enjoy their companionship on a more intimate basis.

"If you are going to be working for Mr. Dalton, it is understandable that you could stay here, but are you sure it is all right if we do also?" the professor asked.

"Yes! Mr. Dalton was the one who brought it up before I had a chance to ask him," Ken said.

"That is certainly kind of him," said the professor with feeling. "This is such a nice place! I know Rachel and the children would love to stay here."

The old but serviceable furniture Mr. Dalton's mother had used was still there. The spacious kitchen had two big windows over the sink that looked out on the orchard that surrounded the house. An assortment of dishes, tableware, pots, and pans were in the cabinets and drawers. Along the wall opposite the sink was a refrigerator that was humming merrily. A gas stove was located on another wall, and in the center of the room was a yellow Formica table with six chairs.

Off the kitchen was the dining room with a long table and a china cabinet. The large living room was furnished with two couches, three overstuffed chairs, some lamp stands, and a piano. Two of the three bedrooms had double beds. When Ken told the Meyers he and Benjamin had been doing fine without a bed so they would take the room with no bed, they protested, but Ken was adamant. The linen closet had an ample supply of bedding. Cupboards in each of the two bathrooms had plenty of towels and washrags. It appeared all they would need was a supply of groceries.

The only bad part of moving into the house was leaving Mrs. Schmidt. She had become a real friend, but when Ken told her about the house, she was genuinely happy for them.

"My goodness," she said. "A body can stay cramped up with three in the same bedroom for only so long. It's going to be good to have some elbow room!"

The Meyers and Ken wasted no time gathering their meager belongings and moving into the house.

Chapter 4

Bill Dalton showed Ken how to pull out the old trees using a logging chain and a big Caterpillar tractor, as well as where to drag the uprooted trees.

"This is going to make quite a mess," he said, "but it will make a lot of good firewood. We can use some of it in our fireplace, and I'll spread the word around that anyone who wants some can come and cut all they want. Then I'll contact some outfits that sell firewood in the city. They will probably take the rest of the big stuff; then we'll have to clean up whatever is left and burn it after it has dried out some. It will burn better after a year or two." Mr. Dalton watched while Ken pulled out a tree, then waved and walked off through the orchard toward his house.

Ken enjoyed driving the big tractor, feeling the surge of power as it pulled out even the most stubborn trees. He was fascinated with the way it could spin around when he pulled the lever that stopped one of the tracks. It was a challenge to see how many trees he could pull out during the day, but he adopted a slower pace when once he didn't take time to secure the chain around the tree very well and in starting forward the chain came loose and whipped around, narrowly missing him.

He shuddered to think of what could have happened if the heavy chain had hit him and realized it was more important to do the job safely than to do it fast.

Pulling out each tree didn't take nearly as much time as dragging it to the area where Mr. Dalton wanted the uprooted trees. The trees created quite a jumble. Ken kept pushing them together, but they still took up a lot of space. Mr. Dalton had told him not to pack the trees too tightly so the people who wanted to cut firewood could get to them easily.

Ken marveled at the size of the Dalton farm. He had seen many acres of orchards, a large pasture, and some crop land, but there was still vacant land where the uprooted trees could be left for eventual disposal.

Mrs. Dalton dropped by to welcome her new neighbors. She brought a loaf of bread, a big berry pie, and a large box of produce from her garden. Mrs. Meyer shyly accepted the gifts and tried to make her visitor welcome but seemed frustrated that she was not able to converse the way she wanted to. Mrs. Dalton didn't seem to mind the lack of communication but soon announced she needed to get back to prepare lunch for her husband.

She left saying, "Don't you hesitate to let me know if there is anything I can do to help you, dear."

Mrs. Meyer seemed to understand the intent of her words and accompanied Mrs. Dalton to the door and bade her good-bye. Mrs. Meyer was pleased as she looked through the box of produce and found more than two dozen ears of sweet corn, a large bunch of green beans, some onions, three cantaloupes, and several tomatoes. She used several of these items in preparing supper.

When Ken entered the kitchen a few days after moving into the house, Mrs. Meyer was searching through the cupboards looking a little disappointed. He asked the professor if there was something she needed that she didn't have.

He said, "Well, Rachel wanted to make bread, but she doesn't have any flour."

He knew the Meyers were too proud to ask him to get flour for them and that the professor had not received any teaching pay yet, so Ken left to get some in town. On the way, he suddenly thought there might be some other things Mrs. Meyer needed to cook with. He decided to go see Mrs. Schmidt and ask her what basic commodities were normally needed for food preparation. She wrote out a short list for him, and Ken went to the grocery store and bought the items on the list.

Mrs. Meyer was surprised when she saw the things Ken had bought, but she was obviously pleased. Ken felt rewarded not only by her expression of thanks but also with the knowledge he would get to enjoy the food she prepared. That was one of the benefits of living with the Meyers. Ken knew if he had to get his own meals he would not be eating nearly as well. Some of the meals Mrs. Meyer prepared were unlike any he had before, but they were always tasty, and he really looked forward to mealtimes.

It pleased Ken to see how much the Meyers enjoyed the house, especially Mrs. Meyer and Rebecca. In their limited English vocabulary, they tried several times to tell him how much they liked living there. They gave the house a thorough cleaning and washed the windows until they sparkled. They found some vases under the sink and kept the house supplied with several bunches of fresh flowers. Ken came into the house after quitting work one day and found them singing a happy-sounding song while they were dusting and vacuuming. In subsequent days, he often heard them singing, many times in two-part harmony. Their singing seemed to add to the already tranquil, happy atmosphere. Life was good!

Ken had been working on the Dalton farm for almost two weeks. It was Saturday afternoon when Mr. Dalton came by just as Ken had extracted another tree.

"Hey, you're doing great," he said. "At this rate you should have them all out early next week!"

"Yeah, I guess you are right," Ken said. "I kind of hate for this come to an end, though. I have been enjoying it."

"You seem to be one of these fellows who has a positive attitude about everything," Mr. Dalton said as he handed Ken his wages. "You may not like everything I'll have you do as much as this, but I will be surprised if there will be anything that you will dislike. The next thing we need to do is to grade the ground to level it up. When that's done we will lay out the grid to know where to plant the trees in nice, straight rows; then we'll need to dig the holes. I have the trees on order and expect to get them sometime in the next week or two."

"It looks like I'll be getting plenty of exercise digging all the holes," Ken said.

"Well, not too much," Mr. Dalton said. "We'll use the John Deere tractor with an auger attached to the power takeoff. It doesn't take long to dig a hole with that setup. We will probably need to clean some of the holes out with a shovel, but it won't be like digging them from scratch."

"Wow, that sounds fun," Ken said. "I am sure learning some new things!"

"Just keep at it, and we will make a real farmer out of you one of these days," Mr. Dalton said with a smile as he turned and started home.

Ken had driven the tractor into the Dalton's backyard to refill the fuel tank from the big storage tank that was mounted on a stand at the side of the yard when he saw Mrs. Dalton gesturing to him from across the yard. He went across the large open space to Mrs. Dalton and could see she was hot and breathless.

"All of our crazy pigs got out, and some started rooting around in our garden. I chased them out of the garden, but they've scattered to the four winds. I can't even begin to get them back into the pen. Every time I get close to one, it just runs farther away. Bill is at a farmers' co-op meeting, so I would appreciate it if you would help me," she said. "If they would just stay out of the garden, I wouldn't even bother with them, but I hate to have them tear up my garden after all the work I've done on it! If you wouldn't mind herding them into the pen, I'll open and close the gate."

"Sure, Mrs. Dalton, I'll be glad to round them up for you," Ken said. He looked around and saw a pig disappear behind a shed. "How many are there?"

"There should be seven unless some of them have left the country. I almost hope they have! If any of them give too much trouble, let's just shoot them!"

Ken saw a pig come out from behind a farm implement and started for it. The pig saw him coming and began running in the opposite direction. Ken outran it and started it back toward the pen, with the pig doing his best to dodge around Ken. Finally he was able to herd it into the pen, and Mrs. Dalton closed the gate behind it.

"Whew! That was harder than I thought it would be," Ken said, mopping his brow as he started looking for another escapee.

He soon saw another pig near the chicken pen and with difficulty got him started toward the pigpen and finally back inside. That left five more of the fugitives that were still on the loose! They were obviously enjoying their freedom and didn't want to go back into the confines of the pen. By the time he had located the last pig behind the barn and headed it toward the pen, he was panting and out of breath.

As Mrs. Dalton opened the gate to let the pig in, another large pig in the pen, seeing the opportunity to escape, bolted through the open gate. As it darted past, Ken dove for it and succeeded in getting his arms around it. The big pig squealed loudly as it dragged Ken for several feet until Ken's grip gradually slipped off, leaving him lying face down in the dust. He heard Mrs. Dalton laughing as he wearily got up and chased after the pig. When he finally got it back in the pen and Mrs. Dalton had securely shut the gate, Ken was tired out.

"Whew," he said. "I had no idea pigs could be so obstinate and so strong and slippery." He leaned back against the fence to rest.

Mrs. Dalton was smiling broadly as she came over and put her hand on Ken's arm.

"Thank you so much. I'm sorry that was such a chore, but it really was a good show. I wouldn't have wanted to miss it for anything! You come over into the shade, and I'll get you a glass of lemonade."

The lemonade sounded great, and Ken wearily did as she suggested. As he drank the lemonade and ate the cookies Mrs. Dalton brought, she laughed again as she talked about his trying to tackle the pig. Her laugh was infectious, and Ken laughed with her. Mrs. Dalton seemed like such a nice person. As he drank his second glass of lemonade and talked with her, he was glad he had the opportunity to get better acquainted with her, even at the expense of his dignity.

She looked at his face covered with dust mixed with his sweat and said, "You come into the house and take a shower. I can't let you go home looking like you have been in a fight." She got up and pulled on his arm. "I'll get some of Bill's clothes out for you while I wash your things."

Ken protested and said he could wait until he got home to take a bath, but she wouldn't have it.

"Nope," she said. "I got you into this mess, and it's my responsibility to get you cleaned up. Come on!"

Ken reluctantly did as she said, and once he was in the shower, it felt so good he was glad she had insisted. He had just finished dressing when Bill came in, and Mrs. Dalton explained what had happened. He laughed as she related how Ken had tried to tackle the pig.

"You didn't know you were going to get into pig wrestling when you agreed to work for me, did you?"

"You're right. I sure didn't expect anything like that, but I guess it really wasn't all that bad. I think with a little practice I might do a better job!" Ken joked.

Bill said, "Well, I could let them out again if you want to have another try!"

"No thanks. I think I have had enough of that for one day," Ken said.

Bill laughed again and went to see if he could tell how the pigs had gotten out.

Ken thanked Mrs. Dalton for letting him take a shower and the clean clothes and started out to finish refueling the tractor feeling much better than he had a short time before.

"I'll have your clothes ready for you by tomorrow," Mrs. Dalton said as he left the house.

From the time they had moved into the house, Professor Meyer had begun always asking God's blessing on the food at mealtime. Then, in recognition that it was because of Ken that they were in the house, Professor Meyer asked Ken if he could read some Scripture to everyone after supper. Ken felt humbled by this question since Professor Meyer was a mature adult and he was still in his teens, but he quickly told the professor to please do as he felt he should.

Professor Meyer would read a passage of Scripture from a German Bible first in German; then he would translate the passage into English. Sometimes one of the family members would ask a question about the meaning of the text, and the professor would share his understanding of the words. One of the Bible passages the professor discussed at length was the fifty-third chapter of Isaiah. He talked about how Jesus had fulfilled that passage in minute detail, and it was very clear to anyone with an open mind that Jesus was the promised Messiah. He also read some other prophetic passages that foretold Jesus' coming to earth.

After reading and discussing a Bible passage, the professor always prayed a short, sincere prayer thanking God for his goodness and asking for his continued blessing and protection on their lives. The night he read the fifty-third chapter of Isaiah, he prayed fervently that God would open the eyes of the Jewish people to understand that Jesus is the Messiah they have been expecting for hundreds of years.

For Ken this was a new experience. For reasons he couldn't explain, he felt just a little uncomfortable with the praying. The little religious training he had in the orphanage was on a very casual basis. Professor Meyer seemed to take religion much more seriously than anyone Ken had known before.

Although he thought of the orphanage occasionally, Ken no longer had a desire to be back there. Living with the Meyer family was an experience he would not have wanted to miss. The love and respect they consistently demonstrated for each other was a standard he intended to adopt when he had a family of his own.

He never heard a harsh word or saw a discourteous attitude between them. They seemed eager to include him in their family circle and strove hard to speak English so he wouldn't feel left out.

There were a number of parlor games in one of the cupboards, and it became fairly common for the whole family and Ken to enjoy playing some of these in the evenings. It seemed nice to have everyone participating in an activity that promoted togetherness. Some of their favorites were dominos, Chinese checkers, Sorry, and Monopoly.

Sometimes, when the others were involved in other activities, Benjamin asked Ken to play chess with him. Ken had never had the opportunity to learn to play chess but found it to be a kind of mental challenge he enjoyed. Benjamin had been taught to play by his father, and it was some time before Ken was able to give him much competition. The winning of his first game seemed to be a breakthrough event, and after that he beat him frequently. Benjamin was a good sport and seemed pleased with Ken's increased competence in the game, even when he lost—partly because his own skill was improving as he faced stiffer competition.

Mrs. Meyer played the piano beautifully, and sometimes the family would gather around and sing some of the songs they were familiar with. Ken liked to listen to them sing even though the words were in German. At one time while he was listening to the unfamiliar words, he suddenly had a desire to learn what the words were saying. Thanks to Rebecca's informal tutoring, he knew a number of words, but he was far from being able to communicate in German. He decided to ask the professor if he would teach him more of the language. However, with his regular teaching responsibilities, Ken wasn't sure if he would want to do any additional teaching, but he seemed pleased that Ken wanted to learn the German language and gave him the first lesson the same day he asked about it. In a few weeks Ken was able to engage in simple conversation. Rebecca also helped with the learning process. She would ask Ken a question in English, which her father was teaching her, and expect him to respond in German. She became very amused at some of his early answers.

Professor Meyer was enjoying his teaching job. The number of students enrolled in summer school was not great, so he was able to

The Dawning of Destiny

give his students all the individual attention they needed. His classes were made up mostly of students who had previous trouble with math, and he took great pride in being able to get a student to understand a mathematical concept that had previously been obscure. If any student expressed a desire for a private session, the professor gladly accommodated him or her.

Regardless of the other demands for his time, the professor always took time to help Ken with his German lessons. His attitude was typical of the entire Meyer family who always made time to make Ken feel like a part of the family. It gave him a warm feeling to be included in the family circle.

Ken's contentment was not limited to the time he spent with the Meyers. Living on a farm offered so many new experiences, and he was enjoying them all. The Daltons had several animals, including two dogs, some cats, a cow, two horses, chickens, and as Ken well knew, pigs. The horses were especially interesting to Ken. They seemed to like the companionship of humans, especially a horse named Molly. Every time Ken went by the pasture where the horses were kept, Molly would run to the fence to greet him. Sometimes the other horse would join Molly.

One day, as Ken was feeding Molly a carrot, Bill Dalton came up behind him and said, "Why don't you take her for a ride? She could use some exercise. There are a couple saddles over in the barn. You are welcome to saddle up and take her for a ride anytime you want."

He knew by this time Ken would not neglect his work so he could enjoy some other activity. He mentioned the other horse needed exercise too and suggested Ken get someone to ride with him.

A few days later, Ken was caught up with all of the work he was aware of that needed to be done and asked Benjamin if he wanted to go horseback riding. Benjamin was immediately interested and readily joined Ken. They went to the Dalton home and told Bill they would like to accept his offer to let them ride his horses. He took them to the barn, where they got two bridles, and went out to the pasture. True to her nature, Molly immediately came up to them, and Bill put a bridle on her then walked to the other horse that was busy grazing and put a bridle on him. They led both horses to the barn, where Bill demonstrated how to saddle them.

Ken let Benjamin have Molly, who seemed the gentlest, and he took the bigger horse, which was named Bob. They rode around the farm for nearly an hour, with both of them enjoying every minute. After that Benjamin frequently wanted to go riding, and when Ken had the time, he complied with Benjamin's wish. Once Rebecca rode Molly while Benjamin was riding Bob, but she didn't seem to want to repeat the experience.

Ken saw some fishing poles equipped with reels, line, and hooks in the shed. He remembered how inviting it had been when he had seen the people fishing in the river, and he was anxious to give it a try. He showed a rod to Benjamin and asked him if he would like to go fishing sometime. Benjamin wanted to go right away, but since it was nearly suppertime, Ken told him they needed to wait until they had more time.

The next Saturday Ken stopped work a little earlier than usual. When he got to the house, Benjamin was in the front lawn playing with Buddy. Benjamin had spent so much time with Buddy that they both seemed to think he was Benjamin's pet. Ken was glad for this development. If he had to go into military service, Buddy would still have someone to take care of him. He told Benjamin he thought they had enough time to go fishing for a while, and Benjamin was immediately ready to go. Together they dug some worms, gathered the fishing equipment, and went to the stream that ran along the west side of Mr. Dalton's property.

There was something unexpectedly exhilarating about the fishing experience. Ken wondered if it was the fresh, pleasant atmosphere, the sight and musical sound of the stream running over the rocks forming mini waterfalls, or if it was just the excitement of being involved in a brand new adventure. Perhaps all of these elements were involved. Buddy had followed them, and he was happily exploring the new terrain. Soon he discovered a rabbit, which he chased for a short distance before the rabbit disappeared.

Ken didn't know much about fishing, but he knew there had to be bait on the hook to attract the fish. He picked a big worm out of their bait can, ran a fishhook through its middle, leaving both ends wiggling, and dropped it into the stream. Almost immediately he felt a mild tug. He pulled his line out and found remnants of the worm on the hook but no fish. Benjamin had copied his action and had a similar experience.

Ken realized they needed to put the bait on in a way the fish would get the hook in its mouth, as well as the worm. He then threaded a worm onto the hook, leaving only a short length that was not on the hook, and showed Benjamin what he had done. He dropped his line into the water and a few minutes later pulled out a plump, ten-inch fish he learned later was a trout. The feel of the fish fighting against the line produced a new and rather exciting sensation.

As he removed the hook from the fish's mouth, he remembered the boys at the stream where he had given Buddy a drink had carried their fish on a forked stick, so he made one for Benjamin and another for himself. It certainly made it much easier to carry the fish.

The fishing was interrupted by Benjamin's line becoming snagged on some object below the water. Try as he might, he couldn't get the line free. Ken tried to help but finally removed his shoes and socks, rolled up his pants legs, and waded to the spot where the line was caught in a crevice between two rocks. It took only a moment to get it loose.

As Ken was looking into the water, he saw a pretty, symmetrical-shaped object that stood out against the rocks in the stream bed. He picked it up and saw it was a perfectly-shaped large arrowhead. He turned it over in his hand and marveled at the craftsmanship that had gone into making it, certainly without the help of modern tools. How long had it been here, and what had become of the one who had made it? Had the owner been shooting at an animal drinking from the stream or perhaps a bird in the trees along the bank? He wished he could go back in time and watch as the Indian brave notched his arrow and launched it at its intended target.

He waded out of the stream, showed it to Benjamin, and told him a little about the American Indians. With the awareness that Indians had once been in the area, Ken began watching the ground for more Indian artifacts.

When Benjamin caught his first fish, he gave an excited exclamation! He was obviously proud as he held up the wiggling fish, which was bigger than the two Ken had caught. Ken gave him a pat on the back as Benjamin continued to admire his catch.

They changed locations several times as they fished their way up the stream and between them caught seven fish. Finally Ken looked at the sun and decided they should quit for the day. Benjamin was not pleased when Ken told him he thought they should go, but he pulled in his line, picked up his fish, and followed Ken. As they were going past the Dalton home, Mr. Dalton saw them and walked over to take a look at their fish.

"That's a nice mess of fish," he said. "Do you know how to clean them?"

Ken confessed he had no idea how to do it.

Mr. Dalton beckoned to them and led them to a pump in his yard. He pumped water into a pan, took out his pocket knife, and demonstrated with one of the fish how to remove the innards and scrape the slime from the skin.

"That's how it's done, boys. I'll let you have the fun of cleaning the rest of them," he said, rinsing off his knife.

Ken thanked Mr. Dalton for the demonstration, and he and Benjamin started home. Then Ken remembered the arrowhead he had in his pocket, and he took it out and showed it to Bill. Bill looked at it and wondered if it was a spearhead. The Indian may have been trying to spear a fish, and the spearhead could have come off the shaft and become buried in the dirt at the bottom of the stream. Later, the dirt that obscured it must have been washed away.

"Hang on to it," Bill said. "It is in perfect condition and will be a nice souvenir."

Bill told them that over the years he had found three arrowheads on his property and another object that had obviously been shaped by humans, but he had no idea of its purpose. On the way home, Ken decided to give the spearhead to Benjamin.

"Keep this as someone who is going to become a new American, as a memento of one of the earliest Americans," Ken said.

Benjamin was pleased and said he would put it away where he would be sure not lose it. When they got home, they cleaned the rest of the fish and took them to Mrs. Meyer, who didn't seem thrilled to get them. She left the kitchen door and windows open while she cooked them, trying to get rid of the fishy smell. Everyone had all the fish they wanted that night for supper, and they all seemed to enjoy them. Benjamin was proud to have his father eat the biggest fish he caught.

The professor returned from school one day with something obviously on his mind.

That night at the supper table, he said, "It has been a long time since we have been able to attend worship services. There is a little church not far from the school that I think we should visit. We need this, and it would help acquire greater familiarity with the English language."

Mrs. Meyer nodded her agreement.

Thus it was that the whole family and Ken on the next Sunday made their way to the attractive little church. They arrived in the parking lot as three or four other cars were parking. As they walked toward the entrance, several people greeted them with friendly smiles. At the front door, a smiling, middle-aged lady greeted them warmly as she handed them each a bulletin.

"Hello," she said. "How nice to have you join us this morning! I am Mrs. Atkins, the pastor's wife. I do hope you enjoy the service! Please find a seat wherever you wish."

This was the first time Ken had been in a church. From time to time, different ministers had spoken at the orphanage, but it had seemed there was always some distraction going on, and Ken had never really absorbed much of what they were saying. He was curious about what was going to take place.

Most of the pews were pretty well occupied. They came to a pew that had enough space for several, but not for everyone in their group. Ken was about to look for a seat by himself when a young couple looked up and, realizing there was not room for them all, arose with a smile and headed for another pew. Professor Meyer led them into the vacated pew.

After a few minutes, a door on the right of the platform opened, and the pastor, followed by a young man, stepped out and went to the pulpit. His eyes swept over the congregation and paused momentarily as he saw the new family.

"Good morning. It is a joy to once again gather to worship our Lord!" he said. "We are glad to see you all in God's house this Sabbath day, and we want to extend a special welcome our visitors. Let's all get a hymn book and join in praising him as Michael leads us."

The young man stepped forward with a radiant smile and said, "Let's turn to page fifty-eight, *A Mighty Fortress is Our God*."

Ken turned to page fifty-eight and shared the hymnal with Benjamin, even though he didn't think it would be of much help to him. As the lady at the piano began to play, the young man began enthusiastically leading the congregation in singing. The melody immediately sounded familiar to Ken, and he remembered this was a song that the Meyers had sung in German on several occasions. He glanced at Mrs. Meyer, who smiled and nodded her head. He hesitatingly joined in the singing with some of the German words echoing in his head.

The highlight of the service as far as Ken was concerned was when the pastor's daughter, an attractive teenager, sang a special song with such poise and beauty that the remembrance of it lingered long in Ken's mind. In fact, very little of the pastor's sermon penetrated his thoughts.

When the service ended, people crowded around the newcomers, welcoming them and telling them to be sure to come back. Ken could tell Professor Meyer was pleased with reception they had received, and he spoke of the service enthusiastically on the way home. He was obviously impressed with the pastor's sermon. Consequently, attending Sunday worship services at the little church became a regular event. Ken liked going to the services, but there was a lot he didn't understand.

As the summer wore on, Ken continued to complete the various tasks Mr. Dalton assigned him in a very conscientious manner, earning high praise from Mr. Dalton. He had enjoyed leveling the ground where he had pulled out the trees, then helping Mr. Dalton lay out the grid, dig the holes, and finally plant hundreds of the four-feet-high trees. Furrows were dug along each row of trees to provide means of irrigating them. It was very satisfying to look over the newly planted orchard and see the neat rows of small, leafless trees, knowing that before long they would have leaves and in a few years bear fruit.

Bill had said he would like to get some firewood from the trees Ken had pulled out before it had all been taken by others, so when Ken had an hour or two between other chores, he would spend time cutting firewood using a one man cross-cut saw. Even though it was hard work, he enjoyed it. After several days of that, he noticed his arm muscles were getting hard. When he had enough wood cut for a load, he would use Bill's pickup to take it to the house, where he stacked it neatly in the place Bill wanted it.

A small peach orchard gave Ken another project to work on. As the peaches grew in size, their increasing weight bent the limbs over to an alarming degree. Mr. Dalton asked Ken to thin the peaches to keep the limbs from breaking. He told Ken it would also allow the nutrition from the tree to go into fewer peaches, making them larger than if the trees hadn't been thinned. Ken followed Mr. Dalton's instruction and carefully removed the peaches that were crowding others. It seemed a shame to waste the promising-looking fruit, but it was rewarding to see the branches relieved of their drooping, stressed look. Mr. Dalton looked over the results of Ken's efforts and said it was a good job.

Vegetation Mr. Dalton called "vetch" had been planted in the apple orchard to provide nitrogen to the soil. Ken was disking these plants into the ground when Mr. Dalton walked into the path of the tractor and stopped him.

After greeting Ken he said, "I have been working you pretty hard. I want you to take off Saturday and go to the county fair. I doubt you have had the chance to go to one, but it's something you should see at least once."

"That sounds interesting. What is there to see at the fair?" Ken asked.

"Oh, there are a lot of exhibits of animals that kids in 4H or Future Farmers of America have raised, and exhibits of agricultural products, baked goods, canned fruits, quilts, things like that, where ribbons and prizes are given to the person who the judges think have the best entry. Then there are booths where you can try your hand at winning some sort of prize, carnival rides, horse racing, fireworks, and other things. There will be several different food vendors, and someone told me they even have a gospel quartet performing this year. Go. You will be glad you did. I'm going to give you a bonus so you will have some extra money to spend there. You certainly deserve it."

"How could I refuse an offer like that?" Ken said with a smile. "I would like to go, and I guess I'll see if the Meyers want to go too."

The Meyers thought it would be a chance to see a side of American culture they hadn't seen before, so they were interested when Ken told them about the fair. Mrs. Meyer made several sandwiches to take with them for lunch, hoping there would be a nice place at the fairgrounds where they could eat them. They left early Saturday morning and were among the first arrivals at the gate to the fairgrounds. Benjamin especially was excited.

The pens for the animals were just inside the gate, and they stopped at each of the pens to see the sleek-looking horses, cattle, sheep, and pigs. The young people who had raised the livestock were in several of the pens, brushing their entry in order to make the most favorable appearance. Mrs. Meyer and Rebecca enjoyed watching the baby animals and were especially entranced with some little lambs. There was a huge hog that must have weighed about five-hundred pounds that reminded Ken of the battle he had with the Daltons' runaway pigs. The Meyers had been told about his experience with the pigs, so they laughed when he remarked if the Daltons' pigs had been that big he would still be chasing them.

There were several booths where hucksters were challenging the crowds to try to win a prize by knocking over a pyramid of imitation milk bottles with some baseballs, hit some moving objects with an air rifle, toss pennies into various-sized dishes, and other similar activities. They watched while some tried their luck at some of these concessions and concluded it had to be harder than it looked. There were not many prizes being won. Benjamin seemed to want to try hitting some balloons with darts, so Ken paid for a set of darts. He watched as Benjamin threw his five darts without hitting any balloons. Benjamin seemed disappointed, so Ken got another set.

He handed these to Benjamin, but he said, "No. You try it."

Ken agreed to throw three of the darts. He broke a balloon and was given a little ceramic dog as a prize, which he gave to Benjamin.

Another stand was selling all sorts of rather attractive costume jewelry and other trinkets. Rebecca was admiring a necklace, and when Ken saw she liked it, he bought it for her. She objected but seemed pleased when he gave it to her. Mrs. Meyer seemed interested in it and was examining it with Rebecca, so Ken bought her one too. When he handed it to her, she scolded him and told him to take it back. Ken pointed to the sign that said, "No Returns." He told her he had used the extra money Mr. Dalton had given him for enjoying the fair, so she shook her head as she put the necklace around her neck, but she was smiling.

There was the usual merry-go-round blaring loud music and all sorts of other whirling, gyrating rides, which were eliciting screams from some of the riders. Ken told Benjamin he should try the merry-go-round and bought him a ticket. The rest of them watched as he went around, and he obviously enjoyed the experience.

The Ferris wheel looked interesting to Ken, and he suggested they all take a ride on it. No one objected, so he stood in line to buy the tickets. He had been carrying a basket that had their lunch in it, and when he reached the ticket stand, he set it down while paying for the tickets. As he reached out to take the tickets, out of the corner of his eye he saw someone take the basket. He turned around in time to see a man with the basket merge with the crowd and rush away.

Ken handed the tickets to Benjamin and immediately gave chase, following the thief as he dodged through the crowd. When the man saw Ken was about to catch him, he threw the basket to one side and ran off in the opposite direction. Ken went to the basket and found it had come open and the sandwiches had spilled out in the dirt, where some of them were trampled on by the crowd. He reluctantly picked up the ruined food, threw it in a nearby trash barrel, and went back to the Ferris wheel carrying the empty basket. The others were disappointed that their food was gone, but Ken told them they could get something from one of the vendors.

The man selling tickets let them leave the picnic basket behind his ticket counter while they were on the Ferris wheel, and everyone seemed to enjoy the new experience, although the downward motion of the wheel elicited a few exclamations from Rebecca and Rachel on the first few cycles. Benjamin thought it was great fun. It was interesting to be at the top, especially when it stopped to let new riders get on. From there they were able to get a bird's eye view of the crowd and a lot of the activities. Ken tried to spot the thief but saw no sign of him. He was not sure what he would have done if he had caught him. It did make him angry to have him take the lunch they were looking forward to eating. Then he thought maybe the guy was hungry and didn't have money to buy any food, and his anger abated.

Ken had seen the food stands from the Ferris wheel, and when it was about noon, he led the group to them. They went by many of the stands to see what was being sold and saw several foods that were new to them, as well as some they were familiar with, like hamburgers and hot dogs.

Ken told everyone to decide what they wanted. The professor and Mrs. Meyer finally said they would like deli sandwiches. Rebecca and Benjamin each took a corn dog, and Ken thought the pizza looked good and asked for a big slice of that. They all also had a bottle of soda and an Eskimo Pie, which was a chocolate-covered ice cream bar.

Professor Meyer tried to pay for the food, but Ken insisted they use the special money Mr. Dalton had given him. Benjamin was interested in the cotton candy, so after he finished his ice cream, Ken got a stick of that for him. He offered everyone a taste, but Rebecca was the only one that accepted his offer. Benjamin ended up with a sticky face and hands and looked for some time before he found a water hydrant at the base of a drinking fountain, where he rinsed off.

In the afternoon they sat in some stands overlooking an arena and watched teams of big work horses pulling against each other to see which team was the strongest. After that there was a horse race between about a dozen horses. One of the horses was ridden by a girl, and Rebecca was excited when it looked like she might win but had to settle for second place. Then a man with a balance pole walked across the arena between two towers on a tight wire that was approximately fifty feet in the air. Mrs. Meyer and Rebecca were holding their breath while he nonchalantly sauntered across, stopping in the middle to lie down. When he got to the other end of the wire, he got on a bicycle and rode it back across on the wire. Ken asked Benjamin if he would like to try that, and Benjamin vigorously shook his head.

They waited for the next performance of the gospel quartet and were impressed with the great harmony and inspirational songs they heard. When that was over, they left the arena and looked around a while longer, but they decided they did not want to stay around until after dark to see the fireworks and started for home. The Meyers all thanked Ken and told him it had been a fun time, and he was pleased that it was obvious they had genuinely enjoyed it. It made him feel good to be able to treat his surrogate family to the new experiences.

As summer was drawing to a close, Ken thought about all the new experiences he had gone through. How glad he was that he had made the decision to hitchhike and shook his head as he thought about how close he had come to missing all of the things that had enriched his life so much. How ridiculous his dread of leaving the orphanage seemed now! He knew it would probably not be long before he would be leaving this idyllic life and venturing into the unknown again. But whatever the future held for him, he felt prepared to face it with much more optimism than he had when he left the orphanage. Of all the things he had experienced, he felt it was his intimate association with the Meyer family that had most affected his outlook on life. He knew he would forever treasure the relationship he had with them and was as concerned about their future as he was his own.

Professor Meyer had won the hearts of his students with his teaching ability and his pleasant demeanor. Near the end of summer school, the principal had told him Mrs. Kline's baby was due anytime, and she had decided to stay home and take care of her baby for at least a year. He told Professor Meyer everyone was pleased with his teaching and asked if he would consider teaching during the regular school term.

The professor had received two invitations to be interviewed for teaching positions on the college level, but as he considered these offers, he didn't feel clear about following up on either one. When the high school principal wanted him to remain at the high school, he immediately had a feeling perhaps this was what he was supposed to do. True, the pay would not be as good, but he liked the small town environment and felt it would be a good place for his children to experience going to an English-speaking school. He also felt drawn to the church they had been attending, and both his children had friends in the church they were enjoying.

After talking to his wife and praying about it, he informed the principal he would stay and teach as requested. Then he asked Mr. Dalton if he could rent the house they were staying in for the next school term. Mr. Dalton said he would be very happy to have them rent the house for as long as they wanted and named a very reasonable rent figure.

August 26 was the date the orphanage had picked for Ken's birthday. From lack of any other evidence, they had assumed he was about a year old when he went into the orphanage and had taken the day he arrived there as his birthday. The state required the orphanage to keep the age of each child on record. A friendly doctor agreed a year was a reasonable estimate of his age and helped the orphanage obtain a substitute birth certificate for him showing August 26, 1924, as his official birth date.

Ken knew he was required to register for the draft when he was eighteen. He supposed there was probably a grace period for registering, but he didn't know what it was, so he decided he might as well get it over with and register on his birthday. As this day approached, Ken told Mr. Dalton he needed to take time off work on his birthday to register for the draft.

Mr. Dalton said, "Sure, no problem," and asked when his birthday was. When Ken told him, he said, "Wow. That's next week."

On the morning of his birthday, a few minutes before nine, Ken was standing outside the draft board office waiting for it to open. He was soon joined by another young man Ken vaguely remembered seeing before somewhere in town.

"Well, it looks like we are going to get to help win the war, doesn't it?" the young man said cheerfully. "I sure hope it's not over before we can get in on it."

Ken really didn't know how to take this remark. He could understand this fellow's desire for adventure, but when people were dying, it just didn't seem right to not want it to be over as soon as possible.

Draftees were being selected by lottery, so Ken said, "Then I guess you will be hoping they pick your number right away."

"Ha!" the young man said. "I'm going to register, but I'm not going to wait for them to draft me. If you're drafted, they can put you in any service they want to. I'm going to join the Marines before they get a chance to put me somewhere else!"

"Why do you want to go into the Marines?" Ken asked.

"Because they are the best!" the aspiring marine replied. "A lot of times they are the first ones to go in and soften up the enemy. After the hard part's done, the army is able to take over. Every time there is an extra hard job, they send in the Marines. Besides, my dad was a marine in the last war. He has a bunch of medals! I want to be just like him."

"Well, good luck to you," Ken said as the doors to the draft board office opened. Twenty minutes later he had finished registering and headed back to the Dalton farm. As he went, he thought about what the young man had said. Was it better to volunteer to join a specific branch of the service rather than waiting to be drafted? If so, which branch would he want to go into? He had no way of knowing if his father had been in the last war, so he had no tradition to follow like his acquaintance did.

It was just after noon while Ken was irrigating the newly planted trees when Mr. Dalton came by.

"Well, I got my registering out of the way this morning," he said, then asked, "Bill, were you in the last war?"

"Sure was, son," Mr. Dalton said. "It was no picnic. That's where I got my limp."

"If you knew you had to go into military service, which branch would you prefer to be in if you had your choice?" Ken asked.

Mr. Dalton thought for a moment. "You know, I think I might like to be in the air force. I'm sort of fascinated with airplanes. But I don't know; the navy might be good. But I think the most important thing would be to be involved in something that would be of benefit after the war is over, rather than just carrying a rifle like I did. I think some parts of the military use a lot of technical skills now, and experience in some of these might be pretty valuable in civilian life. But I really don't think the draft board will pay a lot of attention to what anyone wants to get into. It probably depends more on where they need men most."

"What would you think of volunteering in order to get into a particular service?" Ken asked.

Mr. Dalton stroked his chin in thought. "I suppose that might be a good option rather than waiting to be drafted. You have no way of knowing when your draft number might come up, but it seems pretty sure that it will happen eventually. I guess that's something you are going to have to decide for yourself. I sure wouldn't want to tell you what to do. Some of life's decisions can have some real unexpected consequences!" he said as he walked away.

The more Ken thought about volunteering, the more desirable it seemed, but which service would be best for him? After thinking about it for a while, he made up his mind; the air force sounded more appealing to him than any of the other options he knew about. He realized Mr. Dalton's suggestion that the air force might be the choice he would make was influencing him some, but he had also been intrigued with airplanes ever since he had seen one doing aerobatics near the orphanage when he was about twelve. If there was any possibility he could become a pilot, he couldn't think of any activity that sounded more interesting. He decided to apply for admission to the air force right away before the draft board had a chance to put him in another branch of service.

He had reset the irrigation water to a new set of furrows when he noticed some of the irrigation ditches were somewhat obstructed with weeds, so he set to work cleaning them out while waiting for the water to soak the soil around the trees.

Late in the afternoon, Mr. Dalton came by and asked Ken if he had decided what he was going to do. Ken told him he planned to talk to the recruiting office within the next few days and would most likely join the air force.

Mr. Dalton nodded his head.

"I sort of figured you would volunteer for something," he said, "but we are going to hate to see you go. I was hoping to have you around for peach and apple harvest." Then he said, "The afternoon is about gone. You may as well turn the head of water back into the main ditch and quit for the day. Come over to my place for a while. You need to see the twin calves my milk cow delivered day before yesterday! They're really cute little rascals."

Ken walked with Mr. Dalton to his home. As they went through the lawn toward the barn, Ken noticed a tablecloth on the picnic table, which was beside a brick barbeque. He sort of wondered about it. When they got to the corral, they leaned on the rail fence and watched the frisky little calves and their antics for a while. Then he asked Mr. Dalton about his experiences during the war.

"Well, I was only in combat for about three months when I got wounded, and before I got out of the hospital, the war ended," Mr.

Dalton said. "But that was long enough. I don't think I'll tell you about that. I don't want to give you any more to worry about in case you should end up in combat. But let me give you some tips. If you do join up, just do exactly what you are told and keep your mouth shut, especially during basic training. I saw one fellow talk back some, and the noncoms made his life miserable all through basic training. He spent about half his time on KP or cleaning the latrine. At least during basic training be careful about volunteering for anything. It most likely won't be anything you especially want to do. I remember one time when the sergeant asked if anyone knew shorthand. When one fellow raised his hand, the sergeant said, 'Good. Come with me. We are shorthanded for the latrine detail!'"

Ken laughed and said, "That sounds like some good advice. I will try to remember those tips. Guess I'd better head home. I don't want to keep the Meyers waiting for supper."

"Okay," Mr. Dalton said with a grin. "Let's go."

When they got back to the lawn, Ken was surprised to see the Meyers and Mrs. Dalton sitting at the picnic table.

"Welcome to your party," Mr. Dalton said. "We don't want to send you off to win the war without celebrating your birthday!"

Ken was speechless; this was so unexpected. He didn't even know that anyone knew this was his birthday; then he remembered mentioning it to Mr. Dalton when he told him he needed to take off time to register for the draft. Back in the orphanage, birthdays were nothing very special because it was not unusual for the two or three children to have birthdays during the week. Celebrations were simple. All the birthday children would be given a cupcake with a lighted candle on it, and everyone would sing the happy birthday song to them. He stood there open-mouthed until Mrs. Dalton went to him, took his arm, and led him to the table.

"Sit down!" she ordered. Then, "Okay, Bill, the steaks are ready. Go to it!" And she handed him a big platter heaped with thick steaks.

There were glowing coals in the barbeque, and as Mr. Dalton took the steaks over to it, he said, "Okay, everyone tell me how you want your steak. If you want it raw, I can guarantee to get it right. Anything else you take your chances, but I will *try* to get it like you want it!"

Ken had never eaten meat that tasted as good as the barbequed steaks. Mrs. Dalton had marinated them overnight, and Mr. Dalton had doused them with barbeque sauce as he cooked them. There were also big potato and macaroni salads, as well as potato chips and lemonade.

When everyone had finished their steaks and salads, Mrs. Dalton went into the house and returned with a chocolate frosted cake with eighteen lighted candles. After everyone had sung "happy birthday" and Ken had blown out the candles, Mrs. Dalton cut the cake and put a huge slice on Ken's plate. Meanwhile, Mr. Dalton brought over an ice cream freezer and dished out big bowls of vanilla ice cream for everyone.

Ken ate the cake and ice cream and felt more stuffed than he ever remembered. He could not imagine a birthday being any nicer, when suddenly Mrs. Dalton handed him a rather small wrapped package and Benjamin handed him another. Ken felt even more overwhelmed and just sat holding the packages, shaking his head.

"Well, open them!" said Mrs. Dalton.

Ken opened the first package he had received and found a nice wristwatch. He was elated. He had not thought about it before, but he knew he was going to enjoy it. He put it on, admired it for a while, and thanked the Daltons. He had become pretty good at estimating the time from the sun's position, but it was going to be nice to have a more precise way of knowing the time.

He opened the other package and found a nice billfold. There was a section of plastic compartments for pictures. There was a nice snap-shot of the Meyer family and one of the house they were living in. He thanked the Meyers, but he knew his words of thanks for either gift did not adequately express the appreciation he felt. He was sure he would treasure the memory of this day the rest of his life.

A few days later, Ken returned from the recruiting office and announced he had signed up to join the air force and was to report for induction in two weeks. Each of the Meyer family members took this news with obvious regret. The next two weeks flew by. Ken was filled with mixed emotions; he was excited about what the future in the air force held for him, but the closer the time to report came, the more he realized how much he was going to miss the farm and being with the Meyer family and the Daltons.

When the day to leave arrived, he went to the Dalton's home, shook Bill's hand, and hugged Mrs. Dalton. He told them this had been the best summer of his life, and he was really going to miss working for them. Bill told him if he ever wanted a job again to be sure to come see him.

It was especially hard to tell the Meyers good-bye. He tried to tell them how much he had enjoyed his time with them and what a special time in his life it had been. They had filled a void in his life that had been yearning for satisfaction for as far back as he could remember.

As Professor Meyer shook his hand, he said, "We are the ones who have been blessed! You helped us in so many ways. I just do not know how we would have got along without your help. You have been the Lord's special agent!"

Mrs. Meyer had tears in her eyes as she hugged him good-bye. Ken was surprised to feel some tears well up in his own eyes as he returned the hug; then he spontaneously hugged Rebecca and Benjamin. The professor had the final words.

"We will most certainly pray for you often."

Chapter 5

The first day at the induction center was rather exciting to those who had an adventurous nature and repulsive to some who had been drafted from a life they were content with and had no desire to leave. Young men from all walks of life were being thrown together and given the same treatment regardless of whether they came from a well-to-do, sophisticated lifestyle, the slums of a city, or the remotest hills of Appalachia. Some made it obvious they thought being herded around like animals was way beneath their dignity. Their attitude, whatever it was, made absolutely no difference in the way they were treated.

After being sworn in and receiving an official welcome to the air force by the base commander, the new recruits were herded into the barbershop, where they all received a "GI" haircut, much to the distress of some who were proud of their wavy or curly hair. Some of the barbers took fiendish pleasure in asking some among those who looked as if they were especially proud of their hair how they wanted it cut. They would listen carefully as their victim would give precise instruction on how they wanted to look; then the barber would proceed to mow off their beloved locks even shorter than for those who did not seem to care so much.

"You call yourself a barber?" one disgusted recruit said to the one who cut his hair.

The "barber" laughed. "Heck no! I never cut hair in my life before yesterday. I was working at the New York City Sewage Disposal Plant before I got drafted. But this is fun. I just may go into barbering when I am discharged!"

After laughing at each other's haircuts, the recruits were marched to the dispensary, where they received a vaccination, three immunization shots, and more rigorous physical tests than the screening tests they had received at the recruiting centers. Then they were taken to the quartermaster's building and issued summer and winter Class A uniforms as well as "fatigues," some high-top shoes, and an overcoat. They were also given a "mess kit" containing a knife, fork, and spoon mounted on a common ring; a canteen with a metal cup designed to fit around the bottom; a towel and washrag; and a duffle bag to put their new possessions in. They were told to carry their loaded duffle bags as they were led to the barracks and assigned a bunk. Then they were told to dress themselves in their new fatigues.

A trip to the mess hall introduced them to the type of meals they could anticipate in their military career. In the afternoon they were herded outside and told to "police the area," which primarily involved picking up the numerous widely-dispersed cigarette butts from the grounds. There were so many Ken suspected those picked up were saved and scattered for the next batch of recruits to have something to do that would impress to them that they were under the control of forces that could involve them in any menial task they chose. Almost before he realized it, the day was gone, and Ken climbed into his bunk to spend his first night as an air force private.

The shrill whistle sounded, awakening Ken from a deep sleep. He heard groans from some of the other recruits. He looked at his watch; it was five o'clock.

"Make up your bunks and fall out in the company street in fifteen minutes!" yelled a sergeant standing in the open doorway.

It was their first full day in camp, and they were scheduled to undergo intelligence, aptitude, and agility tests to determine how the air force could make best use of the new recruits' abilities.

"This is sure a lousy way to start the day," said the fellow in the bunk next to Ken. "I need about three more hours of sleep! And fifteen minutes isn't enough time to wash up and get out there dressed right, let alone having to make up our beds too!"

"I guess we have to just do the best we can," Ken said as he quickly dressed and made his bed. He had just finished washing up when the whistle blew again.

"All right, you mamas' boys, fall out and line up for roll call, and I mean *now*," the sergeant yelled in a loud voice.

Ken quickly joined the recruits crowding out the door and stepped into line. The sergeant waited until the stream of personnel ceased then raised a clipboard as two more fellows dashed out the door. The sergeant frowned but started calling roll. He had read off about a dozen names that all met with a "here" response when another recruit came hurrying out the door.

"Okay, soldier. What's your name?" the sergeant asked.

"Alvin Holowell," the recruit said with an apprehensive smile.

The sergeant looked for his name on the roll, checked it off, and made a notation.

"Holowell," he said, "immediately after you finish taking your tests, report to the mess hall for KP." He then resumed his roll call.

"You are going to go to breakfast; then you are to clean up the barracks until it shines! At 0730 hours, you will stand inspection. Stand beside your bunk at attention when the inspecting officer comes in. At 0800 you will go to Building A for testing. Dismissed," the sergeant said.

In the mess hall, Ken joined the line filing past the serving counter. He picked up a stainless-steel tray and some utensils. As he made his way along the counter, a server plunked a big glob of powdered eggs in his tray. In quick succession he received a thick slice of something he learned was called Spam, some fried potatoes, and some limp pancakes. As he ate, Ken thought how different this food tasted than Mrs. Meyer's. It was a lot closer to the food he had in the orphanage.

Three hours later, sweating heavily in the rather hot, stuffy room, Ken pondered the questions on the multi-page form before him. Some of the questions seemed pretty easy, but others required careful reading and real concentration.

The sergeant administering the test had said, "This is a multiple-choice IQ test. You have one hour to take it. Take time to understand the questions before you answer them. It is more important to get the questions right than to answer them all. If you should finish before the time is up, recheck your answers. Absolutely no talking, and anyone caught trying to copy someone else's answers will have reason to regret it!"

Ken tried hard to finish the test, but there were still several questions he had not answered when the sergeant said, "Time! Lay your pencils down and turn your test papers over."

A corporal immediately began gathering the papers.

When all the papers had been collected, the sergeant said, "Okay, take a break and be back in your seats in fifteen minutes."

As they were going out the door, the fellow behind Ken groaned and said, "That was the fastest hour I've ever seen. Did you finish?"

"No!" Ken said. "Did you?"

"No," he said. "I didn't even get to look at the questions on the last page. To complicate things, I got a nosebleed and had to spend time sopping up the blood!" He held up a blood-spotted handkerchief as proof of his statement.

"Wow!" Ken said. "That's a bad break. You ought to tell the sergeant. Maybe he would let you take the test over."

"No, I don't think I'm going to do that. He might put it on my records. I would like to get into pilot training, and they might think nosebleeds would be a problem and not let me into the program."

"Do you have them often?" Ken asked.

"Not very often, but it seems like it is always at an inconvenient time."

By this time they had joined the line at the drinking fountain. Ken took a better look at his new acquaintance. He had a clean-cut, amiable appearance and wasn't holding a cigarette, which to Ken was a plus.

Ken's mouth was dry from the tension built up while taking the test, and the drinking fountain water was tepid but thirst-quenching. He and his acquaintance talked about some of the questions on the test and speculated about their future in the air force. Ken learned his fellow recruit was from Philadelphia and was planning to go to college to become a mechanical engineer before the war had sidetracked his plans.

"What made you decide on that career?" Ken asked.

"My dad is a mechanical engineer, and he thinks it's a real good occupation. He has described what mechanical engineering involves, and it sounds like something I would enjoy doing. And Dad says he thinks there will be increasing demand for more mechanical engineers in the future, and they can get a pretty good salary. What sort of occupation are you planning on going into?" he asked.

"I haven't really given it a lot of thought," Ken said. "I've been an orphan since I was a baby, so I didn't have a father to advise me about an occupation."

"Talk about bad breaks! That's one of the worst I've ever heard of. I just don't know how I could have got along without my dad and mom. I hope things work out for you."

"Thanks, but it really hasn't been all that bad," Ken said. "I'm sure I will get it all figured out in due time. I think this time in the air force is going to be a good experience and maybe just what I need to help me decide what I want to do with my life." He unconsciously echoed the words Mr. Tanner had said just before he left the orphanage.

After returning from the break, the next hour was spent taking an aptitude test. The test didn't require nearly as much concentration as the IQ test. Ken wondered sometimes which of the answers would help him the most toward becoming a pilot, but he tried to answer every question honestly. It was difficult to decide which option best fit him on some of the multiple-choice questions, but he finished the test, and looking back over it he felt he had checked the most appropriate answers.

"Okay," said the sergeant. "Time's up! Stay in your seat while your papers are gathered up. Watch the bulletin board. In a day or so you will see your name posted with a time to come in and review the results of your tests."

After breakfast on the second day after completing the tests, there was a rush to the bulletin board. When Ken was finally able to get close enough to view the posted notices, he saw his name indicating he was to report to Building D at 1330 hours. There was a buzz of excitement as everyone wondered how the results of the tests were going to affect their future.

There were no other scheduled activities, so Ken eventually wandered over to the recreation hall. There were three table-tennis tables and two pool tables as well as a cabinet with several decks of playing cards. A couple card games were underway, and both pool tables and all three table-tennis tables were in use.

Ken was fascinated with the table-tennis activities. At one of the tables, there were two fellows who were obviously very experienced players. Ken marveled at their abilities to return the ball to each other at high speed for several minutes before one of them slammed the ball out of reach of his opponent. The game was still going on when those playing at one of the other tables laid down their paddles. Ken suddenly became aware that his nosebleed acquaintance was by his side.

"Want to play?" his new friend asked.

"I sure would like to, but I've never played before," Ken said. "If you play like these guys, I wouldn't get the ball back even once."

The fellow laughed. "I sure wish I could play like that, but I've only played a few times, and I want to learn to play better. Come on. Let's give it a try. My name is Robert."

"Okay. I'm Ken. If you are willing to put up with a rank beginner, I would really like to learn to play."

Ken could tell Robert was a better player than he had let on, but he seemed glad to be helping someone learn to play. He showed Ken how to hold the paddle, explained the system of scoring, and started hitting slow practice serves to Ken. It was not long before it became apparent he had a natural talent for the game, and they were able to play a game that was better than Ken had expected but far from the performance of the two experienced players he had watched. After twenty minutes or so, they laid down their paddles so others that were waiting could have a turn at the use of the table.

"Thanks, Robert," Ken said. "That was really fun!"

"Yeah, that was fun. We'll have to do it again first chance we get," was the response.

"It's a deal," Ken said. "I will look forward to that."

Finally it was close to 1330 hours. Ken wondered why they couldn't just say 1:30 like everyone was used to instead of complicating the issue. He made his way to Building D and entered. A corporal at a desk asked his name, made a checkmark on a list of names, and told him to have a seat beside three recruits who were waiting for their interviews. Others soon joined those waiting. Soon a recruit who had just completed his interview came down the hall and out the door. The three fellows who had appointments before Ken were in turn led down the hall to the officer who discussed the results of their testing with them.

When the last of the three came out, the corporal said, "Okay, Ryan. You're up," and led Ken to a room where a lieutenant was seated behind a desk.

The lieutenant looked at a document before him and asked, "Kenneth Ryan?"

When Ken responded, "Yes, sir," the lieutenant told him to be seated in the chair in front of his desk.

He opened a folder and examined the papers in front of him, then said, "Congratulations. Your tests show you have a high IQ, good physical coordination, and excellent mechanical aptitude. You are in great shape physically with one small exception. Although you have good eyesight, one of your eyes has only 20/30 vision. This means you are not eligible for pilot training, like so many of you recruits want. But the air force can make good use of your rather impressive qualifications in several different classifications.

"We are not going to give you a classification until after you finish basic training. The air force is expanding at such a rapid pace the top brass think in a few more weeks they will have a better picture of where you fellows can best be used." The officer stood and shook Ken's hand. "Good luck," he said. "I think you will do well in whatever classification you go into."

Ken left with mixed emotions. He was disappointed to learn he was excluded from pilot training, but the officer's upbeat attitude when talking about his qualifications made him feel good.

Two days later there were three different lists of names on the bulletin board. Ken's name was on a list of personnel that were to be shipped out the next day. The notice said they were to be in front of the orderly room at 0830 hours with their equipment packed in their duffle bags with the exception of their canteen and mess kit, which they were to keep in their possession. Their canteen was to be filled with water. There was nothing in the notice that indicated where they would be going.

The next morning, in front of the orderly room, a sergeant with a clipboard came out and conducted roll call. It was about 0900 hours when several olive drab busses stopped in front of the waiting recruits. They were told to get on one of the buses. After about twenty minutes the buses stopped at the train station, where a train and a few non-commissioned officers were waiting. The recruits were told to take their duffle bags to the baggage car next to the caboose then get aboard one of the passenger cars. This was to be their home for the next several days.

To most of the recruits, being on the troop train was a rather boring experience. Typically some would be sleeping, a few reading, and some card games would be in process, and sometimes a game of dice. The times when everyone lost interest in other activities was when the train stopped in some city or town. Then there was a rush for the windows on the platform side, where a few times there were women and young ladies who handed in soft drinks, donuts, cookies, and other goodies. Sometimes there were also some older men who seemed to want to see those who were eventually going to be engaged in fighting for their country.

The zealous attention by the civilians and obvious desire to please gave those on the train a feeling of importance and bravado. It was not unusual for the more brazen of the troops to try to talk some of the young ladies into giving them their addresses with the promise to write to them with firsthand accounts of the progress of the war when they got into battle. Some of the better-looking servicemen were successful in obtaining several addresses.

Ken enjoyed the excitement and goodies when the train was in a station, but when it was moving, he was much more interested in seeing the scenery than the activities most of the recruits were engaged in. As he was admiring the landscape, a sergeant tapped him on the shoulder and told him he was being assigned guard duty. He handed him a helmet liner to wear, which gave him more of an official military look.

The only instruction he received was to stand on the platform between two of the cars. He wasn't sure if he was supposed to stop servicemen from going from one car to another, but he hadn't been told to do that, so he just watched the passing scenery with a less restricted view than he had when looking out the window. He thought perhaps the main purpose of his being there might be to impress the civilian population that this was a well-organized military operation.

He saw many things that interested him but was distressed to see evidence of extreme poverty in some areas. On the outskirts of some of the towns and cities, he saw several very small, unpainted shacks with smoke coming out of a stovepipe, sometimes with rather raggedy-looking children playing outside. He was astonished to see one such shack with a big, shiny, new-looking car parked outside. The contrast was almost unbelievable.

The next day he was given KP duty. Apparently the fact he wasn't engaged in any of the activities with the others made him a target for assignment to special duties. He was taken to a boxcar that had a big pile of potatoes on the floor. Another fellow was already engaged in peeling the potatoes, and Ken was handed a paring knife and told to help finish the job.

Even though it was considered a menial chore, Ken was sort of glad to be doing something useful. During their two-hour task, as the pile of unpeeled potatoes slowly shrunk, they talked about the basic training that awaited them at their destination and wondered how rough it was going to be. Ken's fellow worker confessed he was a little fearful of going through it. Among other things, he told Ken he was he was a graduate of Notre Dame. Ken wasn't sure if this was true, but it was interesting to consider what a leveling process takes place in military service if it was true.

There were the very boring times for everyone when for reasons unknown the train would pull into a siding outside a town and stay for several hours. Boxes of "C" rations were distributed some mornings, supposedly containing food for the whole day. They were not always the same but could contain cans of powdered eggs and ham, hash, pork and beans, or similar items and other things like a few crackers of strange composition and a chocolate bar. The canned food was eaten cold from the can. Once, they traveled back through the train to a car rigged up as a kitchen, where they received some hot food in their mess kit.

Another time, after almost three days on the train, they were marched through the streets of an unknown city to a large hall set up to feed the troops. This was welcomed with enthusiasm, not only for the improvement in the food but also the opportunity to get some exercise after sitting for so long. Ken heard some muttering when they had to get back on the train.

Mid-afternoon on the fourth day, the train stopped in what they learned was San Antonio, Texas. They disembarked and stood beside the open baggage car door while two men loudly announced the name printed on each duffel bag in indelible ink and threw it out to be reclaimed by its owner. Then, carrying their duffel bags, they were marched through the streets the short distance to Kelly Field, which was to be their home for the next twelve weeks while they received basic training.

The new arrivals were lined up in a rather narrow, graveled street between two rows of squad tents. A businesslike older soldier in a uniform with six stripes stood in front of the group with a clipboard in his hand. Ken learned the stripes meant he was a master sergeant, which implied he had been in military service for quite a while.

"Okay," the sergeant said in a loud voice. "Let's make sure we understand each other. You have started a new life. You are not your own anymore; you belong to Uncle Sam! In the next few weeks, you are going to do things you don't want to do, eat food you don't want to eat, and probably live with some jerks you would rather not be with! Some of you aren't going to be able to take it, and we will have to send you home to mama! We will make men out of the rest of you and prepare you to serve your country as real soldiers rather than a bunch of disorganized hoodlums. This will help you and your buddies stay alive and will help our military be the most effective in combat or whatever you are involved with."

The sergeant paused then continued. "Now, the way to stay out of trouble is to listen real close to what your noncoms are telling you and do exactly as you are told. That will make it easier for all of us. Right now you are all going to be assigned to a tent. Tent numbers are posted in front of each tent. As I call your name and your assigned tent number, lock that number into your head. I don't want anyone coming back asking me to tell him again what his tent number is!"

With that he called the roll and gave the tent assignments. When he finished he said, "Okay, go to your tent and leave your duffle bag; then report back here within five minutes. Dismissed!"

Ken's tent number was B-11. He found it was only a short distance away, and he was the first one to arrive. He saw a mesh-covered ventilation opening in the middle of the eight-man squad tent and thought it might provide some fresh air to help compensate for the smoke he was sure would be present. Then he thought he would probably get more fresh air closer to the entry, so he put his duffle bag on the first cot on the left just inside the tent. Others were coming in as he made his way back out to stand in line again. He nodded as he passed them but didn't take time to talk to them.

When all the recruits had returned, the sergeant called them to attention then announced, "Now, Corporal Hayes is going to take you over to quartermaster's to get some blankets. Don't expect sheets and a pillow; we are not running the Hilton here! Okay, corporal!"

Corporal Hayes was a short, redheaded, red-faced man who obviously enjoyed being in charge.

"All right, recruits. Form up in columns of four," he yelled. "This is going to be sloppy until you learn how to march!"

They did as they were instructed and were soon marching haphazardly toward the quartermaster's quonset hut, where they were each handed two woolen, olive drab blankets. As they marched back, Ken thought back to life sleeping in the orphanage dormitory.

Guess living with a tent full of others can't be much different, he thought. *I just hope the other guys are easy to get along with.*

Just then the fellow in front of Ken dropped one of his blankets, and before he realized it, Ken's foot became tangled in the blanket. He stumbled and lunged into the fellow, knocking him into the person in front of him, and they both fell down. Ken stopped abruptly, and the fellow behind him ran into him, causing him to fall on top the two prostrate men. This stopped the whole column that was behind them.

"Halt!" the corporal yelled to stop the part of the column that was ahead of the source of confusion. He went storming back, very red in the face.

"Okay," he shouted. "What is going on here?" By this time everyone was back on their feet. Ken was struck with an impulse to laugh, which he suppressed, but could not keep a smile from creeping onto his face.

The corporal was visibly angry. "Oh, so you think it's funny. What's your name, soldier?"

Try as he would, Ken could not stop smiling even though he knew it was irritating the corporal.

"Ryan, Kenneth Ryan," he said. He stood at attention, hoping this act of subservience would help placate the corporal's anger.

"Okay, Ryan, who's responsible for this chaos?" the angry corporal yelled.

In the confusion, the blanket had been retrieved by the fellow who dropped it. Ken quickly realized he didn't want to be a tattler, so he said, "I guess it was my fault, sir!"

The corporal seemed somewhat appeased by Ken's docile attitude but took out a notebook and made some notes.

"Ryan, you are not in kindergarten anymore, so don't behave like you think you are. You can expect to be on KP or guard duty or both very soon!"

With that he put the notebook away and gave the command to march on. When they arrived at their company street, the corporal yelled, "Halt! Fall out! Make up your beds, and be ready for mess call in thirty minutes!"

The fellow who had dropped his blanket turned to Ken. "Hey, I'm sorry I got you into trouble," he said. "Why didn't you tell him about the blanket?"

"Well, he was already mad at me. I didn't see any point in both of us getting in trouble," Ken said with a smile.

"Well, thanks. I owe you one. My name is Don. I'm in A-21. Let me know if there's any way I can return the favor." Don held out his hand.

"Ah, that's okay," Ken said as he shook the proffered hand. "Don't worry about it."

When Ken got back to the tent, two of his tent mates were already there. He greeted them, and then another fellow entered.

"Hey," he said. "You're the guy that had the run-in with the corporal, aren't you?"

"Yeah, that's me," said Ken, grimacing. "Not a very good way to start an air force career."

"What was that all about?" asked the newcomer, making his way to the cot next to Ken's. "I was ten or twelve ranks behind you, so I didn't see what happened."

"Well, I tripped over a blanket the guy in front of me dropped and sort of fell against him, and he fell over and knocked the person down who was in front of him. Then the fellow behind me knocked me down on top the other two," Ken said, although he would have preferred to just forget about the whole episode.

"Wow! The corporal made that big a fuss over that? I thought a fight or a riot had broken out!" said his tent mate, laughing.

A deeply suntanned, older man had entered the tent in time to hear Ken's explanation. "Aw, don't worry about that yo-yo. I've seen his kind before. I did a hitch in the army a few years ago, and some guys when they get a couple stripes feel like they are a big shot and are just looking for ways to show their authority. Of course, the brass like to have guys like that for basic training to get recruits used to obeying commands regardless of whether they make sense or not! But I guess he is liable to make your life miserable for a while. Just try to stay out of his way."

As the rest of those assigned to B-11 made their way into the tent, another recruit recognized Ken as the one who had the run-in with the corporal, and some others gathered around him wanting to know the details of what happened. Ken reluctantly went through it again. He was surprised when everyone was laughing and acting as if he was a dignitary, then realized the arrogant attitude of the corporal made him pretty unlikable, so Ken's confrontation with him made Ken sort of a hero. From that moment on, he was the most popular member of B-11.

Everyone quickly made up their cots. Two blankets didn't take long to put in place. When the beds were made, everyone sat down on their cots, and several lit cigarettes. The older fellow had a slight smile as he looked around at his companions.

With a pronounced Texas drawl, he said, "Well, boys, looks like we are going to have to put up with each other for a few weeks. Like I told some of you, a few years ago, I served a hitch in the army, so I might be able to give you some advice if you need it." He had taken the first cot on the opposite side of the tent from Ken. Ken liked him from the start. It seemed good to be with someone who knew the ropes. He learned his name was Chet Dawson.

As he got acquainted with the rest of B-11's occupants over the next few days, Ken felt they were an interesting group of guys to be thrown in with, although some had rather unique personalities. Ken was impressed with Jim Purlee, who had taken a cot at the rear of the tent. He was a congenial person with a ready smile who seemed to constantly exude good humor. He seemed to enjoy life regardless of whatever demands basic training made of him.

Charles Radkin tended to be a little morose; he was regretting his decision to volunteer but admitted he had been deathly afraid of being placed in the infantry if he had waited to be drafted.

Mickey Sawyer was inclined to be a braggart and came up with some pretty tall tales that may have had some element of truth but were not taken seriously by most. Fred Stewart spoke rapidly with a deep Alabama accent that made him difficult to understand. He sometimes played a harmonica that sounded all right for a while but eventually became a little tiresome.

Pete Barrow was a pleasant person, but those in B-11 eventually became aware that he seemed to have an aversion to taking a shower. About the fourth week, he finally responded to the unanimous request from his tent mates to try out the showers, and the atmosphere in B-11 was significantly improved.

Ralph Davis always had something to complain about in a rather joking way. He also had the rather revolting habit of chewing tobacco. When he was inside the tent, he would spit into a clear glass pop bottle, a sight that turned most stomachs.

But despite their differences, in a short time there was a feeling of camaraderie among them.

Although there was a lot of complaining from some others, Ken enjoyed the challenges of basic training. Sergeant White was in charge of training Ken's platoon. Ken had thought Corporal Hayes might fulfill this role, and he knew he could expect some harassment if this were the case. However, Ken did find Corporal Hayes' promise of KP was fulfilled early. The same day he was warned, his name was posted on the bulletin board instructing him to report to the mess hall at 0430 hours the next morning.

Although KP was considered punishment by some, it was sort of interesting to Ken to see what was involved in preparing large quantities of food. The mess sergeant seemed a little surprised with the way Ken promptly completed all the tasks assigned him, including washing a huge pile of pots and pans without complaint.

Ken fully expected to be assigned this task more frequently than his tent mates in subsequent days, but with the exception of Chet, they seemed to get KP about as often as he did. It was probable that Chet's prior service in the army gave him special status and exemption from KP, and he rarely even got guard duty. In fact, he was appointed acting corporal and squad leader. The residents of B-11 made up Chet's squad.

There seemed to be a lot of emphasis on marching when Chet led his squad as one line in the platoon. The close order or marching drill seemed like sort of a game. It was amusing to see one fellow who seemed to not be able to tell his right from his left, which sometimes created a lot of confusion when he turned the opposite direction than the rest of the troops.

Ken thought how agitated Corporal Hayes would have become over this, but Sergeant White finally put a rock in the guy's right hand and said, "When I say 'column right,' or 'right face,' turn in this direction." That seemed to solve the problem. Chet told his tent mates later that it was not real uncommon to run across fellows with that problem, and the way Sergeant White dealt with it implied he had experienced it before.

Ken was impressed with Sergeant White. He dealt with the troops on a professional level; he expected and received instant response to his commands and drove them hard. But he showed his compassion one hot day while marching when a fellow a few ranks ahead of Ken fainted and fell hard on his face in the dust. Sergeant White immediately sent a runner to the dispensary to get medical help and stayed with the fallen recruit until an ambulance arrived. It was only then that training resumed.

Although calisthenics and the one and two-mile runs were Ken's least favorite parts of basic training, he was pleased to find he had no difficulty keeping up during the runs and doing the number of push-ups and other exercises the instructor asked for. Some of the fellows had real problems with these at first, but most finally built up their endurance to be able to meet the demands.

Ken did find his "dog tags" to be a real nuisance, particularly during calisthenics when they were constantly flopping around. They were required to wear these at all times on a chain around their neck. The metal tags were stamped with their name, serial number, and religious affiliation. When the weather turned cold, they were uncomfortable unless kept away from the skin or in continuous contact with it.

Ken really enjoyed the times on the rifle range. He had never fired a gun before, but it was challenging to see how well he did and how much he improved with time. He soon earned his marksman rating and eventually became a qualified sharpshooter. He sort of wondered why learning to shoot a rifle was of value to air force personnel, although he was aware some of the fellows might become aerial gunners, but they would be using machine guns. Chet said you never knew for sure what was going to happen in time of war, so it was important for everyone to know how to shoot if the need arose.

The trainees also received classroom instruction on military history, military customs and courtesies, dress and appearance, aircraft recognition, and security. They also were briefed on chemical warfare and the characteristics of different types of poisonous gases. As part of this training, they were issued gas masks and required to enter a tent filled with chlorine gas and don their masks after smelling the gas. A chemical warfare specialist stayed inside the tent with his mask on and watched to make sure everyone put their mask on properly. Ken was glad to have the gas mask in case it was needed, but it seemed clammy and pretty uncomfortable, and he hoped he would never have to use it. Most of the subjects seemed interesting to him, which was not surprising because he had always liked learning new things.

Almost five weeks of training had passed when it was announced that on the following day they would stand inspection in their Class A uniforms and would receive their first pay. The night before the inspection, the recruits sat out on the company street polishing their shoes. Determined to do a good job, almost everyone applied multiple coats of shoe polish paste, interspersed with vigorous buffing. One individualist had a jar of liquid shoe polish and for the most part leaned back with his hands behind his head amusedly watching the energetic efforts of his companions.

Ken wasn't close enough to see the results of his efforts, but when he saw this fellow's lackadaisical approach to shoe-shining, he thought, *That guy is probably going to be in big trouble tomorrow.*

Much to his surprise and those who had had similar thoughts, that fellow was the only one the inspecting officer complimented on having a good shine.

After the inspection was over, the trainees were told to line up in single file in front of an officer seated before a table which had stacks of five, ten, and one-dollar bills. They were to approach the officer, salute, and state their name, rank, and serial number, and then they were handed their monthly pay of twenty-one dollars, consisting of two fives, one ten, and a one-dollar bill. A sergeant seated beside the officer was documenting the process.

Ken had saved almost sixty dollars from his work on the Dalton farm, but he was glad to add his military pay to the billfold the Meyers had given him, and he felt well-to-do. Everyone was anxious to have the chance to spend some of their pay at some place besides the PX, or post exchange, so they were happy when it was announced they were to receive six-hour passes the coming weekend. Ken was as anxious as anyone to see the sights of San Antonio but was disappointed to find he was assigned to guard duty and would not get a pass.

Ken had completed his guard duty and was lying on his cot when he heard some raucous singing, and then three of his tent mates staggered into the tent looking very disheveled, obviously drunk.

"Theses gotta be the ri tent this time; there's ole Ken," said Mickey, who hiccoughed then belched loudly.

Ralph and Charles laughed uproariously. Ralph started to lie down on his cot, and he fell between it and the cot next to his. All three were again were seized with spasms of laughter. Then suddenly Ralph vomited. Ken quickly escaped to the outside air. He had never been around anyone who used alcohol that he knew of, but with the display of disgusting behavior he had witnessed, he silently vowed he would never start using this mind-numbing substance that made such fools out of people.

The twelve weeks of basic training were almost over. It had been an interesting experience. Ken was glad for the things he had learned and for the physical conditioning he had received, but he was looking forward to the next phase of his air force career. During the last week at Kelly Field, the trainees were brought into a classroom and told that as an experiment they were going to be given the opportunity to state what classification they would like to have. They were each given a sheet of paper with a list of classifications printed on it.

"The paper you have lists the classifications that are in greatest need of more personnel," said the sergeant who was conducting the meeting. "Sign your name and serial number at the top. Read this list carefully; then put a number one by your first choice and a two by your second. There is no assurance that you will get either of your choices; our screening officer may decide your particular qualifications indicate you should be in another classification. In the final analysis, it is the air force who will decide, but allowing you to express your preferences is a starting point."

As he looked at the classifications listed, Ken remembered Bill Dalton had said he thought it would be good to try to get some experience that would be helpful after he went back to civilian life. With this in mind, as his first choice he listed electronics repairman. For his second choice, he listed aircraft mechanic. He left the classroom hoping he had done the best thing. He wondered how his choices might affect where his life's paths were going to lead and was struck with the thought if he could just see into the future, the choices he listed might have been different.

Chapter 6

A week later, Ken was on his way to Keesler Field near Biloxi, Mississippi, to attend electronics school along with seven other recruits. None of his tent mates were in the group, and he was only slightly acquainted with two of the others who were with him.

He was pleased that his first choice for a classification had been granted. Apparently the air force's need for personnel in that classification and his aptitudes coincided with his stated preference.

For whatever the reason, he was happy he was being sent to learn about a subject that could be useful in civilian life. As far as Ken knew, the field of electronics was relatively new, but the article he had read in *Popular Science* in the hospital waiting room indicated electronics would be involved in the development of many new products, as well as improving existing devices such as radio and particularly television, which was still pretty much in its infancy but thought to have the potential of becoming a universally popular mass-media device.

Ken had been surprised when he had been called into the orderly room and was told he was being appointed acting corporal and was given orders for everyone in the group being sent to Keesler Field and responsibility for seeing they got to their destination. He had told his tent mates good-bye that morning with some regret; in the twelve weeks he had spent with them, he had developed some valued friendships. But as he looked out the window of the train that was carrying him to his new assignment, he was glad to be exploring some more of the big world that had been unknown to him only a few months before.

At Keesler Field, Ken and his companions found they were assigned space in a two-story wooden barracks along with men from other bases, rather than the tents they had at Kelly Field. Ken sort of missed the informality of the tent, and there were more inspections than they had before. To be acceptable for the white-glove inspections, there could not be a speck of dust anywhere without someone getting a demerit. Bunks had to be made up so tight a quarter would bounce when dropped on the blanket. Uniforms were to be hung in an orderly manner, with brass buttons shining. Socks, underwear, and other items in their footlockers had to be neatly arranged. Latrine detail was a common punishment for minor offenses, and the least favorite of all details.

Since they were sent to Keesler Field to be taught electronics, Ken was a little curious at the continued emphasis on drilling and physical conditioning, which did not seem to be of any value in repairing or maintaining electronic equipment. After running for one or two miles, Ken's clothes were drenched with sweat, and he could hardly wait to get into the showers. He was glad to find that laundry facilities were available on base because his sweaty clothes required frequent laundering.

He was very interested in the electronics classes, but the training was intense. In addition to the other required activities, classes were in progress for five hours most weekdays. There were quizzes almost every day and a test at the end of every week. Ken was gratified that his test results were tied with two others for the highest scores in the class. They were told those who successfully completed the course would be given corporal ratings.

The deeper Ken got into the electronics course, the more intrigued he was with the subject. Eventually the class was assigned the task of designing and building a three-vacuum-tube radio. Ken approached this project with enthusiasm. Formal class instruction was interesting, but it seemed like the most real learning took place in the lab, where there was test equipment, tools, and parts for hands-on experiments.

At the end of the third week, everyone was given an eight-hour pass. Ken went into town with a classmate named Lou Williams. They went to the USO and had some donuts and a Coca-Cola. The USO provided stationary and pens, so Lou spent quite some time writing a letter to his family. Ken followed his example and wrote a short letter to the Meyers and another to the Daltons. He gave a brief account of his experiences since he had seen them and told them that he missed them and Mrs. Meyer's cooking. It seemed nice to be able to write "Free" in the stamp location, a convenient perk for servicemen who might not have ready access to stamps.

After putting their letters in the USO mailbox, Ken and Lou went out to explore the city of Biloxi. The only thing of interest they saw was a theater marquee advertising the film *The Adventures of Robin Hood* in Technicolor starring Errol Flynn and Olivia de Havilland and decided to see it. It was a nice distraction from the routine of military life, and they enjoyed it.

After they got out of the movie, Lou said, "We have a couple more hours before we need to head back to base. I really like to skate. They must have a roller or ice rink in a city this large. Why don't we see if we can find one and skate for little while?"

Although this was a new activity to Ken, he agreed, and they stopped a passing teenage boy and learned from him there was a roller rink several blocks away.

When Ken and Lou walked up to the skate rental counter, the man behind the counter asked their shoe sizes and placed the skates in front of them. Ken started to hand him the posted rental fee, but he said, "No charge for servicemen."

"You sure aren't going to get rich with that policy," Lou said.

"Hey, see all those girls out there?" said the proprietor. "Why do you think they are here?"

Ken and Lou looked at the skaters going by and could see that a large percentage were girls in their late teens interspersed with about two dozen servicemen and a few older people.

"You fellows are good for business," said the proprietor with a smile. "Come back anytime."

Ken felt pretty awkward and within the first twenty feet fell down twice, but after floundering around the rink several times, he began to feel a little more comfortable. He was still going much slower than the majority of the skaters and stayed next to the railing so he could grab it if he needed to. Suddenly he felt someone run into him and knock him over. He looked up to see a girl looking back over her shoulder at him smiling broadly.

Yeah, thought Ken, *I guess it's pretty funny to watch a beginner try to learn to skate. Guess as slow as I'm going, it's not any wonder that I get run into once in a while.*

He got to his feet and resumed his efforts to improve. After several more rounds, he was beginning to enjoy the activity. A few minutes later, he again felt someone run into him and knock him down. He looked up and saw the same girl looking back at him laughing.

Why, that little imp! he thought. *I think she did that on purpose.* He shook his head. *What did I do to her to make her mad at me?*

When Ken got up after the third time he got knocked down, he kept looking back over his shoulder so he could attempt to stay out of the way when his persecutor came by. While he was looking back, he ran into another serviceman who was just learning to skate, and they both sprawled on the floor.

Ken was embarrassed. "Sorry," he said as he helped the other guy up. "I wasn't looking where I was going."

The other fellow grinned. "Aw, that's okay," he said. "I've been falling down ever since I got here. What's one more time?"

Ken stopped at the rest area and sat down on one of the benches.

The proprietor came over and said, "I see you've met Rosalie."

At first Ken didn't know what he was talking about. Then he said, "Do you mean that girl that keeps knocking me down?"

The proprietor smiled. "Yeah, that's Rosalie."

"Why does she do that?" Ken asked.

"Apparently she has taken a shine to you and is trying to get you to chase her," said the proprietor.

Ken looked out on the floor and could see Rosalie zipping around, obviously a seasoned skater. "Well, that's a joke," Ken said. "I couldn't catch her even if I wanted to!"

"Oh, she would eventually let you catch her," said the proprietor. "She's had a lot of experience with that game."

Just then Rosalie stopped at the railing in front of Ken and looked at him with a big smile on her face.

Ken jokingly shook his fist at her, and she laughed and skated off.

"Well, I'm not going to try to catch her," Ken said. "I think I would prefer girls who are more on the shy side."

"You are sure different than most of the guys Rosalie has been after," said the proprietor.

Ken decided he didn't want to get knocked down anymore, so he went to a soft drink dispensing machine and got a coke, sat down, and drank it while watching the skaters. He marveled at how some seemed to be able to skate backwards just as well as forward. Ken wished he could just be comfortable skating forward. In a little while Lou skated in and sat beside Ken.

"Maybe we had better be starting back to the base," Ken said. "We don't want any demerits to tarnish our spotless records!"

"Yeah, I suppose you are right," Lou said, and he began taking his skates off.

"You boys come back," the proprietor said again as they left.

About the middle of the fourth week, Ken received a letter and a package from the Meyers. He tore the letter open eagerly and noted that all of them had written something, but the professor and Benjamin had written the most. The professor wrote they were still attending the little church and that he had been asked to teach an adult Bible class, which he was enjoying. His teaching in the public school was going well, and he was very glad he had agreed to teach there during the current school year but thought he would probably go back to higher education the next year.

He concluded by saying, "We think so much of you; you helped us over a very critical time in our lives, and we will never forget it. You are such a fine young man. There are many pitfalls out there in the world. I pray you will conduct yourself in a manner in which you will have no cause to later regret. May the Lord bless you and keep you safe from all harm. We pray for you daily."

Mrs. Meyer's part was short, primarily telling Ken how much they missed having him around and again thanking him for all the help he had been to them and how much she was still enjoying the nice house. She said her English was improving, but she still needed her husband's help to write the note to him.

Rebecca wrote about her classes at school and said she was really enjoying school and being able to converse in English. She also mentioned that with Mr. Dalton's permission she and her mother had painted the kitchen, which she thought was fun except for the fumes. It was now a very light yellow.

Benjamin's part contained several markovers. Ken thought probably the professor had read what he had written and pointed out the words that were misspelled. Ken really laughed when he read Benjamin's account of going fishing, just he and Buddy. Buddy had discovered a skunk and got sprayed at close range. Some spray got in his eyes, and in trying to get away, he ran into a bush and got all tangled up. He was yelping like he was in a lot of pain, and when Benjamin went to help him get loose, he got sprayed too.

He said, "Mother made me bury my clothes, and she put a big pan of water outside and made me wash off several times, but she still couldn't stand the smell. She wouldn't let me into the house, and I had to eat and sleep out on the porch for two days. And of course, I didn't go to school during that time. Mr. Dalton heard about it and brought over some tomato juice and told me to bathe with that, which really helped. I think I'm back to normal now; at least Mom will let me into the house. I sure hope Buddy has learned to stay away from skunks. I know I have!"

Several fellows had gathered around his cot, and Ken shared Benjamin's experience with the skunk, causing most of them to laugh. Then Ken realized the main reason they were there was because he had a package. Usually when anyone got a package, it contained something to eat, most of the time cookies, which were almost always shared with the rest of the fellows. So Ken put the letter back in the envelope and opened the package.

As anticipated, the package contained several dozen cookies. They were a kind that Mrs. Meyer had made before, and though Ken didn't know what to call them, they were delicious. As his companions helped themselves to the treats, he regretted seeing them disappear so fast. Everyone exclaimed over how good they were, and some kept coming back for more.

Finally Steve Winters, who had the bunk next to Ken, said, "Okay, give the guy a break. Don't eat them *all*! They are his cookies, and he ought to get to save some for later."

Ken suspected Steve's intervention might be in hope that he might get some more himself. Down in the bottom of the package, there was a smaller package, and Ken opened it to find a pocket-size New Testament. He flipped through it then carefully put it in his footlocker.

Two days later, Ken was surprised to see his name and two others posted on the bulletin board with instructions to report to the headquarters building at 0800 hours the next day.

Oh no, thought Ken. *What's this all about? I'm supposed to be in class, but I guess this takes precedence.* But he did hate to miss class.

The next morning he reported as instructed and was directed by a corporal to a room where one of the other fellows was already seated. The third fellow showed up shortly. In a few minutes their commanding officer, Captain Henning, entered the room, followed by a major and a staff sergeant. All three enlisted men immediately stood at attention.

"At ease. Be seated," said the captain. "I don't know if you fellows have learned yet that when you are in the military service you never know what to expect next. This is one of those times. The air force has decided it needs to give higher priority to some classifications they are anticipating a greater demand for. Upon reviewing your previous testing, Major Harding here thinks you fellows may have the qualifications they are looking for in a particular category. Consequently he wants you to take some further testing, and depending on the results of these tests, you may be assigned a different classification."

Ken kept hoping the captain would say what the other classification was, but he turned to the major and said, "Major, they are all yours," and left the room.

Major Harding seemed to be less pompous than most of the officers Ken had seen. He smiled as he said, "You men are going to undergo some pretty extensive testing, which will probably take the rest of the day and possibly part of tomorrow. I am going to have a short interview with each of you separately while the other two are working on their first test. This test will evaluate your basic understanding of mathematics. It could take close to an hour to complete. When I call you for your interview, give your test papers to Sergeant Perkins to hold until you come back, and he will return your papers to you to finish."

He paused, looked at some papers he had in his hand, and asked, "Which of you is Private Ryan?" Ken raised his hand. "Come with me, Ryan," said the major. "You will start your test when I have finished with you."

The major led Ken to a separate room and told him to be seated in front of a large desk. He became quite informal and asked Ken a lot of questions about his private life: how he liked the air force so far; how he felt abut the war; if he had got along well with his father; if he had any enemies while he was growing up; what he liked to do for recreation; if he had any fear of being in small, closed places; and several other questions. Ken was puzzled over the seeming irrelevance of the questions and wondered how they could possibly have anything to do with any air force classification.

Finally the major said, "That's all for now, Ryan. When you get back to the other room, send in Private Wilcox, and you can start your math test."

He learned later this had been an initial psychological screening test, but he was to find that a more detailed psychological test that would take nearly an hour was ahead of him.

Ken finished the math test and gave it to the sergeant. He was then given another aptitude test, perhaps to confirm the results of the previous test he had taken. When he completed the aptitude test, he was given a form in an envelope and told to report to the infirmary for another physical examination. He was told the form would be filled out by a doctor in the infirmary, and he was to bring back the completed form. This examination was more extensive than any of the previous exams he had received. Shortly after he returned to the headquarters building, Ken and the other two were told to go to lunch and report back at 1300 hours.

On the way to the mess hall, Wayne asked, "Do you guys have any clue what this is all about?"

Ken and James both replied they had no idea.

"They are acting so mysterious that maybe they are going to train us to be spies!" Wayne joked.

"Whatever it is, I think I would rather stay here and keep learning more about electronics," Ken said, "but I guess I'll know better when we find out what classification they are testing us for."

The afternoon was filled with more testing, including psychological, coordination, and agility tests. When the tests were finished, the three were told to report back the next day at 0900 hours. Ken left the building feeling mentally exhausted.

The next morning the three trainees were escorted into the room they had been in the previous day. Shortly, Major Harding and the officer who had conducted the more extensive psychological testing entered. Again, the major told them to be at ease.

"Well, fellows, you can relax. Our testing is complete. Private Fisher, we are going to let you continue with your electronics training. You may be dismissed and report to your regular classroom. Ryan and Wilcox will remain here."

After Private Fisher left, the major continued. "We have not told you what this is about partly because we were tying to make this as stressful as possible to see how you stand up under stress. Now we can tell you. The air force anticipates a need for a lot more navigators. A new class has just started at Mather Field in California, and they have a few more openings they would like to fill. We think you two will be excellent candidates for this class.

"You might like to know the position of navigator requires higher qualifications than any of the other aircraft crew members, including pilots. You both demonstrated a high proficiency in understanding mathematical concepts. You have good emotional stability and did well on all the screening tests relating to navigator responsibilities. We have been asked to get you into the navigator class as soon as possible.

"There will be a plane leaving this base at 0900 hours tomorrow, which will take you to Mather. Here is a copy of orders for each of you. Take these by and show them to your electronics instructor so he will know you haven't gone AWOL; then pack up and be outside headquarters at 0800 hours tomorrow morning, where there will be transportation to take you to your plane. Unless you have some questions, you are dismissed. Good luck!"

Ken's head was reeling. He had a lot of questions but didn't think of any that seemed important enough to ask the major. Besides, the major didn't really seem to want questions, even though he had suggested that possibility. Ken wasn't sure he would have chosen to drop out of electronics and go into navigation, but he wasn't offered a choice. But he again felt that stirring of excitement over what the future held in this new assignment. One positive factor was that navigation involved flying, and he felt a pretty strong desire to experience that.

When they boarded the plane carrying their packed duffle bags, Ken and James learned the plane was from Mather Field and was on a navigation training mission, so providing them transportation had been a secondary purpose of the flight. They sat down in one of the bench seats extending along the fuselage on each side. Ken watched out a window as the plane taxied to the runway where it sat for a couple minutes. Then with the engines roaring loudly, the plane started down the runway gathering speed until he felt it suddenly lurch into the air. Ken watched the ground rapidly drop away and the objects on the ground grow smaller and smaller. What an exhilarating sensation! As he had anticipated, this was going to add to the enjoyment of his new assignment!

The trip to Mather was a very pleasant experience for Ken. He had enjoyed traveling by car and by train, but being able to see a panoramic view of vast areas of land provided a perspective far different from ground travel. He was fascinated by the differences in terrain: low, tree-covered hills; prairie grasslands; arid deserts; the Grand Canyon; evergreen-covered mountains dotted with lakes—they were all a treat to see.

When the plane was descending after crossing the mighty Sierras, he could see two converging rivers and a number of rice paddies and other crops. It seemed to be basically an agricultural area with a few farm buildings in the midst of the broad fields. At the confluence of the rivers, there was a fairly good-sized city but no especially tall buildings. As the plane approached the base, he saw a small settlement among a number of grape arbors. He learned later this was the town of Rancho Cordova, and the nearby city was Sacramento.

After landing, Ken and James were processed in and were assigned to a barracks reserved for navigator trainees. They were told they had only forty-five minutes to get their dinner before the mess hall closed. They had missed lunch, so they were pretty hungry.

Ken thought the food was quite a bit better than they had at Keesler. He was surprised that the nine-hour trip had been so tiring, but he later learned changing time zones in a relatively short time contributed to the tiredness. When they got back to the barracks, both he and James stretched out on their cots and were soon asleep.

The navigator class had been underway for three days, so Ken and James were given private sessions to bring them up to speed. Even during the first session, Ken could tell he was going to enjoy the challenge of this new career. He learned he was now called a cadet and would receive a commission as a second lieutenant upon successful completion of the course, which was a pleasant surprise.

His enthusiasm remained high during the nearly nine months of training. During this time, he and the others were subjected to more screening tests, such as spending several hours breathing oxygen in a reduced atmospheric pressure chamber to assess their ability to function for long periods at high altitudes.

A primary emphasis was placed on honing the mathematical skills involved in navigating. He learned to use basic navigation instruments such as the gyrocompass, the sextant, and the drift meter. He learned the constellations in the sky, which provided a basic means of navigation to supplement the other methods if needed.

Radio beams provided another navigational tool but were of limited value in many cases because of the way they fanned out the farther they were from the source. Navigators were also required to learn Morse code, which Ken found to be relatively easy. He also spent nearly a week at aerial gunnery school. He had enjoyed his time on the rifle range, but it was more challenging to fire the fifty-caliber machine guns.

Ken had been in navigator training for almost three weeks before he felt he could take time to write a short letter to the Meyers and thank them for the package. He explained his change in status and location and that he hadn't really had time to write before. He wrote how much he and his barrack mates back at Keesler Field had enjoyed the cookies. He also thanked them for the New Testament and said his day was so full of scheduled activities that he hadn't had time to read much of it. He promised he would read it more often when he had more time.

After being in the program for several weeks, the cadets were able to get an occasional pass. Thanks to a few who had cars, they were able to tour the many historical places of interest.

Sutter's Fort, the first permanent settlement in the area by those of European ancestry, was a major attraction with its antique equipment and furnishings. They also made a trip to Sutter's Mill in the Sierra foothills, where Sutter's foreman, James Marshall, made the discovery of gold in the sawmill race that started the 1849 gold rush. The gold rush had resulted in a population boom, and a business section sprang up along the river, which became the embryo of the city that became California's capitol. It also became the terminus of the western end of the transcontinental railroad and the pony express system. Tourists enjoyed looking at the old buildings and reminiscing about the historical period that had brought them into existence.

Then there was a brief trip to beautiful San Francisco, with several little sailing ships decorating the bay with their snow-white sails against the blue-green of the bay. Ken's adventurous nature was being gratified.

The navigation training officers were under pressure to develop a number of proficient navigators as soon as possible. Consequently the training proceeded at a rate that was difficult to keep up with, even for the most qualified candidates. In addition to meeting the classroom requirements, after a few months there were several training missions—a number of them at night—to assess each individual's ability to put theory into practice. Ken was among those who demonstrated excellent performance during these flights, never failing to direct the plane to its desired destination.

Those in Ken's class who managed to successfully meet the requirements graduated on October 7, 1943, just a little over a year after Ken had gone into the air force. They were given an allotment to use for the purchase of officers' uniforms and at the graduation exercises were given shiny, new second lieutenant's bars. The base photographer took pictures of the graduating class and then individual pictures of each of the new officers. Ken sent a copy of his photo to the Meyers along with a short letter.

The air war in Europe was taking a terrible toll on the planes and flyers of the Allies. Replacements of both equipment and personnel were badly needed. Consequently, just two days after graduation, Ken and several of his fellow graduates were on their way to Dow Field, near Bangor, Maine, to help form up flight crews. The crews were to man new B-17G bombers just off the assembly line. Ken had a few training flights in an earlier model B-17, and he liked the plane.

Several members of the crew Ken was assigned to had been training together for a couple weeks. Two others besides Ken were new: the copilot and the flight engineer/top turret gunner. When they gathered to take their first training flight, Lieutenant Douglas Murphy, the pilot, welcomed the new personnel and introduced those who were already members of his crew. He was already acquainted with the new copilot, Lieutenant Keith Anderson, whom he had met during flight training.

When he introduced Technical Sergeant Hal Hannigan, he commented on how fortunate they were to have such a well-qualified flight engineer. Hal had been an instructor, training others in aircraft maintenance before he had requested flight status, and was especially well-versed on all the B-17 systems.

"In fact, I think we have an exceptionally well-qualified crew all the way around!" Lieutenant Murphy said proudly.

As Ken looked around at the crew members, they seemed like a great group of men, and he was glad to be on a crew with them. He was especially impressed with Sergeant Hannigan. He radiated good humor and seemed to bond with the other crew members right from the start.

The bombardier was Lieutenant Jim Wright. Ken was to spend many hours behind him in their separate compartment during flights. The smallest crew member was Staff Sergeant Ralph Sullivan, who would occupy the cramped position of ball turret gunner beneath the belly of the plane. Staff Sergeant Bill Williams, the tail gunner, was also somewhat shorter in stature than the others. The two waist gunners were Staff Sergeants Wayne Dixon and Ralph Armstrong. The last man on the crew was Staff Sergeant Peter Morse, the radio operator.

During the next two weeks, the new crew had three training missions. Ken demonstrated his competence in navigating and won the praise of the pilots. Since it was customary for the crew to name their plane, during this time it became sort of a contest to see who could suggest the best name. Several names were considered, but when the copilot suggested "Luck of the Irish" since the names of four of the crew members implied they were of Irish heritage, it quickly gained favor and was soon voted on and accepted. Before they were able to get the name applied to the nose of the plane, they received orders to prepare for deployment to England.

The officers on each of the flight crews were assigned a room together in the officers' quarters. The day before they were to leave, as Jim, the bombardier, started out the door of their quarters, he turned and said, "I'm going to go into town, Ken. I want to get some writing tablets and some pencils. I want to use our flight time to write some letters to my wife and some of my relatives. Want to come along?"

"That sounds more interesting than just hanging around here," Ken said as he got up off his cot and reached for his cap.

He felt it would be a good chance to get better acquainted with Jim. When they went out the door, they felt some strong gusts of wind and had to hang on to their caps. They checked a Jeep out of the motor pool, made their way into town, and soon obtained the items Jim wanted.

Jim said, "I really like milkshakes. We don't know when we will have another chance to have one. Why don't we go to that ice cream parlor across the street and have 'one for the road'?"

"Okay," Ken said. "I've never had one but would like to see what they are like."

They went into the little ice cream parlor, and while drinking their milkshakes, they learned more about each other's background. Jim was a little older than the rest of their crew. He was married, and his wife was expecting a baby in a few months. He had been working with his father in the construction business when he had been drafted and placed in bombardier training. He told Ken he had a premonition he was not going to survive the war and was very concerned about his wife and baby.

Thirty minutes later, when they went outside, they found it was beginning to rain. The wind, which had been gusting before, was now blowing hard. They ran to the Jeep and were pretty wet by the time they got there. It wasn't much better in the Jeep, even with the canvas roof over them. The rain was increasing in intensity, and with the open sides of the Jeep, the wind was blowing the rain in on them in sheets.

The windshield wipers were not even beginning to keep the windshield clear. Jim had to stick his head out the side to see to drive.

As they were going around a corner a short distance from the entrance to the base, they saw a terrible wreck. A fuel truck coming from the base had collided with a small sedan, and the sedan was on fire. Jim quickly stopped the Jeep, and they ran up to the sedan and tried to open the door on the driver's side, but it was jammed shut.

Ken ran around to the other side of the car. The flames were licking the front of the passenger compartment. He yanked hard on the door. It came open, and he saw a woman and a young girl, both unconscious. He quickly lifted the girl out and placed her under a tree by the side of the road. When he got back to the car, Jim was dragging the woman out, and together they carried her away from the car. Then Jim went to check on the driver of the truck while Ken tried to assess the injuries of the woman and girl.

The woman had a gash on her forehead that was bleeding badly. Ken swabbed up the blood with his handkerchief then folded it and laid it on her forehead. Then he went to check the little girl for injuries. Just then the gas tank blew up, and the car was enveloped in flame.

Ken saw the little girl had a big bruise forming on her forehead, but he saw only minor bleeding. He felt for her pulse and was able to find one, but it seemed rather weak. Probably attributable to the cold rain in her face, the woman regained consciousness. When she saw her daughter, she screamed, "Susan!" Ken told her he didn't think she was hurt seriously, but they had better get them both to a doctor.

"Take us to the base hospital," she said in an anguished voice. "I'm Colonel Ross's wife. They will treat us there!"

Jim came back to report the driver of the truck had been a little stunned but had recovered and had backed the truck away from the burning vehicle. Ken and Jim loaded Mrs. Ross into the passenger side of the front seat of the Jeep, and Ken got into the backseat, holding her daughter. Mrs. Ross turned toward her daughter with tears mixed with the rain on her face. Her forehead was still bleeding, and she continued to hold Ken's handkerchief against the wound.

The sentries at the gate seemed apprehensive when they saw the Jeep rapidly approaching the gate. They stepped into the path of the Jeep with upraised hands.

Jim stopped the Jeep and said, "This is an emergency! Colonel Ross's wife and daughter were in a bad accident and need to get to the hospital!"

The sentries immediately stepped back, saluted, and waved the vehicle through. Jim quickly drove to the emergency entrance of the base hospital. Mrs. Ross was now shaking violently from shock and cold, and Jim escorted her into the hospital while Ken carried her daughter, who was still unconscious.

The receptionist at the admitting desk asked for Mrs. Ross's identification, but it was in her purse, which was still in the burning car. She then asked Ken and Jim their names, which she wrote on the admitting paperwork. Ken asked the receptionist if she would call the base fire department to tell them about the burning vehicle and then the motor pool to tell them they better send a tow truck to get the wrecked car off the road before it caused more accidents.

When they were getting back into the Jeep, Ken suggested they check on the truck driver again, and Jim agreed. When they got back to the scene of the accident, they saw that the flames from the car had died down some. The driver, a corporal from the base, had pulled the truck off the road and was standing near the burning vehicle with a worried look on his face. He was apparently prepared to try to warn any other vehicles of the hazard, but Ken was afraid he might not be very visible in the rainstorm and was putting his life in jeopardy unnecessarily. The flames from the fire were much more visible than he was. He saluted as Ken and Jim stopped beside him.

"It looks like you're okay," Jim said, "but we will take you to the hospital if you think you have a problem."

"No, sir. I'm pretty cold, but otherwise I'm fine. How are the others?" the truck driver asked.

"I think they will be all right," Jim said. "They are being cared for at the hospital now. What happened here?"

that Ireland should soon be visible, and after ten or fifteen minutes, Lieutenant Murphy reported he had sighted the Irish coast.

"Wish we were landing in Ireland. I've got some relatives down there and probably some of you do too. Maybe we'll get a chance to visit sometime while we're in England. We had better be asking our parents and grandparents if they can tell us how to locate our Irish relatives."

The group of planes passed over Northern Ireland and landed at Prestwick Field in Scotland in near darkness. The crews were glad to be back on the ground. Most of them had slept some during the flight, but they were all tired and glad to get out of the confines of the planes. They spent the night at Prestwick; then mid-morning the next day, they went on to Bassingbourn Air Base near Cambridge, England, which was to be their permanent base.

Bassingbourn was a former British Royal Air Force base and was furnished with amenities more elaborate than most bases. This was considered the most desirable of all the American Air Force bases in England, but the new crews did not know the hand of fate had assigned them to the most preferred base.

As they began to land, they saw long rows of B-17s and one area where badly damaged planes were grouped out of the way of the planes that would be taking off for their missions over the continent. The control tower directed them to a place to park the plane. As he stepped off the plane, Ken felt a twinge of mild exhilaration. A light fog created a slightly mysterious atmosphere, and it seemed so different from any place he had ever been. It was not hard to realize he was in a foreign country. This was a time of major transition, not only in his geographical location but from his life of relative serenity to one which would involve inevitable danger and possible terror.

Two Jeeps arrived and took the crew of *Luck of the Irish* and their luggage to their quarters. The pilots of *Luck of the Irish*, the bombardier, and Ken were assigned a room together in the officers' quarters.

The next day they received a base orientation and a warm welcome from Colonel Wray, the base commander. He told them they faced a hazardous and difficult task, but crippling Germany's industrial might was vital to ultimate victory for the Allies, and the bombing raids by the Eighth Air Force were expected to play a major role in accomplishing that objective. Several other officers assigned to the base also greeted them enthusiastically. It was always a boost to their morale to have their depleted numbers reinforced.

During the next two weeks, they flew three more training missions in conjunction with other B-17s to hone formation flying skills prior to being subjected to combat conditions. It had been demonstrated in previous missions that tight formations provided better protection against enemy fighters, and it took practice for the pilots to get comfortable flying with their wingtips within a few yards of those of other planes.

The crew members all seemed anxious to start performing the job they were trained to do, but seeing a flight of bombers return to base with diminished numbers and severe damage to some of the planes did create some degree of apprehension. However, a ground crew member had painted "Luck of the Irish" in precise letters on the nose of their plane along with a bright green shamrock, and the crew in general considered this to be an omen of good fortune.

The RAF had attempted daylight bombing early in the war and had suffered heavy losses. They had concluded the bombing raids should be made under the cloak of darkness. In forming the US Eighth Air Force, Major General Ira Eaker had maintained the raids would be more effective and cause fewer civilian casualties if conducted during the daylight hours. Also, the Norden bombsight, which was considered to be a valuable enhancement to bombing accuracy, would be of limited value in darkness. Consequently the Eighth Air Force was committed to daylight bombing. Then, on November 15, the day came that they had been anticipating: assignment to a mission over the continent. That morning, Sergeant Hannigan, along with the ground crew chief, had carefully checked the plane over and pronounced it ready to go.

Clad in their fleece-lined flight jackets, they met in the briefing room and were shown a map of their route to the target, which was the German submarine yards at St. Nazaire on the southwestern coast of France. German U-boats were sinking a significant number of ships carrying materials and personnel to England, and the raid was an attempt to keep more of these subs from being produced and destroy those being serviced. The briefing officer stated the Germans were trying desperately to protect these installations and had continued to increase the number of anti-aircraft guns in the area.

"You will have good fighter escort, so your major concern will be the flak. Be sure to wear your flak jackets. Good luck. We hope to put that operation out of business for a good long time!" the briefing officer said at the conclusion of his briefing.

Tensions were high that morning in *Luck of the Irish*, but they were glad to finally get a chance to put the training they had received to use. As their plane took off in a light mist, Ken felt a surge of adrenaline. This sort of seemed like a dream. Forty planes were assigned to this mission, but two turned back after being in the air for a short time, presumably because some system was not performing properly.

Even though all the bombers were depending on the navigator in the lead plane to get them to the target, Ken was required to know the position of their plane at all times. Following the prescribed procedures, he periodically gave this information to the radio operator over the intercom, where it was entered in a log along with the time and pertinent observations of other crew members.

The formation flew south for several miles before turning east in order to get around the Brittany peninsula and minimize the length of time spent over the continent. About twenty minutes before reaching the coast, the crew of *Luck of the Irish* was glad to see a squadron of P-47 Thunderbolts appear, waggling their wings in greeting.

German radar had apparently given warning of the impending attack, and a few minutes before they reached the coast, a Messerschmitt streaked through the formation, hotly pursued by a P-38. Although Ken occasionally caught glimpses of aerial dog fights in the distance, that was the only German plane he saw that had penetrated the formation.

The American fighters were apparently accomplishing their assignment of keeping the German fighters away from the bombers.

Ken informed the crew that they were approximately five minutes from the target. As the lead planes neared the coastline, he could see several white puffs of smoke, which he knew were bursts of flak. The closer they got to the submarine yards, the thicker the flak got, and their plane was constantly buffeted by concussion from the explosions. Looking out the side window, he saw a plane with one engine smoking, but it seemed to be holding its place in formation.

As they got over the target, the bombardier announced he had released the load of bombs. Ken hoped the bombs achieved their intended purpose but couldn't help wondering how much death and suffering would occur along with the damage to their target. He was glad he wasn't the bombardier and wondered if it bothered Jim to be the one who released the bombs.

"We did it, guys. Let's go home!" said the pilot.

However, they were exposed to the heavy flak for several more minutes as the formation made a wide sweeping turn and headed back out to sea. Ken looked out the side window and saw one of the bombers going down. He watched as three parachutes appeared; then the plane disappeared from view. He stood in order to see down farther but could see no more parachutes.

"Dear God, help the rest of those fellows get out," he said fervently with his hand on the New Testament he was carrying in his shirt pocket.

He realized he had really not done a lot of praying before, but this prayer rose unbidden to his lips, and he resolved to develop more of a prayer life. The next time he looked out the window, he saw another bomber slowly drop one wing and then begin tumbling toward the earth. He didn't see any parachutes. He wondered how many more planes had gone down that he had not seen. When the formation crossed the coastline, the bursts of flak ceased, and Ken breathed a prayer of thanks.

Back at Bassingbourn, the plane landed, completing their first mission. As the crew climbed out of the plane, they had a feeling bordering on jubilation; they were now an experienced combat crew. At the same time there was a feeling of remorse over those who had been shot down, and knowing it could just as well have been them weighed on their minds. Even Hal Hannigan was not quite his usual, jovial self.

"Thank the good Lord for bringing us back," he said. "I hope all those fellows that went down got out okay."

As Hal unzipped his bomber jacket, Ken saw the bulge in Hal's left shirt pocket. He was sure he wasn't a smoker, so he suspected Hal too was carrying a New Testament. It gave him a good feeling to think they might have a common bond.

It was established practice for a symbol of a bomb to be placed on the plane's fuselage as a record of how many combat missions the plane had accomplished. The crew stood and proudly watched as the ground crew chief painted this symbol on *Luck of the Irish*. Hal resumed his typical good humor.

"Well, guys, only twenty-four more to go, and we can go home!" he said enthusiastically.

Several groans were heard from other members of the crew. It was common knowledge that very few planes had survived twenty-five missions. Then they went to the post-mission debriefing, where they were asked to report the details of the mission. One of the first questions asked was in regard to the planes that had gone down. Who had last seen them, how many parachutes were deployed, whether the plane was on fire, and what part of the plane was damaged.

Some crews were able to provide information relating to these questions, which was recorded by a clerk. One plane was reported to have one engine smoking, and another engine appeared to be feathered, providing no power to the plane. This plane was lagging behind, but the last it was seen it was still in the air over the ocean and headed home.

Two days later, they were shown aerial photos of the results of their mission. To their disappointment, the mission had not achieved as much damage as had been hoped. A critique of the mission was given with a discussion of what might have improved their effectiveness. It was also reported that the crew of the plane that had been falling behind had gone down in the English Channel and had been rescued. It was gratifying to learn provisions were in place to save crews that went down in the ocean, but Ken fervently hoped their crew would never need these services. He had never had the opportunity to learn to swim.

The mission had impressed upon Ken the uncertainty of life, and for the first time, he began to think seriously about what lay beyond death. He remembered Professor Meyer seemed to feel the answers to all of life's problems were in the Bible. He wished he had asked some questions when the professor read the scriptures to the family. He also remembered hearing terms like "born again" and "everlasting life" in the little church he had attended with the Meyers and now wished he had paid more attention when these subjects were brought up.

He felt drawn to Hal, who seemed to exhibit such peace and optimism. Maybe he could shed some light on spiritual matters. On impulse, he went to the orderly room and asked which barracks Sergeant Hal Hannigan was in. The corporal on duty checked the records and gave him Hal's barracks number.

Hal was sitting on his cot writing a letter when he looked up and saw Ken approaching.

"Well, hello," Hal said. "What can I do for you?"

"Do you feel like taking a little walk?" asked Ken. "I need to talk to someone."

"Sure, why not!" said Hal, rather mystified. They went out of the barracks and started walking with no particular destination in mind. "What's on your mind?" Hal asked.

Ken wasn't sure how to begin. "Some of the things you have said led me to believe you are a Christian, and isn't that a New Testament you have in your shirt pocket?"

Hal broke into a broad smile. "Yes to both questions!" He pulled out a worn New Testament and held it up. "I have had this for some time, but it has become a lot more meaningful to me in the last few years."

Ken took his New Testament out and said, "This was sent to me by some good friends while I was in basic training, but I haven't really read it that much, and I haven't understood much of what I have read. I'm sure there must be lot of answers in here if I knew where to look for them."

"Yes, Ken. There are answers to all of life's problems. Sometimes they may be a little hard to find, but they are there," Hal said.

"So do you know where to look for an answer when you have a problem?" Ken asked.

"Well, it's not like you might find an answer that relates specifically to a minor problem you have. For instance, if you can't find the keys to your car, you are not going to be able to look in the Bible and see in big glowing letters, 'look under the cushions on the couch,' but there are general principles that cover every situation in life. But I think in understanding the Bible, it helps to have the big picture," Hal said. "Would you mind if I gave my version of what it's all about?"

"Please do," said Ken. "I would be very interested in hearing that."

By this time they had reached the perimeter of the base and were leaning against the fence. There was a field with some kind of plants on the other side. Two men were apparently harvesting the crop.

"Okay," Hal said. "Just remember I'm not a theologian, but I think my understanding of the way the pieces fit together is in agreement with the Bible, and that's what's important. Well, to start with, God is a God of love, or as the Bible says, he *is* love. So he apparently had a desire to share that love not with just anything but with something that could appreciate and return that love.

"He didn't want to create a bunch of mechanical robots who would only serve him because they were programmed to do so. Instead, in his great creative mind, he conceived of a being with intelligence, emotions, and the ability to choose to serve the God of creation. In other words, mankind. This had its hazards because if he gave this being the ability to choose to serve him, it could also choose to rebel.

"This being would need an environment to exist in, so God created the world out of nothing. He made it a place of beauty with all the things man and his descendants would need to lead happy, productive lives. Then he made Adam and Eve and the provision for exercising their free will by putting *one* tree in the Garden of Eden and told them in strong terms to not eat its fruit. All the other trees they were free to eat from, but this one they were told to avoid at the cost of death. Then Satan entered the picture and convinced them God was holding out on them and it would be to their advantage to eat the forbidden fruit.

"As God had warned them, their disobedience brought about spiritual and eventually physical death. Since Adam was the father of all mankind, this sentence of death was passed down through all generations to you and me and everyone else. One aspect of that penalty was a nature inclined to evil so that all of Adam's descendants have followed him in sinning.

"God's righteous nature requires that the price of disobedience be paid as warned in order to restore mankind to the kind of future he had planned for them. To pay the penalty for violating God's laws, God established the practice of accepting the death of sacrificed animals as atonement for man's sin. This was a temporary measure and foreshadowed the death of Jesus on the cross as the sinless Son of God, the once-for-all, perfect sacrifice for mankind's sins.

"But again, free will enters the picture. We can choose to accept Jesus as the atonement for our sins, or we can ignore his invitation and choose to suffer the ultimate penalty of spiritual death in a place of everlasting punishment. The Bible says we must be 'born again.' This is not a physical but a spiritual birth, whereby our spirits are brought into harmony with and in submission to God. Then the Holy Spirit, the third member of the trinity, opens our mind to understand the Bible in a way not possible on our own.

"Okay, that's the way I see it. What do you think?" Hal glanced sideways to see if he could read Ken's expression.

"Wow, that's a lot to think about," Ken said. "Where would I find this in the Bible?"

Hal laughed. "Well, it's not like you would find all that in one place. That was sort of a summary from Genesis to Revelation. But I think I would recommend that a person who is just beginning to read the Bible start with the book of John. Romans has some really great theological truths in it too. I really like Romans."

"How long did it take you to sort all this out?" Ken asked.

"Well, my dad is a Baptist pastor, so I've been going to church all my life, and I've picked up some beliefs all along the way. But it was not until I was about thirteen that I really understood what it was all about and committed myself to be a real Christian," Hal said.

"Hal, were you afraid when we were on that mission?" Ken asked. "You know it could have just as well been us that went down."

"I sure was, but it makes a big difference when we know we have accepted Jesus as our Savior and that we are going to end up in an infinitely better place," Hal said. "We all try to avoid death, but it is something all of us will have to face sometime. If you think about it, it doesn't really matter a whole lot whether we live a short life or a long one here on earth. In comparison to eternity, it is just the blink of an eye. And probably once we are in heaven, we will think, 'Wow, this is so great! I wish I had come here sooner!'"

The two men in the field had been working their way toward the fence where Ken and Hal were standing as they were picking something from the low plants. One of them raised his hand in a friendly salute. Ken and Hal returned the greeting.

"Wonder what they are harvesting," Hal said. Then he looked closely at the plants just on the other side of the fence. "Why, that looks sort of like what we had in the mess hall a while ago," he said. "I wonder what it's called. It was called a lot of very uncomplimentary names in the mess hall."

"It beats me," said Ken. "I think they had some of that in the officers' mess too, but I didn't take any."

The men in the field kept drawing closer until they were only a short distance away.

"Hello, gentlemen," Hal said. "Could I ask you what that is you are picking?"

The older man who had greeted them came over to the fence and extended his hand. "Hello, chaps," he said in an intriguing accent. "I'm

Cedric Sutherland." He pointed at the other man. "That's my man, Tom. These are brussels sprouts. Don't you have them in America?"

"If we do, I sure don't remember seeing any," said Hal, and Ken agreed.

"Surely you have had them with your meals here at Bassingbourn; your supply officer purchased some from me just a few days ago."

"Yes, we had some of those today," Hal said with an unconscious grimace that showed he hadn't particularly enjoyed them.

"Now, now, lads," said Mr. Sutherland, "don't get down on brussels sprouts! For most people they are a tasty vegetable if they are cooked right. But when they are overcooked, they can have a slight sulfurous taste that is a bit unpleasant. I suspect your cooks didn't get it right. You come over to the manor, and the Mrs. will cook some for you that I think you will like."

He pointed to a building barely visible through the trees and shrubbery. "Come over any time. We want to treat you Yanks right, now you've signed on to help us whip the Hun! Even though we get wakened when you chaps start off in the early morning hours, we are glad to know that madman and his cohorts are getting paid back for what they have done to us with their bombing. Have you lads been to London?"

"No. We haven't yet, but I sure want to see London sometime," Hal said.

"Are you chaps flyers or ground crew?" Mr. Sutherland asked.

"We are on a flight crew," Hal said.

"You need to see the results of the bombing we had during the blitz. Those Krauts thought they could make us throw up our hands and give up with all that bombing, but it just stiffened our backs! I think it will make you feel keener about your bombing raids when you see what their bombs did to our cities. You should at least go to Cambridge; it is only about ten miles from here. They got some pretty serious bombing. Even the base here got bombed, and I got a bomb in my field about two hundred meters from my house."

"That must have been really frightening. Did it cause any damage?" Ken asked.

"It did destroy some of my crops, but there was no major damage. It made a big hole in the field that we had to fill in, and we had to pick up some fragments that were spread over quite an area, but I was glad they wasted the bomb there instead of on the base here.

"Our lads used to have Lancasters and Spitfires based here, you know. I think every last one of our Spits that would fly was in the air that night. Our boys shot down some of the blighters. I was out watching the show. It did give us a bit of a fright when the bomb went off, but I was nearly two years in the trenches in the last war, and nothing seems too bad after that.

"But the job you lads are doing has to be quite frightening too. I've seen some of your planes come back looking like they couldn't possibly stay in the air, and I'm told there have been many of them that didn't make it back."

"We have only been on one mission," Ken said, "but I have to admit I was scared. At least if we don't get shot down, we do get to come back to hot showers and a good bed when the mission is over. That is something you folks didn't have in the ground war."

"Well now, living in the trenches was certainly no picnic. But it does take brave men to do the job you are doing up there where you don't have any place to hide, even though, as you say, there may be some advantages over ground combat. But we do need both. The bombing should jolly well be softening them up, but to get the job done, we are going to have to go in on the ground again. The way it looks, it shouldn't be too long before our chaps will be back on the continent. As to that, Tom there lost a leg from wounds he got at Dunkirk. You might never know, but he is walking on an artificial limb," Mr. Sutherland said.

Tom had continued to work as Mr. Sutherland was talking.

"We heard a lot about the bombing while it was going on. It sure sounded like a terrible time. I'm sure you folks were really glad when it ended," Hal said.

"Well, it hasn't ended completely; we are still getting some buzz bombs, especially around London, but it's nothing compared to the blitz. But you are right. We were grateful to our lads in the RAF and the Almighty when the worst was over. Well, chaps, we must finish up here. 'Tis already quite past the time m'wife was expecting me to come to supper. But you lads come over and visit any time. The old girl has several relatives in America, and she always wants to find out if any of you Yanks have met any of them!"

"Okay, Mr. Sutherland. We will sure try to do that sometime," Hal said. "Thanks for the lowdown on the brussels sprouts. I think I'm going to see if I can tell our cooks to be sure not to overcook them next time they are on the menu. We enjoyed talking to you. So long!"

"You Yanks do have some quaint expressions," Mr. Sutherland said with a rather puzzled look on his face. "All right then. Cheerio! Come see us soon!"

"We enjoyed meeting you. Thank you for the invitation," Ken said; then to show he was willing to adapt to the English culture, he echoed Mr. Sutherland's parting greeting.

As they were going back to their barracks, Ken said, "I think it would be interesting to go visit Mr. Sutherland and his wife and see what an English home is like. He sure seemed like a nice person."

"Okay, let's do it," Hal said. "We won't always have this opportunity. We might as well take advantage of it."

As they parted to go to their separate barracks, Ken said, "I'm going to be thinking about what you told me, and I'm going to take your suggestion and start reading the book of John."

"Great!" Hal said. "I would be glad to try to explain anything else to you that you have questions about any time."

As Ken walked on to his barracks, his mind mulled over what Hal had told him. He had a feeling he was on the verge of an exciting new discovery. When he got to his room, he sat on his cot, took out his New Testament, and turned to the book of John and read several chapters, then turned to Romans. He suddenly remembered Professor Meyer reading some of these same passages in his nightly readings.

Thinking of the Meyers reminded him he should give them his new mailing address, so he decided he would write while they were on his mind. He knew his mail would be censured, so he felt a little inhibited in his writing. He did tell them he was now overseas, that he was reading the New Testament they gave him, and that he had a Christian friend who was helping him understand it. He closed with, "I really do appreciate your prayers."

As he was finishing his letter, his roommates came in discussing the movie they had seen at the base theater. Ken was glad they had allowed him a period of solitude.

That night he lay awake in his bed for some time thinking about Hal's words and the Scripture passages he had read. For the first time he grasped the significance of Jesus as the Son of God coming into human existence and giving himself as the perfect sinless sacrifice for the atonement of the sins of mankind.

He lifted his heart silently in prayer and thanked his heavenly Father for his love and Jesus' sacrifice that had provided the way to escape the penalty of sin and opened the way to eternal life. He confessed his need of a savior and told God he wanted to experience the new birth that had been described to Nicodemus by Jesus in the third chapter of John. As he lay in his bed looking up into the darkness, it felt good to know with all his heart he had turned his life over to the great God who controlled his destiny.

That night he dreamed he was back in the house in the orchard with the Meyers. Everyone was in the living room. Mrs. Meyer and Rebecca were sitting on the piano bench while Mrs. Meyer played. They were singing a beautiful song that stirred a chord deep within Ken's breast, and he wanted it to go on forever. Then suddenly they both turned into angels in white, shining garments and the scene faded away, but the music kept echoing in his head.

The next morning Ken woke up with a feeling of joy and peace that he had never before experienced. He felt so alive, so clean. Then he was awed as he realized this was the witness of the Holy Spirit that he had been born again, as he had read in John's Gospel the night before. He just couldn't wait to tell Hal what had happened to him!

As he started out of the officers' quarters, he saw a lieutenant by a bicycle rack that had about three dozen bicycles in it. He had a glum look on his face. Ken greeted him, and he returned the greeting then asked Ken if he had a bicycle.

"No, I don't, but I've noticed they are pretty popular around here. Why? Do you have one for sale?" Ken asked.

"No, not for sale, but here's one you can just have if you want it. I'm Richard Horrell. This bicycle belonged to Bill Hopkins, my copilot. He caught some flak over St. Nazaire, and he died yesterday afternoon. We are sending his personal effects to his family, but someone might as well get some use out of the bicycle. If you haven't biked around the country yet, you need to try it; there is a lot of nice scenery to see."

"That does sound interesting," Ken said, "but it doesn't seem right to take it for nothing."

"Hey, don't worry about it. It used to belong to a guy whose plane went down somewhere in the channel. Bill didn't pay anything for it either. If you want it, just go to the orderly room and have them make you a tag like these others on the rack and paste it over Bill's tag."

"Well, okay. You have convinced me. I would like to have it. Thanks," Ken said. He introduced himself to Richard and learned he was the pilot of *The St. Louis Express* and had flown nine missions. Then he went to the orderly room and got a tag for his new possession's parking place.

Hal was overjoyed to hear that Ken had been born again. He suggested he and Ken have daily Bible studies together when feasible, and Ken enthusiastically agreed. They found a quiet place and began that morning. Then Ken told Hal about his new bicycle.

"Hal, why don't we see if we can find one for you and take in some of the scenery around here?" he said.

Hal liked the idea, so he asked some of the fellows who had been there longer where everyone was getting their bicycles. He was told there was a bicycle dealer in Cambridge, but if he wanted to save himself the trip, talk to Sergeant Harris. It seemed anytime you wanted anything, Sergeant Harris was the man to see. Following the directions given to them, Hal and Ken located Sergeant Harris.

"Sure," Sergeant Harris said, "I can get you a good bike. A brand new single speed will cost you seven pounds, or a three speed will cost you seven pounds, ten shillings. It may take a day or two to get either one to you."

"A single speed would be just fine, but don't you have any that are used?" Hal asked.

"As a matter of fact, I can give you a single speed that's in real good condition and looks practically new for only six pounds," Sergeant Harris said.

"Let me look at that one," Hal said.

"Okay. You gentlemen just hang around for a few minutes, and I will bring the little beauty over. Before I go, is there anything else you need? Watches, rings, knives, picture frames, cigarette lighters, billfolds, souvenirs to send home? Just name it!"

"No. The bicycle is the only thing I'm really interested in at the moment," Hal said.

"How about you, sir? Can I get anything for you?" Sergeant Harris asked Ken.

"No thanks. I can't think of anything I need," Ken said.

"All right. Just wait here, and I will be back in a little bit." With that Sergeant Harris strode purposefully away.

After he was gone, Hal said, "You know, I've run into people like him before. I think he likes to deal. I'll bet I can get that bike for five pounds!"

"This is going to be fun to watch!" Ken said.

Sergeant Harris came back riding the bicycle, stopped in front of Hal, and presented it to him with a flourish. "Here she is," he said. "Ain't she a beaut!"

Hal walked around the bicycle, not saying anything for a couple minutes. Then he said, "I don't know. The tires look a little worn, and there are a few scratches in the paint."

Sergeant Harris rubbed his chin. "Course them scratches aren't going to affect the way she rides, but tell you what, since there is a teensy bit of wear on the tires, I guess I can let it go for five pounds, ten shillings."

Hal studied the bicycle for another minute or so. "Well, thanks," he said finally, "but I think I'll wait and see if I might be able to find a little cheaper one." He looked at Ken with a "let's go" toss of his head and turned to leave.

"Well now, just a minute," said Sergeant Harris. "Instead of having to put this baby back into storage, I guess I could let you have it for five pounds."

Hal looked at the ground as if weighing this offer. "Well, I guess I can go the five pounds," he said, and he slowly took the money out of his billfold.

Sergeant Harris took the money with a rather rueful smile and said, "Okay, she's all yours. And you fellows remember, if you need anything else, be sure to come to me!"

"That was a real education!" Ken said as they walked away with Hal wheeling the bicycle.

The first time Ken and Hal got together to tour the countryside on their bicycles, Hal watched curiously as Ken struggled to keep the bicycle upright.

Ken saw Hal looking at him and said, "It's going to take me a while to get the hang of this."

He told Hal that was the first time he had ever been on a bicycle; there hadn't been any bicycles at his orphanage. After ten or fifteen minutes, his riding had improved significantly. Hal told him he was impressed that he was riding so well after such a short time.

Three times in the next few days, Ken and Hal traveled some of the narrow, winding roads, enjoying the green, picturesque landscapes. Cozy little cottages and larger manors were common sights, some with thatched roofs but most with slate or tile. Always there were green hedges, other shrubbery, and many flowers. They saw several other American servicemen with bicycles, and occasionally a small car would zoom past with a wave after honking to let them know they were coming. Once in a while, a two-decker bus would pass.

"Those things sure look top-heavy. I am surprised they don't turn over on some of the curves," Ken said.

It seemed so strange to see the cars driving on the left side of the road, and even though he had seen that was the custom in England, he found himself cringing the first few times he saw two vehicles approaching each other and pass on the left.

On the third trip, as they were stopped admiring an especially pretty scene, Hal said, "I wish we had a camera. I would like to be able to send some pictures of this pretty scenery to my family."

"Well, I guess we could go see Sergeant Harris," Ken said.

"Yeah. Let's do that," Hal said.

When they got back to the base, they went to Sergeant Harris's barracks but were told he had left the base and that he was probably out scrounging for things to replenish his stock of merchandise. They learned pawn shops were some of his primary sources of supply.

"How is he able to conduct a business while he is in the air force?" Hal asked one of the men they were talking to.

"Well, he is in charge of the maintenance of the vehicles in the motor pool, so he can check out a truck or Jeep at any time to road-test it. So he goes into town and checks out the pawn shops and who knows what else. He and his guys do keep everything running good, and a lot of times there isn't much for them to do. There are locked cabinets in the garage for storing tools and parts, and he uses some of those for his stuff."

"But doesn't his commanding officer know what's going on?" Hal asked.

"I'm sure he must know, but Harris keeps him supplied with cigars and other goodies, so he's not about to put a stop to a good thing. But then Harris is not violating any regulation that we know of. Actually, he is a pretty nice guy, and most of the fellows seem to think the prices he asks for the stuff he sells are reasonable."

"Well, it sounds like he has covered all the bases. Thanks. We will try to catch him later," Hal said. Then, as they were leaving, Hal muttered, "He probably has a better income than the base commander!"

Ken laughed and agreed it was possible.

Then Hal said, "Guess we could go to a pawn shop ourselves and cut out the middleman."

"We could do that, but I sort of admire Sergeant Harris's ambition, and he probably has checked out the best shops to deal with. They may even give him lower prices since he is a regular customer," Ken said. "Why don't we see what he has to offer, and if he doesn't have something we want, we can always try the other places."

"I guess that's the best thing to do," Hal said. "Who knows what else we are going to want from him. Maybe the more things we get from him, the better prices he'll give us."

The next afternoon, when Ken went by Hal's barracks, he didn't see Hal anywhere. He really wanted to have Hal with him, but since he had started out to see Sergeant Harris, he decided to continue.

Sergeant Harris was playing cards with some other fellows. When he looked up and saw Ken, he said, "Well, fellows, here's a customer. Business before pleasure," and he laid his cards aside, ignoring the objections of the other players. "What can I do for you, sir?" he asked.

Ken greeted him and said, "Sorry to interrupt your game, but I'm in the market for a camera. What can you do for me?"

"Sir, you are in luck!" Sergeant Harris said. "I have several good cameras I can offer you. Would you be interested in a top-of-the-line Leica or something like a good thirty-five millimeter single-lens reflex Pentax, or just a Kodak Brownie?"

Ken had never had a camera and knew hardly anything about them, but since the sergeant seemed to imply he had offered the cameras in descending order of value and cost, he thought the Pentax might be a good middle course. "Let me see the Pentax," Ken said.

"Okay, sir. Wait right here. I will be back in a jiffy," Sergeant Harris said. He disappeared and returned in a short time with a nice-looking camera. "I'm not really an expert on cameras, but I've been told this is a real good one, and it comes equipped with this nice, leather carrying case."

Ken took the camera and looked at it carefully. There were some adjusting mechanisms that looked rather mysterious to him, but he thought Hal might know what they were for. "I might be interested in this depending on the price," Ken said. "What do you want for it?"

"Well, sir, when that camera was new, it probably sold for ten or eleven pounds, and it still seems to be as good as new. But since you are a repeat customer, I can let you have this for only seven pounds. That includes a thirty-day money-back guarantee if you have any kind of problem with it!"

Ken remembered how Hal had been able to negotiate the price of the bicycle down and momentarily thought about trying that but decided against it. "Do you have film for it?" he asked.

"Sir, you can get all the thirty-five millimeter film you want in the PX; I don't stock that."

"All right, I guess I will take it." He took out his billfold and handed Sergeant Harris a ten-pound note, and Sergeant Harris gave him three pounds in change.

"Thanks, sir! Remember to tell your friends where you got this bargain!" Sergeant Harris said as he carefully tucked the money into his pocket.

Ken went to the post exchange and bought two rolls of film. He was sitting on his bed examining his purchase when Jim, the bombardier, came in. Photography had been one of his hobbies, and he carefully explained to Ken how to make the adjustments to get good pictures.

"The thing to do is look at the information that comes with the film and set your adjustments based on that particular film's sensitivity. This little sheet shows pictorially what settings you should use under various light conditions. And you need to remember to set your focus adjustment for the approximate distance to the object you want to photograph." He showed Ken how to make the adjustments for the aperture, focus, and time of exposure. He loaded the film into the camera and said, "Okay, you are ready to go. Maybe you can take this with you on the next mission and snap a picture of old Adolph from thirty thousand feet!"

Ken and Hal had agreed to ride their bicycles to Cambridge the next day if they didn't get a call to fly. When they met outside the officers' quarters, Ken showed Hal the camera.

"I don't know much about cameras, but that looks like a nice one," Hal said. "It's going to be great to have some pictures to send home and to help us remember all the sights we saw on our trips when we get old and forgetful!"

On their way to Cambridge, they stopped and took pictures of some quaint cottages and scenery they thought was especially attractive, sometimes with one or the other of them in the foreground. They took pictures of each other sitting beside a canal with a gingerbread-decorated house in the background. A woman with a cute little girl was walking down the road, and Ken asked the mother if they could take a picture of the little girl. The mother seemed pleased he wanted a picture of her daughter and told her to smile for the snapshot.

As Mr. Sutherland had expected, Ken and Hal were awed by the devastation the German bombs had caused in Cambridge. They stopped to take a picture of two middle-aged men who were working in a huge pile of debris, the remains of a large bombed-out building.

One of the workmen who was throwing some of the stones into a truck saw them and said, "Quite a muddle, isn't it, lads? You can see they really gave it to us, but one day all this will be gone, and there will be a nice, new building here."

"How tall was this building?" Ken asked. "It sure made a lot of rubble."

"I think t'was four or five flights if m' memory serves me proper. You see how high the stones are toward the back side; they were just about as high on this end b'fore we started the clearing."

"That's a lot debris to get rid of," Hal said. "How long do you think it will take you to clean it all up?"

"Hard t'say, mates. It depends some on what we run into. Three days ago we found two bodies. They'd been here several months, y'know, and they were pretty far along. There's sure to be more. When that 'appens we have to stop work and call the authorities to come to try to identify the remains before they are disturbed too much. Sometimes the things around them give a clue. Then too, sometimes we get called out to help on some other stint that someone needs a hand with. We can't spare many men to work on the clearing. I'm sure you know a good lot of our chaps are in the military, and others are makin' war materials. After the war is over, we will have more hands for clearing.

"But you lads need to go see the good things we have here, not just the ruins! Cambridge has a lot of history. We were invaded by the Romans in the first century. That hill over there is where they had their encampment. The remains of some of their structures are still around. Then we had the Danes, the Saxons, the Vikings, and the Normans. They all made their mark. And be sure to take a look at our university; it is hundreds of years old and famous 'round the world! There are many settings that make for better photographs than this pile of stones."

"Yes, we do want to take pictures of the good things too. This is still a beautiful city, but I would have liked to have seen it before the bombing. It's hard to visualize what it looked like then," Ken said. "Thanks for taking time to talk to us. We had better let you get back to work."

They mounted their bicycles and went slowly down the street. They saw several signs with arrows that pointed the way to air raid shelters. They were somewhat appalled to see several children happily playing in heaps of rubble.

Ken was impressed with the friendliness of the people. Everyone appeared to be glad to see them, and they were greeted with smiles and waves. There seemed to be a spirit of optimism that was a little out of place in the midst of the devastation surrounding them.

They looked around for some time and took some pictures of scenes and buildings that particularly impressed them. They came to a bridge crossing a pretty river and paused to watch some of the little boats. A distinguished-looking, nicely-dressed gentleman with a white mustache and a cane was strolling across the bridge toward them. He smiled as he approached and stopped in front of them.

"Hello, lads. Nice to have you visit our city. Would you be wanting any directions or information?" he asked.

"Well, yes. Thank you. I was just wondering what you call this pretty river," Ken said.

"This gentlemen, is the Cam, and it is probably the reason the city was started here hundreds of years ago. We do have a strong affection for it. But we have many other smashing things to see in Cambridge. Have you been in the city before?"

"No, sir. This is our first visit, but I hope not our last," Ken said. "We were told you have a famous university here. Which way would we go to find that?"

"Well now, you could go in several directions. You see, the university is comprised of several colleges, and they are not all grouped together. But if you continue in the way you are going, you will soon see one of the prettiest campuses. I spent several years on that campus many years ago."

"Hey, I just figured something out!" Hal said suddenly. "The Cam River and a bridge must be where Cambridge got its name! Is this by any chance the bridge that it was named after?"

"Sorry to disappoint you, lad. Many people are under the impression that sort of thing is what happened, but just the opposite is the true story. The river was originally called the Granta, but some felt it should be changed to the Cam, which does seem to fit in with the city's name quite well. I think you might like to enjoy the Cam by doing some punting."

When Ken asked what he meant by that, he explained the little boats they saw were called "punts." These could be rented not too far from where they were. He also recommended they take time to visit the Fitzwilliam Museum and told them how to find it. They thanked the English gentleman and agreed they were going to take his advice and rent a punt.

The punting was an enjoyable experience. There was a feeling of camaraderie among those in the punts. Everyone involved in this sport seemed to be in a festive mood and seemed glad to see American servicemen joining them in their activity. They went upstream for a while, thinking it would make their return trip easier, but the river was flowing slowly, so it was not difficult to go either direction.

They had rented the punt for an hour and were able to see many interesting sights along the river they would not have seen without the punt. When they took it back, they asked the attendant where they could get something to eat. He pointed to a nearby fish and chip shop and told them that was a favorite of his. They followed his suggestion and were impressed with the tasty food that was new to them.

Acting on the advice from the gentleman on the bridge, they decided to visit the Fitzwilliam Museum. They learned it had been established in 1816. Inside there were numerous displays of antique furniture, paintings, old coins, ancient manuscripts, and sculptures. They spent about an hour looking around and decided it was time to head back to their base.

By the time they got back to the base, they had used up both rolls of film, and Ken wished he had bought more. He took the film to the post exchange, where it would be sent out to a local photography shop for developing.

Chapter 8

Ken woke up to the sound of voices. An enlisted man was standing in the open doorway and had just awakened Lieutenant Murphy.

"Sir, you need to have your men get to the mess hall for breakfast at 0400; then report to the briefing room at 0430. You are scheduled to fly today," the corporal said.

This news was no surprise. They had been told the previous day to stand by for a possible mission.

"Well, I guess that's what we are here for. Do you know where we are going?" Lieutenant Murphy asked.

"No, sir, they never give out that information before the briefing," the messenger said as he closed the door.

Ken felt a wave of foreboding as he swung out of bed. He knew their first mission had been a relatively safe one compared to the bombing of targets deeper into enemy territory, and their losses had been comparatively light. The odds were their next mission would be more hazardous.

The crowd in the briefing room was hushed as the briefing officer strode to the front and flipped back the cover over the map of Europe.

Ken heard a few low groans as they saw the red line that showed their route extending deep into Germany. It appeared to be about a hundred miles from Berlin.

"Gentlemen, your target for today is the Focke Wulf plant at Oschersleben," the briefing officer began. "As you know, men and materials continue to build up for the eventual invasion of the continent by ground forces. As a measure to help assure success of that undertaking, it is important for us to have absolute control of the air at that time. Putting this Focke Wulf plant out of business will be a step in that direction.

"Our planes from other bases will hit other aircraft plants in the same area as part of this mission. You will have P-47 and P-38 escort part of the way to the target; then due to their limited range, they will turn back, and some of our P-51s will take over. The P-51s will get you started home. When they start getting low on fuel, they will leave, and some Spitfires will escort you on your last leg back to England."

He proceeded to give information about locations of known concentrations of antiaircraft emplacements, the best approach to the target, and other vital information such as radio frequencies and codes to be used if absolutely necessary. As navigator, Ken was aware this information might be essential to the performance of a successful mission and being able to survive the mission hazards, so he listened intently and took several notes.

Luck of the Irish sat waiting to take off on the gray, foggy morning on that January 11, 1944, another day that would be forever etched in Ken's memory. The bombers were scheduled to take off at 0530, but a report of the heavy overcast over the continent put the mission in question. Finally, word came that the overcast seemed to be dissipating, and it was thought by the time the planes reached the target area the weather would permit the mission to be carried out successfully.

Even though it was still foggy at the base, shortly after 0645, the flare signaling takeoff was to begin was seen. Six-hundred and sixty-three planes from the various air bases were assigned to take part in the mission.

Once in the air at about twenty-five thousand feet altitude, the planes encountered difficulty in locating other groups that were to be part of the massive formation. The planes from Bassingbourn were finally able to join with the planes from the other bases, and they headed for Germany and their assigned targets.

Most of the time Ken kept his attention focused on his navigating responsibilities, providing periodic updates of their position. The crew was in a rather somber mood, and communications over the intercom were terse and to the point, unlike their training missions when there had been a lot of lighthearted banter.

The intermittent banks of fog added to the feeling of uneasiness. It was sometimes difficult to see even the closest planes in the formation. The only consolation was they would be more difficult for the German fighters and antiaircraft batteries to see, although it had been learned the Germans were beginning to use radar to help aim some of their antiaircraft fire.

The formation consisted of three levels, spaced to provide maximum firepower on all sides toward enemy fighters. The bombers maintained an altitude of nearly five miles high, putting as much distance between them and the antiaircraft batteries as possible. At that altitude, supplementary oxygen was essential, and the oxygen mask was another encumbrance that had to be endured as part of the job. The fifty-degrees-below cold was also a major discomfort, particularly for the waist gunners, who fired their weapons through open windows.

Over the continent, enemy fighters began attacking intermittently, the fog hindering their attacks to some extent. The American fighters had not been able to locate the formation for some time due to the fog and imposition of radio silence. After they appeared, there was a period of reprieve from the enemy onslaughts. As Ken again calculated their position and the remaining distance to the target, he felt a little melancholy over how slowly they seemed to be approaching the target.

Eventually the short range escort planes had to leave them, and the enemy planes resumed their attacks. The intercom was alive with almost constant reports of approaching enemy planes accompanied by the chatter of machine gun fire. As the formation neared the target, the enemy fighters ceased their attacks, and the bomber formation entered an intense barrage of flak. Ken looked up from his navigating duties to see a B-17 slowly twisting then burst into flames. *Luck of the Irish* shuddered as a burst of flak hit it.

"Is everybody okay?" Lieutenant Murphy asked over the intercom.

Replies came back from each member of the crew that they were unhurt, but one of the waist gunners reported a gaping hole in the fuselage near him. Just then another burst of flak tore through the left wing. From the top turret, Sergeant Hannigan reported part of the left wing had been blown off. *Luck of the Irish* seemed relatively unaffected by the damage.

Even though they were cumbersome, Ken was glad to be wearing a flak jacket. It became routine to hear the sound of new hits from the flak. Fortunately, these were fragments from explosions that were some distance from the plane. It was doubtful that a plane could survive a direct hit from an antiaircraft shell, which would explode on impact.

To increase the accuracy of the bombing, the B-17s were designed to allow the bombardier to remotely assume control of the plane as the plane began its bombing run, and shortly after Ken reported they were five minutes from the target, Jim was in control. He bent over his bombsight, watching for the landmarks that would indicate the target was going to be coming into view. Another burst of flak jarred the plane, but Jim stayed focused on his task.

Finally he said, "Target in sight," and after a moment's pause, "Bombs away!"

With a tension-filled sigh, Lieutenant Murphy immediately resumed control of the plane. It took a lot of willpower to keep his hands off the controls while the plane was making its bombing run.

The lead planes in the formation had begun turning to head back, and soon, much to the gratification of the crew, *Luck of the Irish* was going west. It seemed good to be headed home even though they knew there were still many dangerous miles ahead of them. The intensity of the flak decreased as they left the target area, but suddenly several enemy fighters started attacking, unopposed by any friendly fighters.

Ken felt so vulnerable. Sometimes he could see enemy fighters approaching on what looked like a collision course and felt an absurd impulse to dodge out of the way. He was sure Lieutenant Murphy would feel the same impulse to take evasive action but knew this was out of the question in the tight formation. It was difficult enough to keep from colliding with the other planes even when no fighters were attacking them.

"Where are those P-51s?" Lieutenant Murphy said in exasperation.

It was later learned they had arrived some time before the bombers and had to return to base before they ran out of fuel. The policy of maintaining radio silence made coordinating activities very difficult. Ken saw another B-17 going down. He didn't see any parachutes. Tracers from the fifty-caliber machine guns were streaking across the sky from most of the bombers. The intercom was busy with reports of approaching enemy aircraft from various crew members. Occasionally there were reports of an enemy plane going down, including one claimed by Sergeant Sullivan, the ball turret gunner.

Ken occasionally caught glimpses of German planes as they hurtled through the formation with tracers from the bombers' guns following. Those pilots were enemies, but Ken sort of admired their bravery for being willing to subject themselves to the combined firepower of hundreds of well-armed bombers. He again calculated their position and was a little depressed to see how far they had yet to go. Each minute seemed like it was ten minutes long. Suddenly there was a series of sharp shocks accompanied by a short groan.

"Did someone get hit?" Lieutenant Murphy asked immediately. "Report your status."

"Radio. Yeah, I'm pretty bad, I think," Sergeant Morse said weakly.

"Ken, could you go check on him?" Lieutenant Murphy asked. "We need the guys to stay with the guns."

Even the bombardier was now manning the nose gun.

"I'm on my way," Ken said as he took off his intercom and system oxygen supply and grabbed his emergency oxygen cylinder. He made his way up through the access port and back to the radio operator's position. He took one look at Peter and knew he had received a fatal wound. He was no longer conscious, and blood was running out of his mouth. Ken felt his throat for a heartbeat, and even as he did, he felt it fade away. Tears welled in Ken's eyes. He hadn't really known Peter all that well, but it was distressing to know he would be making no more flights with them. He unsnapped Peter's throat microphone, held it to his lips, and said, "Peter's gone."

There was a moment of silence; then Lieutenant Murphy said, "While you are up, will you also check on Hal? I can't raise him."

A feeling of dread rose in Ken's mind as he made his way to the top turret. He found Hal unconscious, with his head resting on his guns. Ken was relieved that he was still breathing, but his oxygen mask was in shreds yet still providing him with some oxygen. Ken quickly put his emergency oxygen supply on him.

He was horrified to see that Hal's left foot was shattered and bleeding profusely. Ken removed a shoestring and tied it tightly around the ankle. This stopped the major source of bleeding, but there were several places on Hal's upper leg and hip and one on his head where flak fragments had made wounds that caused significant bleeding. The low atmospheric pressure made the bleeding much worse than it would have been at ground level. There was a pool of blood on the floor with more dripping into it.

Ken reported the situation and said, "It's really bad. There's no way to stop all the bleeding. We still have a long way to go. I'm sure he will be bled out before we get back."

There was a short interval of silence; then Lieutenant Murphy said, "I guess you know what we have to do. I'll have Keith take the controls, and I'll help."

They had been told if a crew member was wounded so badly that they wouldn't live to get back to England they should be dropped, in hopes some German doctor would provide medical aid. The Red Cross had informed the air force they had encountered an American flyer in a POW camp who told them he had survived in that way. Ken recoiled at the thought but realized that was Hal's only chance. He quickly took Hal's handkerchief from his back pocket and wrapped it around the bloody remains of the shattered foot, then added his own. There was a canvas bag that contained some tools that Ken emptied out, and then he inserted the foot into the bag and tied it around the ankle.

Maybe that will keep the dirt out when he lands, Ken thought.

Lieutenant Murphy had arrived. Together they put Hal's parachute on him and carried him to the bomb bay. They laid him beside the open bay, and Lieutenant Murphy signaled he would pull the parachute release. He had the ring in his hand as they rolled Hal out, and they watched as the parachute blossomed and was immediately out of sight. Ken realized his face was wet with tears, and he saw tears glinting in Lieutenant Murphy's eyes.

He prayed, "Oh God, Hal is one of your servants. Please watch over him."

His mind turned to what Hal had said about death. He had said death was something everyone had to go through sometime and in the big picture it really didn't matter much when it occurred in a person's life if the life had been committed to God. He felt a little better when he remembered that, but he was really going to miss Hal's companionship. He had known Hal for a relatively short time but felt like he was a close friend.

The homeward trip seemed to take an agonizingly long time. The only relief from the German fighter attacks was when the formation was going through dense overcast. The Germans were desperately trying to prove the daylight bombings were too costly to continue, and many in the bombers were wondering if the results were really worth the sacrifice.

Finally, when the formation was twenty or thirty miles from the coast, a squadron of Spitfires arrived and engaged the attackers in combat. After the planes reached their base, the weary crews stumbled from the planes, grateful to be among those who had survived. At the Bassingbourn base, the final tally showed that 17 percent of the planes that went on the mission were lost, and almost all of the planes that came back had minor to major battle damage. Of the 663 planes assigned to the mission, only 238 had reached their target. The rest had either been called back by the commanders at some bases with the belief that the weather would not permit a successful mission or had been shot down or badly damaged, causing them to turn back before reaching the target.

The weather over the continent the next few weeks was not conducive to flying missions, but it didn't matter too much since so many of the bombers were in need of repair. *Luck of the Irish* needed a new left wing in addition to a lot of surface patching. The ground crew obtained an undamaged wing for *Luck* from another plane that had suffered major damage to the fuselage and tail section and was destined for the scrap heap. In addition to three rather major holes in *Luck*, the crew chief reported they had patched fifty-nine smaller holes.

Besides the death of the radio operator and the severe wounds suffered by the flight engineer, the right waist gunner had received a wound in his shoulder as well as frostbite to his nose. Ken was grateful to have escaped unscathed.

In a day or so, Ken had recovered from the weariness he had felt after returning from the Oschersleben mission but was still under a cloud of depression because of Hal's fate. It was their commanding officer's responsibility to send word to the families of the flyers who had been shot down, but Ken had helped get Hal's personal possessions together to send to his family. He had included some of the better snapshots he had taken of Hal.

As he thought about Hal and his friendship, Ken found himself walking to the fence where he and Hal had talked. He stood there recalling their conversation and the change it had made in his life. He desperately hoped they had done the right thing for Hal and prayed he had received the medical care he needed. He thought about the enjoyment they had touring the countryside together and their visit to Cambridge. Then he remembered Cedric Sutherland's invitation to visit, which they had not followed up on as they intended. On an impulse, he climbed over the fence and made his way toward the building Mr. Sutherland had pointed out.

The Sutherlands were obviously better off than the average Englishman. Their house was large and well-maintained, and there was a nicely-painted white picket fence along the front of the house. A sleek, sporty-looking car was standing in the circular driveway. There were several outbuildings, and Ken could see a cow and some sheep inside a fenced pasture. A collie came running toward him from the side of the barn barking; then Mr. Sutherland came into view.

"That'll do, Shep," he said, and the dog immediately stopped barking.

As he came up to Ken wagging his tail, Ken thought about Buddy and realized he missed him. He petted the now friendly dog as Mr. Sutherland stopped in front of him.

"You sure have a nice dog, Mr. Sutherland," Ken said.

"Let's just leave it at Cedric," Mr. Sutherland said. "I don't go much for formality. Aye, Shep is a very important member of our household. He does help so with the sheep, but how nice you have come to visit!" He warmly shook Ken's hand and said, "You are just in time for tea. The wife will be pleased. Come on to the house."

He took Ken by the arm, turned him toward the house, and sort of propelled him to the door. He opened the door and gestured for Ken to enter. As he closed the door behind him, he announced, "Flora! We've a guest for tea!"

A pleasant-looking woman that sort of reminded Ken of Mrs. Schmidt came bustling into the room with her hands outstretched. "Oh, I am pleased, I am. I jus' luv talkin' w' you Yanks. You've such an engagin' way of speakin.'"

Mrs. Sutherland probably thought the smile on Ken's face was due to his friendliness, but amusement over her words and accent certainly played a part. He was struck by the irony that his speech apparently sounded as strange to her as hers did to him. She was obviously from a different community than Mr. Sutherland; her accent was quite different.

"Y' come on into the parlor and make yourself easy while I fetch the tea," she said.

She led the way into a nicely furnished room, motioned toward an ornate, overstuffed chair, and hurried away. Cedric had followed them and took a chair opposite Ken. There was a nice charcoal fire burning in the fireplace and a cozy feel to the room. Ken noted the contrast with his comparatively spartan barracks room.

"Why didn't you bring your chum with you, the one you were talking to at the end of my field?" Mr. Sutherland asked.

Ken wasn't really ready to talk about it, but after a pause he said, "On our last mission, he was wounded badly and losing so much blood that we didn't think he could live until we got back. We dropped him over Germany, hoping the Germans would get him to a doctor."

Ken was embarrassed to feel tears forming in his eyes, and he wiped them away with his hand.

Cedric put his hand on Ken's knee. "'Tis all right, lad. I lost some good mates in the first war. I know exactly how it is. You did your best by him; that's all anyone can do. The military will do all they can to save him so they can try to get information from him, if for no other reason."

Ken was grateful when Mrs. Sutherland came back into the room carrying a tray, which she put down on a low table. She brought a cup and saucer over and put it on a stand beside his chair, then returned with a pot of tea.

She filled his cup and asked, "'Ow many lumps, love?"

Ken was a little perplexed, but when she stood in front of him holding a cube of white substance with some tongs, he realized she must be talking about sugar. He had never seen sugar in lumps before.

"Oh, I don't need any sugar," Ken said. "I've heard you folks are rationed on a lot of things, and I wouldn't want to use up your rations."

"Fiddlesticks," Mrs. Sutherland said as she put three lumps in his tea.

"Actually, lad, when I saw the war coming, I laid a few things by to tide us over," Cedric said. He paused then said rather sheepishly, "Of course, we are not supposed to do that, but as the saying goes, we got ours before the hoarders got it all!"

Ken laughed; then Mr. Sutherland continued.

"But I didn't take our sugar from the general supply. I had it imported direct from Cuba, so we are not really depriving anyone."

Then Mrs. Sutherland placed a saucer containing some kind of pastry beside Ken. "Eat up, love, and give us a call when you want more."

Ken took a bite of the pastry. "This is delicious!" he said. "What do you call this?"

"Oh, that is a scone. You 'aven't 'ad them b'fore?" Mrs. Sutherland asked.

"No, I don't remember having anything like this," Ken said. "Did you make them?"

"Why, of course," she said. "What kind of pastries did your mum make?"

Ken explained that he had grown up in an orphanage, and he couldn't even remember his mother. Mrs. Sutherland seemed to be distressed to hear he had never known a mother's love and asked him several questions about his life in the orphanage. Ken answered her questions but looked for an opportunity to change the subject.

"You sure have a nice place here. Have you lived here long?" he asked.

Cedric smiled. "Actually, I was born right here in this house. This place has been in my family for fifteen generations. The land was deeded to my ancestor, William Sutherland, in 1416 by King Edward the Fifth for spectacular bravery in the battle of Agincourt. But of course, this house is much more recent. It wasn't the way it is now until around 1755. The walls could tell many tales of happenings over the years, mostly pleasant events, but some rather crude. There have been a few black sheep in the family, but most were fine people and honorable citizens."

Hearing Mr. Sutherland refer to a long family history made Ken wistfully wish he had some sort of family history to claim.

The Sutherlands seemed to be very pleased that Ken had visited them. He felt their warmth, and as they chatted, he felt his mood lifting. Mrs. Sutherland poured him another cup of tea and insisted he eat another scone. By the time Ken rose to leave a couple hours later, he was feeling very much at home and in a much better frame of mind.

"Do come back, lad. We did so enjoy your visit," Mrs. Sutherland said, and Cedric echoed her sentiment.

As Ken walked back across the field to the base, he felt refreshed. He was sure he would be visiting the Sutherlands again unless providentially hindered. But he wished again that Hal had been there to go with him.

The day after visiting the Sutherlands, Ken decided he would get a haircut. As he entered the base barbershop, there was someone getting out of the barber chair that looked familiar. Then he remembered it was the face he had seen across the table-tennis table back in the induction center.

"Robert!" he exclaimed. "It's good to see you again!"

Robert's face lighted with sudden recognition. "Ken, isn't it? What a nice surprise to run into you! It looks like you have done well. Aren't those navigator wings you are wearing?"

"Yes, you are right," Ken said. "And it looks like that bloody nose didn't keep you from becoming a pilot."

"Yes, I did train to be a pilot, but I really wanted to be a fighter pilot. But I guess bombers are better than nothing. Well, actually, I'm copilot on the *American Beauty*. We just got in from the States the day before yesterday, so we haven't had any missions yet. How about you? Have you been here long?

"Just long enough to get in two missions," Ken said. "If you want to wait until I get my hair cut, maybe we could stop by the recreation hall for a game of table tennis! If I remember right, after our game at the induction center, we agreed to have another one the first chance we got."

"You're right!" said Robert. "We did agree to do that, and this is our first chance! I'm ready for another game." He sat down and waited until the barber was finished with Ken.

The two of them walked around the base talking about the widely different paths their training had taken them then had brought them together again.

"I'm kind of eager to get in on the action, but I hear it's been pretty rough. How about the missions you were on?" Robert asked. "Tell me about it. Was it bad?"

Ken didn't want to drag up those depressing emotions again, so he just said, "Yes, it was bad, but you are going to find out about that soon enough yourself. Let's go have that game of table tennis."

They played several games, and Ken was pleased to find his performance had improved quite a bit by the time they played the last game.

Although Ken hadn't told Robert about Hal's fate, he did tell what good times they had touring the country roads on bicycles. Before they parted that evening, Ken told Robert anytime he was interested in seeing the scenery, he knew where he could get a bicycle for him to use.

"Well, I'm not scheduled for anything tomorrow that I know of," Robert said. "That does sound fun. How about tomorrow?"

Ken said that was fine with him, and they agreed to meet at the bicycle rack outside Ken's barracks about 0830 hours the next day.

The next morning after breakfast, Ken went to Hal's barracks and brought his bicycle back for Robert to use. Robert appeared promptly at 0830 hours, eager to see some of the interesting things Ken had told him about. Ken wanted to take Robert on a road he and Hal had been on that he thought had some especially nice scenery, but due to the light fog and the numerous crossroads, they missed the road Ken wanted.

Eventually, he was satisfied with the road they were on since it had some scenery that was new to him, and Robert seemed to be enjoying it. He told Ken he'd had a bicycle since he was a small boy and had spent many hours a day riding it. It had been several months since he had been on a bicycle, and it seemed good to get to ride again. He had ridden his bicycle to school and used it for several years delivering newspapers. When he was in the Boy Scouts, he had taken a three-day trip on his bicycle with some other scouts to earn a merit badge and told Ken about some of the experiences they'd had while on the trip. He was surprised when Ken told him the bicycle he was on was the first one he had ever ridden.

They rode for quite a distance, stopping occasionally to take pictures or to talk to one of the local people. One old fellow felt he had to tell them all about the trip he and his wife had taken to America to visit some relatives who had emigrated to Chicago and had become American citizens. They didn't want to be rude, so they endured about ten minutes of rather boring details of the event. Robert was fascinated with the English dialects and how different they seemed to be in communities that were fairly short distances from each other.

Ken looked at his watch and saw it was a little past noon.

"Robert, are you getting hungry? I think it's about time we look for a place to have something to eat," he said.

"I think I could go for some lunch," Robert said, "but 'Rob' sounds more natural to me than Robert. That's what I have been called for as far back as I can remember."

"Okay. That's easy enough," Ken responded.

A few minutes later, they saw a man coming toward them in a horse-drawn, two-wheeled cart. As they neared him, he stopped, and they stopped their bicycles by the side of the cart.

"I guess you blokes are Yanks. You lads don't get out this way often. In fact, it's been a fortnight since I saw the last pair that looked like Yanks."

"Yes, sir, you are right. We are Yanks, and we are looking for a place to get something to eat. Is there a restaurant near here?" Ken asked.

"Well now, there is a rather posh pub just down the road called Saint George and Dragon that serves food. The fare there is quite good. You can't go wrong with Saint George's. They have capital bitters and ales too."

"That is an interesting name for a business. Do you happen to know why the owner gave it a name like that?"

"That I don't know, lad. It has been around for quite more than a hundred years, I fancy. It seems it was pretty small when it first opened, and I expect the owner was trying a name that would get people's attention. It is much larger than it was years ago. If you look carefully, you can see where the additions have been made." He paused.

"There's a tale about the place that may interest you. It is told there were two peddlers who were passing through. At mealtime, one who had carried his nosh sat under a tree outside as he ate. The other went into Saint George's for a bite. At that time, it seems the owner had hired a serving girl who was quite surly and had quite a beastly temper. That day, the owner had stepped out, and when the peddler ordered his fare, he was served quite rudely.

"A bit later, the outside peddler was surprised to see the other come bolting out with dishes being thrown after him. Upon inquiring the cause, the one fleeing the girl's wrath said, 'Why, I don't know, mate! After I ate my fare, I thought I would see if I could sell some of my wares. I 'ad in me mind the owner's name was George, and I told the maid I would like to show my wares, but I would rather talk to George, and she began throwing things! I just now remember his name is Charlie!'"

Ken and Robert laughed at the rather improbable tale, and Ken said, "So, I guess she thought the peddler was implying she was the dragon!"

"If the tale be true, take comfort that hussy is no longer there. You will be served quite nicely. Give it a try." The man raised his hand in a parting gesture, clucked to his horse, and started on.

"Thanks," Ken called after him.

Robert said, "That is really a strange name to give a place of business!"

"It does sound strange, but I don't think it is too unusual. We saw several names on businesses in Cambridge that seemed pretty strange to us. I think if we get a chance to go to London we will see a lot more," Ken said.

"I really want to see London," Robert said. "How about we try to do that soon?"

"Okay, I'm really looking forward to seeing it too," Ken said.

They continued down the road until they came to a building with a sign announcing it was Saint George and Dragon. It looked more like a rather large house than it did a business, except for the sign. They went in and saw several people were already seated at small, round tables covered with white tablecloths. They were greeted graciously by the hostess, who escorted them to a table. She handed them each a menu and left.

Ken and Robert looked at the menu but couldn't decide what to order.

When a waitress came, they asked her what she recommended, and she suggested shepherd pie with lamb and a pastry, and they took her suggestion.

The other customers seemed friendly, but Ken and Robert could tell the presence of Americans was unusual, and they felt their every move and word was being observed closely. Feeling a little self-conscious while they were waiting for their food, Ken's gaze turned to the many items of silverware in front of him.

He thought, *I know I'm going to look like a hick. I have no idea the proper way to use all these utensils!*

He was curious about how the local people were using all the silverware, and when he glanced at those at a nearby table, he was intrigued to see they were eating with their fork in their left hand, which conflicted with the table manners he had been taught at the orphanage. *Oh well,* he thought, *maybe they will realize we have different customs and not expect us to know which implement we should use throughout the meal.*

Ken and Robert's conversation as they ate was rather constrained, and although the food was good, they were happy to get away from the friendly surveillance and back out on the road again.

They had gone quite a distance and had taken several turns, so when they started back, they found it difficult to retrace their steps. The light fog added to the difficulty. Ken resolved to get a map of the area.

"It's kind of embarrassing to be a navigator and have trouble finding your way home!" he said.

Twice they stopped and asked the general direction to Bassingbourn. Finally Ken saw a building that looked familiar and realized they had come upon the Sutherland estate from the side opposite the base.

"Let's stop in here for a little while," Ken said. "I know these folks."

Shep barked twice when he saw the bicycles approaching the house but soon recognized Ken and welcomed him with enthusiastic tail-wagging. The Sutherlands seemed happy to see Ken again, gave Robert a friendly greeting, and insisted they come in for tea.

"So nice you have a new chum now that you've lost the other one,"

Cedric said. "I see you chaps have been out cycling. I hope you saw some interesting sights."

"Cedric, your country is so pretty and green with so many interesting, winding roads, pretty plants, picturesque houses, canals, and quaint little towns. I think practically everything we saw was interesting," Ken said. "We had lunch at a place called Saint George and Dragon. We thought that was sort of a strange name for a place of business."

"Apparently you went east, toward the coast. That would be just a few miles from Colchester. We've been there several times over the years. The name is not really too unusual. I know of two other pubs with the same name, but they are not at all near each other. I should not be surprised if there were not more that I don't know about. The name does stir up thoughts of a rather favorite tale of bravery and conquest," Cedric said. "Puts people in a good frame of mind, it does."

They chatted with the Sutherlands a while longer; then Ken said, "We had better be getting back to the base. We have been gone since fairly early this morning, and everyone may begin to think we have gone AWOL!"

They thanked the Sutherlands for the tea and crumpets, mounted their bicycles, and were on their way.

"What did Mr. Sutherland mean when he talked about you losing your chum?" Robert asked.

"Our flight engineer was named Hal Hannigan. We had a lot in common, but on our last mission, he was wounded badly, and we had to drop him over Germany in hopes he would get the medical attention he wouldn't survive without," Ken said slowly. "That's his bicycle you are riding."

After a long pause, Robert said, "Well, I hope he got that care and is on the way to complete recovery."

"Even if he does make it, he will never be the same. I'm sure he is going to lose his left foot if nothing else, and he had some other pretty serious wounds. I really don't think he had much of a chance, but Hal said if we are prepared to meet God, it doesn't really matter too much when we die."

"He is sure right about that!" said Robert. "I take it he was a Christian then?"

"That's right, and he helped me become one too!" Ken said.

"I am really glad to hear that," Robert said. "Count me in! About two years ago, I was just drifting along through life when a girl I really liked persuaded me to go to a revival meeting, and I got saved! We are planning to get married when this is all over."

Robert's words were a big boost to Ken's morale. One of the reasons he felt so bad about not having Hal around anymore was that he really wanted Christian companionship. Suddenly he now had a new source to look to for that companionship!

"You know, when I think back, I remember feeling like there was something different about you when we met at the induction center," Ken said. "I guess it was divinely ordained that we would end up at the same base!"

Chapter 9

The ninety-first bomb group had received some replacement planes, and most of those damaged during the Oschersleben mission that were judged to be repairable had been restored to flying condition. However, to the exasperation of bomber command, the weather over both the continent and England was not at all conducive to flying. Consequently most of the service personnel that requested passes received them. Ken and Robert had agreed to go to London soon, so they took advantage of this opportunity and obtained three-day passes.

They considered checking a Jeep out of the motor pool, but they thought it would be interesting to experience riding in the little English train cars. The cars were made up of compartments. Every compartment had a door that opened to the platform and two bench seats that faced each other with room for several people on each side. Above the seats on both sides of the compartment was a place for luggage, composed of some brackets mounted on the walls with heavy netting strung between them.

The train bound for London whistled and came puffing into the station. It stopped with a squeal of brakes, and Ken opened the door of the compartment in front of them. There was only one person in the compartment, an American GI snuggled down inside his overcoat as if trying to shut out the world. Ken greeted him as he entered, and the lone serviceman listlessly acknowledged the greeting. His overcoat covered all indications of rank and military affiliation, but Ken assumed he was probably in the air force.

Ken and Robert carried on a light conversation for a few minutes; then Ken asked their fellow passenger, "Are you going to London?"

"Yes, sir, I am," was the response.

"This will be our first time," Ken said. "Have you been there before?"

"Yes, I have. Several times."

"How long have you been in England?" Ken asked.

"I've been here almost a year."

"You must be in the air force. Where are you stationed?" Ken asked.

"I'm at the bomber base at Bury St. Edmonds. About a hundred miles north of London.

"What kind of duty are you involved with?" Ken asked.

There was a pause; then their fellow passenger said, "I don't really have permanent assignment right now. Sometimes I help out in the orderly room, sometimes in the spare parts hangar, and with some maintenance." He paused again. "I *was* a waist gunner for twelve missions, but the last mission I was on, there were eleven planes that went out, and the plane I was on was the only one that made it back. I just couldn't take it any longer. I guess I had a mental breakdown. So I let my crew down." He looked very distressed, and Ken was sorry he had asked him questions that turned out to be discomforting.

"My goodness," Ken said. "That would shake up *anybody*! You have certainly done your part. I'm sure no one thinks any less of you." Then, to change the subject, he asked their new acquaintance to tell them about some of the interesting places to see in London.

The serviceman seemed to relax some and described some of the sights he thought were especially worthwhile.

"I suppose there is someplace we can get a map that shows how to get to all these places," Robert said.

"Yes, the Red Cross keeps some to give out to servicemen, but one good way to hit all the most important sights is to hire a taxi to take you around. For a couple pounds, the driver will give you a two or three-hour tour. Some of the places you will probably want to go back to later when you can spend more time."

"Hey, I like that idea!" Robert said.

"There are some things you'll want to see that you won't need a taxi for, like the subway, or the Underground as the British call it. I've been sort of fascinated by that. That's where a lot of Londoners went for safety during the blitz. It is also a great way to get around London."

"We will make a point of checking that out," Ken said.

The three continued talking until at one of the stops there was a sign that said "Waterloo Station."

"If you are planning to go to the Red Cross, this is a good place to get out. That's where I stay when I'm in London. It doesn't cost anything. But there are several hotels in the area if you like more privacy."

"The Red Cross sounds okay to me," Ken said. "How about it, Rob?"

"Fine with me," Robert said.

As the train came to a stop, they stood, took their bags from the luggage rack, and quickly stepped out on the platform to make way for a group of people waiting to enter the compartment they were leaving.

As they walked toward the Red Cross, Ken told their new acquaintance they would be glad to have him join them when they took a taxi tour if he was interested.

The GI smiled for the first time, apparently pleased with this gesture of friendship.

"Thanks, but I've done it before, and I have a date with a girl I met here a couple months back," he said.

They made arrangements for beds at the Red Cross and left their bags in a locker they were assigned. They went back to the reception desk and got a map, which highlighted the places of interest and where to take the Underground trains that would take them to some of the sights they wanted to see.

"You boys had better have some coffee and doughnuts before you start out," said the friendly Red Cross lady. "It's pretty damp and cold out there."

"Shall we take time to accept this kind lady's suggestion, Ken?" Robert asked. "I think I could go for some."

"Well, we do have three days. I think we can take time to have some free refreshments!" Ken said.

They took a seat at a table, and a hostess immediately brought them some coffee and doughnuts. As soon as their plate was empty or their coffee was getting low, they were offered more.

Ken looked at the two or three dozen servicemen sitting around the tables. Some were talking to others, some were writing letters, but most of them had a cup of coffee and a paper plate with doughnuts.

"You know, I think it is really great that there are places like this for servicemen to come thanks to the Red Cross and whoever provides the support for the expenses. This is sort of like having a home away from home."

After they had finished their second cup of coffee and a few more doughnuts, Ken said, "I think we might as well get going unless you would like another round."

"I've had plenty of doughnuts and coffee to last a while," Robert said. "I'm ready to start seeing the sights."

"Okay," Ken said. "Let's go."

There was a small vehicle with a sign indicating it was a taxi parked in front of the building the Red Cross was using. As Ken and Robert walked toward it, the driver opened his door and stepped out.

"'Ello, mates. Is it th' tour you'd be wantin'?"

"Yes, we are thinking of taking a sightseeing tour, but we would like to know the cost," Ken said.

"Ah, yes. You Yanks are all for it, three, sometimes four tours a day I do, showin' London. Two pounds will get you to th' principle sights; three will give you th' grand tour," the cabbie said.

"That sounds fine," Ken said. Then to Robert, "Which tour do we want?"

"Why don't we go with the two-pound tour? By the time we finish that, it will probably be time for lunch," Robert said.

"Okay," Ken said. "Let's go. Along with whatever else you are going to show us, we would like to see some of the damage from the bombing."

"Don't worry, lad, of that you will see enough and to spare," the cabbie said.

At Buckingham Palace, they got out and looked through the fence at the impressive-looking building. In spite of the presence of a number of imposing-looking guards in tall bearskin hats and red jackets, the gate was locked. Ken wondered if it was for security purposes during the war or if this was standard practice. It would certainly be demoralizing to the British people to have their king assassinated.

The cabbie said the palace had been built in 1703 and had been the residence of the British monarchs since Queen Victoria's reign. He told them the tall, ornate structure in front of the palace was Queen Victoria's monument. He talked proudly of "good old George," the present king, who resided there with Queen Mary and Princess Margaret. Princess Elizabeth was supporting the war effort by serving in the Women's Auxiliary Territorial Service. Ken snapped some photographs of the castle and the guards and took one with Robert standing in the foreground.

"I wish the king would come out," Robert said. "I would like to be able to say I saw a king."

"I guess we should have phoned ahead and told him we were coming," Ken joked.

After a few minutes, the cabbie said, "We'd best be on our way, lads."

They got back into the cab and were taken to the Tower of London. The cab driver said this was the source of a lot of interesting history. Many famous people had been imprisoned there, with beheadings, murders, and tales of ghosts. The driver recommended they return and spend the hour or so it took for a tower guide to escort them through the tower and grounds and discuss the rather dramatic history.

Even though most of the rubble had been cleared away, they saw the evidence of the vast devastation around St. Paul's Cathedral, caused by the bombing. They were told the area was the site of many deaths and a massive fire that brave firemen battled for hours with inadequate water supplies pumped from the Thames River. With their heroic efforts, they were able to keep the fires from reaching St. Paul's. Several firemen were among those who lost their lives there. They heard one five-hundred-pound bomb landed quite near St. Paul's but failed to explode, which the British considered divine intervention.

Inside they noted the burial places of British notables such as the Duke of Wellington, Admiral Nelson, and Christopher Wren, the architect of St. Paul's. They were encouraged to take the 530 steps to the Golden Gallery, an observation platform on top of St. Paul's that provided a panoramic view of London. They were told to check out "the whispering gallery," a circular walkway about halfway up the dome where you could hear a whisper on the opposite side 112 feet away.

The cab driver took them to see the Houses of Parliament with Big Ben in the tower, Westminster Abby, and Piccadilly Circus, and showed them several other areas where there was evidence of extensive bomb damage, especially near the docks. The taxi driver had shown them a lot of interesting things, and when he stopped back in front of the Red Cross, Ken thanked him and handed him the two-pounds fare he had asked for. Robert then handed him a crown tip, which delighted the cabbie.

"You Yanks are a generous lot," he said. "'Twould be m' pleasure to take you out again. Now look to the nipper over there. 'E does a smashing bit w' the shoes. 'Is sire was put down during the bombin,' and th' lad tries to 'elp wi' th' provender for th' brood."

Ken and Robert glanced in the direction the cabbie was looking and saw a boy with a shoeshine kit looking expectantly toward them.

"Oh well," Robert said as they walked away from the cab. "I don't think I really need a shine, but I guess I'll help the—what was it the cab driver called him?"

"A nipper," Ken said. "Yeah, I guess I'll get one too. But I wonder if he is in cahoots with the cabbie!"

"Hey, that is possible!" Robert said. "He sure did some good advertising for the 'nipper.'"

As they drew close to the boy, he said with a broad smile, "If it is a polish you'd be wantin,' I'm 'ere to give you a fine one!"

"And what would a 'fine one' cost?" asked Robert.

"For fine gentl'men th' likes o' you, one shillin' would bear th' cost!"

"Is that the price for both of us or for one?" Ken joked.

"Oh, sir. I was meanin' for one, but if it pleases you, I will do both."

Ken laughed and tousled the boy's head. "I was just joking. A shilling each is fine."

The boy looked relieved and said, "Who would be first then?"

Robert put his foot on the box and asked, "Do you know that cab driver there?"

"Oh yes, sir. 'Twas 'im who put me onto this polishing bit, and 'e's th' one who came to th' flat the night m' father was put down. They were mates, y' know. Hosin' th' fire when a wall fell on m' father. 'E's been very kind to Mum. When 'e's a fare down by th' greens market, many times 'e's brought greens to th' flat."

"Do you mean vegetables like brussels sprouts?" Ken asked.

"Oh yes, sir, and potatoes and cabbage and chard. Whatever is on that day."

Ken felt a new respect for their cab driver. The boy finished shining Robert's shoes, and Robert gave him two shillings.

"I do thank you, sir!" he said, looking pleased.

When the boy was nearly finished with Ken's shoes, he asked, "Is there a place near here that sells fish and chips?"

"Oh yes, sir. Ver' close. Y' see the bobby on the next corner? Just past 'im on this side of th' street, there's a fine place. I 'ad their fare once," he said rather wistfully.

"What is your name?" Robert asked.

"Edward, sir," was the response.

"Edward, have you eaten lunch?" Robert asked.

"Well, no, sir. I don't always take lunch."

"Why don't you take us to that fish and chip place, and I'll buy your lunch," Robert said.

Ken nodded his agreement.

"That's very kind of you sir, but—" He paused, not sure what to say.

"Fine. Let's go," Robert said as Edward put the finishing swipes on Ken's shoes.

Ken handed him a half crown, and Edward started to give him change, but Ken waved it away.

"Like the man says, let's go."

Edward picked up his shoeshine box and slung it over his shoulder by the strap that was attached, and they started toward the fish and chip shop. Along the way they asked Edward to tell them about some of the shops with strange sounding names and other unusual sights they were seeing.

Edward ate his fish and chips with such relish that Robert was glad he had asked him to come along. He had obviously been hungry.

"I've heard children were evacuated from the big cities to the country during the blitz. Where were you during that time?" Robert asked.

"I stayed right 'ere in London, sir. Mum and Father wanted me to go out, but I brought them 'round into letting me stay. My younger brother and sister did go out for some months, but they are here now."

"Did you stay in the Underground any during the bombing?" Ken asked.

"Oh yes. Mum and I slept there many a night. Other nights we kept ourselves in a shelter a little nearer our flat, but sometimes there wasn't room for us."

"Did any bombs land near you?"

"Well, sir, there was one that left us without 'earing for a span, even tho' we were in the shelter. We did 'ave to climb over some stones on the steps when we went out."

Ken and Robert continued to ask Edward about life during the blitz. He proudly talked about the bravery of the RAF, the police, firefighters, and ambulance drivers who continued to serve in the midst of the bombing. He told of ordinance men who risked their lives disarming unexploded bombs and related instances of seeing the actions of some of these brave men as he and his mother were making their way to the shelter.

As a semi-humorous yet rather distressing sidelight, he told the popular story of the lady in the next flat who closed her oven door as she rushed out to the air raid shelter, only to find on her return that her cat had taken refuge in the oven when it heard the sirens. The charcoal fire beneath the oven was still smoldering, and she became known in the neighborhood as "the woman who cooked the cat."

They told Edward about the sights they had seen on the taxi tour and asked him if there were any interesting sights nearby. Edward told them there were some within easy walking distance and named several of them. Almost before they realized it, an hour had passed.

Edward suddenly said, "I do thank you for the fish and chips. I'd best be getting back on the job. Mum won't let me be polishin' tomorrow since it is the Sabbath. She'll be wantin' us all in the services."

"Say," Robert said, "why don't we see if we can get Edward to take us on a walking tour tomorrow afternoon? He probably knows the best way to get to some of things that we want to see."

"Great idea," Ken said. "How about it, Edward?"

"Well, I would have to see if it's a'right with Mum. I'd be for it if she's favorable."

"If she will give you permission, why don't you meet us in front of the Red Cross at one o'clock?" Ken said.

"Aw'ri, governor. One o'clock it is, if I'm not forbidden," Edward said with a broad smile. With that he turned to go back to the Red Cross in hopes of finding some more customers.

Ken and Robert looked around idly at some of the shops. Robert said he needed something to hold his unruly hair in place and wondered where to look for hair oil. They saw a sign on a store that announced it was an apothecary.

"Robert, I think that's what the English call a drugstore. You might try in here," Ken suggested.

"Okay," Robert said, and when they entered Robert asked if they had any Brylcreem or Vaseline hair oil.

"No," the clerk said, "but if it's 'air tonic you are wantin,' some seem to like this one."

He held up a bottle of a rose-colored liquid. Robert thought that was probably equivalent to American hair oils, so he paid the clerk, and they left the shop with the new purchase. Later, when Robert opened the bottle, he found the contents had an overpowering perfume smell, and he threw it away.

After looking around a little more, they decided to go back to the Red Cross. As they went in they waved at Edward, who was in the process of trying to sell his shoeshine services to a couple American servicemen. As they entered the building, they saw a poster advertising a live performance by Irving Berlin and his troupe at a local theater with the title *This is the Army*.

"Hey, that might be worthwhile!" Robert said. "I think that guy Berlin is the person who wrote *God Bless America,* which is a great song. Why don't we take that in?"

"Okay. That does sound interesting," Ken said.

This is the Army was a very entertaining show highlighted by the song by that title that Berlin wrote. All the performers were American servicemen, some of whom were made up to play the part of females, which they did quite convincingly as hostesses at the Stage Door Canteen. Much of it was humorous, and a patriotic theme was stressed throughout the show.

Berlin himself appeared in WWI army uniform and sang his song of that era: "Oh how I hate to get up in the morning." He introduced a new song he had written that he was trying to popularize with the title *My British Buddy*. It just didn't seem to Ken and Robert to be of the quality of his other songs in the performance, but overall the show was great, and they were glad they went.

The next morning Robert said, "I think I would like to go to a service at one of the cathedrals and see what it's like. The church I attended with my girlfriend would look pretty primitive compared to the cathedrals, but I'll bet what goes on inside isn't any better."

Ken readily agreed that it was a great idea. They checked their map and saw where the closest one was and obtained the time of services from a Red Cross hostess. They arrived at the cathedral about ten minutes before the service was to start. There was quite a crowd of people entering before them. An usher greeted them enthusiastically and took them to a seat near the front. The dome rose above them so high it sort of gave the impression that they were outside. A large choir sang a beautiful hymn, and the elaborately-robed minister gave a rather dry sermon but did include some worthwhile thoughts. It did not seem to Ken that it was as inspirational as the services he had attended with the Meyers.

As they made their way out of the door, Ken saw the usher who had seated them and remarked, "You really had a big crowd this morning."

"Ah, yes," the usher said. "'Tis the war, you know. The bombings have brought many back who sadly had given up the services."

As they moved on past the usher, Robert said, "It's really a shame it takes something like a war to get people to church."

Ken and Robert stopped at a restaurant they saw on the way back to the Red Cross and had lunch. At one o'clock, they were standing in front of the Red Cross wondering if Edward was able to get permission to be their guide; then they saw him approaching with a woman they assumed was his mother and two children.

Robert and Ken removed their caps as the group stopped in front of them, and Edward said, "This is my mum. She wanted to see if you are proper gentlemen for me to be wi.'"

The lady flushed and said, "Now, Edward, you needn't be tellin' that, but I did want to see what kind of chaps you are b'fore letting Edward go wi' you."

Robert quickly said, "Oh, that is certainly the right thing for a mother to do. You have a fine boy there, and you wouldn't want him to stay long around people who would be a bad influence. We just enjoyed talking with him, and he seems to know all about some of the places we would like to see, so we thought maybe he could be our tour guide. We will surely watch out for him, if you will let him go with us."

"Well, now I see you, m' mind is put at ease. I fancy I'm a mite over-protectin' of 'im. 'E's 'ad to step into 'is father's shoes, you know."

"Yes, we heard about your husband's death during the blitz and can understand a little of how hard it has been for you and your children. But Edward seems to be trying hard to fill the place your husband's death left," Robert said.

"Yes, and it is ver' proud of 'im, I am. 'E's named after King Edward the Seventh, Queen Victoria's son, y' know, and 'e 'as been behavin' like royalty since a small child!"

"Ma'am, we would be glad for you and your children to go with us if you would care to," Ken said.

"'Tis a nice thought, but Edward will go with you. We would be a bother." With that she bid them good-bye and started back the way they had come.

Edward led the Americans to Charring Cross, which was considered to be the heart of London. He then took them the fairly short distance to Trafalgar Square, which had a monument commemorating Admiral Nelson's naval victory during the Napoleonic wars. They spent a little while watching the pigeons compete for the scraps of bread being thrown to them by spectators.

Hyde Park was their next destination, where several different people were standing on their boxes loudly promoting some cause or denouncing the government for some policy they didn't agree with. A few of these speakers had drawn quite a crowd of listeners, but one man continued to harangue loudly even though it didn't appear anyone was listening to him.

They then visited the British Museum and were fascinated with the display of ancient objects from previous civilizations. Over two hours flew by as they looked at the various exhibits; then Edward told them he had promised his mother he would be home by five o'clock.

"We surely wouldn't want you to disobey your mother," Robert said, and they immediately started back to the Red Cross.

At the Red Cross they thanked Edward for being their tour guide, and Ken handed him a sovereign. He went happily down the street toward his home.

Almost before they realized it, the first two days of their leave were gone and it was Monday. Ken and Robert were supposed to report back to their base by seven o'clock in the evening. They wanted to be sure to experience riding on the Underground and checked their map for points of interest they could travel to.

"Too bad Edward is in school today. He could have made sure we took the right trains," Robert said. "But then since you are a navigator, you should be able to get us where we are going!"

Ken smiled. "I will do my best, but remember I don't have my instruments! But if we get too confused, we can always ask a bobby for directions."

They went to the nearest Underground station and were intrigued by the two levels of boarding platforms and the long escalators providing access to the platforms. Neither Ken nor Robert had seen an escalator before, and they got a lot of enjoyment out of riding up and down on them. They decided they would take their cab driver's recommendation and go through the Tower of London. It took only a short time for the Underground train to get to the station nearest the tower.

Tour groups left the tower entrance every hour, and Ken and Robert had to wait a while until the next tour started. They saw more of the colorful, red-jacketed guards they had seen at Buckingham Palace. Finally they were summoned to begin the tour by a man in a colorful costume known as a yeoman warder, also called a beefeater. The latter term was thought to have been an ancient derogatory reference to the fact that these "pampered guards," or tower custodians, regularly had beef to eat while most of the general populace had little or none.

The tour guide seemed to get a lot of enjoyment out of relating the history of the tower to the dozen or more people in his tour group. His colorful accounts of the happenings there made the tour quite interesting. He told them the construction of the tower was completed in 1098 under William the Conqueror. It had served as a fortress, a palace, and a prison. It currently housed the Royal Mint and the Royal Observatory, and the crown jewels were kept there in recognition that there was no place better protected.

Several notables had been imprisoned there, some of whom were executed. One of the more famous was Anne Boleyn, the wife of King Henry VIII. As the story went, she was executed because she was accused of adultery, but most people thought the real reason was because she had outraged the king by giving birth to a daughter rather than a son to occupy the throne. Her daughter, Elizabeth, was imprisoned there by Mary, her half sister, who wanted the throne herself. Public outcry brought about the release of Elizabeth, who eventually assumed the throne as Queen Elizabeth I. Tradition had it that Anne Boleyn's ghost still wandered about the tower.

Ken and Robert left the tour with a new appreciation of British history and a desire to learn more. They looked up some more points of interest on their map and proved to themselves they could understand how to use the Underground to get around London, even when it meant changing trains.

Everywhere they went, they were greeted with welcoming smiles, with the exception of a few of the British servicemen. American servicemen got significantly higher pay and were therefore more likely to attract girls who were looking for someone who could take them to dinner and other types of entertainment that cost money. This made some British servicemen resent the Americans, but most of them were happy to have comrades to help them fight their common enemy.

Among the places of interest they were told they should see was Madame Tussaud's Wax Museum. When they visited this museum, they found life-size replicas of famous people, both good and bad—

even Hitler and Mussolini. They were amazed at how lifelike the figures were. There were no name tags on the exhibits, and they didn't
know who some of the figures represented. The creator of the museum
apparently thought the persons represented were so well-known to
most people it would be an insult to post their name.

There was a young lady seated at a counter who appeared to be a
hostess. Robert embarrassed himself when he asked her if there was a
figure of King George in the museum. Ken really laughed at him when
they realized the girl was only wax. They were not able to spend much
time there since they wanted to be sure to catch a train that would get
them back to their base on time.

They began their return trip mid-afternoon. As the train stopped
at a station just outside London, a British sailor entered their compartment. He immediately swung into one of the overhead luggage racks
and was soon asleep. Later he awoke, and Ken commented he was surprised to see that someone could sleep there.

"Oh, this is jolly good sleepin,' mate. I could sleep on a clothesline
wi'out the pins!" the sailor said, and promptly went back to sleep.

Then, recalling they had heard that British sailors slept in ham-
mocks, they realized the luggage rack was not really much different.

As they left the train station at their destination, Ken said, "Well, that
was a fun trip, but there were a lot of things we didn't have time to see."

"We'll just have to go back," Robert agreed, "and we ought to go to
Scotland sometime. One of the guys in my barracks says there's a real
impressive castle in Edinburgh that everyone ought to see, and I would
like to go by Loch Ness to see if we could spot the sea monster!"

"We will just have to do that," Ken said. "We will see if we can get a
picture of you on Nessie's back!"

The stretch of bad weather that had kept the bombers on the ground
improved some, and clear weather was forecast for the following day.
Lieutenant Murphy announced in view of the predicted good weather
there would be a training flight to make sure their plane was function-

ing properly after its extensive repairs, and the crew was ready to perform their duties with top performance.

The next day, *Luck of the Irish* took off and made its way in a northerly direction, and before long they were looking down at the beautiful city of Glasgow. They flew around the city, and in the distance they saw a large ship, the *Queen Mary*, making its way out of the Firth of Clyde. Although designed as a luxurious passenger liner, it had been pressed into service transporting thousands of troops to England. The majestic ship was making its way back for another load of troops. Spitfires were crisscrossing the sky above the ship looking for any U-boats that might be lurking in hopes of torpedoing the ship as it made its way out to sea. Once at sea, the ship was difficult prey for the U-boats, thanks to its superior speed.

Nearby were the shipyards where the *Queen Mary*, the *Queen Elizabeth*, and many other British ships had been built, and others were under construction. Earlier in the war, these shipyards and docks had been the target of several German air raids. The British had eventually achieved dominance of the air over Britain, and with the exception of an occasional high-flying observation plane, the skies were free of German aircraft.

Lieutenant Murphy obtained clearance from the tower, and the plane landed at the spacious Glasgow airport for a short stay. The crew was pleased. Everyone had wanted to visit Scotland, and this had been the first opportunity for all of them, although they had stayed overnight at Prestwick Field when they had first arrived in the British Isles.

They were captivated by the delightful brogue they heard from the Scottish people, but the Scots seemed more reserved than the British, and they did not sense nearly as warm a reception. They were impressed with Glasgow's wide streets and several well-maintained parks. There was not enough time to do much sightseeing, but they did go to see a cathedral that was said to have been built in the 1100s and got a brief look at a beautiful botanical garden.

They saw a Red Cross and stopped by for a cold drink. While there they were told a photographer was taking pictures of American servicemen dressed in kilts and complete Scottish attire. As a lark, they each submitted themselves to being photographed.

The stay was short, but Ken enjoyed the experience and planned to get back to Glasgow and Edinburgh with Robert at the first opportunity. The afternoon was pretty well gone when they arrived back at the airport. They took off and went north while gaining altitude. As they began to turn, Ken looked at a map he had and reported to the crew if they would look out the left side of the plane they could see Loch Lomond in the distance.

Someone started singing softly, "You take the low road, and I'll take the high road…"

Chapter 10

Ken's heart jumped as the briefing officer unveiled the map of Europe. The line of red yarn led to today's target: Berlin! He heard some groans and some low curse words. This would be his fifth mission, and the experiences from the previous missions made surviving twenty-five missions seem pretty unlikely. There had been the crew of the *Memphis Belle* and a few others who had accomplished this and had been sent home, but a far larger percentage had not even come close to completing twenty-five missions.

They now had the advantage of long-range P-51 fighter support, which the earlier missions didn't have, but the casualty rate was still high. *Luck of the Irish* had returned from the February 24 bombing of Schweinfurt with a badly wounded ball turret gunner, an inoperative engine, and many flak holes. The left waist gunner would have probably been killed or at least wounded badly if he had not been wearing his flak jacket. The ground crew had only the day before restored their plane to flying status. Considering the damage they had sustained during other missions, an attack on Berlin sounded exceptionally hazardous. It seemed probable the Germans would go all out to defend their capital.

Ken concentrated intently on what the briefing officer was saying to be sure he didn't miss any information that was important to navigators and the success of the mission. He was determined to do a good job navigating, even while feeling apprehensive over a mission so deep into enemy territory.

When the briefing officer had finished talking about the target, fighter support, the expected strength of resistance, the weather, and other considerations regarding the conduct of the mission, the security officer strode to the front and began his usual instruction.

"Remember, do not talk about the target even if the mission is scrubbed. Sometimes it seems apparent that the Germans have somehow been given information about our missions. If this does happen, it makes the mission just that much more difficult.

"There is of course the possibility some of you may become POWs. Do not take billfolds or anything else that provides any information other than your name, rank, and serial number. Be sure to wear your GI shoes. These will be a help if you are shot down and are evading capture. Most of you know if you should go down over France there's a good chance the French Resistance patriots will help you get back to England. Anyone who has not been briefed on POW behavior, remain here for a while after the others have left."

Ken joined the large group of men gathered in front of the Protestant chaplain while he prayed for their protection and safe return. It was a little strange that many men who seemed to be completely irreligious always wanted to be included in these prayers. Catholic and Jewish chaplains were also praying with others who were of their faiths. As Ken walked to his quarters, he reflected on how much greater his fears would have been if he had not committed his life to God.

A Jeep was not designed to accommodate ten men plus a driver, but as usual, the whole crew was piled onto a single Jeep as it took them to their plane. As they approached the plane in the pre-dawn darkness, they were greeted by their ground crew chief. He had checked out the plane and found no problem with any of the systems. Ground crews developed a strong affection for the plane they maintained and its crew, and the flight crew appreciated the crew chief's sincere good wishes as they boarded. They had a new copilot on this mission. Lieutenant Anderson had been assigned as first pilot on another plane.

In some ways, the tension of waiting to take off was harder than the time in flight. There was always the desire to get started and get it over with. The waiting that morning of March 6, thanks to the clearer weather, was much shorter than on some previous missions. It took about a half hour for the planes from Bassingbourn to climb to twenty-eight thousand feet and join with planes from other bases to compose a several hundred plane formation.

As they came to the European coast, they were gratified to see their escort planes approach, as usual wagging their wings in greeting. Ken envied the freedom they had to zoom around apparently wherever they wanted to go instead of being committed to a steady, unwavering path. However, he knew the strength of the bomber's own defenses depended on maintaining positions that provided for keeping all sides of the formation protected with maximum firepower. He did fervently wish the speed of the B-17 was as great as that of the fighters.

Ken glanced out the side window and saw that enemy fighters had appeared, forcing some of the P-47s to drop their long-range fuel tanks in order to engage the enemy planes in combat. Those P-47s that still had their auxiliary fuel tanks would be able to stay with the formation nearly halfway to the target before dropping their external tanks and starting back to base. He hoped the P-51s would show up as planned to take over when the P-47s had to leave. Even the P-51s did not have the fuel capacity to stay in the air as long as it took the bombers to get to the target and back.

As usual, even though the primary navigation was being performed by the navigator in the lead plane, it was Ken's responsibility to know where his plane was at all times. There had been several instances when the lead plane had gone down, and other planes had to assume the lead position, which emphasized the importance of every navigator staying on the job. Also, periodic reports to the radioman of their position would be used in conjunction with observations from other crew members to record locations of heavy flak concentrations and other information that might be of value to future missions. Bomber command also wanted to know the precise location of any planes that were shot down.

Ken was glad he had something to occupy his mind, to make the time go a little faster. Every time he was asked for an estimate of the time and distance to the target, he had a ready response. All the crew members who manned guns spent their time scanning the sky for fighters. The American fighters kept the German planes away from the bombers for the most part, but occasionally some crew member would report a ME 109 or a FW 190 plunging through the formation with guns blazing.

Ken wondered if Robert's plane was in the formation. He had been on a mission a few days before during which his plane had received no damage and overall mission causalities were unusually light. Due to needed repairs, *Luck of the Irish* had not been available to take part in that mission.

In spite of the improbability, Ken hoped this Berlin mission would turn out the same way as that experienced by the one Robert was on. However, it would be surprising if the Germans didn't have exceptionally strong defenses to protect their capital with its large population and many industries.

It seemed a shame that there were so many important manufacturing plants in the area around Berlin; it was inevitable that innocent civilians would be killed. He wondered how the majority of the German people felt about the war and if they realized they were reaping a harvest sown by Hitler and the German military.

Flak was relatively light in most places. The route had been chosen to avoid most of the known areas of heavy antiaircraft concentrations, but as they passed north of Hannover, the flak became intense. Ken heard the now familiar sound of metal tearing through the fuselage.

Lieutenant Murphy asked everyone to check in, and no one reported being wounded. A few minutes later, the barrage of flak ceased.

Suddenly, there were what seemed to be dozens of German fighters flashing through the formation. It appeared the German high command had ordered up more attack planes than the Americans had enough fighters to keep engaged. The intercom was in constant use with reports from almost every gunner of approaching enemy aircraft. The continuous rattling of machine guns over the roar of the engines and chatter on the intercom created a cacophony of confusion. The biting fifty-degrees-below cold added to the stress.

In the midst of the confusion, Ken's mind turned back to two nights before when he and Robert had visited the Sutherlands again. A cozy fire burned in the fireplace as they leisurely sipped their tea and ate Mrs. Sutherland's delicious pastries. Shep would come to Ken once in a while and lay his head on his knee and wait for a pat, then go to lie in front of the fireplace. The Sutherlands had asked many questions about their lives in America. These questions were most often answered by Robert, whose life had been more typical of the average American.

When Ken and Robert related some of the interesting English history they had learned on their trip to London, the Sutherlands elaborated on some events that the tour guides had talked about. Ken asked the Sutherlands if they had seen the film *The Adventures of Robin Hood* and wanted to know how much of the film was historically accurate. Mr. Sutherland said it was hard to know how much about Robin Hood was true because there were so many contradictory tales and that some skeptics doubted there even was such a person.

Cedric told them about the new black lamb that had been born that morning and wanted them to go to the barn to see it before they went back to their base. It was a picture of tranquility, so unlike his present situation. Then he thought how satisfying the peace and quiet he had experienced on the Dalton farm had been. He wished the circumstances he was in were just a nightmare and that he could wake up and find that he was in the house in the orchard with the Meyer family. He wondered what the Meyers and the Daltons were doing at that time, and he visualized Mr. Meyer praying for his safety.

Shortly after one of the waist gunners reported that he had shot down an enemy plane, the massive fighter attack suddenly ceased. Ken thought the planes may have returned to their base to replenish their ammunition. There was relative quiet for some time; then about twenty minutes from the target, the fighter attacks resumed. The German planes were trying desperately to prevent the bombers from reaching their target, sometimes almost colliding with the bombers.

As their plane drew near the target, there was a series of shocks as an enemy fighter sprayed the tail section of their plane with machine gun and cannon fire. Ken looked up just as the German fighter flashed past. He winced. It looked like the plane had barely missed their left wing.

When Lieutenant Murphy asked the crew to report, there was no response from the tail gunner. That close to the target, it was especially important for the navigator to stay on the job, so Lieutenant Murphy sent the radio operator to check on him.

When he got to the tail, he found cannon or machine gun slugs had penetrated Sergeant William's flak jacket, and he was very obviously dead. He reported this to the pilot and said he would stay on the tail guns for a while until the severity of fighter attack lessened, but when he checked the guns, he found they had been badly damaged. He worked with them for a while but saw there was no hope to get them working properly, so he returned to his normal responsibilities.

As the formation approached the outskirts of Berlin, the fighter attack broke off, and the heaviest concentration of flak Ken had seen began. Their plane was continuously being jarred by the concussion, and frequently there would be the unmistakable sound that the bomber had been hit with fragments of flak. Ken was grateful the B-17 could withstand so much damage and still stay in the air.

There were no further reports of injury to the crew. Ken saw a B-17 going down and waited anxiously for the sight of parachutes but didn't see any. Then he was horrified to see a person tumbling through the formation with no parachute. He looked down at his parachute at his side to assure himself he could reach it rapidly if the need arose.

Ken reported their plane was just a few minutes from the target, and soon the plane was again under the control of the bombardier. With the concussion from the flak bursts constantly jarring the plane, he was having trouble looking through the bombsight. Finally Jim reported the bombs had been dropped, and Ken was relieved to know their assignment was completed and they would be heading home. As they were turning, there was another jarring as an intense burst of flak hit the plane.

A little later, the pilot announced, "Well, boys, both of the engines on the right side have been hit. The inboard engine is on fire and was sputtering, and the outboard engine has quit. I had to feather them both."

There was silence as that news sank in. There was concern that the engine fire might spread to the fuel supply, and even if it didn't, everyone knew they would not be able to stay with the formation, which increased their chances of being shot down. There had been some early missions when the formation as a whole had slowed to help protect planes with disabled engines, but bomber command had issued instructions for the formation to maintain normal speed with the thought that a slower speed would provide more opportunity for the enemy to shoot down more of the bombers.

The fire gradually died down and went out, but the engine was still emitting smoke. Lieutenant Murphy increased the RPM of the two remaining engines above the "red line," or what was considered the maximum sustainable engine speed, but the plane slipped back through the formation until they were alone. They knew they were exceptionally vulnerable with no tail guns; however, the enemy fighters were apparently regrouping for another massive attack, so they had at least a temporary reprieve.

About twenty minutes after they had left Berlin, the bomber formation was nearly out of sight. Then they saw German fighter planes return and again begin attacking the formation. The *Luck of the Irish* crew fully expected to be attacked, but the fighters apparently were so intent upon attacking the formation that they didn't notice their plane.

It was not long before only the sharpest of eyes could still see the American planes. Then Lieutenant Murphy saw a bank of clouds not quite on their course but in the same general direction. He immediately turned their plane toward the clouds, which offered a place to hide from their enemy.

After fifteen tension-filled minutes, the plane was surrounded by whiteness. The smoke from the engine blended in with the clouds, leaving no evidence of their presence, and there was a chance that after hiding for a while they could continue to escape detection by the fighters as the bomber formation drew them farther away.

Lieutenant Murphy reduced the speed of the remaining engines to normal cruising RPM to provide relief for the overworked engines. The extreme cold had helped keep the air-cooled engines from getting excessively hot, and they seemed not to have suffered any from being overstressed, but it was unlikely they could have continued much longer without some damage and possible catastrophic failure.

The clouds stayed with them for nearly thirty minutes. When they broke out into bright sunshine, they were still more than four-hundred miles from their base. The engine was now emitting only wisps of smoke. The crew scanned the sky for enemy fighters but didn't see any.

There had been several instances when lone bombers had returned to base long after the rest of the planes, in at least one case when the plane was flying on just one engine. Remembering these occasions gave the crew hope. A song came to mind that Ken had heard on an American Forces radio broadcast with the title "Coming in On a Wing and a Prayer," which seemed appropriate for their situation.

Suddenly, they began getting some flak, which increased in intensity in the next few minutes. Ken had plotted their position and knew because of the detour they had taken to get into the clouds they were passing over the outskirts of Hannover. Since they were the only target in the sky, the antiaircraft guns were all concentrating on their plane.

The bursts of flak kept getting closer and closer as the antiaircraft batteries homed in on their position and altitude. Then the plane shook violently as a blast hit the nose of the plane. Jim had been standing at the nose gun, and the explosion knocked him to the back of the compartment. Ken grabbed his emergency oxygen bottle and immediately went to him.

With horror, Ken saw his face and particularly his neck was pouring forth large amounts of blood. One eye had been penetrated with shrapnel. Ken knew the war was over for him.

As he started to put his regular oxygen supply back on, there was suddenly another massive explosion at the rear of the plane, apparently obliterating the tail. The plane's nose began rising, slowly at first then with increasing speed until the plane stalled and slowly began tumbling backwards.

Ken was thankful for the quick release provision on the flak jacket and quickly shed the cumbersome equipment. He grabbed his parachute and with effort managed to strap it on. The plane was spinning, and Ken had to exert all his strength to make his way to the bailout portal. With his last ounce of energy, he finally pushed himself through the portal, and everything went black as something struck his head with a forceful blow.

In the first moments after Ken opened his eyes, he had no idea where he was or what had happened to him. He was in a hazy, dreamlike state. Something was seriously wrong, but he just couldn't think of what it was. His head was whirling, he saw flashes of color, and he hurt all over, especially his head.

Slowly he began to remember he had been flying a mission. As his eyes began to focus, he was looking into the sky but didn't see any other planes in the formation. Then he realized he wasn't in a plane. He was lying on his back in a field with the edge of his parachute draped over the lower part of his body. What was he doing here? His head was throbbing with pain, and blood was running down the side of his head. He put his hand to the source of pain and felt a gash. When he looked at his hand, his fingers were covered with blood.

Then it all slowly came back to him. Luck had run out for *Luck of the Irish* and its crew. He began to remember the desperate struggle he had getting out of the plane and the blow to his head. He didn't remember pulling the rip cord. How had his parachute been opened? Did anyone else get out?

He weakly pushed himself up on his elbow to look for others. What he saw caused him to collapse back to the ground. A man was coming toward him with his face twisted with anger. He had a club in his hand. A little ways behind him, struggling to catch up, was a woman.

The man reached Ken and in a voice filled with rage spoke words Ken had never heard from the Meyers, but he knew the man was calling him some derogatory names. Ken was almost resigned to his fate. He knew a lot of misery had no doubt resulted from the American bombings, and he wasn't surprised the German people were angry.

But he prayed, "Dear Lord, thank you for helping me escape from the plane. Now would you please somehow get me out of this mess?"

The man seemed to have finished voicing his anger and raised the club. The woman arrived just then, out of breath, and pushed her way between Ken and the man. She spoke to the man in scolding tones, and Ken gathered she was his wife. Ken didn't understand all her words, but it seemed she was saying he wasn't responsible for the war. He was just doing as his superiors had ordered him to do.

Her words did not seem to have any effect on the man's fury. He appeared to be determined to vent his anger with the club and was yelling for the woman to get out of his way, but with surprising alacrity she kept herself between Ken and his aggressor. Ken was grateful for the woman's intervention and knew if it had not been for her he very probably would have been beaten to death.

The argument between the two Germans standing over him was interrupted by the arrival of a military vehicle with two soldiers who jumped out and told the civilians to step back, which the man did very reluctantly. They searched Ken for weapons; then one of the soldiers looked briefly at the gash on his head, went to the vehicle, and came back with a first aid kit. He quickly applied a bandage to the wound and secured it with some adhesive tape. Ken thanked him in English, and after a moment he curtly nodded his head.

Ken decided he would not reveal that he understood some German so they would feel freer to talk about what they were going to do with him. He was pretty sure the main reason they wanted to keep him alive was to try to get some military information from him, but they didn't show any evidence of hatred.

The soldiers each took an arm and lifted him to his feet. He was very dizzy and found that he had sprained an ankle and limped badly in the few steps he took to the vehicle. The soldiers helped him into the vehicle, which was the German equivalent of a Jeep. One of them quickly bundled up the parachute and placed it beside the driver's seat then went back and carefully examined the ground Ken had been lying on. Ken thought he was probably looking for anything that might be of interest to their interrogators.

Ken looked quickly around for other crew members. He didn't see any but knew they could have come down quite a distance from him, but remembering the desperate struggle he had getting out, he felt it was unlikely anyone else made it.

Even though his wound had been bleeding badly, Ken didn't think it was life-threatening, so he was a little surprised when he was taken to a doctor, who closed the gash in his head with several stitches and applied some kind of ointment, a new dressing, and gave him some pain medicine. Then, accompanied by two new guards, he was handcuffed and put in the back of a military vehicle that had the side windows covered. One guard sat beside him.

Ken still hurt all over, especially his head, and he was grateful to the doctor for the painkiller he had been given. Once in a while he got a brief glimpse of a bombed-out area through the front windshield.

They traveled for a few hours; then, as it started to get dark, they stopped where Ken was put into a cell in the village jail. He was given a bowl of barley soup and some coarse bread. It was not very good when compared to food he had been getting at Bassingbourn, but he was grateful for it. There was a thin pad on top of a wooden bench where he laid down and covered himself with the rough blanket that had been placed there. In spite of his aching body and the hard bed, it was not too long before he dropped off into a troubled sleep.

The next day they resumed their journey and just before noon arrived at Dulag Luft, the Luftwaffe interrogation center near Frankfurt. This was apparently standard treatment for downed air force officers. He was taken into a small room with one window, which was covered. The only furniture in the tiny room was a cot.

He was there for two days with minimal amounts of food and nothing to occupy his time except his own thoughts and his aching head. Ken realized this was part of the psychological treatment used by the Germans to make POWs more likely to give the information they wanted. He found himself over and over grieving Jim's death and the unknown fate of the other crew members. Jim's premonition that he was not going to survive the war had been fulfilled.

He marveled over the fact that he had survived and felt sure it was the hand of God that had made it possible. In getting out of the tumbling plane, he felt that he must have had strength beyond his own, and he was still mystified how his parachute had been opened.

God must have plans for me, he thought.

The morning of the third day, he limped badly as he was taken to a room where an interrogation officer was waiting. He was glad his head had stopped spinning and the pain had diminished significantly. He wanted to be clearheaded as he went through the interrogation and not say anything that would compromise security issues.

In spite of the rather intimidating situation, Ken was thankful to be there. The American airmen had been told by the security officer at POW briefings if they were captured, the sooner they could get into the hands of the Luftwaffe, the better their treatment would probably be. The German flyers seemed to have a professional respect for the Allied airmen; they had experienced the terror of aerial warfare and were in a position to empathize. The ground support members of the Luftwaffe seemed to have adopted their flyers' philosophy of treating prisoners humanely.

Judging from the way the civilian had expressed his hatred toward him when he first landed on German soil, which he thought was probably typical of a lot of Germans, he knew from his own experience it was good to be in the hands of the Luftwaffe. The officer acted very friendly and in excellent English asked Ken where his home in the United States was.

"Sir, as you know, the Geneva Convention specifies that I need only give my name, rank, and serial number. I am Lieutenant Kenneth Ryan, serial number 25316552."

The German officer smiled. "Ah yes, Lieutenant Ryan. Your plane, *Luck of the Irish*, crashed a few miles west of Hannover. The markings indicate you were assigned to the ninety-first bomb group based at Bassingbourn. See, we know quite a lot about you already."

Ken's pulse quickened at the mention of his plane. He had had time to grieve over Jim's death, but he was anxious to learn the fate of the other crew members.

"Then there is probably nothing important I could tell you that you don't already know," he said, "but can you tell me about the other members of my crew?"

The Luftwaffe officer frowned. "Lieutenant Ryan, I am the interrogator here." He paused then said, "We do have a lot of information, but we like to verify it from as many sources as possible. What possible harm would it be for you to tell us where you are from?"

Ken knew if he answered this question it would just lead to more questions. Besides, where was he from? He had no home; he could no longer claim the orphanage as his address.

"Sir, that is not for me to decide. Our superior officers instructed us to stay only with the requirements of the Geneva Convention. I'm sure you must tell your military personnel the same thing."

The Luftwaffe officer looked a little uncomfortable then seemed to change tactics.

"You may be interested to learn that I know quite a lot about America. I spent three years at Columbia University in New York City, and I got to do a little traveling around the country. That was a very enjoyable time period for me. Unfortunately, when the war broke out, I was called back to Germany and didn't get to complete my studies.

Who knows, I might even go back there and finish getting my degree after this war is settled."

He then began to talk about the sights he had seen while in America, and Ken knew he was trying to get him to relax and catch him off guard. The interrogation session lasted for nearly an hour, but Ken was certain he had not given any information that would be of help to the German cause. When it was over, the officer stood and shook Ken's hand. Ken was surprised to find he actually liked the man. It was hard to think of him as being an enemy. He was escorted back to his room and two days later was taken back for interrogation by the same officer. Again Ken refused to give information of any kind.

The third time he was interrogated, it was by a different officer who was very harsh, bordering on threats of punishment if his prisoner continued to refuse to answer his questions. Ken was amazed to hear him read from some papers that told of all the bases where he had received training, the date he received his commission, and the date he arrived in England. He wondered how the German officer had obtained that information. He refused to confirm anything the officer said, and he finally seemed to accept the fact that Ken was not going to weaken and closed his notebook. Ken thought he detected a note of grudging admiration as he called for the guard to take Ken back to his room.

The next morning Ken heard his door being unlocked, which was a rather ominous yet welcome sound since it promised relief from his boredom. Two middle-aged guards summoned him to his feet, handcuffed him, and led him out to a vehicle that took them to into Frankfurt.

As they entered the city, Ken saw several bombed-out buildings. One of the guards displayed an obvious loathing for his captive, and Ken heard himself referred to in derogatory terms. The other guard was much more amicable and performed his guard duties with professionalism and a basic concern for Ken's welfare.

When they got out of the vehicle at the train station, some of the civilians pressed in on them and looked at Ken with angry expressions that implied they wanted to get their hands on him, but the guard sternly demanded that they stay away. Ken knew it was probable that many of those in the crowd had suffered loss of family or friends and perhaps damage to their property, so he could understand why they would be angry. He was glad to get into the safety of the train compartment, which was commandeered by his guards.

During their time on the train, his guards treated him humanely but with some reluctance on the part of the surly guard. The other guard seemed to respect Ken as a fellow human being and brought him food and water at mealtimes. Ken's cooperative attitude seemed to soften the hostility he sensed from the unfriendly guard, and they both smiled and returned his handshake when they delivered him to two other German soldiers at the Hamburg railroad station.

Once again he was put into a military vehicle, and several hours later he was turned over to a guard at the gate of Stalag Luft One just north of Barth, near the Baltic Sea.

Chapter 11

Stalag Luft One was a large prison camp reserved for air force officer prisoners of war. Within the confines of the prison, there were thousands of POWs—Royal Air Force flyers from Britain, Canada, Australia, and New Zealand, as well as the Americans, although the RAF personnel were in a separate compound. Early in the war, the camp had been established for RAF prisoners, but eventually the number of Americans far outnumbered those in the RAF, which was attributable to the daylight bombing and the frequent missions with large numbers of aircraft that provided more visible and more numerous targets for the German fighters and antiaircraft guns.

The compound was surrounded by two concentric ten-foot-high fences topped with barbed wire. There were large rolls of barbed wire splayed out between the two fences, which were about ten or twelve feet apart. Several guard towers equipped with searchlights and machine guns were strategically placed around the perimeter. As an added precaution to prevent escapes, a wire had been placed around the perimeter about ten feet inside the inner fence and about eighteen inches high.

Signs posted on the fence announced that anyone on the wrong side of the wire could be shot without warning.

Ken, still limping some from his sprained ankle, was escorted to one of the buildings inside the compound and taken to Colonel Zemke, the senior American officer and camp commandant. The colonel asked Ken questions only an American would be likely to answer correctly to make sure he wasn't being planted by the Germans as a source of information about what was going on inside the camp. It didn't take long for the colonel to be satisfied that Ken was a loyal American. He stood and shook Ken's hand and said, "It wouldn't be reasonable for me to tell you to enjoy your stay here, but I hope you won't find it too unpleasant! Go to the room next door, and Lieutenant Norris will assign you to a barracks."

Lieutenant Norris was a very pleasant person who stood and shook Ken's hand.

"Welcome, you are now the recipient of Herr Hitler's hospitality!" he said with a smile. "I'm sure you will appreciate the elaborate amenities he has provided for you!"

Ken laughed. "Well, I guess I don't really have much choice, but after being locked in that little interrogation room for about five days, so far this looks like it is going to be a real improvement."

"Yeah, I know what you mean; that wasn't much fun," Lieutenant Norris said. He sat down and opened a ledger. "Let's see what sort of deluxe accommodations we can offer you." He leafed through the ledger then stopped and said, "Say, you are in luck! There is a vacancy in a barracks that has a scenic view of the north fence and a nice guard tower, always equipped with at least two guards who will watch out for your welfare! Seriously, I think it's kind of nice to be able to see outside the camp, rather than just looking at a bunch of barracks all the time."

"Sounds good, lieutenant," Ken said. "Sign me up!"

"Just call me Mark," Lieutenant Norris said. "Everyone here is an officer, but hardly anyone ever refers to rank unless it's some high-ranking officer like Colonel Zemke."

Mark took Ken into his barracks and introduced him. The men in the barracks crowded around him and gave him a hearty welcome, asking about his capture and the latest outside news of the progress of the war. New arrivals provided a welcome break in the monotony. Captain Lowell Tighe was the officer in charge of the barracks. He was responsible for maintaining discipline and seeing that the basic needs of those in the barracks were met. He led Ken to a bunk that was on the bottom of a rough three-tiered set of bunks.

"Here are your own private quarters," Lowell said. "Be sure to hang out the 'Do Not Disturb' sign if you don't want the maid bothering you! Here's Jeff Braden; he has the bunk above yours."

"You will be glad to have a considerate guy like me upstairs," Jeff said. "I don't play loud music late at night, and I very seldom throw wild parties! Of course, I will probably step on you sometimes climbing into my bunk, and my bunk squeaks pretty badly when I turn over; other than that you will probably not even notice me. Oh, one thing—you need to be careful to not mess up the nice shine on my shoes that I leave under your bunk at night!"

"Okay, I will be careful," Ken said with a smile. "I wouldn't want to see you have to go out in public with scuffed shoes!"

"Of course, you will have to put up with Jerry," Jeff said. "He has the bunk above me, and I think he gets his exercise by climbing up to his bunk about a dozen times a day. He weighs so much sometimes it feels like we are going to tip over. We get out to about a forty-five degree angle sometimes. Isn't that right, Jerry?"

Jerry just smiled. "Jeff is famous for his exaggerations; other than that he is not a bad guy. He did neglect to tell you he snores!"

"I think that is a case of mistaken identity!" Jeff said indignantly.

After the novelty of their new barracks mate's arrival had worn off, the others began drifting back to their own bunks or activities. Ken was glad for the reprieve; he was tired. The stress of the interrogations and being in the custody of German guards had worn him down. "I guess I'll try out my new bed for a little while," he said and lay down.

After resting a while, Ken took a closer look at his new residence.

There was not much to see; it was pretty plain and colorless. Most of the space was occupied by the bunks, but in the center of the room, there was a rough table with a bench on each side. A bare lightbulb hung over the table. *Well, I guess you wouldn't expect to find anything too fancy in a POW camp,* Ken thought.

Although everyone in the barracks was friendly, John Douglas, whose bunk was near Ken's, seemed to make it his responsibility to help Ken adjust to his new environment. He told Ken when to expect the roll calls, described the food situation and what recreational facilities were available, and shared a little bit about some of the more colorful fellow prisoners.

"One person you need to meet is Pappy Rea. He is a real interesting old fellow. He is in a barracks on the other side of the camp. I will take you to meet him some time if you want to."

"How old is he?" Ken asked. The term "Pappy" certainly implied an advanced degree of maturity.

"Oh, I don't know exactly, but he must be up in his thirties," John said. "He was a fighter pilot in the air force before the war started and loves to defy authority. He has been called before the German commandant so many times they are almost on a first-name basis! He has had several periods of solitary confinement. He has a lot of interesting stories about things that happened here."

"Well, when you have the time, I would like to meet him," Ken said.

"Okay, we have some time to kill before roll call; we might as well go now. We might be lucky and catch him in his barracks. He wanders around a lot seeing what trouble he can stir up!" John said.

As they walked through the maze of barracks, John told Ken that Pappy's name was Jack Rea, but almost everyone called him "Pappy" because he was so much older than most of the fellows. He had been shot down during one of the first missions the Eighth Air Force had conducted. He had lost an eye and received other wounds from shrapnel but had eluded capture for almost three weeks. When the Germans finally caught up with him, he was so weak from lack of food and loss of blood that he just couldn't resist anymore. He was one of the first Americans to be placed in the camp with the RAF prisoners before the two groups were separated.

"Wow! That would sure imply he is a pretty feisty person!" Ken said.

Ken and John went into Pappy's barracks and found him lying in his bunk reading a tattered paperback.

"Pappy, here's a new arrival who might like some advice from an old time prisoner," John said.

Pappy grinned and swung to a sitting position. "My main advice to everyone is to not take any guff! We need to make life just as miserable for these clowns as we can!"

"I hear they have done their part in making life a little miserable for you," Ken said. "Solitary confinement doesn't sound like much fun!"

"Hey, it just gives you more free time to think up ways to aggravate them," Pappy said. "I consider it an accomplishment when I can make them mad enough to put me in solitary!"

"Could I ask what sorts of things you did to qualify for solitary?"

"Well, once they were posting some bulletins that had a picture of Hitler on them. I tore one down, took it over to the guard who was posting them, and spit on Hitler's picture!" Pappy said with a laugh. "That guard came unglued; it was great! I got three weeks for that, but it was worth it! They thought I was getting too fat from all the good food they were providing, so they put me on a weight reduction diet."

He was smiling broadly, as if he really enjoyed recalling the event. Ken could see he was exceptionally thin. *He had better try to stay out of trouble!* Ken thought. *He doesn't look like he could stand much more time in solitary if it always involved deprivation of food!*

They chatted a while longer about prison life, and Pappy related several other amusing experiences.

About a half hour later, John said, "It's about time for roll call. We had better be getting back where we are supposed to form up. We wouldn't show up on the roster for this end of the compound."

"Aw, let 'em wait; it'll do them good!" Pappy said.

Ken and John laughed but started to go as Pappy said, "Remember guys, let's not dance to their tune; we are *Americans!*"

"You were right," Ken said as they went back to their barracks. "He sure is an interesting old fellow! But I don't think I want to pattern my behavior after his. I think I would rather sort of lay low and not create any waves."

John became a special friend, and he and Ken spent quite a bit of time together talking and engaging in some recreational activities. John had been a machinist for a short time in civilian life and liked to make things. He satisfied this desire by spending a good part of his time creating useful objects out of materials from Red Cross parcels. He tried to get Ken to join him in this activity. Ken tried it a few times but just couldn't get interested in it.

There were several fighter pilots in the compound, but most of the prisoners were bomber crew members. Some members of both groups had obvious signs of injuries. Ken saw one fellow who had been horribly burned. It made him grateful that he had survived with minor injuries. The wound on his head was healing but still bothered him some.

He overheard some fighter pilots expressing a desire to be back flying missions again. He knew the war had to continue until victory was achieved, but in spite of being in prison, he was sort of glad to be out of combat. He had seen firsthand death of friends and the likely death of others including his friend Hal. He had also witnessed the devastation of German cities and had wondered how much death and suffering had resulted from the bombing raids he had taken part in. He had to admit to himself he was tired of war, even though he had been in it for a relatively short time.

Ken soon learned the thing that made POW life the hardest to tolerate was the shortage of food. There were few times when the POWs received enough to satisfy their hunger, and inevitably all lost significant amounts of weight. Under the Geneva Convention, the Germans were supposed to provide a fairly extensive list of food items, but the prisoners were fortunate to get a minimal supply of cheese, potatoes, rutabagas, or cabbage and perhaps some barley soup. Sometimes they would receive black bread, which contained a liberal portion of sawdust. There was a shortage of grain in Germany, and even the German people had to eat the sawdust-laden bread sometimes. The sawdust didn't provide any nutrition, but the bulk helped ease the hunger pangs.

Sam Olivas, who lived in the same barracks Ken did, was one of the camp cooks. Occasionally, when a few of the food items supplied to the mess hall had not been used up, Sam would bring some of them to his barracks and provide his buddies with a little extra food. He was able to create some surprisingly tasty dishes from ingredients that seemed to offer little promise of being enjoyable. He had acquired his cooking expertise working in his family's Mexican restaurant in El Paso.

"When we get back home, you fellows come to our restaurant, and I will treat you to a real good meal!" Sam said. "You need to try my tamales. Everyone says I make the best tamales they have ever tasted. I would make you some now if I had the ingredients."

"Hey, Sam, the other day I saw a big rat run under the barracks next door," Charles Downing said. "How about using him for some tamales?"

"You catch him then get me some cornmeal, hot chilies, tomatoes, corn husks, and a few other items, and I'll fix you right up!"

"Oh, now we know what kind of meat you use in your Mexican food! I'm not sure I want to go to El Paso for a free Mexican dinner!" Ken Anderson said.

Sam grinned. "Well, we have to do everything we can to keep prices down! But we don't always use rats; for our best customers we use rattlesnakes or horned toads!"

"It probably doesn't make much difference what he uses in his food if you put his salsa on it," Terry Ward said. "A few days ago I heard a guy say he was from El Paso, so I asked him if he had ever eaten at the Olivas's Mexican restaurant. He said it was his favorite restaurant and he especially liked Sam's hot salsa. He said once a napkin had somehow got in his food that had a lot of that good salsa on it, and he ate half the napkin before he realized it wasn't a tortilla!"

Sam just grinned as hoots of laughter echoed off the bare walls of the barracks.

The food provided by the Germans was at times supplemented by food parcels supplied by the Red Cross. The intent had been to distribute these each week, but their delivery was sporadic and rarely in the quantities that were sufficient for all the prisoners.

Receipt of these parcels was a much-welcomed event. They were supposed to contain enough food to sustain an individual for a week, but it would be difficult to stretch it that far. They were not always the same but could contain two different cans of Spam, corned beef, or stew; a can of either salmon or sardines; a box of crackers or cereal; two chocolate bars or a can of cocoa; a packet of coffee; a can of powdered milk; a can or package of cheese; raisins; margarine; and five packs of cigarettes.

Since no one had any money, a barter system was devised with exchange values of all items in the parcels, and cigarettes were a very frequent medium of exchange. It was a real boon to non-smokers, who seemed to be in the minority. The most highly-prized items in the Red Cross parcels were the chocolate bars, which were each valued at ten packs of cigarettes.

The margarine proved to be useful for making candles. The margarine was melted and poured into an empty can from a Red Cross parcel and part of a webbed belt placed in it for a wick. It was then allowed to harden and became a reasonable substitute for a real candle. Due to the uncertainty of the electrical supply, the margarine candles provided a little illumination that made for better morale than the depressing complete absence of light.

Next to the shortage of food, boredom was the greatest problem. As officers, in compliance with the Geneva Convention, they were not assigned work responsibilities. The only scheduled events were two roll calls a day. The rest of the time everyone had to find some way occupy the long, dreary days.

Some men, such as John, kept themselves busy improvising cooking containers, dishes, or utensils made from empty containers from the Red Cross parcels. The Red Cross and the YMCA had provided some footballs, baseball equipment, and other sports items, but most prisoners just didn't have the energy to use the equipment very often due to their limited amount of food.

One of the most common ways to pass the time was by playing cards, and there were almost always several games in progress. There were also a few chess sets in the compound, which were in almost constant use. Ken sometimes watched the chess games but could tell the playing was beyond his level of expertise so never tried to challenge the winner like more experienced chess players did. Checkers was another game available to the prisoners. Ken watched some of these games, but when compared to chess, it just didn't seem very challenging.

Ken was told about one POW in a different compound that was making a violin, which didn't seem possible with the limited availability of materials and tools. The story went that the man had traded the cigarettes in his Red Cross parcel to a guard for a pen knife he was using to make the violin out of bed slats. He learned later the story was true; the man's name was Clair Cline, and he had done some woodworking in civilian life so had some knowledge of how to proceed.

He had painstakingly shaped the various pieces of the instrument with the knife and had soaked the wood in water until he was able form it into the contours of a factory-made instrument. Glue was obtained from the excess around the legs of the tables and benches. He had even carved the usual f-shaped openings in the resonance chamber cover and had polished it with pumice. Catgut for the strings and a bow were obtained from a guard with more Red Cross cigarettes. It was reported that the violin was so well-made it was difficult to tell it had not been made in a violin factory, and it played beautifully.

Another source of entertainment was the books provided by the YMCA. These were kept in a simple library composed of a large number of mostly dog-eared paperbacks and a few hardcovers, among which were some classics. A checkout system was set up, and everyone was encouraged to finish reading their book as soon as possible so someone else could read it.

Ken had not done much reading before, as there had been few books other than texts at the orphanage. It soon became one of his favorite ways of passing the time. The books he enjoyed most were those containing adventure. There were a few biographical books about explorations of the American West, the South Seas, the Polar Regions, and other world areas that he found especially interesting. He started a book by Shakespeare but wasn't enjoying the archaic language and gave it up.

There were several college graduates and tradesmen who regularly provided instruction in their field of expertise to those who were interested in learning something that could be of value when they were back in civilian life. The courses were very casual, as there were no texts, audio/visual equipment, or blackboards for use in providing instruction. In spite of this, those who were serious about learning were able to significantly increase their knowledge of the subject they were studying.

Ken regularly attended a class on the German language and learned a lot of conversational German. He was also interested in a class conducted by an electronics engineer. Much of the subject matter presented was a repeat of what he had studied in the electronics school at Keesler, but it helped reinforce what he had learned there. He did miss working with the parts and test equipment that he had in his previous course.

In addition to his instruction in theory, the electronics instructor brought a crude radio set he had made to class. A basic rectifier was made using a rusty razor blade, a safety pin, a piece of pencil lead, and wire he had removed from an electrically heated bomber jacket. He had made a capacitor with tinfoil from cigarette packages and an adjustable tuning coil with wire wrapped around a tube he made from cardboard from a Red Cross package. He made an earphone using four nails he had pulled from the wall, with wire wrapped around them, creating a simple electromagnet. When impulses from the primitive radio were fed into this electromagnet, the metal bottom of a corned beef can was deflected, creating sound. He was able to very faintly hear the BBC broadcasts. Ken marveled at his ingenuity.

Even though the homemade radio brought satisfaction to its creator, it was not really needed to know what was going on in the world. There was a clandestine radio in camp that reportedly had been put together by two RAF airmen who had somehow acquired the parts needed to construct it. News from the radio broadcasts was spread through the camp by duplications of written copies of the latest news through an ingenious method created by a professional photographer using only materials available in the camp. This news was always at odds with that given to them by their captors. The German news bulletins would report that their troops had "occupied better defensive positions" rather than retreated. This was typical of their ongoing attempts to put a positive spin on their defeats.

The guards seemed to suspect the existence of the radio, possibly because of having come across one of the camp's "newspapers," which presented a different version of the news than their bulletins. Several times they appeared to be searching for it, but lookouts were always posted when it was in use. The radio was well-hidden behind a wall panel in one of the barracks.

The prisoners were elated when they heard that the June 6 invasion of Europe by the Allies had begun and eagerly plotted their progress on a rough, hand-drawn map. Morale, which had been sagging, now improved with every bit of information regarding gains made by the Allied forces.

The beginning of the invasion offered hope of eventual liberation, but in the meantime, the prisoners had to deal with the harsh realities of prison life. Cleanliness was a real problem, and there was a lot of sickness as a result of the unsanitary conditions. It was not unusual for someone to succumb to one of the mysterious illnesses that swept through the camp.

Although there were basins and faucets in the latrine, most of the time several of the faucets were out of order. About every other week, the men were given an opportunity to take a very brief group shower. Several men would be herded into a room that had ten showerheads and basically just given time to rinse off. They did have bars of soap that had been provided by the Red Cross, but it was sometimes difficult to get the soap rinsed off before being herded out of the shower.

During those times when there was nothing else to occupy his time, Ken's thoughts often turned to the Meyers. In his last letter Professor Meyer said he was still enjoying the little church and his teaching job and was proud of how fast his children had become proficient in the English language. It was a delight to him how they were excelling in their academic studies; both of them were at the top of their classes scholastically in spite of their language handicap. He also mentioned that Mrs. Meyer and Mrs. Dalton had become good friends and were spending a lot of time together and that Mrs. Meyer had learned to drive. His letters always ended "We are praying for you." Ken had a feeling that it was because of their prayers he was still alive.

The Daltons and how good they had been to him were also frequently in his thoughts. Several times he relived his birthday party in his mind and tried to recapture the enjoyment he had experienced. The watch the Daltons had given him had been so useful. He looked at it many times during the day. He no longer had the billfold the Meyers had given him, but he was thankful for the New Testament that he had managed to hold on to throughout his capture, interrogation, and incarceration. As much as he enjoyed the watch, he valued the New Testament much more. He spent a lot of time reading it and memorizing favorite passages. He was awed by the way some of verses that seemed to have obscure meanings suddenly became clear after a period of meditation. He was disturbed that he hadn't been baptized when he read Mark 16:16, which said, "He that believeth and is baptized shall be saved," but he knew God had come into his life. Then he thought about the thief on the cross; he hadn't been baptized, but Jesus told him he was going to be with him in paradise. The thief, like Ken, had not had the opportunity to be baptized, so it seemed it was not held against him.

There were three complete Bibles in the library that were in almost constant use, and it was understood they should be brought back to the library when not in the process of being read. During his imprisonment,

Ken was able to read several of the Old Testament books. He paged through those that didn't look too interesting to him but felt uplifted by others, particularly Genesis, Ruth, Esther, Psalms, Isaiah, and Daniel.

He especially admired the steadfastness of Joseph and Daniel in every trial they faced. He was awed by the revelations regarding the future given to Daniel by the angel Gabriel and their partial fulfillment by the rise to power of Babylon, Persia, Greece, and Rome and the foretelling of the precise time of the advent of Christ.

He was moved by the stories of bravery and conquest in Judges and some of the following books but was dismayed at the recurring cycles of the times when the Israelites forsook God until another national crisis arose. He was amazed at God's patience in dealing with his chosen people when they seemed to be so prone to turn from him to idols and at how they could think for a minute that a man-made god could help them in any way.

Ken's New Testament also had the book of Psalms, and Ken began the practice of lying on his bunk and reading a Psalm every night before going to sleep. Ivan, who was in the bottom bunk next to him, observed this routine and asked him to read aloud. Soon, almost all the men in Ken's barracks would gather each night to hear the "Psalm of the day." Eventually Ken added a brief prayer after each reading.

It was not long until the others began coming to Ken for spiritual advice and encouragement. The harsh conditions and bleak outlook on their future seemed to make most men feel a greater need for spiritual help. Ken was happy to share with them and pray for them. Some started calling him "parson." One very sincere Catholic named Tim asked him if he would hear his confession. Ken's heart was moved with sympathy for this fellow who seemed to want to do his best to serve God in the manner which he had been taught.

He just wasn't sure what to say, but finally he read the eighth and ninth chapter of Hebrews to him, which described how the ministry of earthly priests has been superseded by Christ, who had become the great high priest. He then told Tim to talk to the great high priest, who was always ready to hear confessions and prayers. Ken said he would listen to his prayer to God if Tim wanted him to do that, but any for-giveness would have to come from God. Tim did as Ken suggested and seemed to be encouraged.

Many of the prisoners had suffered a lot of trauma, which sometimes manifested itself in rather bizarre or disturbing behavior. One of the fellows in Ken's barracks always seemed depressed. He had frequent nightmares and would cry out as if in terror during the night, disturbing the other occupants. Once when they were alone, Ken said, "George, something seems to be bothering you. You know, God can help you with that."

George was silent for a while then said, "I really hate to talk about it, but I guess I might as well tell you. Maybe it will help to get it off my chest."

"I think you are right; it might help," Ken said.

George seemed to struggle with how to begin. "Ken, I am respon-sible for the deaths of my crewmates and probably another crew." His eyes filled with tears and he choked up.

Ken waited while he tried to compose himself.

"I was a B-24 copilot," he said. "We were on our way to bomb Schweinfurt when a Focke-Wulf came at us head on. He gave us a machine gun burst that just riddled our pilot; his blood splattered all over me. I glanced over at him, and when I looked back, there was another fighter directly ahead that appeared to be about to collide with us and I panicked! I yanked the plane into another bomber, and we both went down. As far as I know, I am the only one that survived." A sob escaped as he related this.

Ken waited a bit for his emotions to subside. "I can see how this would distress you, but you are going to have to put this behind you. Your actions are certainly understandable, and probably most of us would have done the same thing if we had been in your shoes. In time of war, things like this are bound to happen. You never know what might have happened if you hadn't dodged; it might have been even worse. God allowed you to survive; now you need to use your life to serve him and help other people. The good you can do with your life could far outweigh what you consider to be a tragedy. I think we should pray about this."

Ken prayed a short prayer asking that the load of guilt George was carrying would be taken away and that he would establish a relationship with God that would be uplifting and would result in him being used for great good for God's kingdom and the benefit of others.

When Ken finished praying, George wiped away some tears, shook Ken's hand, and said huskily, "Thanks, I do feel a *lot* better!"

In future days the other residents of their barracks wondered why George had suddenly ceased crying out in the night.

During the first few months Ken was in the prison, there was no chaplain in the compound he was in, but two laymen who had been active in their churches held short, informal meetings each Sunday. A few familiar hymns would be sung, prayer offered, and the exposition of some Scripture would usually be made. Sometimes the talk would be based on Joseph, Daniel, Jeremiah, or Paul as Biblical prisoners who could relate to their circumstances.

Ken was impressed that the prayers almost always included petition to bless and help the guards and the German people; he knew that was the true Christian attitude. Of course, the prayers always included asking God for a rapid conclusion of the war and release from the prison.

Eventually the Red Cross was able to negotiate placement of a chaplain in the compound, which proved to be a blessing to all who valued spiritual emphases. Ken regularly attended the services the chaplain held and felt uplifted by them.

Ken told the chaplain about his desire to be baptized and said he regretted there was not a river or at least a pool of water to make it possible. The chaplain told him although most of the baptisms referred to in the Bible were immersions, there were some instances in the Bible when people had been baptized when they were not at a river or other body of water. He cited Paul's baptism of the Philippian jailor and his family. He said although he preferred immersion, some churches offered the choice of immersion or having water poured or sprinkled on them.

On the basis of the chaplain's words, Ken asked to be sprinkled, and the chaplain complied with his wishes. Ken knew he had done the best he could under the circumstances, but it still seemed to him the symbolism of immersion more nearly identified with the death and resurrection of Jesus, and he knew he would ask to be immersed when the opportunity was available.

It was curious the way different prisoners tolerated their captivity. Some seemed to maintain an upbeat attitude regardless of the circumstances. Others seemed to be continuously despondent, and Ken was told of one man who deliberately crossed the perimeter warning wire knowing it would result in his death.

A couple of interesting men in Ken's compound always manifested good humor and seemed to be doing their best to improve everyone's morale. Their comedy acts were a welcome respite, and everyone enjoyed their clowning. Ken leaned their names were Don Johnston and Bob Vierra. They were together constantly, singing and joking.

Once they made themselves up as Hitler (with a fake mustache) and Mussolini, with chin and chest thrust out strutting around displaying the kind of irrational behavior they thought could be attributed to the persons they were portraying. Some prisoners enjoyed going along with the gag and gave a "heil Hitler" salute to the jokesters. They did make a point of staying out of sight of the guards in case they would take offense at their belittling of their leader.

They seemed to get pleasure out of making fun of a grim-looking guard whom they called "Stony Face." Sometimes when they saw him, in jest they would sing "You are My Sunshine" in two-part harmony, and the guard would give them a rather peculiar look and appeared to be wondering why they were singing. Ken had seen him often but had never seen the somber expression leave his face or heard him speak a word.

At one time the amateur comedians put up a notice announcing a collection was being taken to buy Stony Face some comic books for his birthday, with the thought he might coax a smile out of his face. Although there were other guards far more surly and disagreeable, for some reason they had singled out Stony Face as a target for their teasing.

Ken sometimes wondered what made him look so glum. He surely looked like he had some depressing problem on his mind. Ken's compassionate nature caused him to feel sorry for him, and he always treated him with respect, nodding with a smile when encountering him. Stony Face finally began to respond with a slight nod and the hint of a smile, and once it almost seemed like he winked.

Ken had not been in the camp long when he had taken a walk around the perimeter to see what was outside the compound. On one side, in the distance, he saw a plume of black smoke rising. In the next few days, he noted the smoke seemed to be constant, and he was curious about its significance. A fellow prisoner was going by, and Ken asked him if he had any idea what was going on there.

"I don't know for sure," the man said, "but most seem to think it is a concentration camp for Jewish people. You have probably heard the stories that Hitler is trying to kill all the Jews, and that may be one place where it is happening. Word has it the smoke is from a furnace they use to cremate the bodies."

Ken shuddered to think the Meyers might have been in one of the concentration camps if they had not left Germany when they did. He felt his anger rise and at that moment had a strong desire to get his hands on Hitler and his henchmen to repay them for all the suffering, sorrow, and death they had caused.

Ken enjoyed walking around the perimeter and did this often. It gave him a time of solitude when he could pray and meditate. On one such occasion, some words from a hymn he had heard came into his mind: "When we walk with the Lord in the light of His word, what a glory he sheds on our way." Ken started visualizing Jesus walking along beside him and many times felt his presence and would return to the barracks with his spirit renewed. One day, as Ken was reading Psalm 146, the words "The Lord sets the prisoner free" jumped out at him. Ken pondered the implications.

Sometimes a group of prisoners would get together and try to think of some way to escape. The security officers at their respective bases in England had told them if they became POWs one of their assignments was to try to escape, and the meetings were an attempt to comply with that instruction.

In Ken's compound, tunneling was pretty much out of the question. The barracks were blocked up about two feet above the ground, allowing visibility to the underside. Some thought they might be able to bribe a guard, but the camp authorities had established practices that would make it virtually impossible for a single guard to allow an escape. And then it was unlikely any guard would be willing to risk the consequences even if he could permit an escape. There just didn't seem to be any realistic options.

Ken heard that a few escapes had been attempted, but none had succeeded. But sometimes as he looked at the terrain on the other side of the fence, he fervently wished there was some way to get away from his captors and to freedom. On some crisp days when the wind was blowing toward them, they had heard very faint locomotive whistles coming from the direction of the concentration camp, and Ken thought if someone did escape, he might be able to go to the source of the whistle and sneak aboard a train as it was leaving.

There was a big difference in the guards. Most of them were either older men or combat veterans who had received disabling wounds and were probably used as guards so the younger, physically fit men would be available for combat duties. Some of them were surly and displayed an obvious hatred for their captives. These seemed to take pleasure in making the prisoners stand outside for extended periods for roll call, particularly in the coldest weather and any other hardship they could impose. A few guards were rather friendly and seemed to want to make prison life a little easier to bear.

Ken struck up a casual friendship with an elderly guard named Walter. Ken got the impression Walter heartily disliked his job as guard.

He had been a schoolteacher and seemed to take pleasure in helping Ken learn to become more proficient in use of the German language.

One day he gave Ken a textbook on German grammar. Unfortunately, it was not of much help to Ken, who had learned to converse pretty well in German but had difficulty trying to understand the words describing the subtleties of German grammar. However, it was welcomed by the instructor that was teaching German, and he used it in teaching grammar in some of his classes.

If Walter saw Ken when he was in the compound, he would stop and chat with him for a few minutes. Ken learned he had a son in the German army on the eastern front. The Russian army had acquired a reputation for being willing to sacrifice massive numbers of their troops to advance against the Germans. They were known for their brutality in battle and to any German soldiers who were captured. Walter was very concerned about his son's welfare.

He asked Ken how the American people felt about the war, and Ken told him he thought the country seemed united in its determination to continue the war until victory was achieved. Walter muttered something about hoping it would be soon. He guiltily looked around to make sure he had not been heard by any of the other guards.

Once, he slipped an apple into Ken's hand and shrugged off Ken's expression of thanks. Ken was pretty sure the German commandant, and most of the guards, would strongly disapprove of Water's gestures of friendship toward a supposed enemy. Walter was careful not to be too friendly when there were other guards near.

Occasionally Russian bombers would fly near the compound on their way to bomb Berlin or some other military target. Just after dark one night, Ken again heard the bombers and went to the door and scanned the sky. In the distance he could hear the sound of antiaircraft guns firing at the bombers. Some of the guards in the towers turned their searchlights into the night sky to help pinpoint the location of the bombers.

Suddenly, there was the spectacular sight of a bomber coming down in flames. At first Ken thought maybe it was going to crash into the prison compound and was prepared to run; then he saw it would land a short distance outside the fence. He watched entranced as the plane struck the ground; then there was the earsplitting sound of multiple bombs exploding. The ground shook as if there was a violent earthquake, and the towers swayed like reeds in the wind.

The searchlight on the guard tower near Ken went out as the tower tottered then slowly toppled toward the inside of the compound. He heard expressions of fear from the two guards as it was falling and their loud grunts as the tower smashed to the ground inside the fence. Ken knew they would be unconscious or at the least badly stunned.

A voice in Ken's head said, *Go!* He hesitated briefly, and again he heard, *Go now!* He went through the darkness toward the fence and groped for the tower's supporting timbers, now making a bridge across the fences, then silently made his way along one of them to freedom.

Chapter 12

With his heart thudding inside his chest, Ken made his way cautiously through the darkness to the forest on the side of the compound toward the concentration camp. After looking at the searchlight and the flames from the crashed bomber, he just couldn't see a thing. He desperately hoped his eyes would soon adjust to the darkness.

He felt a wave of sympathy for the bomber crew and wondered if any of them had been able to bail out before the crash. It brought back unpleasant memories of the demise of *Luck of the Irish*.

But he suddenly felt a surge of euphoria as he realized he was free after months of being under the thumb of his captors! However, his freedom could be very temporary unless he was able to get away from the compound before he was discovered. He was frustrated at not being able to go faster; it was difficult to avoid the obstacles even at the slow pace he was going. If he only had a flashlight to use when out of sight of the camp, it would sure help. At least the crashed bomber would probably attract the attention of the guards for a while, which would buy some time for him.

After a few minutes he stopped in a small clearing to look at the stars to make sure he was going in the right direction. He saw that he needed to change directions several degrees. Then he froze as he heard someone coming through the trees. He dropped and lay flat and hoped he was not visible in the darkness. Whoever it was did not seem to have a light. Surely if it was a guard, he would have a flashlight!

His heart was beating wildly; then he heard someone stumble over some unseen object and say softly, "Ow, blasted rock," with a distinctive British accent, to Ken's great relief. The man was making his way across the clearing and was going to pass within a few yards of Ken. Ken stood up and said softly, "Hello, friend!"

The man stopped abruptly and after a moment said, "It's a Yank you're being, I think!" He cautiously came toward Ken. "Just tell me if you are a Yank!"

"You are right. I'm a Yank, and I am sure glad that you are not a German." Ken could dimly sense the man was even taller and huskier than he was, and he had seemed ready to attack if he was not convinced Ken was not an enemy.

"Mate, you've almost scared me out of my pants. 'Ow did you get out?"

"Let's talk about that later," Ken said. "Right now we need to get away from here. Let's head over toward the concentration camp and see if we can catch a train that's leaving."

"No, mate, we don't want to go there straight away. They'll 'ave the dogs on us, you know. We need to lead them on a false trail for a while. I've been planning escape for over a year. I think I've got it down. I've seen a little rough map of this area that one of my chums got from a guard. Let's go over to a stream of water so we can lose the dogs; then we can make our way to th' camp. I'm Andy. Who might you be?"

"Ken."

Ken was suddenly grateful for the unexpected companion. He sure sounded like he knew what he was talking about, and Ken readily followed his lead. Andy said they would go north for a while as if heading toward the coast. As they cautiously made their way through the trees, their eyes began to adjust to the darkness, and soon a faint fringe of light began appearing on the eastern horizon. Before long the partial moon was providing enough light to be some help in making their way around obstacles. Sometime later, they came to a rocky outcropping, and Andy stopped.

"Now this looks like a good place to change directions. You wait 'ere. Don't move your feet. I'll be goin' on a bit; then I'll be walkin' backwards to you. Try to keep me on the same path I went on. If the footprints are overlappin',' it'll be 'arder to tell they're the same both ways."

Andy walked toward a tree about thirty feet ahead; then at the base he stopped and took a packet from his pocket that he said was tobacco that he had pulverized into fine powder. He emptied some of the tobacco there and backed up a few steps, emptying more as he went.

"This ought to give the dogs some trouble. It should muddle their sense of smell and take them some time to find our trail again," he said. "Now tell me if I'm not goin' straight back to where you are."

Ken guided him as he carefully backed to Ken.

"Now you step sideways onto the rocks," Andy instructed. Ken stepped up on the outcropping and out of Andy's way and let him have the lead. They went as far as they could on the outcropping, and when it was no longer above ground, they stepped on individual rocks as far as they could go then went east to find the stream Andy said he had seen on the map.

"I 'ope that crash keeps those blokes busy for a few hours," Andy said.

It was slow going through the forest with just the light of the moon while trying not to leave any evidence of their passing. They walked for over a half hour looking for the stream and were beginning to wonder if the map Andy had seen was a fake; then they were glad to hear the soft sound of flowing water.

Rocks at the edge of the water enabled them to get into the stream without leaving footprints on the bank. They went south up the stream, wading in water that sometimes was almost a foot deep. There were several spots that looked like good places to get out of the stream, but

Andy splashed on for twenty or thirty minutes. Finally he stopped, lifted one foot out of the water and let it drain, then stepped on a rock and let the other foot drain back into the stream. Ken copied his actions.

Leaving the stream behind, they went east on a course they hoped would take them to the concentration camp. They might have passed the camp on the north if it had not been for the putrid smell.

"The railroad must be on the south side," Ken said.

"I think you are right, mate," Andy said.

They made a wide circle around the camp, making sure to stay far enough away that the guards and any dogs would be not alerted, and eventually they came to some train tracks and followed them a little closer to the camp. They stayed in the forest out of sight of the compound but where they would be able to see a train when one came.

It was almost daylight, and they stretched out on the ground to rest while they waited. Andy asked Ken again how he had escaped. Ken described what had happened and asked Andy the same question.

"Like I told you, mate, I 'ave been planning escape for over a year. When the tower searchlight went up and the guards were lookin' for the Ruskie's planes, I thought I might never have a better chance. So I climbed the fence."

Ken looked at him in disbelief. "How in the world did you get over the barbed wire at the top of the fences and that bunch rolled up between the fences?"

"Oh, that was part of m' plannin.' I 'ad my socks on me 'ands, and I threw one of my blankets over th' first fence. Then I threw my other blanket over the nest in the middle and put my leather jacket over th' second fence. I tried to pull my jacket off, but it wouldn't come. Of course, I did get nicked a bit; th' socks and padding 'elped but weren't enough." He smiled as he held up his hands. In the dawning light, Ken could see some scratches on his hands and arms and tears in his clothes.

"Even with the help of covering the barbs, I think that was really a pretty amazing accomplishment. It would be hard enough to get over those fences even if there wasn't any barbed wire, but I'm sure glad you made it and are letting me share your escape plans! What did you plan to do from here on?" Ken asked.

"My plannin' was mainly about gettin' out and 'eading over 'ere to see about gettin' on a train to get some distance fast.

"Then we could 'ead for the Ruskie's lines. But with the fierce fightin' that's goin' on, we might 'ave a time getting through, and I think th' lines are quite a ways away. Of course, they are movin' toward us. That would be a 'elp.

"Another thought is to 'ead for Switzerland, but it's a long way too, and we'd 'ave to go through th' length of Germany. If we went north we'd come up against th' sea. We might be able to steal a boat and get across to Sweden, but there'd be a lot more people on the coast, and we'd 'ave more chance of bein' spotted. We might get some 'elp if we made it to France, but again we'd 'ave to go through a good part of Germany.

"Like I said, my plannin' was mostly around gettin' out and gettin' away from the camp. I don't really know what's best from 'ere on. What's your thoughts, mate?"

"Switzerland sure sounds like a good place to go if it is at all practical, but I think you're right that our first priority should be to get away from here," Ken said. "Maybe we should just do that and see what opens up. Getting on the train would certainly help us get away from here faster. Why don't we stick with that idea for a while to see if it's going to work out?

"Meanwhile, I feel pretty tired. Maybe we should try to get some sleep and rest while we are waiting to see if a train shows up. I think the train will whistle, judging from what we have heard, so we shouldn't have any trouble waking up."

"You're right, mate. We never know when we might 'ave to make a run for it, so we'd best be rested. Good to 'ave you along." Andy yawned and stretched. "My, what I wouldn't give for a Red Cross parcel ri' now," he said as he laid back with his hands behind his head.

Ken was impressed with Andy. He had demonstrated resourcefulness and seemed to be the ideal person to be with in a situation like the one they were in. Ken looked at him with gratefulness to God for this unexpected blessing.

He had a pleasant appearance and in spite of the minimal amount of food in the camp looked rather muscular. Ken suspected he had been a good athlete; being able to scale the prison's perimeter fences attested to that in addition to his physical appearance.

It didn't take long for them to fall asleep.

Ken awoke with a start. It was beginning to rain. He felt a surge of frustration. They had enough to worry about without getting wet and cold. Andy roused, yawned, and looked into the darkening sky.

"Looks like we are in for it, mate," he said cheerfully, "but then this could 'elp throw th' dogs off, so I'm ready for it."

Ken felt a little abashed at Andy's cheerful acceptance of another hardship. They moved to the shelter of a nearby tree that looked denser than the one they were under, hoping it would provide better shelter from the rain.

"'Ow did you come to be in th' 'otel back there, mate?" Andy asked.

Ken told him about being shot down and asked Andy about his story.

"I'm a Spitfire pilot," he said. "I went through th' blitz with no problem. But near two years ago, when I was on escort duty, some flak knocked out my engine. I bailed but didn't get my chute open quite soon enough and landed 'ard enough to break m' leg. The Germans did set th' leg proper and put me in the camp, and I've been itchin' to get out and get back up there again ever since!"

It was still raining a few hours later when they heard a train whistle, and they went a little closer to the compound where they could see the entrance. The train stopped outside the gate and whistled again. Ken and Andy couldn't tell what was inside the boxcars, but Ken shuddered as he realized it must be another load of Jews. Slowly the gate opened, the train went through, and the gate closed. Buildings along the fence blocked their view of the inside of the camp.

"Now, how long do you suppose it will be before it comes out?" Andy mused, not really expecting an answer.

Ken and Andy discussed where it would be best to get on the train. They wanted to be far enough away from the compound that the guards wouldn't see them, but they needed to get on before the train picked up too much speed. It had been traveling rather slowly when it approached the camp, but it would probably go faster when it left.

There was a slight bend in the track a little over a half mile away, and they decided that would be a good place to try to get on. The train should not have picked up too much speed by the time it reached that location. They would stay behind the trees until the locomotive had gone around the bend so the crew wouldn't see them get in one of the boxcars.

"But th' locomotive may come out last unless they 'ave a switching track inside," Andy said. "We just may 'ave to see how it goes before we decide where to get on. But it doesn't seem likely they would want to go far just pushin' the cars."

They agreed it was probable that the short train would be turned around inside the compound.

Then Ken had another depressing thought. "Andy, there was a caboose on the end of that train. There were probably some guards riding in it. That will make it even harder to get on without being seen!"

"You're right. There will be guards, but they probably won't be payin' much attention to th' scenery. It's less likely they would see us than th' engine crew. Why don't we just go a good part of the way to th' turn and wait to see 'ow the train looks before we decide for sure what to do?"

As they made their way toward the place they were going to wait, Andy said, "It does worry me some that they may be lookin' for us 'ere, but this seems th' only way to get some distance fast. I guess we'll just 'ave to take our chances but keep a sharp lookout."

They sat down to watch for the train, and Ken saw Andy was shivering badly. He took his jacket off and handed it to Andy. "Here, take this for a while," he said.

"No, it's awri,' mate. I'm no pansy. I've been cold before. But I do wish I'd spent a little more time getting my jacket off th' wire. But then that might 'ave made all th' difference. I could be back inside or lyin' there with a bullet in m' back."

Ken laid the jacket around Andy's shoulders. "Just take it long enough to warm up a little."

Andy offered no further objection.

Daylight was beginning to fade when the gate opened and the train slowly came out. Ken and Andy stood up, making sure they stayed out of sight, and got ready to get on the train when it came by. As they had hoped, it had been turned around; the engine was in the lead. It stopped, and three guards went through the dozen or so cars, apparently checking for Jewish escapees. One guard went into the caboose but came right back out. They seemed satisfied and to the surprise of Ken and Andy went back inside the compound. While they were making their inspection, two men—apparently the engineer and the fireman—got out of the locomotive cab and went into a little building outside the compound.

Soon smoke was coming from the stovepipe, and Andy said in a disappointed voice, "Why, I do believe they're going to stay th' night there."

"It sure looks like it," Ken said. "It's really too bad. With it starting to get dark, this would have been the perfect time of day to get aboard! I sure hate to stay around here much longer. But they will probably start out first thing tomorrow morning, so I guess if we are going to use the train to get away, we will just have to wait. But if we can't get on the train by sometime tomorrow morning, I think we ought to just start walking."

Ken was shivering now, and Andy handed Ken's coat back to him. Andy looked longingly at the open boxcar doors.

"What would you think of climbin' into one of those boxcars and gettin' out of the rain for a while after it gets good and dark?"

Ken considered the suggestion. He did dislike the idea of going that close to the grim-looking camp, but the rain and cold were going to be pretty hard to bear for whoever was not wearing the jacket.

"Well, the guards might search the cars again before the train leaves, but we should be okay if we make sure to get out of there before daylight. Let's do it!"

About an hour later, they quietly made their way to the boxcar farthest from the gate and climbed in. They followed the side of the boxcar toward the corner then slumped down against the wall. It did seem good to be out of the rain, but there was a stench that was rather unpleasant. They sat shoulder to shoulder for warmth. Ken spread his jacket across their chests.

"I 'ope there's a rat in here somewhere," Andy said softly. "If I can get m' hands on 'im, I'll eat 'im raw, fur and all!"

Ken gave a low laugh. "My, you *are* hungry. I guess now is the time we need to ask God to help us find something to eat."

"Now, mate, I'm afraid it's up to us," Andy said. "If we don't do for ourselves, we're just plain out of luck!"

"Andy, God has answered other prayers for me, and I believe he will answer one for us now," Ken said. Then he prayed softly, "Oh Lord, thank you for helping us so far. Now would you please provide us with some food? Andy is awfully hungry, and I am too. Please show Andy you are a God who cares and does answer prayer."

The two were weary. It seemed good to be out of the rain and in the relative warmth of the boxcar. They were soon asleep. Sometime later, Ken awoke with a start and was horrified to find a flashlight shining in his face. His spirits fell, and his heart began to race wildly! They had failed to escape after all.

Then he heard a low but urgent voice say, "Get out *now*. No noise. Danger is near!"

The flashlight quickly swung around to show some potatoes on the floor just inside the open door, and a hand held up a pocket knife, which was placed on top of the potatoes. In the reflected light, Ken could barely make out first a German uniform then the features of…Stony Face! Ken was astonished. When he had first seen the provisions and the German uniform, he immediately thought it had to be Walter, the friendly guard, but Stony Face? The flashlight disappeared, and Ken immediately woke Andy up.

"We've got to get out of here right now, but be very quiet," he said softly.

As he started to stand up, his hand brushed some cloth on the floor beside him. On an impulse he scooped it up then quickly made his way to the door and quietly slid out of the boxcar. When Andy came out, Ken pushed the cloth material into his hands and picked up the potatoes and the knife.

As they quickly made their way from the boxcar, they heard voices. Looking back over their shoulders, they saw two flashlights going down the line of boxcars, stopping to inspect each one.

They walked on softly, and when they were well beyond hearing distance, Andy said quietly, "That was a close one, mate. 'Ow did you know?"

Ken smiled in the darkness. "God sent an angel to warn us, and look what he brought!" With that he placed one of the large potatoes in Andy's hand.

Andy stopped short, feeling the potato. With a note of wonder, he said, "This does feel like a potato. Is it real, or am I dreamin'?"

Ken gave a low laugh. "Why don't you take a bite and see?"

He heard Andy do as he suggested. "'Tis real. That's for certain. And oh, is it good." He chewed that bite up, smacking his lips, and started to take another bite, then said, "Oh, but I'm not givin' you your turn!" He tried to hand it back to Ken.

"Keep it," Ken said. "We have two more, but maybe we had better make them last."

"My, but you are th' right chap to be with when you can get an angel to bring us food! What's this other bit you 'anded me?" Andy asked.

"I don't know," Ken said. "I felt it as I was getting up, and I thought it might be something we could use."

"'Ere. 'Old th' potato for a bit while I see what it is."

Ken heard Andy rustling around in the darkness.

"Why, I do believe it is an old topcoat! It's not really big enough, but it's going to be a 'elp!"

"Andy, those were our guards looking for us. They evidently thought we might head over this way and try to catch a train." Ken told him about seeing the guard from his prison compound. "We had better get out of here as soon as we can. Maybe we can try the train farther down the track if we can get a few miles from here."

"That's sense, mate. We're terrible lucky we weren't caught back there."

"God helped us!" Ken said quietly.

"Well," Andy paused. "You know, mate, you just might be right!"

The overcast skies hid the light of the moon, and the intense darkness made it difficult to try to go through the dense forest. After fumbling their way along for a while, they decided to just do their best to stay out of the rain while waiting for daylight. They found a tree that was fairly dry close to the trunk and sat down. Ken's pulse was beginning to settle down after their narrow escape but was still higher than normal.

The time they had spent in the boxcar had allowed them to get several hours of sound sleep, and they felt pretty well-rested. When the sky started to lighten, they made their way farther away from the camp. It was slow going at first, but the thought of their narrow escape motivated them to go as fast as they could.

They waded up a small stream for a while then finding a good place to get out left the stream behind. The sky lightened more as they walked on; then, to their relief, the rain stopped, and the sun began to break through the clouds. Andy was in the lead, and Ken was amused at the way he looked with the tattered overcoat around his shoulders. Apparently the coat had been in such bad shape the owner had discarded it and the German guards had ignored it, but Andy seemed to be glad to have it.

As the clouds dissipated, the sun came out in full strength, and they sat on the trunk of a fallen tree for a while and basked in its warmth. Andy had saved a small piece of his potato but decided he would finish it. He put it in his mouth and chewed it for some time before swallowing it. Ken also ate some of a potato. They heard some squirrels chattering and saw one go to a fallen pinecone and began chewing on it. Suddenly Andy stood up.

"I think that little blighter is try'n' to get somethin' to eat out of that pinecone. Isn't there supposed to be some kind of nut in there?" As he approached, the squirrel scampered away with an angry chatter. Andy picked up the pinecone and shook it. Several pine nuts fell out, and Andy picked one up and ate it. "'Ey, mate, these things are good! Let's gather some."

With that he picked up another cone and started removing the kernels. Ken joined him and was impressed with the tasty little morsels. They ate several and put as many as they could gather in a short time in their pockets. They were a real treat.

As they started on their way, Andy said, "Do you think God sent that squirrel?"

Ken smiled. "Very probably!"

"Well, if he keeps 'elpin,' we just may make it through yet!"

They spent the night under the low branches of a dense spruce tree. Ken had cut the last potato in two and had given Andy half. Throughout the day, they had not been able to resist nibbling on their half, and by the time they stopped for the night, neither of them had any left. The pine nuts they had saved were also almost gone, but they were pretty sure they would be able to find some more.

There was something nagging at Ken's mind. He just couldn't put his finger on it. He thought again of the enigma of Stony Face and the reasons for his help. It was all very perplexing, but he felt a deep gratitude toward him and wished there was some way he could repay him for his kindness and prayed that God would reward him abundantly. But what had prompted him to take the risk of helping them?

He shook his head, but suddenly he realized what was bothering him! That warning in the boxcar had been in *English*! It just didn't make sense.

When the escapees awoke the next morning, they were both thirsty.

There were quite a few streams in the area, so they went in search of one. A short distance away they came to a small stream, and as Ken knelt to drink, a large fish darted away. He wondered how raw fish would taste. Then he had a thought.

"Andy, do you have any matches?" he asked.

"That I do, mate. I'm a smoker without any fags. But I do have the matches."

"I wonder if we might be able to spear that fish," Ken said.

Andy expressed his doubts but was ready to give it a try.

Ken finished drinking then looked around until he found a slender seedling tree that was a few feet long. He cut it down and trimmed off the branches. He sharpened one end and handed it to Andy, who had been watching with interest. Andy immediately went to the stream. Ken started cutting another spear for himself, and he heard Andy attempt to spear the fish several times. Ken had just finished his spear when he heard a whoop from Andy. He turned to see Andy on his knees, holding a large, wiggling fish.

Andy stood up laughing. "I wasn't havin' any luck w' the spear, so when I saw 'im go under a rock, I reached down and caught 'im wi' m' 'ands!"

They were reluctant to build a fire, but the thought of having fish for breakfast made them willing to take the chance. Ken figured they must have gone ten or eleven miles from the concentration camp, but as an added margin of safety, they walked on for nearly two hours before searching for wood to build a fire.

They gathered several sticks of wood, and Ken whittled off the wet part and made a small pile of dry shavings, which Andy lit. After a blaze was going, they were able to put on some damp sticks, which slowly ignited. Finally the fire was hot enough that they were able to add larger sticks that were finally ablaze.

While the fire was getting started, Ken had cleaned the fish, silently thanking God again for the knife and the guard's kindness. Then they rigged up a spit to hold the fish over the fire while it cooked. The smell of the cooking fish was torturous.

The fish tasted delicious. Although it didn't completely satisfy their hunger, it did raise their spirits. With the fish, the potatoes, and the pine nuts they had eaten, they felt strengthened.

They continued going in a southerly direction parallel to the railroad, thankful for every mile that four days of walking had put between them and their guards. Still hoping for an opportunity to get on a train, they stayed fairly close to the railroad.

The next day they heard the sound of an approaching train. They eagerly went close to the track and lay down behind a tree to stay out of sight of the locomotive crew. As the locomotive was passing, it seemed to Ken it was traveling too fast to try to get aboard the train.

Andy was more optimistic. "I think we might just be able to catch that beast if we run our best! Now if there is just an open boxcar!" He started to stand up as he looked down the train. Suddenly he fell flat and said, "Stay low, mate! There are guards sitting on top of the caboose with rifles in their hands!"

The train passed, and Andy drew a breath of relief. "That was close! If I had stepped out a little farther, those guards would 'ave probably seen me! I guess that's one train we don't want to ride on!"

As they continued walking, they wondered if it was them the guards had been looking for or if there was some other reason they were posted on top of the caboose.

"I wonder if they saw our tracks in the mud outside the boxcar we were in?" Ken said.

"That could be, mate; we will have to be real careful of our choice of trains."

The next day a stream joined the railroad course. There were some dense bushes on the other side of the stream, and Andy jumped across to look at them.

"Say, mate, there're some striped, green-looking things on these bushes. Would you know if they are good to eat?"

Ken joined Andy and said, "Why, I think that's called a gooseberry! I saw a picture of them in a farm magazine in a hospital waiting room and thought that was really a strange name for a berry. They get ripe later than other berries. I didn't think they looked very good because they are green, but they are supposed to be edible!" He picked one and popped it in his mouth. He made a wry face and said, "Wow, they are kind of sour but don't really taste all that bad."

Andy picked one, ate it, and said, "Well, I've eaten worse things! They are certainly better than nothing."

They stayed by the bush until they had eaten all they wanted. They were not nearly as satisfying as the fish had been, but they were grateful for them.

The railroad and the stream followed the same general course for some time but began to diverge.

"Why don't we stay with the stream for a while and see if there might be something else growing along it that we could eat?" Andy suggested.

As they followed the stream, it was not long before the terrain began to get wilder and more difficult to traverse. They entered a gulch strewn with large boulders and fallen trees, and it was rather slow going as they clambered over the obstacles in their path. Andy was enjoying the challenge and burst out jovially singing, "It's a long way to Tipperary..." but stopped suddenly.

"Oops. I don't suppose it's likely anyone is near, but I 'ad better be quiet in case there is. This would be a jolly good area to 'ide out in for a while if we 'ad some rations. Look. There is a cave we could stay in up there."

A little ways ahead of them, a few yards up the steep bank of the gully, there was an inviting opening. Andy veered off their path to inspect the cave. When he reached the entrance, he peered in and said, "It's a nice place, mate. Too bad we can't—"

Suddenly there was a loud growl, and Andy almost fell over backwards. He came sliding down the bank and began leaping from rock to rock as a big brown bear appeared in the mouth of the cave. Andy was laughing uproariously.

"Guess we wouldn't be interested in sharing space with that furry chap. Let's get out of 'ere in case 'e feels like socializing! 'E probably doesn't get many visitors!"

Ken was torn between fear and amusement. It was highly entertaining to see Andy's reaction to his encounter with the bear, but he was wondering if the bear might be looking for some more food in preparation for his hibernation. As quickly as they could, they crossed the stream and scrambled over the jumble of fallen trees and rocks away from the cave and its inhabitant. He felt relieved as he looked back over his shoulder from time to time and saw no evidence of pursuit. When they were well away from the cave, they stopped and both had a good laugh.

When they started on, Andy said, "Maybe it's time we got out of this ravine with all the obstructions. Let's climb out and go along the ridge for a while."

Ken was ready for a change, and he readily agreed. As Andy started up the bank, Ken said, "I'm going to get a drink before we leave the stream." He lay on his stomach and started drinking.

He heard Andy say, "'Ey, there's some bees. Maybe we can get some honey!"

Ken finished drinking and looked up in time to see Andy start to poke a big, gray, inverted dome-shaped object off a tree branch with a stick. "No, Andy. Wait!" Ken yelled.

It was too late. Andy looked at the nest lying on the ground, apparently still expecting to find some honey.

"Run! I think those are hornets!" Ken yelled.

Ken had been stung in Mr. Dalton's barn, and Bill had pointed out an object he said was a hornet's nest that he was going to have to get rid of, and it looked just like the one Andy had knocked down.

Angry hornets swarmed out of the nest and began attacking their adversary. Andy immediately took flight and soon disappeared over the edge of the gully, running hard and swatting frantically at his attackers. Ken heard some yelps of pain as some of the hornets expressed their outrage with a painful sting.

Ken made a wide berth around the fallen nest and went a little way in the direction he had last seen Andy going. He was sure Andy would be coming back and knew he might miss him if he went too far away. About fifteen minutes later, he saw Andy coming toward him with one eye almost swollen shut, a lopsided grin, and several red bumps on his face.

"Well," Ken said, trying to keep a straight face, "shall we go back and see if we can get some more honey?"

"You know, mate, I've decided I can get along very nicely without any honey," Andy said with a broad but badly distorted smile. "Those little beasties were dreadfully unfriendly. I would have much rather been chased by th' bear!"

Ken laughed but knew Andy was in pain and wished he could offer some relief.

They made their way back toward the railroad. As they started over a low hill bordering the track, Andy suddenly stopped and held out his hand to stop Ken and motioned for him to be quiet. They both lay prone and watched as two German soldiers were walking north along the tracks, obviously looking for something.

After the soldiers were out of sight, Ken and Andy looked at each other.

"It sure looks like they may be after us!" Ken said.

"I think you are right, mate. We 'ad better not get too close to the railroad for a while, but I think we should still follow its general direction."

As they continued their southerly course a few days later, they saw they were approaching a town. They made a wide berth around the town, keeping well out of sight in the forest knowing that the prison commandant could have put out a notice to communities near the prison to be on the lookout for the escaped prisoners. They came to a small clearing where there was a small, rather rustic cabin.

"'Old up, mate," Andy said. "Let's see if we might be able to go in and get some food."

They lay on the ground at the edge of the clearing trying to determine if anyone was in the cabin. They were talking together in low tones when they suddenly heard a sound behind them. They looked around quickly and saw a little old man with a beard just a few paces away. The pine needles on the ground had silenced his footsteps. He was bent over carrying a small deer over his shoulder and an ancient rifle in his right hand.

He had his eyes on the ground, and he looked up just as Andy stood. He was obviously startled and dropped both the deer and the gun and quickly turned around and fled at a surprising rate considering how old he appeared to be.

"Well now, that's what I call real service," Andy said. "Deliverin' our supper right to us!" He quickly picked up the deer and glanced at the gun. "Since I'm goin' to accept 'is gift of this food, I'll leave 'is gun so 'e can get some more. Besides, we don't have any bullets, so it wouldn't do us any good. We'd best be on our way, mate. 'E is probably goin' to raise th' local constable. My, but this will make some fine fare!"

Ken felt bad about taking the old fellow's game, but the prospect of having some meat to eat was really appealing.

"Why don't we 'ead more in th' direction of th' Russian lines," Andy said. "I think there will be less people in that direction than goin' south."

Ken had pretty well memorized a map of Germany, and he knew part of the Baltic Sea extended south for quite a distance from where he estimated they were, so they adopted a southeasterly path, which he thought might get them around the southernmost part of the sea in the least time.

Both the thought of possible pursuit and looking forward to a real feast prompted them to hurry as fast as they could, trying not to leave any evidence they had passed that way. They were glad they were in a heavily forested area that screened them from observation, although the area seemed to be sparsely populated, and it was not likely they would be seen even without all the trees.

Ken estimated they had gone nine or ten miles when they decided to make camp for the night. The anticipation of a good meal prompted them to stop sooner than they might have otherwise. They gathered some firewood and built a fire ring out of some stones. Then with difficulty they cut one of the hind quarters from the deer and speared it through along the bone with a stick, which was to serve as a spit. The stick had a fork in one end that they thought could be used to turn the unbalanced load with the use of another two-foot-long stick between the forks to apply leverage.

They built a low fire and placed some bigger rocks on both sides of the pit to rest the spit on. Andy took over turning the spit while Ken kept the fire supplied with wood. The smell of the cooking meat was tantalizing, and they could hardly wait for it to finish cooking.

Ken was increasingly more thankful for Andy. He was really a pleasant person and had a natural exuberance that was appealing. He seemed to be really enjoying their escape experiences. Again, Ken felt he couldn't have had a better companion to share this adventure with. He looked at Andy and could imagine him in his plane pursuing a German fighter. He asked, "Andy, did you like being in combat?"

Andy seemed a little surprised with the question. He closed his eyes as if imagining he were back in the air. "Mate, just flying a Spit is almost as good as being in 'eaven; then the fun of th' chase is even better. I just don't think there is anything more stimulatin'! I can 'ardly wait to get back up there!"

"Wasn't it pretty scary trying to outmaneuver the German planes?"

Andy laughed. "It seems to me there are two kinds of fighter pilots, sort of like 'awks and sparrows. You can tell th' sparrows are always worrying about getting shot down, and to them it is probably scary. The 'awks just can't wait to get in the game and have a jolly good time. I was a 'awk. The most fun is when th' bloke in the Messerschmitt is good enough to give some real competition!"

Ken recalled seeing Spitfires flitting around the sky in combat with German planes and wondered how many of the pilots had fit Andy's description of a hawk. "Were there many sparrows in your squadron?" he asked.

"No, not many. In the first place, not many of that kind got into flying Spits, and those that did get in usually didn't last too long in combat," Andy said.

Ken thought about Andy's implication that his squadron was made up mainly of "hawks." He doubted if many of them had the same level of enthusiasm for combat that Andy seemed to. He wondered how many of Andy's characteristics he had inherited from his parents.

"What kind of occupation does your father have?" Ken asked.

"'E is a tugboat captain, but 'is real love was playing football. I think you Yanks call it soccer," Andy said. "'E sort of gave that up about the time th' war started, partly because of 'is age, I suppose. 'E was a pretty well-respected player in 'is time."

"Did you play football?" Ken asked.

"I played a bit, but I really liked track and field sports better. I trained for th' decathlon competition in the 1940 Olympics, but they were cancelled because of th' war."

That fit with Ken's impression of Andy. "Do you have any brothers or sisters?" he asked.

"No," Andy said. "I was an only child, and I suppose my folks did spoil me badly."

"What part of England did you live in?" Ken asked. "Your accent sounds like some I heard in London."

"Well, I suppose I do 'ave a bit of th' Cockney accent. I did live in Chiswick, which is a suburb of London. Of course, I lived in Dover until I was about six, but that was a long time ago. 'Ow did you like London? We Brits are pretty proud of it."

"I was only there once on a three-day pass, but I thought it was fascinating," Ken said. "There were so many famous things to see and such interesting history. Saint Paul's Cathedral, the Tower of London, and Buckingham Palace were especially interesting. We would have liked to have seen the king, but I guess he probably stays inside the palace most of the time. Did you ever see him?"

"Aye, I've seen 'im many times," Andy said. "I was one of th' palace guards for a little over a year before th' war but quit to join th' RAF when Hitler started 'is rantin.'"

"Do you mean you were one of those guys with the red jackets and the bearskin hats?"

"That I was, mate. It's a pretty posh job. I may just see if I can get back on when th' war's over. I don't expect there will be much demand for Spitfire pilots."

"Wow! That's really something! You look the part. All of those guys look big like you are. Aren't those hats uncomfortable?" Ken asked.

"They can be a bit grotty if th' weather is 'ot, but most of th' time they are no problem."

"That hat makes you guys look like you are about ten feet tall! Actually, the whole uniform is pretty impressive. How about Churchill? Did you ever see him?" Ken asked.

"I did see 'im when 'e once came to th' palace when I was on duty. To my notion, 'e's a great man. We all love good old George, but it's Winnie that knows 'ow to get us out of th' mess we're in!" Andy said.

The aroma of the roasting meat made them even hungrier, and they started cutting chunks of meat that were still pretty rare from the outside of their roast. They didn't have any salt or other seasonings to put on it, but it tasted wonderful just the way it was. They finished cooking the rest of it and slept that night with very full stomachs.

The next morning they had some more venison for breakfast. They had resumed their journey when early in the afternoon Andy stopped suddenly.

"I 'ope I'm wrong, but I think I 'eard a dog," he said, and he stood still listening.

Then Ken heard the unmistakable sound of a hound baying.

"Well, things were getting a little boring. I guess it's time we 'ad a little excitement! That little man that gave us the deer must have put them on to us," Andy said. "First thing, we need to stash this meat and remember where it is so we can come back and get it unless we get too far away. I'll carry the rest of the leg we cooked, but we will probably have to make a run for it, and taking the rest of it might slow us down."

Ken was amazed at the calm way Andy accepted this turn of events, but it did seem to be characteristic of him. Andy went off at right angles to their path for a few yards and placed the rest of the deer carcass on a tree limb that was as high as he could reach.

The baying sounded like it was still quite a ways away, but now they could tell there was more than one dog.

Andy returned and said, "Come on, mate. We need to try to confuse the dogs by tramping around a bit."

He started walking around randomly, making a wide jumbled path, crossing over his trail many times. Ken followed his example. Then Andy leaped as far as he could from their trail and started off at right angles for a ways then headed back toward the baying parallel to the path they had taken.

"Let's see what we are up against. We are on the downwind side, so the dogs won't smell us."

Ken really wanted to go in the opposite direction, but Andy seemed so confident in what they were doing that Ken was willing to go along. They had gone about a quarter of a mile, and the dogs sounded like they were fairly close. They lay down behind some trees, and after they heard the dogs pass them, Andy went for a look at their pursuers.

He came back and said, "Only two dogs and two men with packs and rifles. That's not bad odds! Let's go, mate!"

With Ken following, Andy started off in a new direction.

"A nice stream would be would be a 'elp. 'Ope there's one close," he said cheerfully.

They walked rapidly away, and the sound of baying grew fainter. A few minutes later, the baying had a different sound.

"Well, I think they're where we milled around a bit. It'll take 'em a while to work it out." But a little later the baying had a new note of excitement. "It does sound like they found our trail already, but I think they must 'ave turned one of the dogs loose to work it out. I think we can run faster than the men with their equipment, but the dog will probably catch up to us unless we can find a stream."

For the next twenty minutes, Ken and Andy ran, but the baying kept getting closer. They broke out of the forest to the shore of a shallow lake.

"This could be a 'elp. Let's wade out a bit."

They went about fifteen feet into the lake to where the water was about three feet deep. They could tell one dog was very near, but the baying from the second dog seemed to be quite a ways away.

"This should do it if th' dog will just come at us right away. We need to get rid of 'im before the others catch up. I just 'ope that dog will cooperate. 'Ere, mate. 'Old this a while, and stand back a bit." He handed Ken the rest of the deer hindquarter.

The dog came running out of the forest and out into the water. "That's it, boy. Just keep comin,'" Andy said as the dog swam toward them snarling.

Andy had tied the arms of the old topcoat loosely around his neck when they started running. Now he removed it and held it in his right hand and held his left arm out to the dog as if inviting him to bite it. When the dog reached him, Andy threw his tattered topcoat over his head, grabbed him, and held the struggling animal under the water until it went limp.

He held it under a little longer then said, "Well, that's one problem down, but I don't think it would work for th' men since they 'ave guns. Let's get out of 'ere! I think we can outrun those blokes, but they could call in some reinforcements and 'ead us off. We've got to find some way to get rid of 'em. I just wish we had a couple rifles! If it comes to it, maybe I'll let 'em chase you while I get behind 'em and way-lay one and take 'is gun! Why didn't I try that when we were b'hind them before?" Andy mused. "I wasn't thinkin' proper!"

The thought horrified Ken. "No, Andy, let's not do that! You might get killed!"

"Well, let's 'old off a while and see if we can think of something else."

They quickly waded out of the lake and headed off in a new direction. A few minutes later, through an opening in the forest, they saw a dirt road.

"Guess we want to stay away from th' road," Andy said, and he started in a different direction.

"Wait, Andy. I think I saw a vehicle, and I don't think anyone was in it!" Ken said.

"Well now, that is something we should check out," Andy said, and they went toward the road until it became evident Ken was right.

They cautiously approached, looking carefully to see if there was anyone around. Then they saw a soldier two or three hundred yards away walking down the narrow dirt road away from the rear of the vehicle holding something to his ear.

"I think that guy is trying to get those other two on a walkie-talkie and can't find a place where he can get reception!" Ken said.

"I 'ope he keeps 'avin' trouble. Let's just see if he was kind enough to leave th' keys!" Andy said.

Going to the vehicle, they were elated to find that the engine was still running.

"'Op in, mate. Let's see I can figure out how to drive this foreign beast!" Andy said.

He released the brake, put the car in gear, and spun the wheels as he accelerated. Ken glanced back to see the soldier turn quickly around with his mouth open.

"Hit it, Andy! He has spotted us!" Ken said.

"Keep your 'ead down, mate! There's liable to be some bullets coming this way."

By the time the soldier had recovered from his surprise and taken his pistol from its holster, the vehicle was traveling away from him at a rapid clip. The only shot that came close went through the center of the windshield.

"This is more like it!" Andy said, and Ken felt jubilant. "By this time I 'ave no idea which direction we're 'eading, but at least we're putting space between us and those German blokes."

They traveled along at a fast pace for about fifteen minutes when they came to a corner that had a high embankment dropping off on one side. Andy stopped.

"I think this might be a good place to 'ide this thing. There's lots of growth out there that should screen it from anyone comin' along the road. I would like to keep going in it, but that bloke with th' walkie-talkie may have called in some reserves to intercept us. You get out, and I'll take it over the edge and make sure it's where nobody can spot it."

"Okay, be careful!" Ken said as he got out. The steep incline looked rather treacherous.

Andy eased the vehicle over the embankment. After sliding down to more level terrain, he slowly drove the vehicle though the trees farther away from the road. Soon he came leaping back up where Ken was waiting. They quickly rubbed out the tracks, leaving no evidence the vehicle had left the road at that point.

"Now we need to get out of 'ere," Andy said. "We've been lucky no one has come by and seen us with th' lorry."

They quickly went into the forest until well out of sight of the road.

They sat down to eat some of their venison and decide which direction they should go. They knew it was not practical to go back and get the deer carcass, but they really hated to abandon it.

"At least we have enough on this hindquarter for a few more meals. After it's gone, I'm sure God will provide something else for us, just like he has done so far," Ken said. He looked at his watch, the sun, and the direction the shadows were cast and pointed to the southeasterly direction they wanted to continue going.

For the next few days, they were extra careful to avoid leaving any tracks or trampled undergrowth and hoped their pursuers had given up looking for them. Several times they waded along a stream for a while in case some more dogs were on their trail. In a few days, all the edible portions of the venison had been eaten, and they took the precaution of burying the bones and scraps and covering the dirt with leaves. Eventually they began to feel pretty confident that they had eluded their pursuers. It seemed good not to have to keep straining to listen for the sound of another dog.

On an unusually warm day, they came upon a pretty beaver pond.

It looked inviting, and Andy looked at it for a few moments then said, "I think I'm goin' to take a bath. It's been a long time since I 'ad a decent one, and I worked up quite a sweat when we were runnin' from th' dog."

"I guess I'd better take one too," Ken said. "You wouldn't want to be around me if I was still sweaty when you are nice and clean!"

They left their clothes on the bank, and Andy dove into the water with a splash.

When he surfaced, he emitted a loud, "Whoo! That's bracing!"

Ken went in a little more cautiously and found the water to be very cold but not unbearable. It did really feel good, and Ken agreed that it was refreshing. They spent a few minutes splashing around in the pond much to the annoyance of the beaver who had apparently built the dam. When they climbed out of the water, they felt pretty cold as they danced around on the bank until they dried off a bit. It seemed a shame to have to put their unwashed clothes back on, but they didn't have any choice.

Chapter 13

The next day they came upon a railroad track going a little more easterly than they had been traveling and started following it. Late in the afternoon, they saw a farm where there was a large barn and several other structures that looked like coops and pens, implying the presence of chickens and other animals.

"Let's stay near 'ere for the night. When it's dark I'll sneak in there and see if I can get a chicken or something to eat," Andy said.

Having some chicken really sounded good to Ken, and he readily agreed. "Shall I go with you?" he asked.

"No, mate. I think just one of us would make less noise and have less chance of gettin' shot," Andy said.

An hour or so after the light in the house blinked out, Andy went off into the night toward the farm. Ken prayed he would get back without harm and that he would be successful in his search for food. It would be pretty difficult to find anything in the dark.

Sometime later, Ken cringed as he heard a dog barking wildly. This continued for several minutes; then the barking gradually tapered off and finally ceased. Ken waited anxiously and nearly an hour later was about ready to conclude the farmer had captured Andy when he heard a low whistle. With relief, he answered with his own whistle. It was not long before Andy appeared.

"Lost me way, mate, but it was worth th' trip, even though that blasted dog made such a ruckus that I gave up getting a chicken!"

He had used the old coat to bundle up several ears of corn he had taken from a corn crib. The corn was dry and the kernels were hard, but when they held it in their mouths a while, it softened enough to chew up. They both ate three ears then lay down to sleep with their hunger pretty well satisfied.

They continued to follow the train track that offered the remote possibility of faster travel than walking. With the lapse of time since their escape, they decided it should be safe to again think about trying to get on a train. For three more days, they walked near the track, which was in general going toward the southeast. They saw only one eastbound train in that time, and they had no chance of getting aboard.

Just before noon on the fourth day, they saw they were approaching a town. The train would probably stop or at least slow down as it went through the town, and there might be a good place to get on before it picked up speed as it left the town.

They circled the town, keeping out of sight, and made their way back to the track. There just didn't seem to be any place to wait to get on a train without being seen. Then too, they had no idea how long it would be until a train came by, so they continued walking.

When they were a few miles away from the town, they heard a train coming toward them from the southeast, and they stopped behind some trees where they wouldn't be seen by the train crew. Then, as the train neared them, they also heard the sound of a rapidly approaching airplane. Soon a Russian fighter plane appeared and began to strafe the locomotive. It made one pass with no visible effect then turned around for a second try. The train had just passed Ken and Andy.

There was a loud noise as the locomotive blew up and derailed, causing several of the boxcars to derail and overturn. Some of the box-cars had burst open, and bedraggled people began emerging. Ken real-ized they were Jews headed for the concentration camp. Most began running toward the forest, while some started opening the doors of the boxcars that were still closed.

Suddenly a dazed-looking German guard who had apparently been in the overturned caboose appeared, and started shooting at the flee-ing Jews. Some of them were obviously hit and dropped to the ground. Then another guard appeared from the other side of the train and started shooting. Those who had not fallen continued to flee into the forest.

The thought that the Meyers could have been among those Jews who were being killed made Ken's anger suddenly rise up in a terrible wrath, and without thinking he ran toward the side of closest guard, who was forty or fifty yards away.

The guard was focused on preventing the Jews from escaping, so he didn't see Ken until he was just a few feet away. He started to swing his gun toward Ken, but Ken seized it, wrenched it from his grasp, and with strength generated by a mighty fury struck him with a skull-crushing blow to the side of the head with the butt. He collapsed in a heap, and Ken thought he probably had killed him.

He turned to see the other guard glance at him and start to turn toward him with his raised gun. Ken quickly brought up the gun in his hands and fired just before the guard did. Ken's shot struck the guard in his shoulder, and he dropped the gun as he fell to the ground.

The guard's shot had struck the ground about thirty feet in front of Ken, but he was startled to hear a bullet whistle over his head from behind him. He turned around and saw there was a third guard lying on the ground with Andy standing over him. Andy picked up the stunned guard's rifle, calmly placed it against his head, and pulled the trigger. Then, seeing the guard Ken had shot struggling to reach his gun, Andy quickly made his way to him and shot him through the heart. He had a big smile as he watched Ken approach.

"Oh, that felt good! I've jus' been achin' to get back at these blighters," he said.

Ken grasped his hand and shook it. "Thanks, Andy! You showed up just in time. If you hadn't knocked that guard over, I would probably be dead!"

"Oh, it was me pleasure," he said. "Just show me another and I'll take him on!"

Ken looked again at the soldier he had clubbed. His anger had dissipated, and he felt a slight pang of remorse. He sort of hoped he wasn't really dead, although he appeared to be. He was an enemy, but he was a human being God had created; it gave Ken no pleasure to believe he had ended the man's earthly existence. Then he wondered how many Jews had escaped being killed by his intervention, and he felt better.

They picked up two of the rifles, and Andy searched the guard's bodies for ammunition. The soldier that Andy had knocked down was a big man. While Andy was gathering his ammunition, he looked at the man's warm-looking jacket and said, "Well now, this bloke won't be needin' 'is jacket anymore, and it should fit me fine. It is in a little better shape than the coat you gave me!" With that he removed the jacket and put it on with a satisfied look. "My, but this is nice," he said. "Glad I didn't put any 'oles in it!"

They looked at the four Jews lying on the ground and found they were all dead. It was probable that some who had fled were wounded. The soldiers were either drunk or shaken badly from the overturned caboose, or their aim toward the fleeing Jews would have resulted in more deaths. They also saw the bodies of the engineer and fireman who had been killed by bullets from the Russian fighter or when the locomotive overturned.

All the Jews who had been fleeing had disappeared, but suddenly they heard a faint call. They made their way toward the voice and found it was coming from one of the boxcars lying on its side. They climbed to the doorway, which was now on top. Some of the Jews had opened the door but apparently left when the guard started shooting. Most of the occupants had managed to get out, but they found the cries had come from a rather young-looking woman and a child that was three or four.

It was startling to see a woman and child after so many months of seeing only men, and for a few moments, Ken and Andy stood looking at them with dazed expressions. The woman seemed to be frightened and held her child close as if trying to protect her. She had apparently been hoping that her cries for help would be answered by some of her fellow Jews, and she wasn't sure what to expect from the foreigners.

Andy dropped into the car, gently extracted the child from her mother's arms, and lifted her up to Ken. The young woman was obviously anxious to rejoin her child and offered no resistance when Andy motioned he was going to lift her out, but when he did she gasped with pain. There was blood dripping off her shoe; the side of the boxcar had splintered, and some sharp ends of wood had pierced her leg.

As Ken helped her to the boxcar surface, he tried to allay the fear on her face by saying in German, "Don't be afraid. We will try to help you."

He was rewarded with a slight, rather strained smile. He waited until Andy climbed out then dropped to the ground, and Andy lowered the woman and child to him.

From his vantage point on top of the boxcar, Ken had looked toward the town they had circled and knew people there must have heard all the noise and that someone would probably be coming to investigate. In a short time, as he had feared, they heard the sound of an engine and looked up to see a rapidly approaching motorcycle with a sidecar. The occupants were German soldiers.

Andy said, "Get on the other side, mate. I'll 'and them over."

Ken jumped across the coupling to the northeast side of the track, and Andy lifted the child to Ken then helped the woman across.

"Get them out of 'ere, mate. I'm going to settle it with these blokes. I'll catch up."

Ken saw him pick up the rifles and settle himself in a defensive position. Ken wished Andy would just flee to the forest with them but knew it wouldn't do any good to try to talk him out of staying. But it would be good to know the Germans were out of commission and not able to pursue them or the fleeing Jews. When they saw the dead German guards, they would certainly want to try to get revenge with whoever had killed them.

"For goodness sake, don't stay long, and be careful," Ken said as they left. He was worried about Andy's enthusiasm in being able to be on the offensive again. He seemed ready to take on the whole German army.

Ken picked up the child and took the rather disoriented woman by the arm, and they hurried into the trees. The woman was limping, and they couldn't go as fast as Ken wanted to. As they went deeper into the forest, they heard several shots. Ken prayed Andy was all right.

After they had gone a few hundred yards into the forest, Ken told the woman to wait there and that he would be back after he checked on his friend. He made his way toward the wrecked train and was aghast to see that more German soldiers had arrived. Some were looking at the Germans who had been killed.

Peering through the branches of a tree, Ken scanned the area but couldn't see Andy anywhere. He assumed he must have come into the forest before the new group of soldiers had showed up and was probably somewhere near. He must have left because he wasn't shooting at the Germans. But which way had he gone?

As Ken started to leave, a German officer straightened up from looking at a body and started pointing into the forest in several different directions including toward Ken. As the soldiers began to move in the directions the officer had pointed, Ken knew he better get the woman and her child farther away. He hurried back, quickly picked up the child, and told the woman they needed to leave immediately.

Their progress was slow. Ken had the woman hold on to his arm, and that did help to go a little faster. They came to a small stream, and the woman pulled away, knelt, and cupped water in her hand for her child to drink, then hurriedly drank some herself.

As they went their way, Ken kept scanning the forest, desperately looking for some sign of Andy. He wanted to call out for him but didn't know how far into the forest the German soldiers would come, and he certainly didn't want to attract their attention. He berated himself for not pointing out to Andy the direction they were going to go. He considered going back a ways looking for him again but knew it could be a risk, and it was unlikely he would find him in the dense forest.

They had been walking for over two hours. By that time the woman seemed exhausted, and they sat down to rest. Ken asked her if she had been injured any place else besides her leg. She said she had been shaken up and felt rather bruised in places, but she was glad she had been holding her daughter and had managed to keep her from getting hurt.

Ken told her his name and asked for theirs. The woman said she was Deborah, and her daughter's name was Hannah. She said they had been forcibly removed from their home near Poznan in Poland by the Germans and placed in the boxcar the previous afternoon along with the other Jews. She tearfully said her husband had been killed by the Germans a few months before while he was trying to help free some of his friends who had been seized and imprisoned.

Ken asked Deborah if she had lived in Germany before moving to Poland, since she spoke German so fluently.

She replied she had lived in Poland all her life. "I think most Polish people speak German, and many speak Russian. Some also speak French, Italian, or Swiss," she said.

Ken had told her he was an American, and she asked him if people spoke German in America. When Ken answered only a very few of the people he knew spoke German, she asked how he had learned the language.

"I know I don't speak German nearly as well as you do, but I learned some from a Jewish family from Germany that I lived with for a few months," he said. "Then I learned more while I was in a German prison camp, some from the guards and some from studying with other prisoners."

"I don't think you are a Jew, but if you lived with a Jewish family, you must not hate the Jewish people."

"My goodness, how could I hate God's chosen people?" Ken said as he realized she was so used to being the target of hatred that she sort of expected it from anyone who was not Jewish. He saw tears glistening in her eyes.

Deborah asked why he had been in prison, and Ken explained he had been a crew member of an American bomber that had been shot down.

She was silent for a while then asked, "Did they decide you had been in prison long enough and let you out?"

Ken laughed. "Not on purpose, they didn't. I'm sure they are still looking for me and would like to put me back in."

Hannah softly told her mother she was still thirsty, and Ken told them to rest there a while longer and he would see if he could find water. He had gone a short distance when off to his right he saw a dirt road going east. He stayed in the forest but went along beside the road for a ways and saw a small building and a barricade across the road. It occurred to him this was probably a German-Polish border crossing, but he didn't see any guards.

Wondering if the guard house had been abandoned, he quietly made his way through the forest to the back of the building and cautiously looked in a small window. There he saw a guard leaning on a table with his head on his arm. He appeared to be asleep. Obviously, this was a minor road that had infrequent need of a border guard.

In the guard's hand, which was resting on the table, there was a bottle. There was also an open box on the table, in which there were cans and other items that looked like food. Ken looked past the guard at a shelf where he could see a stack of similar boxes, and he realized these must be German field rations.

The guard looked like he was in a deep sleep and possibly even drunk. Did he dare go in and take some of the rations? He carefully made his way to the open door. Peering in, he saw the guard hadn't stirred. He quietly went in, and, seeing a burlap sack on the floor, he picked it up and quickly put several boxes of the field rations in the sack. He added a canteen and a small pot with a handle that he thought could be useful. A cot in the corner caught his eye, and he removed a heavy, woolen blanket and quickly made his way out the door into the forest.

Then he had a disturbing thought. Had that been a two-way radio he had seen beside the guard? If so, the guard might report that an intruder had been there which would probably bring more soldiers to the area. But then he wondered how likely it would be for the guard to report that while he was armed and supposedly ready to deal with trespassers, his things were taken from right under his nose.

He thought of David and his companion going into Saul's camp while he and his men were asleep and taking the spear and jug of water. That sleep had been imposed by God, and Ken knew it was possible the guard's sleep was because of God's intervention, but the guard's superiors would probably not be appeased by that line of thought!

Ken felt elated. He had some badly needed food and a blanket, which was going to make it a lot better for his companions. He just wished Andy would show up to share the provisions. As he started back to the others, he had not gone far when he heard some noise. Peering though the foliage, he saw a group of soldiers walking down the road toward the border crossing.

Deborah and Hannah were asleep when he got back. He roused them and told them they needed to leave immediately. As they went north, away from the road, he told Deborah there were some soldiers in the area that would most likely be looking for them since he had taken some things from a border guard.

Twenty minutes later, they came to a stream. Ken rinsed the dipper and gave his Jewish companions a drink. He rinsed and refilled the canteen and clipped it to his belt. They walked until the increasing weight on Ken's arm told him Deborah was very tired. They stopped under a tree, and Ken opened the sack and gave them some of the rations. They ate hungrily, and Deborah told Ken this was the first food they'd had since the morning of the previous day.

Ken was surprised he had heard no complaining from Hannah. She seemed like such a nice little girl, and she was showing she was a little trooper. He told Deborah her daughter seemed to be a special little girl and asked how old she was. Deborah said she was four and would be five next February 14.

"That's Valentine's Day!" exclaimed Ken. "No wonder she is so sweet."

They rested for about an hour; then Ken told them he thought it was important to get farther away from the guard house and any Germans who may have continued their search deep into the forest. Ken lifted Hannah to her feet and could not resist giving her a hug before setting her on his shoulders; then he helped Deborah up.

Ken chose a northeasterly course that he thought would take them both to the border and farther away from the road. Soon they arrived at the border fence. Ken set Hannah on the other side and lifted Deborah across then climbed over himself.

He let Hannah walk for a while then asked if she wanted a ride. She nodded her head, and Ken lifted her to his shoulders. It was such a nice feeling to have Hannah's little arms around his head. After that, every time he asked Hannah if she wanted a ride, she eagerly said yes and held up her arms.

The heavy forests that had provided cover ever since he had left the prison camp seemed to go on forever, but Ken knew he needed to eventually get Deborah and Hannah back to civilization. But he wondered how they could tell they were not walking right back into the hands of the Germans. Even though they were now in Poland, it was occupied by Germany. It was a far greater problem for Deborah and Hannah. For him it meant return to prison camp, probably with some punishment, but for them it meant death.

Perhaps the wisest thing for all of them would still be to go until they came to the German-Russian battle lines then try to find a place to hide until the fighting moved past them to the west. The last he had heard, the Russians were making steady advances, but he had no idea how far away they were. He knew he needed God's guidance.

They continued going northeast until the sunlight was fading, and Ken knew they needed to look for a place to spend the night. It was obvious Deborah could not walk much farther. Ken set Hannah down and told Deborah to wait there while he looked around for a good place to camp. After a short search, he saw a large fallen tree that he decided they should snuggle up against. He went back to the others and brought them to the site he had picked out.

Deborah gratefully sank down against the tree with Hannah beside her. Ken asked Deborah if her injury was still bleeding, and she said she thought it had stopped. He got out more of the field rations. He wanted to see them satisfy their hunger and knew Deborah needed nutrients to rebuild her blood, so he gave them enough for a satisfying meal.

After they had eaten, Ken checked the ground where he was going to make a bed for his companions and cleared it of objects that would be uncomfortable to lie on. He then cut some small, soft spruce boughs then put the blanket on top of the branches. It was wide enough to be underneath as well as over them. He told them they could go to bed there any time they wanted to, and it didn't take them long to decide to take advantage of the makeshift bed. When Ken folded the blanket over them, Hannah smiled so angelically Ken couldn't resist kissing her on the forehead.

In the fading light, Ken thought he saw tears in Deborah's eyes.

"Why are you helping us?" she asked.

Ken wasn't sure he knew how to answer that. Finally he said, "Have you ever helped someone?"

Deborah slowly nodded.

"Why did you help them?" he asked.

"Well, they needed help, and I was there," Deborah said.

Ken smiled. "I think that is the answer to your question; you needed help, and my friend and I were there to give you that help."

"Helping us to get away from the Germans is only part of it," Deborah said. "You could have just left us there, but you are taking care of us like we are family."

"We are *all* part of God's family," Ken said. "We all are related to Adam and Eve, as well as Noah and his wife. And I think all of us have been helped by someone, and it gives us a good feeling to pass it on."

Deborah smiled, cuddled up to Hannah, and closed her eyes.

Ken woke up with the sun in his eyes. He looked toward Deborah and Hannah, still sleeping soundly in each other's arms. He felt a surge of anger. What kind of monsters would try to harm innocent human beings like these? For a moment he wished he was back in his *Luck of the Irish* bomber dropping bombs on Germany.

Then he thought of Walter and Stony Face and what a blessing the potatoes were and particularly the knife that he had used so many times. He knew that not all Germans were bad. Some, perhaps many, were in the grip of forces that they didn't agree with but were unable to resist. But he was very glad that he was no longer in that prison under the control of people who were responsible for so much suffering.

He arose and walked a few hundred yards away from their camp to see if there was a stream nearby where he could wash up, but he didn't find any. He went back to camp and sat down to wait for Deborah to wake up.

When Deborah awoke, she looked around and for a moment seemed bewildered by her surroundings. Then her gaze fell on Ken, and she slowly smiled as the events that accounted for her situation came back to her mind.

"Good morning," Ken said. "How's that leg feeling today?" He had seen some blood dripping off her foot while they were walking, so he knew it was not just a minor scratch.

"It still hurts," she said, "but it is not bleeding anymore."

Kent thought about asking to take a look at it but knew it wouldn't do any good since he didn't have anything to dress it with, and he wasn't sure how Deborah would feel about pulling her long skirt up high enough for him to see the injury.

"Well, we'll hope it is healing fast," he said.

After they had eaten some of the field rations, Ken folded up the blanket and put it back in the burlap sack, and they were ready to continue their journey.

As they started walking again, Ken said, "Well, we don't know where we are going for sure, but at least we are getting farther away from those Germans that were after us!"

"You don't have any particular destination in mind?" Deborah asked.

"Well, my friend and I were thinking about going to the Russian front and seeing if we could somehow get through," Ken said, "but that was a long ways off the last I heard."

"Do you know where we are?" Deborah asked.

"I just have a general idea. We must be in the northern part of Poland, not far from Germany. Do you know anything about this part of the country?" Ken asked.

"I just know there are not many people who live in the north except along the coast. I have an uncle who lives in a small village somewhere east of here. Do you think there's any way we could find our way to Czluchow? I think we would be safe with my uncle since there are so few people who live there."

"I have never heard of that town. I wish I had my maps!" Ken said. "Where is it in relation to Warsaw?"

"I think it is about two hundred kilometers northwest of Warsaw," Deborah said. "I was there about five or six years ago with my father and mother. The train we were on went through Warsaw, and I'm pretty sure we went north and west from there."

"Well, that's something to consider. I think that would make it somewhere around a hundred kilometers east of here. Let's go in an easterly direction, and maybe God will help us find it. That does sound better than trying to get to the Russian lines, except for the difficulty in finding a specific location. Maybe we will run into someone that we can ask!" Ken said.

"I'm sure my uncle would be glad to have us stay with him. He told me that I am his favorite niece!" Deborah said. "He owns the only store in town. The townspeople go to him for everything, and he has helped a lot of them when they needed it. I doubt there are any Germans there, and he is so well-respected I don't think anyone would try to persecute him."

"That sure sounds like a good place to hide out until the war is over," Ken said. "Let's make that our objective!"

Deborah was limping worse than she had the day before. She didn't offer any word of complaint, but her face registered pain. The thought that they might be able to get to her uncle's house seemed to help motivate her to continue walking in spite of the pain. As they walked, she asked him about America and said her husband's uncle had immigrated to New York a few years before the war.

Ken wanted to know more about the persecution the Jews had suffered at the hand of the Germans. Deborah told him it started rather innocuously with the requirement for all Jews to wear a bright yellow Star of David, then progressed to old people being shoved off the sidewalks, to the looting and devastation of the stores of Jewish merchants, and finally the dragging people out of their homes and their deportation to some unknown destination. She told of some of her close acquaintances being brutally mistreated, many who had disappeared in the night. Her own husband had been killed trying to rescue some of his friends who had been seized by the Germans. The Nazis and their sympathizers had shown no mercy even to children, and Deborah had kept Hannah secluded. Then came the day when they had burst into her house and roughly seized her and Hannah. Ken's anger rose up again as he heard Deborah's vivid account of the savage cruelty.

By the fourth day from the guard house where Ken had taken the rations, most of them had been eaten. A little after noon, they came to a clearing in the forest where there was a farmhouse and some fields that had been harvested. Ken asked Deborah if she thought they ought to see if the farmer would help them. Deborah said most of the Polish people in her town seemed to think the Germans were doing the right thing in trying to get rid of the Jews.

"I don't think we should take the chance," she said. "I think I would rather keep on going and try to find my uncle's house."

Ken looked over the part of the field farthest from the house to see if anything had been missed in the harvest. His search rewarded him with a few small potatoes that were on the roots of some of the vines. They alternately walked and rested until the sun was sinking low. The potatoes supplemented the last of the German rations when they camped for the night.

The next morning, Deborah's leg appeared to be bothering her more. Ken was hesitant to ask to see the injury, not sure if it might offend Deborah, but he finally asked to see it. The open wound was just below her knee. It was an angry red and was draining some. Worst of all, a red streak was going up her leg from the wound. He had heard this was an indication of blood poisoning, which could be fatal. Apparently the splintered wood that had penetrated her leg had been contaminated with filth from the floor of the boxcar.

"Deborah!" he said. "We've got to get something to put on this!" Then he bowed his head and prayed aloud. "Dear Jesus, Deborah needs some medical help. Please show us what to do!"

When he opened his eyes, Deborah was looking at him curiously. He knew that in addition to some medication, she needed nourishment to help the injury heal. Even though she was in pain, Deborah seemed eager to be on their way. Before Deborah and Hannah awakened, Ken had taken the pot and gathered quite a few pine nuts, which they had for breakfast before resuming their journey.

In the afternoon they saw a small creature shuffling along in the forest. As they drew closer, they saw it was a porcupine.

"Hey, I've heard the American Indians eat porcupines when they can't find anything else," Ken said. "There must be some meat down under all that armor!"

"But it's not kosher," Deborah said.

Ken stopped. "Deborah, if Hannah was going to die of starvation and you could keep her alive by giving her non-kosher food, would you refuse to let her have it? Think about it."

Slowly Deborah said, "I would do anything to keep her alive."

"Well, God loves us a million times more than you love Hannah. I don't think he would want us to pass up the opportunity to be strengthened by something to eat he has put in our path."

With that Ken quickly found a heavy stick and killed the porcupine and with some difficulty managed to remove the skin and quills. He rinsed the carcass in the nearby stream and laid it on a bush while he gathered wood to make a fire.

While gathering the wood, he saw a large patch of mushrooms. Ken had never eaten mushrooms but knew at least some were edible but others were poisonous. He picked a few, took them to Deborah, and asked if she knew if they were good to eat. She immediately said that her family had gone mushroom hunting many times, and these were a type they had often eaten.

There had been some matches in the field ration parcels. Ken started the fire then rigged up a spit and started roasting their quarry, and soon it smelled as good to their hungry appetites as a leg of beef. He took the border guard's pot back to the patch of mushrooms and filled it.

While the roasting was in process, Ken said earnestly, "Deborah, please believe me when I say your Messiah has come as promised, and his name is Jesus! I heard the Jewish man I almost think of as my father read and discuss the fifty-third chapter of Isaiah. He said it describes Jesus so accurately he didn't see how anyone could not see that he is the Messiah from that chapter alone. He died on the cross as the sinless Lamb of God, the once-for-all, perfect sacrifice for the atonement of our sins, ushering in a new covenant that superseded the Mosaic covenant.

"And in the New Testament book of Acts, it tells of a vision God gave to one of Jesus' Jewish followers where he was shown all kinds of 'unclean' animals. He was told to 'slay and eat,' and when Peter objected because they were not kosher, God told him not to call what he had cleansed unclean. So when it's done, have some of this delicious-smelling meat with a clear conscience!"

Ken's impromptu sermon rang true, and Deborah did seem to feel better about the prospect confronting her.

Their hunger made the roast porcupine and mushrooms taste like a gourmet meal. There hadn't been a lot of meat on the porcupine, but there was enough to satisfy them completely with a little left over that Ken put into the guard's pot to carry with them for their next meal.

One of the books Ken had read in the prison camp told how sailors suffering from scurvy had overcome this condition by chewing on pine needles. Ken thought the nutrients in the pine needles might also help Deborah heal from her injury. He gathered some needles, placed them in the pot with some water, and brewed a tea over the fire. He took it to Deborah and told her why he thought the tea might help her. She didn't seem to enjoy it, but she did drink it all. Then he boiled some water and after it had cooled some poured it over the inflamed wound. Deborah seemed to appreciate his attempts to help her.

The weather was turning colder during the nights. Ken was fairly comfortable with his warm jacket, but he was worried about Deborah and Hannah. He was afraid the blanket was not enough covering to keep them warm at night, and their clothes didn't look heavy enough to keep them warm enough in the daytime.

When Ken was carrying Hannah, he put his coat around her. They were going to have to find shelter or some more warm clothing, and most of all Deborah badly needed medical attention. During the night she occasionally moaned, and Ken was afraid she was not only cold but her wound was hurting worse. From what Deborah had told him, he knew it would be risky to ask someone for help, but they just had to get help from somewhere.

"Dear God, please show us what to do," he prayed.

The next morning Deborah was obviously feeling worse. Her face was flushed, and Ken suspected she had a high temperature. He thought about feeling her forehead but knew it would do nothing to help with the problem. The only thing he could think to do was try to get her to drink a lot of water.

With the field rations gone, there was now room in the burlap sack to tie a knot about halfway down. By putting his belt around the sack under the knot, Ken was able to have the sack dangling at his side, which was a little awkward but allowed him to have both hands free to help Deborah.

When they started to walk, Deborah was struggling to even get started, and Hannah looked concerned about her mother's obviously worsening condition. They could not go far before she would have to rest. By midday, she seemed to collapse and said she didn't think she could go any farther. Ken told Hannah he was going to have to let her walk for a while. He put his jacket on Deborah then picked her up and began carrying her. She didn't really weigh much, but Ken had to stop and rest frequently. He wished big, strong Andy was there to help.

Late in the afternoon, Ken saw several plumes of smoke rising, which indicated there was a village ahead. Ken knew the time had come when they were just going to have to trust God to lead them to the right place. They could go no farther without help.

As he struggled to the edge of a clearing, he saw the village in the distance, and across the small field in front of them, there was a house where there was an elderly woman chopping some wood. Ken made his way toward her, praying she would not be a Nazi sympathizer. As they drew near, the woman saw them, straightened up, and crossed herself. That action was comforting to Ken. When she saw that Deborah was obviously in bad condition, she seemed to lose some of her apprehensions.

When they were close, Ken said, "This lady is very ill. Could you help us?"

The woman glanced at Deborah and sweet little Hannah then back to Ken's honest, pleading face. She put the axe down and said, "Come."

With that she turned and started shuffling to the house behind her. She went in and beckoned for them to follow. She led them to a cot and motioned for Ken to put Deborah down. Ken uttered a sigh of relief. He wasn't sure where this was going to lead, but it seemed so good to get Deborah into shelter and to be able to put her down.

"Is there a doctor we could get to look at the injury she has?" he asked.

The woman looked at Ken, then at Deborah and Hannah. "Jews?" she asked.

Ken considered saying no but decided to trust God. "Yes, they are Jews."

"And you?" the woman asked.

"No, I'm not Jewish, but I am an American," Ken said, surprised at himself for his candor.

"That doctor." The woman almost spat the words. "He's a Nazi! He would have them sent to a camp. Let me see the injury."

Ken felt relief at the woman's words. He was disappointed they couldn't get a doctor to help Deborah but was grateful the woman wasn't a Nazi sympathizer.

"Thank you, God, for leading us here," he said aloud without thinking.

The woman looked at him and smiled. "You pray to our God! That is good!"

The woman looked at the festering wound and the angry red streak and seemed to shudder. She went to the other side of the room and poured some hot water into a basin from a pot that was sitting at the side of the fireplace, then took it to Deborah with some soap and a rag and tenderly washed the wound. She went to the door and threw out the water. Then she went to her cupboard and came back with a jar.

As she was applying some kind of ointment from the jar, she said, "I do not know if this will help, but I do not know what else to do except to make some soup."

Hannah was hovering over her mother, and the woman patted her head as she bent over and asked if she was hungry. Hannah shyly nodded her head.

The soup was good. It seemed to lift Deborah's spirits, even though she was in pain. Ken felt worn out after carrying Deborah for so long, and after having two bowls of hot soup, his head began to nod.

They had learned the woman's name was Karina. She now placed her hand on Ken's arm and said, "Come." She led him through a doorway into a small room that had a narrow bed and gestured toward it. "Rest," she said.

Ken gratefully lay on the bed and immediately fell asleep.

When Ken awoke, the day was starting to dawn. He went into the next room and could make out the old woman sitting in an armchair by the fire.

Oh no! he thought guiltily. *I took Karina's bed, and she had to sit up all night.* He went to the cot Deborah was on with Hannah curled up beside her. As he looked down at her, he saw that she was awake. "Are you feeling any better?" he asked in a low voice.

She weakly grasped his arm and said in a soft, excited voice, "Oh, the most wonderful thing just happened! The Messiah came and stood beside me. He was so beautiful! He said he was the Messiah but his name is Jesus, just like you said! I asked him to forgive me for not accepting him as Messiah. He said I was going to be with him soon, and he took the pain away and filled me with such a peaceful, happy feeling! It will be so wonderful to be with him, but I do hate to leave Hannah. Ken, will you take care of her?"

Ken's voice was choked as he said, "Of course. I will love taking care of her."

Deborah's voice was weaker as she said, "Will you promise?"

Ken said, "Yes, Deborah, I will promise to take care of her as if she were my own child."

"Oh, I'm so glad! Thank you! Tell her about Jesus and that I love her." Then, in a low, weak voice, she said, "I think I'm going now! Good-bye!"

Ken, with tears falling freely from his face, knelt by her bed holding her hand as she left the tumult of the world behind and went to join her Messiah in a blissful eternity. The morning light revealed a radiance on her face, and Ken knew he was in the very presence of God.

Ken didn't know how long he had knelt at the bedside still holding Deborah's hand when he felt Karina beside him.

She looked down at the lovely face and crossed herself. "Poor dear," she said. "I'm glad her troubles are over."

Karina wrapped Deborah's body in an old blanket, and Ken carried her out to the shallow grave he had dug under a tree in Karina's yard. Hannah stood by mutely as Ken offered a prayer to God, thanking him for the privilege of knowing Deborah and for the wonderful vision she had.

When the unofficial funeral service was over and they started back to the house, Karina said softly, "That's one Jew the Gestapo is not going to have the pleasure of putting in the ovens."

Ken sat down on the cot, drew Hannah to him, and hugged her

tightly. She buried her face in his shoulder and wept out her grief. His orphan heart opened wide in sympathy for this brand-new orphan who had suddenly become his responsibility, and the seed of love he had felt for her from the first now sprouted and began to blossom into maturity.

He was glad for the affection he had expressed toward her from the first day and felt it made it easier for her to turn to him for comfort, but for many days he could tell she was under a cloud of depression. She frequently would say she wanted to go be with her mother, and Ken would take her out to the grave and hold her while she wept silently. Ken's heart ached for her, and he constantly looked for ways to focus her attention on other things.

One diversion that seemed to lift Hannah's spirits was watching a little bird that had landed on the windowsill one day. Ken lifted Hannah up to see the bird, and she was captivated as the bird curiously examined its reflection in the window. Ken asked Karina for some bread crumbs and took Hannah outside. The bird flew to the tree by Deborah's grave when they opened the door but watched as Ken put some crumbs on the windowsill. They stood back away from the window and watched the bird until it finally flew away.

They went back into the house, and sometime later Hannah said, "There's the bird!"

They watched through the glass as the bird ate the bread crumbs, much to Hannah's delight. The bird became a regular visitor and a source of entertainment for everyone, but especially Hannah. Hannah named the bird "Otto" and made sure Ken remembered to put some crumbs out for it every day. Ken was so glad to see her coming out of her depression.

There was snow on the ground around Karina's house. Ken had chopped a lot of firewood and had done some much-needed repairs. Karina had told him she had not had the energy to dig many of the potatoes, carrots, and turnips her grandson had planted before he was forced into a German labor camp, so Ken had carefully dug them and put them in her cellar. Cabbages grew well in cold weather, and there were several heads still growing in her garden, which Ken had also gathered and put in her cellar. Karina was elated.

"I wasn't sure I was going to make it through the winter," she said.

It seemed so good to have a place of refuge, and Ken dreaded thinking about leaving. He was concerned about imposing on Karina, and after a couple weeks in her house, he asked her if she would rather that they left.

She said, "Nonsense. You need a place to stay, and I need you!" She said she had been lonely. Her husband had died several years before, and her only son had been killed fighting the Germans when they had invaded Poland.

From time to time Ken went into the forest adjoining Karina's property searching for dead trees to use as firewood. One day he ran across some tracks in the snow he thought were probably made by a deer. He hurried back to the house and asked Karina if she had a gun, explaining that he might be able to get them some venison. Karina went to a chest and took out an ancient rifle and some ammunition for it.

Ken went back to the place he had seen the tracks and started following them, carefully scanning the woods for his prey. After following the tracks for more than an hour, he was nearly ready to give up when he saw some movement ahead. Cautiously peering around a tree, he saw a large buck thirty or forty feet away, pawing at the ice on a stream.

He waited with the rifle at his shoulder while the deer drank; then, as he turned sideways, Ken fired at the side of his head. The deer took a couple leaps and fell to the ground.

Ken had helped Bill Dalton butcher a pig, so he knew it was important to bleed out the deer, and he quickly severed the jugular vein. He felt bad about killing the magnificent animal, but he was glad that he was able to contribute to Karina's food supply.

Getting his game back to Karina's house was not easy. The deer had a large rack of antlers, and Ken estimated it weighed nearly three-hundred pounds. Much of that weight would be gone after dressing the deer, but he knew it would be too difficult to try to do it with his pocket knife. Karina's butcher knife would make the job much easier. He finally got the deer back to Karina's, and even with her big knife and a saw, butchering it was not an easy job. Acting on Karina's instructions, he cut the meat into pieces that would be convenient to use. Karina was overjoyed.

Just outside the house, there was a large, sturdy box that Karina's husband had built for storing meat. The winter cold provided all the refrigeration needed to preserve the meat in top condition, and the venison provided many tasty meals throughout the long, cold winter.

Karina would frequently ask Ken to get some of the vegetables from the cellar. Along with a piece of the meat, they provided the ingredients for the savory soups and stews she made. After rubbing spices into strips of meat, she kept a continuous batch of jerky drying by the side of the fireplace to preserve some of the venison for the summer when it would not be cold enough to keep the meat from spoiling.

It became increasingly obvious Karina was genuinely glad to have Ken and Hannah with her. She seemed to really enjoy their company and cooking for them and would smile happily as they ate the things she prepared for them. She had asked Ken how he had met Deborah and Hannah. When he told her, and how they had sometimes had difficulty finding food, it seemed to prompt her to want do her best to show them they no longer had to worry about getting all they wanted to eat.

Ken was outside getting more firewood to bring in when he saw a bent figure approaching. He didn't know if he had been seen, but he went in the house and told Karina there was someone coming and asked if she knew the person.

She went to the window and said, "It's only Mikolaj! He is an elderly neighbor who comes by sometimes to see if I need anything. He was a good friend of my husband when he was alive. We don't need to be afraid of him; he hates the Nazis even more than I do!"

She opened the door and welcomed him into the house. He greeted her while looking curiously at Ken and Hannah. He reached into his coat pocket and handed Karina two eggs, then more until he had finally given her five. Karina spoke to him in Polish, and Ken could tell she was explaining their presence because he smiled and raised his gnarled hand in greeting. During further conversation, when Karina did most of the talking, he looked mainly at Hannah. Finally he waved and made his way out the door.

Karina explained that he had a goat, and she was asking if he could bring Hannah some milk. The very next day, he knocked on the door with nearly a quart of milk, and every two or three days after that, he would bring more and would sometimes also bring more eggs.

Karina had some children's books, and it became a familiar routine for Ken to sit with Hannah in his lap and tell her the story he thought the pictures portrayed. The words were in Polish, so Ken couldn't read them, but Hannah seemed to enjoy the stories Ken told her. Sometimes Ken heard Karina laughing over the story he was concocting.

Hannah had become his shadow. Many times, when he went out to gather more firewood, she wanted to accompany him, and when she did Karina would bundle her up against the cold. Once, Ken helped her build a small snowman, which she seemed to enjoy.

As the winter wore on, she seemed to be getting over her mother's death, yet Ken was sure it would remain in her memory the rest of her life. Ken had tried to describe how wonderful heaven was and how happy her mother was with Jesus. He had told her that Deborah had asked him to tell her that she loved her.

"And you know what? I love you too," he had said with a hug.

Christmas had been honored in Karina's house as Jesus' birthday and a special meal but without a Christmas tree or decorations. Ken thought he might cut a small tree for Hannah's benefit, but Karina felt the tradition was based on pagan beliefs.

Karina gave Hannah a doll that she said had belonged to her daughter, who had died during a flu epidemic while still a child. Hannah was thrilled with the doll and in the following days spent many hours playing with it. Karina sang some carols, and Ken tried to follow along, but he didn't know many of the German or Polish words. Ken fervently wished he had some gifts to give but was helpless to follow his desires.

The cold winter was passing slowly, with several fairly major snowstorms. Karina had a homemade snow shovel that Ken used to clear the snow from the doorway and a path to the wood pile and the outhouse.

When the snow got deep, Ken was surprised to see that even though Mikolaj didn't deliver the milk quite as often, he did continue to come every few days using snowshoes. He didn't speak German, so Ken asked Karina how to say thank you in Polish. On his next visit, Ken warmly shook his hand and spoke the word of thanks Karina had taught him. Ken also wanted Karina to ask Mikolaj if he could help him in any way. When she relayed this message, the old man smiled and shook his head.

Soon it was Valentine's Day. Ken remembered Deborah had told him Hannah would be five years old on Valentine's Day. Ken and Karina tried to make it special, but Ken was again frustrated that he had nothing to give her. Karina made a special dinner with a roast, potatoes and gravy, and a cake.

Ken told Hannah when they got back to the United States he would get a birthday present for her. When he mentioned going to the United States, she said she didn't need a birthday present. She would rather they stayed with Karina. Ken was sure knowing her mother was buried there was the primary reason she wanted to stay. It was going to be hard to explain to her they had to go.

As the winter of 1944 to 1945 passed, they were gratified to hear the progress being made in defeating the German armies on both fronts. Ken had repaired Karina's radio, and they listened to the BBC, which Ken would interpret for Karina, or a Swiss station that Karina would interpret for Ken. Once in a while, Ken could hear a little of the American Forces Network, but it was pretty faint. Sometimes in scanning the radio channels they would hear the ranting of Hitler, which they turned away from as quickly as possible. They frequently listened to a station that broadcast classical music, which Hannah always seemed to enjoy. Sometimes Ken would hear her humming some of the tunes she had heard and thought she must have some innate musical ability.

They were apprehensive as the broadcasts reported the eastern front battle lines were drawing nearer. They wondered what they should do to avoid any possible confrontation with the combatants but didn't think it would be much safer to try to hide in the forest, and they couldn't predict when the armies would arrive in their area.

Their concerns turned out to be baseless. The German army was in full retreat when they drew near and completely bypassed the little village. A few days later, they were happy to hear the news the Russian armies were on German soil and before long were besieging Berlin.

Finally, on May 7, they heard that Germany had surrendered to the Allies. It was a time of rejoicing. They celebrated the occasion with a special meal Karina made.

Chapter 14

Even though Karina was glad the war was over, she hated to think that her guests who had helped dispel her loneliness through the long winter would be leaving. She was grateful when Ken told her they would stay long enough to do everything he could think of that would help her and asked her to tell him if there was something that needed to be done that he wasn't aware of.

He spent nearly two weeks gathering, chopping, and stacking a supply of wood that would last her for many months and planted a garden with every kind of seed she had. During the winter, he had fixed everything he could that needed fixing but examined the house again for anything he might have missed.

Karina expressed her gratitude for everything Ken had done, but Ken felt he was still greatly in her debt. He often wondered what would have become of them if they had not happened upon her home but felt sure God had directed them there.

In spite of Ken's desire to get back to his fellow countrymen, it was hard to leave Karina's little house. It had been a sanctuary at a time when it was greatly needed, and Karina had treated them so kindly and shared her food so generously. During the long winter they had developed an intimacy and mutual appreciation. Karina said she had almost come to think of them as family and really dreaded thinking about them leaving.

Before they left, Ken prayed with her that her grandson would soon return and would be able to help her with her needs. She hugged them both with tears when they left. She had packed some provisions for them and insisted they take a paper bill and a few coins she had. She said they might need to buy some food for Hannah, so Ken reluctantly took them but promised himself he would reward her many-fold for her generosity when he had the resources. He had her write her address on a piece of paper and put it in the inside pocket of his jacket.

When they heard the war was over, Ken had put a rough cross at the head of Deborah's grave. He had not done this before because he thought it might spawn some questions that could create some problems, although it was unlikely anyone would come by Karina's rather isolated home unless they were a friend.

When they went out the door as they were leaving, Hannah pulled Ken over to the grave where she stood and wept a silent good-bye. After a few minutes Ken gently told her they needed to go but would try to come back sometime. As they left, Ken turned around to wave a last good-bye. Karina was standing in the doorway with her handkerchief in her hand, obviously weeping. What a blessing she had been.

Ken had decided he and Hannah would head for Berlin. He had heard on the radio that first the Russian and then American troops had entered Berlin, and it was probable they would still be there. The Russians would no doubt be occupying the territory between them and Berlin, but it shouldn't be a problem passing through to the American troops.

Karina had used the burlap sack Ken had taken from the German guard to make a rough knapsack with shoulder straps. Ken really appreciated the shoulder straps; they made it so much easier to carry the blanket and the pot he had taken from the guard as well as the food

Karina had given them for the trip. He carried the German guard's canteen clipped to his belt.

Hannah started out carrying the doll Karina had given her, but after a few miles she asked that it be put in the knapsack. He asked her if she wanted a ride, but at first she didn't accept the offer. Ken was glad that she had the energy to feel like walking. It was a nice, bright day. Hannah seemed to be happy, which made him feel good. He had feared having to leave her mother's grave behind might make her depressed for some time.

In Karina's house, Ken had started teaching Hannah some English words; now, as they walked along, he used the time to teach her more words. He had explained to her these would be the words they would be using in America. She proved to be a quick learner, and Ken was proud of her.

During the winter at Karina's house, Ken had asked Hannah if she wanted to call him Ken or something else. He was a little surprised when she shyly said she would like to call him the Polish equivalent of "daddy." Now he told her she might want to switch to the English word but to continue to use the Polish word if she would rather, and it seemed she was more comfortable to continue to use the word she was familiar with.

Karina had told Ken how to get on the narrow dirt road that would take them in the direction of Berlin. It was probably not much more than 120 miles away, which wouldn't have been too bad if he was by himself, but he was sort of dreading the long walk for Hannah's sake. He doubted the money Karina had given him was enough for bus or train fare. Even if it was enough, it was unlikely buses would be running on the minor road they were on, and he had not seen a train track since that fateful day he met Deborah and Hannah.

He wished they at least had a bicycle, but it was doubtful he had enough money to buy even an old one. He didn't know the value of the bill or the coins and what their purchasing power would be but thought if the opportunity presented itself he might see if anyone was willing to sell a bicycle for the amount of money he had.

There was also the possibility he might need the money to buy food after Karina's provisions were used up as Karina had suggested, so he wasn't sure he should consider spending it on something besides food. However, with a bicycle they could travel faster, so the food they had wouldn't have to last as long. He just wasn't sure what would be the best thing to do, but so far there had been no opportunity to even try to buy a bicycle.

They stopped under a roadside tree about noon and ate some of the food Karina had bundled up for them. She had made some venison sandwiches and had sent enough of the jerky she had made to last for some time as well as a big loaf of her heavy, dark bread, which Ken had grown quite fond of. She also packaged up some polenta that they could use for breakfast. They drank some water from the canteen, and Ken was glad they didn't have to depend on finding a stream every time they wanted a drink.

He let Hannah rest for a while then said they should go but if she wanted a ride to tell him. Later they passed through a small village and felt the curious stares of the villagers. Some of them waved back when Ken lifted his hand in greeting. An elderly man came out of a building just ahead of them and went to an old bicycle that was leaning against the building. Ken asked him in German if he wanted to sell his bicycle, but he obviously didn't understand German. Ken told Hannah to ask him in Polish if he wanted to sell his bicycle. When Hannah relayed this question, the old man smiled and shook his head.

They had not gone far after lunch when Hannah gave up and said she would like a ride. Ken lifted her to his shoulders and soon felt her relax and fall asleep, and she slept for over an hour but stayed on his shoulders for quite a while after she awoke. Ken was able to walk faster when Hannah wasn't walking beside him, although it was surprising how fast she could go with her quick footsteps.

When the afternoon sun started getting low on the horizon, Ken started looking for a place to spend the night. There was a stand of trees ahead fairly close to the road, which looked promising. They found a nice spot to camp under the trees and settled down to eat more of the food Karina had provided.

There were a lot of pine needles under the tree, which provided a nice place to prepare a place to sleep. As he lay there under the blanket with Hannah snuggling beside him, Ken thought back how different this night in the woods was from those when they were fleeing from the Germans. It seemed so good to be going toward friends rather than fleeing from the enemy.

Ken let Hannah sleep until she awakened the next morning. He had built a fire, and they had some polenta for breakfast. They had eaten this often before at Karina's house. Ken was not impressed with the taste, but Hannah seemed to like it. It was probable that she had eaten quite a bit of it in her short lifetime and was used to it.

When they resumed their journey, he kept hoping for another opportunity to try to buy a bicycle, but they seemed to be in a fairly sparsely populated area and saw few people. They crossed a stream where Ken refilled their canteen with fresh water. A short time later, a farmer with a horse-drawn cart stopped and beckoned for them to come and ride in the cart. The ride was a nice break from walking, and Hannah seemed to enjoy the new experience. After a mile or so, the farmer turned off on a side road and stopped to let them off.

In the late afternoon, the sky was beginning to darken, and Ken was hoping it was not going to rain. By the time they had stopped for the night, it was looking more and more threatening. He looked around to see if there was any place they could find shelter if needed. Through the trees he could see glimpses of some kind of unpainted building. That seemed to be the only possibility other than a dense tree that would help some.

They had nearly finished eating when the rain began to fall. Ken quickly put their belongings in the homemade knapsack and told Hannah they needed to hurry to try to find some place to get out of the rain. They ran toward the building he had seen, and they found it was an old barn. The door opened easily, and Ken didn't think the owners would mind them going in to get out of the rain.

It was rather dark inside, so they went in cautiously to be sure they didn't stumble over anything. They sat down, and Ken asked Hannah if she had enough to eat, and she said she did. The floor seemed to be covered with a soft layer of fingernail-sized leaves, which were probably the remnants of alfalfa hay. Spending the night in the barn would mean they would not only have a drier bed but a softer one.

Ken was startled to hear someone clear his throat. He rose to his feet not knowing what to expect and asked who was there.

There was a low chuckle, and a voice said, "Don't be alarmed. I mean no harm! I'm a soldier who is on his way back to Germany. I can tell you are not a Russian, and since you have a child with you, it is unlikely you would be a threat to me." The man arose, came toward Ken, and said his name was Karl. "Where are you from?" he asked. "You don't sound like a German!"

Ken wondered if the man found out he was an American he would still consider him to be an enemy. His eyes had begun to adjust to the darkness, and he could see the man was wearing a rumpled uniform and had a pistol in a holster on his belt, which probably meant he was an officer.

"You do know the war is over, don't you?" Ken asked.

"Oh yes, I know that, and I can't tell you how glad I am. I was beginning to think I would never see my wife and children again. You are an American, aren't you?"

"Yes, I am an American, but we are no longer enemies, are we?" Ken said a little apprehensively.

"No, my friend. I have never considered the Americans to be the enemy. Our main enemies were our own leaders, especially Hitler, who got us into the war."

Ken was relieved. "Well, I'm sure glad to hear that," he said. "What are you doing here? I thought the German armies had all gone back to Germany, judging by what I heard on the radio."

Karl told him he had been on the Russian front, and near the end of the war he had received a leg wound and was at a medical aid station in a rear area getting his wound dressed when his unit was overrun by the Russians and systematically executed. He barely managed to escape but had been unable to link up with any other unit. He had been limping toward Germany ever since. He was not able to go very fast because his leg wound was still bothering him. Even though the war was over, he didn't know if he could trust the Russians to not continue to express their hatred of the Germans, so he was doing his best to avoid them.

"I have such a longing to get home. I'm hoping that I will find my family is all right. I haven't heard from them for several months, and I'm sure they are worried about me," he said. He said he had three children all under age ten.

Karl asked Ken how he and Hannah happened to be there. Ken reluctantly told him he had been on a bomber that had been shot down and was now trying to get back to his countrymen. To Ken's relief, Karl didn't seem offended that he had helped bomb his country. They talked for some time about their experiences and what the world was going to be like now that the war was over.

Ken finally asked Karl if he was hungry. Karl told him the last food he had was a rabbit he had shot three days before, but he had finished eating it the previous day. Ken shared some of the food Karina had given them, trusting that the rest would last them or that they would be able to find more. Karl expressed his thanks and immediately sat down and hungrily devoured the food. They finally bid each other goodnight and lay down to sleep.

When Ken awoke, the rain had stopped, and Karl was in the process of leaving. He said he wanted to continue his journey without delay. He thought he would be able to reach his home in a few more days if he kept at it. He was still concerned with the possibility of meeting some Russian troops but said he guessed he would just have to take his chances. Ken gave him several strips of jerky. He shook hands with Ken and thanked him again for the food. He patted Hannah on the head and left. Ken and Hannah soon left too and went back toward the road where Ken built a fire and fixed some polenta and jerky for breakfast, and they soon resumed their journey.

Mid-morning, they heard a vehicle coming from behind them. Ken didn't know if hitchhiking was a custom in Europe, but he turned around and held out his thumb. An American Jeep stopped, but the two men in it wore Russian uniforms. The uniform and insignia worn by the passenger indicated he was an officer, but Ken had no idea what his rank was.

He was sitting in the front seat beside the driver. It seemed that high-ranking American officers always sat in the backseat, so Ken wondered if this was an indication the Russian was not a high-ranking officer, but he suspected Russian customs might be different than American customs.

The Russian officer asked in accented but understandable English, "Is that an American flying jacket you are wearing?"

"Yes, sir, it is," Ken said as he saluted. He had no idea whether he was saluting an equal or a superior.

"And are you an American flyer?"

"Yes, sir, I am. I was in a plane that was shot down near Hannover several months ago." Ken said.

"Have you spent all this time avoiding capture?"

"No, sir," Ken said. "I spent several months in Stalag Luft One near Barth, Germany."

"Ah yes, we liberated that camp a month or two ago. Were you there then?"

"No, sir. I escaped from there about ten months ago," Ken said.

The Russian looked at Ken with open admiration. "I thought escape from that camp was not possible. And who is your little friend?"

Ken explained he was there when her mother died, and he had promised to take care of her daughter.

"Where are you going?" the officer then wanted to know.

"I want to get back to the American troops. I thought I would try to get to Berlin. I think there will be some there," Ken said.

"Get in. We will take you there," the Russian said.

Gratefully, Ken lifted Hannah into the backseat of the Jeep and climbed in himself. A few minutes later he wasn't sure it had been the right thing to do. The driver sped down the narrow dirt road at a high rate of speed, skidding around corners and bouncing over rough places. His officer seemed unconcerned. Hannah's eyes were wide with terror. Ken wondered if she had ever ridden in a motor vehicle before, and if she hadn't, this ride would be extra terrifying. He drew Hannah up against him, and she hung on tight.

"Lord, don't let us survive the war just to get killed by this maniac after the war is over!" he prayed silently.

Before long the road joined another more major road that had a lot less curves and bumps, but the driver was still going much faster than Ken was comfortable with. About seventy or eighty miles from Berlin, they turned onto another road where they began to meet convoys of Russian tanks and armored cars and hundreds of foot soldiers on their way back to Russia. The driver of the Jeep had to slow down considerably, much to Ken's relief.

After several hours of enduring the rough ride, the city of Berlin was visible on the horizon. As they entered the city, the devastation caused by the Allied bombing was visible almost everywhere.

What a waste. All those beautiful buildings that had probably been built over a period of hundreds of years destroyed in just a few years because of one man's lunacy and the desire for power that he and his collaborators apparently had, Ken thought.

The American sentry at the Brandenburg Gate saluted as the Jeep stopped. Ken gratefully lifted Hannah out, saluted the Russian officer, and thanked him for the ride. The officer nonchalantly returned salute, and the Jeep drove away. Hannah seemed a little overwhelmed and clung tightly to Ken's hand.

"How can I get in touch with the air force?" Ken asked the sentry after identifying himself as an American serviceman. The sentry reached for the walkie-talkie hanging on his belt.

"I need to speak to the air force rep," he said. After a short wait, he said, "Captain, I have a man here wanting to contact the air force. He looks air force." Another pause, then, "Yes, sir." He handed the radio to Ken. "He wants to speak to you."

As requested, Ken gave his name, rank, and serial number and the base where he had been stationed. There was a long pause while apparently some records were being checked. The voice on the radio asked Ken to give his serial number again.

After a short pause, the voice said, "Okay, Ryan, we'll send someone to get you, but you might like to know you are listed as killed in action!"

In a few minutes a Jeep arrived, and the driver asked if he was Lieutenant Ryan. When Ken told him he was, the driver told him to get in. He looked curiously at Hannah as Ken lifted her into the Jeep but made no comment. Five minutes later they were at the temporary American Forces headquarters.

"Go on in, Lieutenant," the driver said. "They are expecting you."

Ken was directed to the duty officer he had talked to on the walkie-talkie. In response to the officer's questioning, Ken spent the first few minutes explaining what had really happened to him, contrary to the reports of his demise. Then Ken related the story of how he had acquired responsibility for Hannah's welfare and said he had to find a way to get her back to the States. He had been told that just a few days before the ninety-first bomb group had been sent back to the States for eventual deployment to the Pacific theater so assumed he should be going too. The officer listened sympathetically but shook his head.

"I just don't know how I can help you," he said. "Air force regulations do not permit civilians to use military transport systems." He paused then said, "If anyone in this office can help you, it would be General Ross. He's from the Pentagon and has been here to help set up the administration of our occupying forces. Let me see if I can get him to see you. Come with me." He arose and started down a hallway.

Ken and Hannah followed him to a closed office door where he stopped and rapped.

"Yes?" came from within, and the officer opened the door.

"Sir, there is a Lieutenant Ryan here to see you about some way to transport a civilian to the States."

"Captain, you know that is not in my area of authority. He needs to talk to the American Embassy when it gets in operation," the voice said.

"I thought so, sir, but I thought I'd check with you to see if you knew any other way." He started to close the door but heard, "Wait!" The captain reopened the door. "Did you say Lieutenant Ryan?"

"Yes, sir," the captain said.

"Would that be Kenneth Ryan?"

The captain turned to Ken, who nodded his head.

"Yes, sir, it is Kenneth Ryan," the captain said.

"Send him in," were the words from the office.

Ken entered the office with Hannah in front of him. He saluted and stood before the general wonderingly.

"Lieutenant Ryan, were you at Dow Field in October of 1943?"

"Yes, sir, I was," Ken replied.

"Did you see an accident between a car and a fuel truck a short ways outside the base?" the general asked.

"Yes, sir," Ken answered.

General Ross stood up, came around the desk, and held out his hand. "Lieutenant, you and a Lieutenant Wright saved the lives of my wife and daughter!"

Ken shook the outstretched hand and stood, not knowing what to say. He remembered the woman had said she was the wife of Colonel Ross. Evidently he had been promoted. The general said from what his wife had told him, then seeing the wrecked car, it was clear if his wife and daughter had not been pulled from the burning car they would not have survived. He said he was also thankful they had received medical treatment so promptly.

"Have they recovered from the effects of the accident?" Ken asked.

"Yes. They suffered no permanent harm. My daughter did have a concussion, but she recovered rapidly. My wife had some bad burns on her legs that healed all right, and she still has a scar on her forehead, but that's a minor problem. We owe you a big debt of gratitude. Now, tell me how you came to have this lovely child in your custody."

Ken told the general he had promised her dying mother to take care of her daughter, but the general kept asking for more detail until Ken found himself telling about his escape from the prison camp and the intervening events leading to helping Deborah and Hannah escape from the Germans.

The general shook his head. "Lieutenant, you have an outstanding character. Do you just make a practice of going around rescuing people?"

Ken grinned. "No, sir. Just as the occasion demands," he said jokingly.

"Lieutenant, I want men like you on my staff!" The general went around to the other side of his desk, opened a drawer, and took out two sheets of paper. He wrote for a while on each sheet then pressed a button on his desk.

The general's door was opened by a staff sergeant. "Yes, sir?"

"Sergeant, type these up right away and bring them back for my signature. I want to wire them to Washington within the next hour. And get someone to come up with a uniform and bars for Captain Ryan."

"Yes, sir!" the sergeant said as he closed the door.

The general observed the look of bewilderment on Ken's face. He smiled and said, "One of those papers promotes you to the rank of captain retroactive back to the first of the year. The other paper assigned you to my staff. I will be leaving in three days to go back to Washington, and I want you with me.

"Now, about this beautiful young lady. I do not officially have the authority to take her to the States. The embassy is in the process of being reactivated, but I'm sure they are not ready to do business yet. Even when they get going, their activities are controlled by all sorts of regulations. It would probably take a long time to work through all the red tape. Since you are responsible for her and have to go to Washington in three days, you can't wait to wade through that red tape. Let's just see if something unofficial might develop." He smiled.

He stood up, walked to the door, and escorted Ken and Hannah to the front of the building. He told the officer on duty to arrange temporary billets for Ken and Hannah and transportation to the airport Friday morning. As he left, the general said, "I will see you at the airport. We will be going on a C-47. It should be near the operations hangar."

Ken was dazed as he left the American Armed Forces headquarters.

Once again he felt the hand of God was orchestrating the affairs of his life. He marveled at how a seemingly random event a few years before could have such an important consequence for his and Hannah's lives.

On Friday morning, a corporal arrived at the quarters being used as a temporary barracks where three other officers besides Ken and Hannah had spent the night. The corporal asked for Captain Ryan. Ken stood up, took Hannah by the hand, and followed him to a Jeep parked outside.

When Ken and Hannah were dropped off at the airport, there was no sign of the general. Ken took Hannah to look at the C-47 on the tarmac near the hangar and told her that was probably the airplane they would be riding in before long. The C-47 was known as "The Workhorse of the Air" to the American troops and had been indispensable in carrying cargo, ferrying troops, and dropping paratroopers into battle.

Hannah had seen planes in the sky but had never seen one up close. She clung to Ken, and he thought she was a little fearful with the thought of being up in the sky. A pilot came down the ladder out of the plane. Ken asked him if this was the plane General Ross would be flying on, and he said it was.

The pilot, copilot, and the crew chief had gone through the pre-flight procedures, and the plane was ready to go when the general arrived. He returned Ken's salute and smiled as he glanced at Ken's captain bars glistening in the sun.

He patted Hannah on the head, glanced to make sure the pilots were listening, and said, "Now, you understand I can't authorize transporting any non-military personnel, but I'm going to go into the hangar for a cup of coffee, and I don't want to know what happens while I'm gone." He turned and walked away.

As he disappeared into the hangar, the pilot smiled and said, "All aboard for America!"

Ken helped Hannah up the ladder, and they made their way to the rear of the plane. A short time later, the general climbed aboard and did not look in their direction. The plane took off, and they were on their way.

Hannah soon got over her initial fear and seemed fascinated to look out the window at the tiny buildings and other objects on the ground.

This was the first time Ken had been in the air since the day they were shot down, and it brought back distressing memories of that occasion and the loss of his comrades. He looked down at the extensive bomb damage and wondered if any of the devastation he was looking at had been caused by *Luck of the Irish* on her last mission. Germany looked a lot different from three thousand feet than it had from twenty-eight thousand feet.

Four days later, they arrived at the Washington National Airport after stops in England, Iceland, and Newfoundland. They landed in a section of the airport devoted to military aircraft and were not subjected to the normal customs and immigration requirements imposed on civilians. General Ross told Ken he was going to take them to his home in Arlington, Virginia (fairly near the Pentagon), to stay for a few days.

"Just long enough to get on board at the Pentagon and collect your back pay. Then you are getting a thirty-day furlough."

He had telephoned his wife from the airport, and she met them at the door with a smile. She threw her arms around Ken and said, "This is such a wonderful surprise! I've wanted so much to thank you for saving us! I was beginning to think we would never see you again. And how's your friend? I want to thank him too!"

After a pause, Ken said, "Mrs. Ross, I'm afraid he won't be coming back. He died over Germany."

Mrs. Ross put her hand to her mouth. "Oh, I am sorry. I didn't mean to bring up sad thoughts." Then she motioned toward her daughter and said, "This is the young lady you saved."

The daughter had grown noticeably and now appeared to be near her teens. She came forward and shyly said, "Thank you for saving us. Mother has talked about you often."

Mrs. Ross turned to Hannah and said, "And who is this darling little angel?"

Ken said, "Well, it's sort of a long story, but to make the proverbial long story short, I was there when her mother died, and she asked me to promise to take care of Hannah. Of course, I would have done it even if she hadn't asked for my promise," he hastened to add.

"Oh my, that is sad that she lost her mother. How fortunate for the child you were willing to assume responsibility for her. I doubt there are many young men your age that would be willing to accept the obligation to care for someone else's child. But she does seem like such a lovely little girl," Mrs. Ross said. "I'm sure you have enjoyed her."

"More than you could possibly know," Ken said.

He pondered Mrs. Ross's wonder at his taking responsibility for Hannah. He had not even considered for a moment not taking care of her. Was it his life in the orphanage that gave him a heart for the welfare of children, or was this God's love being expressed through him? All he knew was that Hannah was precious to him, and he didn't think of her as a burden or an inconvenience.

Mrs. Ross was a gracious hostess. It was obvious she was doing her best to make her guests feel comfortable and welcome. It was interesting to see Hannah look with wonder around the spacious home with its rather elaborate decor. For a while she clung to Ken's side. Then Susan brought in a tiny kitten, and Hannah was enchanted. She played with the kitten and laughed at the kitten's antics when Susan trailed a piece of yarn around in front of it.

Ken said, "Susan, could you tell her what that is called? She needs to learn English."

Susan promptly told Hannah that was a kitten and after that seemed to take pleasure in trying to teach her more English words. After a while Susan led Hannah to some shelves of books and showed her some Little Golden Books. Although Hannah didn't understand most of the words, she seemed absorbed with the colorful pictures as she sat in Susan's lap while Susan read to her.

General Ross barbequed steaks for dinner, and as they sat down to eat, Ken's mind involuntarily turned back to the barbequed steaks at his birthday party on the Dalton ranch and was again seized with a nostalgic desire to go back there.

Hannah looked at all the food before them incredulously. It was hard for her to believe the amount and variety of the food before her was real, certainly far beyond anything she had seen before. Ken was also impressed. It was the most lavish display of food he had ever seen too. Hannah was the center of attention as she sampled each new dish, and Mrs. Ross especially was pleased to see how much she was enjoying it. Ken gave the Ross family his sincere compliments for the extraordinarily fine meal.

Mrs. Ross was charmed with the mature behavior Hannah displayed for such a young child. "Oh, you must leave her with us while you are in Washington!" she said.

General Ross had told Ken day care was provided for Pentagon personnel, but seeing the way Hannah was bonding with Susan and winning Mrs. Ross's heart, this did seem like a better option, at least until his furlough.

When Ken collected his back pay, one of the first things he did was go to the Polish Embassy and inquire about the best way to get Polish money to Karina. Following the advice he got, he sent her a sum that he thought would be about as much as she would get in a year from her small pension. He planned to also enlist the aid of someone who could write Polish and send a letter thanking her again for providing a refuge for them when they needed it so desperately. With funds from his back pay, he hoped he would also be able to buy a used car, which he wanted in order to be able to travel to the Dalton farm during his furlough.

Based on what Deborah had told him, Ken knew Hannah had lived through a period of poverty and deprivation, and he wondered if she might be suffering any ill effects. She seemed to be healthy as far as Ken could tell, but he wanted to have a doctor examine her to see if she had any health problems that were not apparent. He asked Mrs. Ross if she could recommend a good doctor he could take her to. She called the pediatrician their family had used and insisted on getting an early appointment. When the doctor examined Hannah, he said she seemed to be in good health. He did find a slight rash on her stomach, and he prescribed some ointment that he said would clear it up.

Ken was processed into the Pentagon and given an identification badge. He was told to report to a Major Howe, who greeted him warmly, having been told by General Ross to expect him. The major sent him to an orientation meeting and told him just to familiarize himself with the organization for the few days he would be there before his furlough. He would be given his duty assignment upon his return.

As he checked out of the Pentagon to start his furlough, Ken marveled at the events that had led him to be there at the seat of America's military command. As interesting as it was, Ken was pretty sure he didn't want to spend his life in the military. He had been planning to go to college on the GI bill to become an electronics engineer, but lately he was beginning to wonder if God was calling him into the ministry.

When General Ross had told him he was going to get a thirty-day furlough, Ken's thoughts had turned immediately to the Meyers, and the Daltons, and his happy times with them. What better way was there to spend the time than to visit them? But based on the last few letters he had from the Meyers, it was probable the professor was now teaching in a university, which would mean they had moved.

He was anxious for the Meyers to see Hannah. He was sure they would love her and would see right away what a special little girl she was. They were just that kind of people. He also wanted Hannah to see the Dalton farm and the animals, so he planned to go there for a day or two and find out from them where the Meyers had gone, then on to see them if they were not too far away.

Chapter 15

Mrs. Ross had told Ken about an aged acquaintance who had decided to give up driving and was going to sell her car. Ken went to see her and was impressed with the 1938 Pontiac and how well it had been maintained. The odometer read just over seventeen thousand miles. The woman was captivated with the handsome young serviceman and his service during the war and insisted he take the car for much less than she could have gotten for it. Automobile production had been curtailed during the war, so good cars were in great demand. Ken could hardly believe that his very first car was such a nice one.

When it was time for Ken's furlong to start, he gave the Rosses' his heartfelt expression of thanks for their help and their hospitality. General Ross had helped overcome the seeming insurmountable problem of getting Hannah into the country. Then having arrived in the country without any resources, their hospitality had been invaluable.

As they traveled down the highway toward the Dalton farm, he was glad to get away from the city with the constant hustle and bustle. Hannah was happy and seemed to enjoy watching the rural landscapes, especially when there were animals grazing in the pastures. Mrs. Ross and Susan had taken her shopping and bought her some pretty clothes. It was unlikely she had ever had clothes that were designed for appearance as well as serviceability, and Ken could tell she was proud of them.

Ken had given her a teddy bear, and the bear and the doll Karina had given her were her constant companions. When she wasn't holding them, she would carefully set them in the seat beside her. She seemed awed by the car and had visually examined the interior several times and kept feeling the upholstery as if she couldn't believe how soft it was.

"I like this car," she said. "It's better than the one in Germany that we rode in. I didn't like that one."

"I didn't like that one very well either, especially the way the man was driving," Ken said. "But that ride sure helped us out, even though it was uncomfortable at the time. We might still be in Germany if we hadn't got that ride." He knew it was because of General Ross they were now in the States. If they had got to Berlin just a few days later, they would have missed him.

"I guess I'm glad we did get the ride then," Hannah said. "I like being in America."

Ken remembered Hannah had liked the music on Karina's radio, so he turned on the car radio and told Hannah to see if she could find some music that she would like to listen to. She scanned the stations until she found one that was playing classical music then sat back and was obviously enjoying it.

"We need to get you some kind of music lessons. I think you must have some musical talent," Ken said. "Who knows, you might turn out to be a famous concert pianist!"

They stopped at a roadside café and got some hamburgers and French fries for lunch—a first for Hannah. She ate part of the hamburger with obvious enjoyment, but she especially liked the French fries. Then Ken bought some strawberry ice-cream cones, and Hannah's eyes widened as she took her first bite.

"Ooh, this is good!" she said.

"Did you have anything like this when you were in Poland?" Ken asked.

Hannah thought for a moment then said, "I think we had something cold like this once long ago."

The Daltons were surprised and overjoyed to see Ken, and they greeted him as if he were their own son. It was hard for them to believe that the young teenager who had worked for them just a few years before was now a captain in the air force! They were curious about his having Hannah with him, but like everyone else they were captivated by her and did their best to make her feel welcome.

The Daltons wanted to hear about everything Ken had gone through since he had left their place and asked more and more questions until Ken had given them a fairly detailed account of his military career. He showed them he still had the watch they had given him and told them how much he had appreciated having it. It had served him well through all sorts of circumstances. The Daltons were pleased to hear that the watch had been useful, but they were especially interested in hearing the details of how he had become Hannah's guardian.

Ken gave a brief account of how he had met Hannah and her mother and their struggles to survive in the forest until they came to Karina's house. They marveled over the way the crisis in his life had been met and acknowledged there had to be some divine intervention behind it.

"I'm so glad that terrible war is over," Mrs. Dalton said. "There were several boys in our little community that didn't come back, but I am so glad you were able to survive all that you went through!"

Ken wondered if the aspiring marine he had met when registering for the draft may have been one of those who hadn't come back. He had heard the battles in the Pacific had taken a terrible toll on the American forces, especially the Marines, who had been engaged in some of the most violent battles. But even with the high losses among the Marines, he had been told the casualty rate of the air force flight crews was even higher.

Ken finally got a chance to ask where the Meyers had gone. He was dismayed to find that the Daltons didn't know where they were.

Professor Meyer had told Mr. Dalton the name of university where he was going to teach, but he couldn't remember what it was. The opportunity had come up suddenly, and the university had wanted Professor Meyer to report to their institution right away.

"Sorry. I guess my memory isn't as good as it used to be," Bill said, "but I'll keep thinking. Maybe it will come back to me."

"Well, maybe Mrs. Schmidt will know," Ken said.

"I'm sorry to have to tell you, but she had a heart attack and died over a year ago," Mrs. Dalton said.

Ken was saddened to hear of Mrs. Schmidt's death and frustrated that he now knew of no one who could tell him where the Meyers were. It was a major disappointment. His primary reason for making the trip had failed to achieve what he had hoped. He resolved to persistently beseech God to somehow help him find out where the Meyers were.

Ken had planned to stay in a motel, but the Daltons insisted he and Hannah stay with them.

"We want you to stay as long as you can!" Mrs. Dalton said.

Ken had intended to stay only a day or two in the area, but since he didn't know where to find the Meyers, there didn't seem to be any urgency to leave, especially with the Daltons urging him to stay. He had to admit to himself that it was therapeutic to be back in the tranquil atmosphere of the farm. It seemed so good to be able to just relax without any major worries or responsibilities.

Hannah was also enjoying the farm. It pleased him to see how interested she was in all the Daltons' animals: dogs, cats, horses, cows, pigs, and chickens. She seemed fascinated with them all. Her favorite seemed to be Molly, the horse. At first Ken held her as she patted Molly's nose, but in a couple days she would run to the corral fence and pat Molly as she lowered her head to Hannah's touch and loved to give her an apple or carrot. She was thrilled when Ken put her in the saddle and led Molly around with her gripping the saddle horn.

In the mornings she seemed as if she could hardly wait to get outside and visit her animal friends. She loved to go with Mrs. Dalton to feed the chickens. Mrs. Dalton would let her scatter handfuls of wheat on the ground and watch as the chickens hurriedly picked up the wheat, as if making sure they got their share. Helping Mrs. Dalton gather the eggs was another thing she enjoyed.

The cherry harvest was underway again at the Dalton farm. Ken took Hannah with him as they rode Molly to look at the activity that had been Ken's introduction to the farm. He listened to the good-natured bantering of the harvest crew and recalled the contented feeling he had received from being on the crew. If he had not had Hannah with him, he might have donned some picking gear and picked a few trees.

He went by to look at the trees he had helped plant. Bill had told him this was the first year the young orchard had been mature enough to bear a crop. These trees had not been harvested yet, and Ken picked some cherries and gave them to Hannah. She smacked her lips as she tasted the succulent fruit and asked for more. Ken ate some too and was proud of the part he had in getting the orchard started.

After they had eaten all the cherries they wanted, he turned Molly toward the house where he had lived with the Meyers. He had so many good memories of the time he had spent there he wanted to see it again. Bill had said his hired man and his family were now living there. As they got in sight of the house, they saw a girl a little younger than Hannah swinging gently in the swing in the front yard holding a cute, little, black puppy in her lap.

Hannah asked to get down from Molly's back then went over to the little girl and said hello to her but wasn't sure how to communicate further in English. The girl stopped swinging, and Hannah reached out to pat the puppy. After she had patted it a few times, the girl held it out to her. Hannah hugged the puppy then pointed to Molly. Leading the little girl by the hand, she took her over to pet Molly. Ken was amused that Hannah would reciprocate the little girl's sharing her pet by sharing Molly with her.

After a few minutes, the little girl led Hannah to the porch, where she had some dolls seated around a doll table. The two began playing together like old friends. It gave Ken pleasure to see Hannah enjoying herself with someone near her own age.

While he was watching them, the mother came to the door. Ken led Molly over to the porch and introduced himself. He told her he had lived in the house a few years before and that he was staying with the Daltons for a few days. He told her that Hannah's mother had died and he had assumed responsibility for her.

"Oh, the poor little thing!" the mother exclaimed. "I'm so glad you brought her by. Amy seems to be enjoying playing with her so much. Do bring her back as often as you can!"

The lady told Ken her name was Diana Johnson. They talked together for some time with Mrs. Johnson asking more about Hannah and how Ken had become responsible for her and even shed a few tears of sympathy. Ken had told her Hannah didn't understand much English, and when he thought they should leave, he told Hannah in German it was time to go.

Hannah stood up reluctantly and asked Ken the girl's name. Ken told her, and Hannah asked if they could give Amy a ride on Molly. Ken explained Hannah's request to Mrs. Johnson, who had no objection, so Ken set them both in the saddle and led Molly around for a while with Amy hanging on to the saddle horn and Hannah hanging on to Amy.

When the ride was over, as they started to leave, Mrs. Johnson said, "Do please bring Hannah back tomorrow if you can! Amy has been lonesome, and they have had such a nice time playing."

Ken said he might just do that.

The days passed swiftly, and every day after Hannah had visited her animal friends, she wanted to go to Amy's house. Mrs. Johnson always seemed glad to have her, and Ken got so he would leave her there for several hours while he fixed a fence, weeded the garden, or worked on some other project.

Although a large part of the wood from the trees Ken had pulled out had been taken for firewood, there were still a lot of the smaller branches and trimmings left. He remembered Mr. Dalton had said this would need to be burned, so he told Bill he would like to finish the job he had started. He used the John Deere tractor and pushed the wood into several piles with the grader blade; then he ignited a few at a time until they all had been burned.

When Sunday came, Ken wanted to visit the church he had attended with the Meyers. He wished he had a suit to wear, but he had not taken time to buy any civilian clothes except for some Levis and a shirt to wear around the farm. He didn't want to wear them to church. Everyone felt like you should wear your best clothes to church to honor God. He knew his uniform looked good but thought he would feel a little conspicuous. He resolved to buy a suit in the near future.

Ken was pleased when he found the Daltons had begun attending church there. A lady he didn't remember was acting as greeter that morning, but she recognized him and told him it was good to see him again as she handed him a bulletin. She spoke to Hannah and told Ken there was a children's service in the annex if Hannah would rather be with the children than in the adult service. Ken wasn't sure if Hannah would want to be away from him but said he would take her to the annex and see if she wanted to stay.

When they entered the room where the children were, Hannah saw Amy and immediately pulled away to go sit beside her. Mrs. Atkins, the pastor's wife, was getting ready to conduct the children's service, and she greeted Ken warmly and told him it was so good to see him again and know that he had survived the war. She did seem curious about Hannah being with him but didn't ask for an explanation.

Ken was uplifted and inspired by the singing and Reverend Atkins's message. It seemed so much more meaningful than the sermons he had heard before he went into the air force, and he realized his becoming a Christian was what made the difference. Reverend Atkins heartily greeted him after the service and told him how much they were missing the Meyers.

"That family helped us so much," the pastor said. "Professor Meyer was an excellent Bible teacher, and Mrs. Meyer played the piano sometimes when our regular pianist wasn't available. The girl helped out in the nursery a lot, and the boy took over mowing our lawn. We were really sorry to have them leave. Besides all the help they gave, they were a great family to have around."

"Do you know where they went?" Ken asked.

"No, I don't," Reverend Atkins said. "I know the professor had some offers for interviews he was considering, but I don't have any idea where they ended up."

When Ken went to the annex to get Hannah, he met Mrs. Johnson coming out with Amy and Hannah.

When she saw him, she said, "Oh, it's so good to see you in our church! We would like for you and Hannah to have lunch with us unless you have other plans."

Ken thanked her for the invitation but said Mrs. Dalton had prepared some things for lunch and had a roast in the oven. He didn't think after all the trouble she had gone to that he should go somewhere else.

Mrs. Johnson said, "Well, how about letting Hannah come with Amy if you are committed? They seem to enjoy each other so much, and I really enjoy her too. She is such a sweetie!"

Ken asked Hannah if she would like to go to Amy's house for lunch, and she said she would. He told Mrs. Johnson if she really wanted to take Hannah he would come by and pick her up sometime after lunch.

Mrs. Johnson said, "Well, don't hurry. Give them some time to play."

Ken sort of hated to not take Hannah back to the Daltons' but knew she would enjoy being with Amy more.

There was something so very satisfying about farm life away from the crowds and clamor of cosmopolitan areas. There was always something interesting to do and a sense of freedom that contrasted strongly with life in the military. Then there was such satisfaction in seeing the plants and trees mature and produce the crop God designed them for. Farming was one of the occupations Ken knew he would enjoy, but he didn't think it was likely he would become a farmer. He wanted to be open to God's leading, and at least at this point, he did not feel that was the direction he should go with his life.

It was time to go back to Washington. Over three weeks had passed, and Ken needed to get back and find an apartment close to the Pentagon and make sure Hannah could participate in the Pentagon's day care program until it was time for her to go to kindergarten. He had been pleased with how much English Hannah had picked up in the time she spent with Amy. She had demonstrated she was a fast learner, and he thought her being with the other children in day care would give her pretty good command of the language in a relatively short time. He hoped that by the time she started kindergarten she would be able to understand what all the teachers were telling her.

When they left the Dalton farm, Hannah was crestfallen. She had enjoyed the animals and Amy so much, and it was hard to leave them behind. Ken told her they would come back for another visit sometime, and she soon got over her somber state of mind.

After traveling an hour or so, Ken saw the car was getting a little low on gasoline, so at the next town, he stopped at a station to refill the tank. As he was getting out of the car, he saw another man in uniform in a car just starting to leave the station. With a closer look, he realized it was his fellow POW Don Johnston, one of the camp comedians. Ken stepped up to the car and said, "I'll bet you are missing that good Stalag food and soft bed as much as I am!"

Don looked at him, and although they were not personally acquainted, he remembered seeing Ken in the camp. As for Don, his antics made him and his fellow comedian known by name to almost everyone in the camp.

"Yeah, you are right! It's hard to get used to normal life after all that luxury! Say! Aren't you the guy that escaped the night the bomber crashed outside the camp?" Don asked.

"That was me," Ken admitted.

"You might like to know the German commandant was very annoyed, and he sort of took it out on us!" Don said with a big grin. "We spent a lot of time in roll calls the next week or so, and all the guys in your barracks were really grilled, but we were really proud you escaped. Pappy Rea really razzed the guards about them letting you escape; they were about ready to string him up!"

They spent several minutes reminiscing about their POW days, and Don wanted to know more about Ken's escape.

"It was the bomber crash that created the opportunity," Ken said and described some of the details of his escape. "I'm sure you remember the guard you called Stony Face. He really helped me and my English friend that escaped the same night. We would probably have been captured if it hadn't been for him. I just can't figure why he would risk himself to help us. He sure wasn't very friendly in the camp."

Don smiled. "I think I may be able to shed some light on that. On our flight back to the States, I was on the same plane as Colonel Zemke, our camp commandant. I mentioned Stony Face to him, and he told me that Stony Face had been a member of the OSS, a spy agency. He was raised in Germany but had immigrated to the States and lived here for about twenty years.

"When the war clouds started gathering, the OSS was recruiting native Germans to go back to Germany and pose as loyal Germans while serving as undercover agents. Stony Face, whose name was Herman Schultz, wanted to be of service to his adopted country and accepted the assignment. He posed as a businessman who was a distributor of imports.

"Unfortunately, the German military was in need of additional manpower, and he was drafted into military service and was placed in Stalag Luft One as a guard. This thwarted the desires of the OSS for his services, although he was able to provide some information about the prison camp, but he couldn't afford to be too friendly to us prisoners for fear of drawing suspicion."

"Well, that explains a lot!" Ken said. "I'm really glad to find that out!"

Don said his furlong was almost over and he needed to get started back to his base. They exchanged addresses and promised to stay in touch.

Ken decided he would go by the orphanage. He wanted to show Hannah where he had lived and see if Mr. Tanner was still there. He felt a little guilty for not following through on the plans Mr. Tanner made for him when he left the orphanage and wanted to repay the eighteen dollars Mr. Tanner had given him.

A feeling of nostalgia came over him as he drove into the orphanage parking lot. Everything looked pretty much the same, and it brought back a host of mostly pleasant memories. Many of the children were involved in an outside activity, and Ken was enthusiastically greeted by some of the younger orphans that he had been especially fond of. He told Hannah that was where he used to live, and she seemed awed with the thought of living with so many other children.

Mr. Tanner looked up when Ken approached his desk and spoke to him. He stood up, held out his hand, and said, "Well, this is a nice surprise! I've thought about you many times and wondered how you were doing. All of us on the staff thought you would do well in life, but I just didn't think about you becoming a captain in the air force so soon! Tell me a little about your life after you left here." He looked down quizzically at the eighteen dollars Ken laid on his desk.

"Mr. Tanner, the money you gave me started me off on a real interesting adventure. You may have heard I didn't go to the job you arranged for me, although I intended to, and I didn't use the money you gave me the way you expected."

Ken related how in the bus station he had thought about Larry's hitchhiking and on impulse decided to try it, which led him into contact with a family that needed his help and how things had developed from that point. He gave a brief account of his life in the military, told Mr. Tanner how he had acquired responsibility for Hannah, and said he planned to adopt her.

"I think she is a very fortunate little girl," Mr. Tanner said. "I thought maybe you were bringing us a new child to take in."

Ken talked a little longer then bid Mr. Tanner good-bye and thanked him again for the adventure he had started him on. As he started to leave, Mr. Tanner slipped the eighteen dollars into Ken's pocket.

There was a great demand for housing in the Arlington area to accommodate the needs of the thousands of Pentagon personnel. Ken was able to find a nice apartment fairly near the Pentagon that had good subway service nearby so he wouldn't have to spend time battling the traffic. It was also fairly near the Ross family's home, and Mrs. Ross said she would be glad to pick Hannah up from day care if Ken was delayed for some reason. There was an elementary school two blocks away where he planned to enroll Hannah for the next school term.

The lady in charge of admitting Pentagon dependents into the day care program was very accommodating. She did ask for proof Ken was on staff at the Pentagon, and Ken showed her his identification badge and gave her Major Howe's office telephone number in case she needed further verification. Since he planned to formally adopt her, he enrolled Hannah under the name of Hannah Ryan.

The lady called one of the day care personnel and told her to give Ken and Hannah a tour of the area. Ken was very impressed with the personnel, the spacious facilities, and the equipment the children had to occupy their time. Hannah also seemed intrigued with all the activities and didn't seem to be intimidated by so many children as Ken had feared she might be.

Ken's duties as part of General Ross's staff were interesting, but he didn't particularly care for the constant hustle and bustle and found himself longing for the tranquility of the Dalton farm. Even though he felt like he was sort of out of his element, he conscientiously did his best to complete every assignment in a way that satisfied Major Howe, his immediate superior.

Still, he kept looking forward to the time when the war with Japan would be over and he could go back into civilian life. It was gratifying to hear of the progress of the war in the Pacific; then, on August 6, 1945, the atomic bomb was dropped on Hiroshima, followed by a second atomic bomb on Nagasaki on August 9. There was great rejoicing in the nation when the Japanese formally surrendered to General Douglas MacArthur on the battleship *Missouri*, and President Harry Truman proclaimed September 2, 1945, as "VJ Day."

With the war over, activities at the Pentagon seemed to proceed at a somewhat less hectic pace, but one new element that Ken was involved in was helping process the thousands of troops who were being discharged. With his access to the records, he looked for information on each of the men on his crew, but as he suspected, they were all listed as killed in action, including Hal.

When he looked for his friend Robert's records, he was happy to find nothing to indicate he was dead or even missing. He promised himself he would try to get in contact with him.

Then he thought of Andy and the experiences they had gone through together. He wanted to find out what had happened to him, but he didn't have access to the records of British servicemen; he didn't even know his last name. He decided when he had the time he would send an inquiry to the RAF and describe Andy as a Spitfire pilot who had been shot down somewhere around 1942, hoping with his first name and physical description that would be enough information to identify him.

Many of the personnel at the Pentagon wanted to make the military a career. Others like Ken requested to be discharged when their services were no longer needed. He was told he would probably be released somewhere around May or June 1946. Ken was satisfied with that. It would give him time to check out various universities or colleges and apply for admission for the fall term.

One of Ken's duties involved liaison between the Pentagon and Walter Reed Army Medical Center. Thousands of troops had been wounded during the war, many seriously who required delicate surgery and long recuperation times. Medical histories were constantly being reviewed to determine which cases had completed the surgery or treatment they needed and could be released to other medical facilities for recuperation in order to make room for other soldiers who needed the expertise available at Walter Reed.

One morning, Ken went to the hospital administrator with a list of names and their medical status to discuss which ones could be admitted. As he was telling the receptionist that he had an appointment with the hospital administrator, a nurse came to the desk. She had overheard Ken state his name, and she curiously looked at his face.

When Ken turned to go to his appointment, the nurse asked, "Captain Ryan, did you know there is a Kenneth Ryan who is a patient here, and he looks a lot like you?"

Ken told the nurse it was news to him, and he asked which room he was in. The nurse looked at the list of patients on her clipboard and gave Ken the room number. When Ken finished his business with the administrator, he went to see the other Kenneth Ryan.

When he walked into the room, the patient was lying on the bed reading a magazine. His left leg had been amputated just below the knee. He looked up, and when he saw Ken he had a look of astonishment. As the nurse had told him, Ken saw immediately there was a fairly close resemblance between them. Ken went to the bed and offered his hand.

"Hello, Kenneth Ryan. My name is Kenneth Ryan!"

The patient looked even more incredulous and said, "Captain, it is a pleasure to meet you, but does it strike you that we look a lot alike as well as having the same name?"

"Yes. I'm here because a nurse told me she thought the same thing. It really is a coincidence, isn't it?"

"Yes, it certainly is. I've met a few other Ryans, but I don't remember meeting any outside of our family who looked anything like me! And the only other Kenneth Ryan I've heard of was an uncle that I was named after. I don't remember ever seeing him. What family of Ryans did you get your name from?"

A thought that had flashed through Ken's mind when the nurse had first told him about the other Kenneth Ryan came back in a way that quickened his pulse. Could he be related to this Ryan? "How is it that you don't remember seeing your uncle?" he asked. "He must have been a close family member for you to be named after him."

"The way I remember it, nobody really knows what happened to him. It seems like I heard my uncle and aunt and their baby went on a trip and just disappeared."

Ken's head was reeling. "Kenneth," he said, "I think I may have been that baby. You and I may be cousins!" Ken related his story of being raised in the orphanage, why he had been put there, and how he had been given his father's name since no one knew what he had been named.

The patient seemed excited by Ken's story. "Now, doesn't that beat all! This is like a fairy tale! Let's call my mom and see if she can shed any light on this!"

He picked up the bedside telephone and told the operator the number he wanted. A few minutes later the patient was telling his mother that he might have his Uncle Kenneth's son in his room and explained the circumstances. He listened a while then said, "Mother wants to know if you have a dark brown birthmark on your right calf."

Ken felt a flood of emotion as he pulled up the right leg of his pants, clearly showing he did have a birthmark there. Knowing about that birthmark was pretty positive proof Kenneth's mother had seen him as a baby or at least had known about him. The patient told his mother Ken did have a birthmark on his right calf, and he had seen it. After listening for a minute or so, he told Ken his mother wanted to talk to him. The mother was in tears.

"I just can't believe it, after all these years. Your mother was so proud of you! You were so perfect in every way except for that birthmark. Your mother wanted to get it removed, but your father just laughed and said it was nothing to worry about! I'm so glad you do have it so we know you are ours and also to finally find out what became of you and your parents!"

Ken learned he had been named Kenton. His mother had wanted to name him Kenneth after his father, but Ken's father thought since his slightly older cousin had been named Kenneth it would be better to name their baby something else. On family gatherings, having two Kenneths near the same age could be confusing when trying to get their attention.

Ken was told his mother's name had been Judy, and the aunt he was talking to was Dorothy, who was married to his father's brother. Ken felt like he had a million questions to ask but heard the operator ask him to release the line for someone else's use. He reluctantly said good-bye and hung up, promising to call later.

Ken talked to the patient for almost two hours. He learned he had six uncles and aunts, four on his father's side and two on his mother's. He also had seventeen cousins with the males outnumbering the females ten to seven. After getting an overview of his family's history, he asked the patient how he had lost his leg and learned he was a paratrooper who had been hit by a mortar fragment during the Battle of the Bulge. He was being fitted with a prosthesis and expected to be leaving the hospital soon.

Ken asked the patient for his parents' address and phone number. He wanted to be sure to be able to get in touch with the family he had never expected to know. The patient assured him they would have a great family reunion sometime in the near future. Ken left with his heart singing praise to God for this unexpected blessing.

He was pleased to find out what his real name was and that it was so similar to the name Kenneth. He pronounced Kenton a couple times and liked it. He also liked the thought that the "Ken" he had been called most of the time still fit. Then he thought another shortened version of Kenton could be "Kent," which he thought he might like even better than Ken. Of course, there were a long string of military records documenting his name as Kenneth, which might cause some minor problems in the future, but he would face that when it came.

The next day Ken called his aunt Dorothy again. He had not had a chance to find out some things about his parents that he had wondered about often. Some of the questions he asked his aunt called on his uncle Richard to answer.

Ken learned he had been born when his father was twenty-three or twenty-four. He was his parents' only child, so he didn't have any siblings. His father had served in the infantry during World War I, had been wounded in the Battle of Meuse-Argonne, and received a medal for heroism. The wound had healed with no lasting effects.

Ken's grandfather had operated a gold mine near Tin Cup, Colorado, for several years, and he had passed an interest in rocks and minerals on to his sons. This interest was a factor that influenced Ken's father to enroll in the Colorado School of Mines with the goal of earning a degree in geology. He had successfully completed three years at the School of Mines and needed one more year to graduate.

Ken's Uncle Richard had been about a year and a half older than Ken's father, and he related some of the good times they had together growing up. Ken was intrigued to learn that his mother was the younger sister of his aunt Dorothy. It was no wonder there was so much similarity between Ken and his cousin Kenneth when they had received the same basic genetic makeup from both sides of the families.

It was gratifying to be finding out about some things he had wondered about as far back as he could remember. He was looking forward to meeting more of his relatives and learning more family history.

Chapter 16

One thing that weighed on Ken's mind was that he hadn't brought Hannah into the country through the proper legal process. He wanted to formally adopt her and was afraid bypassing the immigration laws might be a barrier to adoption. He didn't know what was involved in the adoption process but was sure questions were bound to come up regarding Hannah's background that would reveal her alien status. He decided to see if he could somehow arrange for her to be a legal immigrant.

He had her dress in her prettiest clothes and carefully combed her hair. She was an unusually attractive child, and he thought anyone at the immigration office who saw her would be moved to do their best to help with the problem. He had looked up the address of the citizenship and immigration office, and they took the subway to the stop nearest their destination.

As he started into the official-looking building hand in hand with Hannah, he was astounded to see Mrs. Meyer coming out the door. She glanced at him and stopped abruptly as the color drained from her face. She dropped the papers she was carrying and covered her mouth with her hands.

"Ken," she said in a trembling voice, "is that you?"

Then Ken realized it was not Mrs. Meyer but Rebecca, all grown up! He spontaneously stepped forward and embraced her. "Oh thank God! I'm *so* glad to see you!" he said.

She returned his embrace and looked up with shining eyes. "Oh, Ken, we were told your plane went down and there were no survivors! I can't believe it's really you! We just never expected to see you again!"

"I was beginning to think the same about you and your family! I didn't know how to find you. I've thought so often about all of you and the happy times I had living with you. I was so anxious to see you again, partly to have you meet my daughter, Hannah!"

"Oh?" she said uncertainly.

"I should have said adopted daughter, or at least I plan to adopt her. I met her and her mother through some strange circumstances. Her mother asked me to care for her when she was dying." He turned around and picked Hannah up, and she put her arm around his neck and smiled shyly at Rebecca. "She's Jewish. That's one reason I wanted her to meet you." Ken paused then said, "I guess the main reason is that I feel like you folks are sort of like family to me, so I wanted to share what has become so precious to me with you."

Rebecca looked at Hannah with love written on her face. "Hannah, it is so nice to meet you! You and I are going to be great friends!"

"Why don't you repeat that in German? She has learned a lot of English but still doesn't know it nearly as well as German," Ken said. "I want to be sure she understands that!"

Rebecca repeated her statement in German then held out her hands to Hannah. Hannah removed her arm from around Ken's neck and reached out to Rebecca, who took her and hugged her tightly, and Hannah looked pleased.

They walked together for a while then found a bench and talked for over an hour. Ken explained he had started to inquire at the immigration office about how to get legal status for Hannah and asked Rebecca how she happened to be there. She said she had been checking on the

Meyer family's applications for citizenship and had sought advice on any way to expedite them.

Ken said, "This definitely has to be an answer to prayer. Being here at the same time on the same day in the same city is just too unlikely to be a coincidence!"

Ken asked Rebecca if she and her folks were living in Washington now. She told him she was attending the University of Virginia in Charlottesville and was living on campus, but her folks were living in Baltimore. She had really wanted to go to the University of Maryland where her father was now teaching foreign languages, but she couldn't pass up the full scholastic scholarship offered to her by the University of Virginia. The distance between Charlottesville and Baltimore was not great, and she was able to see her family fairly often.

Ken wanted to know all about her family and was told Professor Meyer was enjoying his teaching position and Mrs. Meyer was taking some classes there and planned to get a degree in English and literature. Benjamin was in high school and still at the top of his class scholastically. They reminisced about the good times they had together at the Dalton farm.

Ken looked at Rebecca with admiration. It just didn't seem possible that this beautiful, poised young lady was the same one he had regarded as just sort of a nice little sister. He also noticed her speech didn't have the slightest trace of foreign accent.

Suddenly Rebecca looked at her watch and said she needed to catch her train back to the university. The University of Virginia was about an hour and a half away by train. Ken and Hannah walked with her to the depot after he made sure he had obtained her address and the address of her family and both telephone numbers. Rebecca said it might be hard to reach her by phone since the phones in the dormitory were so often in use.

"Have you had a chance to look around at all the sights here in Washington?" Ken asked.

"No, I haven't, but I want to do that sometime," Rebecca said.

"I haven't taken time to do it either, but I've been told there are a lot of historical places that every American should see, and I think that would also apply to anyone on the verge of becoming a citizen! How about coming here some Saturday soon, and we can explore the sights together," Ken said.

"I would love to do that. In fact, I think I could spare time to come next Saturday if that would fit in with your schedule."

"Great!" Ken said. "My schedule for Saturday is wide open."

"If I remember right, there is a train that gets to Washington about nine o'clock, if you wouldn't mind getting up that early," she said with a hint of the mischievousness she had often displayed at the Dalton farm.

"I think I might be able to struggle out of bed by that time!" Ken said. "Let's plan on that."

Ken watched her get on the train with a warm, happy feeling in his breast. It seemed so good to see Rebecca, know where she was staying, and find out where her folks were after almost despairing of ever seeing any of them again. He planned to give high priority to going to see the rest of the family soon.

Ken went about his duties during the week in a blissful state of mind with the next Saturday never far from his thoughts. He told some of the others in his office he was planning on going sightseeing the next Saturday and wanted to be sure to see all the most historically significant sights in Washington. He asked opinions about where he should go. He was told by his coworkers it took much more than a day to see the multitude of historical places and other sights everyone should see. He was given several varying opinions about the best way to spend the day.

When Saturday came, Ken and Hannah were at the train station well ahead of Rebecca's scheduled arrival time. Hannah seemed as happy as Ken was to see Rebecca step off the train, and after greeting Ken, she picked Hannah up and gave her a hug. Ken suggested they catch a bus to the National Mall and just decide where they wanted to spend their time after they got there.

The bus stopped to let them out a short ways from the Capitol building. Ken looked at the map of the area he had obtained and saw they were not far from the Supreme Court building. Since the other places they would be visiting in the mall were on the other side of the Capitol, he suggested they take a look at the Supreme Court building before going to the Capitol. Rebecca agreed, and after a short walk they entered the impressive-looking building and joined a tour group that was just leaving.

A tour guide talked about the history of the institution and the contributions of some of the great men who had served on the court. They were impressed with the scriptural references etched in various places and the image of Moses as the great lawgiver intimating the Ten Commandments provided a basis for the laws governing the citizens of the United States.

After nearly an hour at the Supreme Court, they went on to the Capitol, where they joined another tour that took the better part of an hour going through the building while the guide talked about some of the interesting aspects of its history and those who had served there.

Congress was not in session, but the guide opened the door to the auditorium where they met and said, "And here, folks, is where bills are voted on that may become laws that we all need to live by whether we like them or not."

After leaving the Capitol, they went by Grant's memorial and stopped briefly. Rebecca said she had written a report about the Civil War for a high school history class she was in, and she related some of the interesting things about Grant she had learned. She thought the memorial was a fitting tribute to a man she had learned to admire.

Rebecca and Ken had both heard a lot about the various museums associated with the Smithsonian Institution and were eager to visit some that were of special interest to them. Ken wanted to see the exhibits in the National Air Museum, and he asked Rebecca if she would mind going there first.

Rebecca said, "Of course, that would be of special interest to you, and I would like to see it too!"

Ken was especially interested in exhibits of some of the earliest aircraft and was fascinated to see the 1894 Lilienthal glider and the plane that the Wright brothers used in first demonstrating powered flight was possible in 1903.

Another interesting exhibit was *The Spirit of Saint Louis*, with which Charles Lindberg demonstrated it was possible to fly from America to Europe. Ken had crossed the Atlantic in a B-17 and a C-47, but doing it with a small, single engine plane like *The Spirit of Saint Louis* didn't appeal to him at all. A plane that had belonged to Amelia Earhart was also on display, as well as several others of historical interest.

After about an hour they left the National Air Museum and went into the Arts and Industries Building where exhibits of early inventions were on display, including the first telegraph instrument, the first sewing machine, the first automobile, and the first telephone. There were also several of Thomas Edison's inventions. Ken marveled at his creative mind.

They were trying to get a basic idea of which exhibits would be of greatest interest to them, planning to return and spend more time on those they were especially interested in. With this in mind they reluctantly left the Arts and Industries Building and went into the Natural History Building and started looking at the exhibits of anthropology, archaeology, botany, geology, paleontology, and zoology. Here again they found a mind-boggling quantity of interesting things to see. After looking at the large display of American Indian artifacts and the posted information about their life and culture, it was past noon, and when Ken asked Hannah if she was getting hungry, she said, "A little bit."

They left the museum, stopped outside at a little sidewalk café in the mall, and got some sandwiches and soft drinks and ate them while sitting on a bench in the sun while they talked. Not far from them there was a decorative fountain with water cascading down through several layers of concrete basins. While Ken and Rebecca were talking, Hannah wandered over for a closer look at the fountain. At the base was a large pool where people had tossed coins as if it were a wishing well. Hannah seemed interested in looking at all the coins.

"I'm afraid this is pretty boring for Hannah," Rebecca said.

"It is really surprising how contented she seems to be in any kind of situation," Ken said, and he told her how good Hannah had been when they had been fleeing from the Germans, never crying or complaining even when he knew she was tired and hungry.

When they had finished eating, they decided they would go back into the Natural History Building for a while. As they were going toward the entry, they almost collided with a well-dressed man and woman coming toward them with eyes on the concrete walkway, obviously looking for something. The woman looked as if she were very agitated.

As they started past, Ken said, "Did you folks lose something that we could watch for?"

The couple stopped, and the woman said, "Yes, I did lose my wedding ring. I know I had it when I came here, but a few minutes ago I noticed it's not on my finger. I suppose by this time someone has found it and it's probably gone forever, but I'm going to keep looking for a while longer."

"We will watch out for it," Ken said. "Can you give us a phone number where we can reach you in case we should find it?"

With that the man said, "I don't think it's any use worrying about it. We are just going to have to accept the fact that it's gone, but here's my card just in case."

Ken glanced at the card and saw the name Senator Avery W. Hughes. "Well, we will keep our eyes open anyhow, Senator."

"Thank you," the woman said tearfully, and she and her husband went on down the mall with eyes still on the walkway.

Ken showed Hannah the ring on Rebecca's finger and told Hannah to watch for a ring with a pretty stone in it. He thought the senator's wife might have lost it in the museum and that they could watch for it as they went around to the various exhibits.

"It's over there," Hannah said, pointing.

"Oh, where do you think it is?" Ken asked, not really taking her seriously and not even bothering to look in the direction she was pointing.

Hannah took his hand and pulled him toward the fountain. She pointed in the water, and Ken saw a ring a few feet from the edge of the pool.

"For goodness sake, you are right!" Ken said, hardly believing it even after seeing it. Ken told Hannah to hold his coat, rolled up his sleeve, and was just able to reach the ring. "Hannah, if this is the right ring, you are going to make that lady very happy!" he said. "Let's hurry and catch up with those folks!"

The senator and his wife had been walking slowly and were not far away. The woman was astonished when Ken handed her the ring and asked if that was the ring she was looking for.

"Oh yes! I can just hardly believe it! Thank you, thank you, thank you!" she said with tears in her eyes.

"Well, Hannah here is the one that noticed it in the fountain. She's the one that deserves the thanks," Ken said as he put his hand on Hannah's head.

The woman held her hand to her mouth. "Oh, I remember now. It must have come off when I threw a handful of pennies into the fountain!" she said. "I had it resized several years ago when I put on some weight, but recently I have been on a diet, and it is a little loose now."

She knelt down and gave Hannah a hug. "Thank you so much, honey. This is our anniversary. We've been married twenty-five years today, and I have treasured my ring ever since our wedding day!" The woman stood up and said to Rebecca, "You are too young to have a child this age. This must be your little sister. She looks so much like you!"

"I surely wouldn't mind having her for a little sister, but she is really an orphan that Ken brought back from Germany," Rebecca said.

The woman wanted to know the circumstances, and once again Ken gave a brief account of how he had acquired responsibility for Hannah.

They talked a little while longer; then the senator held out his hand and said, "Thanks again for your help. The rest of the day is going to be much more enjoyable for both of us! You have my card. Let me know if I can do anything for you."

"Thank you, Senator. It has been a pleasure meeting you folks," Ken said.

As they were leaving, the senator slipped a ten-dollar bill into Hannah's hand.

After the couple walked away, Ken said, "Well, Hannah, it looks like you have a start toward your college fund!"

"That was sure interesting," Rebecca said. "Imagine us meeting a United States senator!"

"And we have his offer of help if we need it!" Ken said, and he thought if he had any trouble getting legal status for Hannah he might ask for the senator's help.

They were in a happy mood as they went back to the Natural History Building and spent more time there than they intended to. When they came out, they decided to go to the Washington Monument and the Lincoln Memorial before it got too late. Again they were impressed with the scriptural quotations that were engraved in these attractions.

Time was growing short, and they wanted to be sure to see the White House, which was not far away. They didn't have time to take a tour of this historic attraction but went to the front of the building and stood looking at it for a few minutes, talking about some of the great men who had lived there. The current occupant was Harry Truman, and they were wishing he would go by so they could catch a glimpse of him, but it was not to be.

As they went to catch a bus to take them back to the train station, Rebecca told Ken how much she had enjoyed the day. Ken also thought it was a very worthwhile experience, but he knew what made it special was seeing all the sights with Rebecca.

"We need to get your folks to come with us to see these things sometime," Ken said.

Rebecca agreed that would be something to plan on doing.

"Could Hannah come to see you next weekend?" Ken asked. "I think she would like to see what a university looks like. Now that she has a start on her college fund, she might want to go to college there someday!"

She smiled. "I would be happy for Hannah to come see me next weekend. She can even bring you if she wants to."

"Well, I was kind of hoping she might want to do that," Ken said. "Tell us where we can meet you and what time."

She gave him the information he wanted, and as Ken watched her train leave, he was hoping the week would pass rapidly.

Ken and Hannah met Rebecca the next Sunday afternoon and spent several hours with her, walking around the beautiful campus grounds. Ken was looking very handsome in his uniform, and many of the girls going by cast envious looks at Rebecca.

They looked at the stately buildings, and Rebecca told Ken the university had been established in 1819 by Thomas Jefferson, one of the eight US presidents from the state of Virginia. She showed Ken where her dormitory was and the buildings where she attended classes.

Ken asked her what academic goal she was working toward. She said she hadn't decided for sure, but the first year was pretty standard for all degrees and would be a step in preparation for the premed course she was thinking of taking. She said she didn't think she wanted to become a brain surgeon or any exotic specialty but thought she might enjoy being a pediatrician or a family doctor. As an alternative, she was considering becoming a teacher. It boggled his mind to think of his little cherry-picking companion possibly becoming a doctor.

Rebecca had asked Ken what happened to him when he got shot down, and he had put her off with a question about her parents. Now she asked again and said she really wanted to know. Ken decided he might as well tell her about it and satisfy her curiosity.

She tensed up and seemed to live the experience with him as he briefly described the last mission he was on, the engines becoming disabled, and finally the series of flak bursts that had brought their plane down. He told her about feeling the plane begin to go into a backward spin and barely managing to claw his way to the bailout portal, then landing and becoming a POW.

With her persistent questioning, he described his escape, his meeting with Deborah and Hannah, and their eventually finding refuge in Karina's house. He left out a lot of details and tried to satisfy her with an overall view. Even the abbreviated account of his experiences brought tears to her eyes at times.

Ken then demanded equal time and asked Rebecca for a more in-depth account of her life since they left the Dalton farm. She told him her life had not been nearly as exciting as his had been but described in greater detail what had happened to the Meyer family since he had seen them.

Then with some nostalgia, they again talked about some of their experiences on the Dalton farm and agreed that had been a special time in their lives. Ken told Rebecca all about his visit with the Daltons when he went on his furlough and how being there brought back so many special memories of the times he had spent with her family and the Daltons.

When the afternoon was drawing to a close, Ken told Rebecca he was really looking forward to seeing her parents again and planned to call them and go see them the next weekend if it was convenient for them. He asked if she could go with him. She said she had two major tests coming up the next week that she needed to prepare for and reluctantly said she didn't think she should go. Then Ken asked if he could come to see her again the weekend after seeing her folks, and she readily agreed.

The Meyers were so happy to see Ken. Rebecca had written about her providential encounter with him, and he had called them to let them know he was planning to visit them. As Professor Meyer heartily gripped his hand, Ken saw that tears were just below the surface. Mrs. Meyer greeted him with a warm embrace and tears of joy.

The professor said they had prayed for him every day since he had left the Dalton farm until they heard his plane had been shot down with no survivors. Ken asked how they got this misinformation.

Professor Meyer told him another professor friend of his had a brother in the war department. After almost a year of not hearing from Ken, Professor Meyer had asked his friend if he could find out anything about Ken. About a month later they got the news they dreaded. A British undercover agent had by chance watched a bomber at high altitude being shot down and crash into the ground near him. He had watched it from the time it was hit and saw no parachutes, which implied Ken's chute had been opened close to the ground, out of the range of his vision. It was also possible that his attention had been drawn to the descending bomber. He had reported to his contact that a B-17 had gone down on the outskirts of Hannover with no survivors. When this was relayed to the American Bomber Command, they had determined this had to be *Luck of the Irish* and had accepted the reputable agent's report of no survivors as authentic.

Ken told them he believed it was because of their prayers he had survived, and they were pleased to believe their prayers for his safety had been answered.

"God is so good!" Professor Meyer said.

They asked many questions about his experiences. As Ken had anticipated, they also displayed an instant love for Hannah and set about finding ways to entertain her.

Ken saw the picture of himself in his uniform that he had sent them on the fireplace mantle.

The professor saw him looking at it and said, "We didn't put that up because we knew you were coming. We have displayed it ever since we got it!"

Benjamin had grown so much it was hard to believe he was the same boy. He brought the Indian spearhead Ken had found in the stream by Mr. Dalton's farm and showed Ken he still had it, bringing back pleasant memories of that occasion. Benjamin said when his history class had been assigned the task of giving an oral report, he decided to make his report on the American Indians. He had included their experience of finding the spearhead and had received an A on his report. Ken told him he wanted to take him to see the Smithsonian American Indian exhibits sometime, and Benjamin was enthusiastic over this prospect.

Buddy seemed to recognize Ken and enthusiastically greeted him. It was so good to see them all again, including Buddy.

Ken told them again how much he had appreciated their prayers, and even more important than his survival, he believed it was because of their influence and prayers that he had become a born-again Christian. He showed them the much-worn New Testament they had sent him and told them he had received so much comfort from it, especially during his imprisonment. He knew the story of Hannah's mother and her vision would be especially meaningful to them, and as he had suspected, they were deeply moved by it and rejoiced that Ken's commitment had allowed God to use him to point one of their race to their Messiah. They urged Ken to come back as often as he could.

The next weekend, Ken and Hannah were back at the University of Virginia. Rebecca asked Ken to wait in the lobby of her dorm for a while. She wanted her roommates to see Hannah and to show Hannah her room. They were gone for quite a while, and when they came back, Hannah had a new hair-do with ribbons in her hair, a string of beads, and smelled of perfume. Rebecca said every one of her roommates wanted to kidnap Hannah and had such fun fixing her up. Hannah was all smiles.

Ken and Rebecca laughed when Hannah said, "I think I like college better than kindergarten!"

As they walked around the campus, Ken asked Rebecca how she had done with the tests she had studied for. She said she was satisfied with the grades she got.

"I suppose that means you got an A on both of them," Ken said, and Rebecca admitted that was true.

Ken told Rebecca about his visit with her parents and how good it had been to see them again. He also told Rebecca about his providential meeting with his cousin and how he had learned he had a lot of blood relatives that he wanted to meet but didn't think they would ever replace the feeling he had for the Meyer family.

"I sort of think of your parents as my father and mother, and Benjamin as a little brother, but—" He paused and looked at Rebecca. "I'm not at all sure I want to consider their daughter as my sister anymore."

Rebecca digested this with a slight smile but made no comment.

They sat down on a park bench overlooking a little lake. Ken had bought a sack of popcorn for Hannah, and she was busy feeding some ducks in the lake. Ken and Rebecca talked for a while; then the conversation turned to Hannah.

Finally Ken said, "You know what she needs most is a mother. I wonder where I could find a nice mother for her. Since she is Jewish, it would be extra nice if she had a Jewish mother, and of course she would have to be able to love Hannah, and it wouldn't hurt a bit if she were beautiful and intelligent. Where would I look for someone like that?"

Rebecca silently looked at him with a rather quizzical smile and finally said, "Well, I guess you could always try the classified ads!"

Ken seemed to consider that suggestion then said, "Yes, I guess I could do that, but maybe I could save some money and just ask around. Another thing to consider is that person might have to be willing to be a pastor's wife, depending on how the Lord leads. It could be a pretty uncertain life. Would you happen to know anyone who might be willing to take on the job?"

Rebecca's smile grew brighter, and her eyes glistened as she said softly, "You know, I just might be able to think of someone who would be *very* happy to take on the job!"

Ken reached into his pocket and pulled out an ornate little box, which he handed to Rebecca. She took the box with obvious excitement and opened it. Just under the lid was a folded note.

Unfolding the note with trembling fingers, she read, "I love you so much. *Please, please*, marry me!"

Underneath the note there was a beautiful diamond ring. Rebecca gave a little exclamation of joy. Hannah came skipping over and watched as a radiant Rebecca removed the ring from the box and slipped it on her left ring finger.

"You have no idea how often and for how long I've dreamed of becoming your wife!" she said happily as she looked up at him. Ken leaned over and gave her a lingering kiss.

"Oh, that's another thing I have looked forward to!" she said with a sigh. Ken immediately repeated the rather obvious request for another kiss, even more lingering than the first one.

They looked up to see Hannah looking at them curiously, and they both reached out and drew her into their arms in a three-way love-filled hug.

listen|imagine|view|experience

AUDIO BOOK DOWNLOAD INCLUDED WITH THIS BOOK!

In your hands you hold a complete digital entertainment package. Besides purchasing the paper version of this book, this book includes a free download of the audio version of this book. Simply use the code listed below when visiting our website. Once downloaded to your computer, you can listen to the book through your computer's speakers, burn it to an audio CD or save the file to your portable music device (such as Apple's popular iPod) and listen on the go!

How to get your free audio book digital download:

1. Visit www.tatepublishing.com and click on the e|LIVE logo on the home page.
2. Enter the following coupon code:
   1df8-a2f0-8ee2-ff4b-0291-e501-6c61-edc9
3. Download the audio book from your e|LIVE digital locker and begin enjoying your new digital entertainment package today!